The Chronicles of Allysa

Volume 1

The Throw Away

Book one

By Roxy A'nod

ROXY A'NOD

Printed in the United States of America

ISBN 10: 0-9884629-3-1
ISBN 13: 978-0-9884629-3-9

Author: Roxy A'nod

Published by Koi Publications

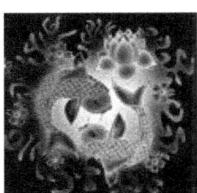

Div. of Lushious Ent
KoiPublications@gmail.com

ROXY A'NOD

DEDICATION

Dedicated to strong women with logic

That starts as a child.

Who struggles through many obstacles.

Therefore, to prosper takes a while.

She earns respect with determination

As she makes her way

To fulfill what she dreams to do

And intends to say.

Roxy A'nod

ROXY A'NOD

TABLE OF CONTENTS

CHAPTER

ROXY A'NOD

CHAPTER ONE

As the Story Goes

While walking through a Paris park observing how beautiful the trees are when evolving toward their dormant stage, I noticed an elderly couple on a bench smooching. They really needed to get a room; however, taking the time to realize how beautiful life gets as you grow older, I understand the feeling of getting better.

Barely middle age myself the couple made me think about my man and with them still having the hots for each other, made me reflect on that man and our affair. Our group of friends never let us forget the passion of our love and I'm always aware of my blessings by giving thanks while figuring ways to continue them. So... my lover is at home waiting for me, but I'm taking a walk to make him want me... more.

Really, I needed a break since I prepared all night for our group of friends. We're looking forward to reminiscing the many years we've enjoyed life and everything together. Then plan for the continuance of our expectations and listen to stories regarding growing into the people we are that make my soul happy.

But... life didn't start out that way. No, it was bad. However, I have looked at my life as a chronicle of events with people, places, and things that brought my life into perspective. Yeah, everybody has a life with many starting badly. However, in life's journey factors enter that's subject to change your life with your decisions making your life good or bad, create the individual, and hopefully make life delightfully interesting.

You must give serious consideration to the choices made in life since everyone and everything judge you by those choices. What we choose may take away that freedom of choice and then render the world's insensitive choices on others for whom you're responsible. Choices made by others that became fact, uniquely contributed to the way I came about life.

I never knew my parents and only knew them by the terrible things my adoptive father said. As a child I know I wasn't by myself with this type of childhood; however, everyone's life is unique and so was mine in a way.

The story I heard... my parents were heroin, cocaine, crack, whatever gets you high and available addicts. Told that often and the fact they didn't want me I never judged and had an inquisitive notion about them, but I heard nothing good.

Born a preemie, my mother and I didn't have a chance to bond. Everyone figured I would die, and when I didn't, the story went my father drank and beat us trying to kill us anyway. I'm guessing my mother and me. But what I knew:

- I was born addicted to a cocktail of drugs.
- I had terrible headaches that went on for hours sometimes causing me to lose consciousness.
- My father was African American and my mother Caucasian.
- I was only 3.02 lbs.
- The Director of an agency hired by the state to place and monitor orphaned children, adopted me just after my sixth birthday.
- A traumatic injury caused a scar, and I lost all memory of my early child hood,
  And this was my world then...

One of my earliest memories was a woman taking me to this large brick house with many rooms. I had short hair with a large scar on my scalp that started about ½ inch from my forehead and went back almost to the hairline on my neck. I had to wear a helmet to protect my head for a long time. My hair grew covering the scar, but for years, kids teased calling me Butt-head.

My adopted father, John Morgan, who I called The Director or AD, had a big dopey son age 11 and two daughters ages 15 & 17 when I arrived. He also had another small child staying there, but the child soon disappeared. My AD's wife died while having his son, and my AD lived in a large pretty house with three floors and eight bedrooms.

My AD's system that ran the household was the help stayed downstairs and the men stayed on the third floor. His rule; women were born to serve men or suffer punishment. I knew I received more than my share of punishment since I did more than my share of ignoring them. His daughters went along with the program, but after a while of phony fanfare and bullshit, reality sat in and he beat me terribly on the regular. He was wicked, and they all ran on the same tracks.

The house was spooky. I had only been there for about two months and every night I heard something creeping up and down an endless hallway. I didn't know what. All I saw was a shadow go past the bottom of my door. That was my signal to run into the closet and hide. At first, it just went past the door, but it twisted the doorknob and one night it came in. I thought I had lost my mind. Pinching myself, I listened trying to figure with many things going through my mind while in the closet tangled up in clothes hiding. I was petite and could hide anywhere, but this situation went on for about two months. I never had enough courage to see what was going on, and no one paid me any mind when I said something. The family only noticed me to assign work.

The daughters just looked at me, then whispered and laughed. They took turns taking out their frustration on me with words at first, but later they beat the shit out of me... for a while anyway. The two sisters were his dead wife's children by another man and acted like a bunch of COWS. They had to work too, but didn't care and they smelled like they looked... very unpleasant, but they were depressed, and had given up all hope. My soul wouldn't allow me to be that way.

My adoptive family was strange to say the lease and the other people who worked in or around the house stayed out the family's way, but I will explain my early life, the people, and things I dealt with. Maybe it will explain some of the choices I made and help you to understand me, The Throw Away.

My favorite house employee was the cook Adja, who was of African descent I think. I don't remember hearing her talk or I guess say something I understood. Her eyes were the windows of her soul and that's where I understood her. She arrived exactly at 9:00 am and left before dark. If a storm made it dark, she stepped. She always kept her bag packed.

At first, she seemed bothered by my presence in her world, the kitchen. I stayed there since it was the safest place for me while she was at work, and I learned to read Adja's thoughts through her eyes. She helped me that way. I figured out by just observing what she did how to stay out her way, help her, and hide when necessary. This helped me to survive other people. Once, Adja made me hide from a person dispatched from my AD's alleged agency to help me with my problems. I found out that person reported everything I said to my AD. Later I saw Adja reading the Bible that she left open at certain pages since the story helped me.

Adja hid me for the last time from the director shaking her head no with her eyes showing disapproval of my AD and what she saw happening. Before she left that day, Adja's eyes showed sadness; then, tears when she left that evening never to return. I was nine and my AD blamed me for her leaving with me gaining all the responsibility of the kitchen which turned out to be a good thing. I was already doing most the other house chores, so that gave me the power of running the house. It kept me well organized and proved to be a very effective bargaining tool.

The off and on garner/driver couldn't or wouldn't speak English, even though, I saw him and Adja talking once. He did his work not getting involved without ever stepping in the house. After the gardener stop working for my AD, he saw me running home hard. I was late, and he picked me up without saying a word dropping me off within eyesight of the house. When he left I think I heard his tires squeal as if there was a curse on the area. Which brings me to the son who got him fired over a lie.

The Son was an ASSHOLE and the director, my AD, treated him as if he was the little director, and he made us understand we had better do the same. The son had me doing stupid shit sometimes for the fun of it and other times because... he wasn't that smart. Then a little after Adja left, my AD announced to his son he would give me to him as a present for his bride. So I had to use my time wisely to get lost or die.

My AD? He was a real piece of work and made himself look like an angel of light, but in reality, he was a demon of darkness forcing his will on whom ever he felt he had power over. He had power over his daughters and power over the people who worked under him, those who were hypothetically there to take care of the abandon children and protect us, The Throw Aways.

Upon arrival at my AD's house at 6 years old, I ran away often, which prompted a visit from a social worker. I made it known about how spooky it was there and wanted to leave. That's when my AD came into my room saying he was there to comfort me. He told me no one else cared. My parents had thrown me away, like garbage, but I was special to him, because he had chosen me (as if he was GOD). Then he told me,

"It can be hard and scary for you since something can happen and there's no one to miss you or even wonder, but Allysa, I want you to know I'm here to comfort and protect you, but you must comfort me." Then he proceeded to sodomize me for years.

I didn't know any better concerning the action at first and it didn't bother me while I looked forward to our time together with his attention. I felt I was special enough for him to give me a little of his time when he came home.

His habit was to come straight to my room whenever he came in. I learned how to use this as a bargaining tool by watching how the daughters evaded work. My mode of thinking stayed innocent even though I felt bothered somehow by what I was doing and thinking. I think it was Adja's eyes. She looked at me different with concern and sorrow.

My AD's wish was for us to be home taught, so there were no friends, and omission of certain lessons totally with my AD training me to keep my mouth closed to all others. My well-being depended on it with us managing to keep up the appearance of a family to outsiders. That was important since my AD was a very important person to the city.

Every Christmas and Easter political allies and friends of my AD, who were Government and Military Officials from Washington, came with their families. Then my AD would dress me up showing me to all who came and the city by taking his family out shopping with the other families. It was a grand occasion that started the Christmas shopping seasons and pictures with the Mayor shaking hands to start a drive for the disadvantage and orphaned children. This took place during the lighting of a huge Christmas tree and donation declaration announcements from the wealthy with a long speech given by my AD and his friends encouraging adoption. Then he kept me in front to make it known I was one of those children and he adopted me.

Christmas and Easter were the only times he took me shopping with camera men following taking pictures of him buying expensive shit for me he returned for refunds later... and he wanted me to smile. I received my worse beatings during that time because after a while I never smiled.

My early life sucked, (no pun intended). When I realized my AD's actions, my life became terrible. I was eight and didn't want to continue our little secret as he called it. That's when he started telling me daily I was a throw away. I wasn't a real person since I could disappear and no one would look for me.

I tried to find my space, but it was hard after our home schoolteacher quit. Whatever happened, she quit only weeks after Adja did the same. The teacher must have left a bad reference on my AD as an employer with her agency since my AD called, but no one came back. This left us going to a local private Catholic School. I was nine at this point and my AD knew I was intelligent since the home schoolteacher urged my AD to have me tested when I was six. The tests proved I had an abnormally high I.Q. with a photographic memory. The Catholic school found out I knew how to apply myself not to have had much social contact, so they tested me again.

I advanced to 7th grade with my school counselor arranging for me to go to Advanced Preparatory Tech (APT) on scholarship, which was a school that trained exceptional children from all over the world. The fact that I was one, strengthen me. The school was on the same campus as my music, voice, and dance classes, which worked out well.

My counselor or growth instructor at APT wanted to help me socially and placed me in every enrichment class available outside the school like extra business classes. I loved my business classes and every outlet it presented since it taught me how to make and work money. I also joined the YMCA at her urging because I was athletic and loved to run and jump. Everyone thought I was quiet and shy, but I understood things better quietly. The trickle of a small mountain stream is not as loud as the oceans' surf, but it's just as important.

Most of the people in my city were Caucasians; a small percent Black, and a fraction of a percent Brown (Spanish origin, Mid-Eastern, and people like me). We didn't see many Asians at all. I was smaller and younger than my classmates, the same color, or just slightly darker with a couple prominent features. Sometimes mistaken to be Caucasian until you inspected me, and most people stared, inspecting, trying to figure because of my mixed race, which seemed like the wrong two. So, I felt most people considered me a freak of nature.

Where I lived wasn't an outright prejudice town. It was more a politically prejudice town like most places. Meaning yes it was there, but it wasn't a problem because everyone there knew their place and stayed in it, so I tried to stay in mine... but where was that?

My AD, was Caucasian and from California. At some point in his life, you could see he had been more liberal in behavior. Liberal enough to be freaky and that gave him his bag of tricks, but with him being wealthy and Caucasian, most everyone accepted and tolerated me. Most Blacks accepted me, but a great deal didn't like me, and that's where I felt I belonged.

Race was never an issue until I made a better grade or seen talking to a popular guy. Then depending on who made the statement the thought was I think I'm cute because I'm white, or black, but too cute suddenly. DUMB SHIT! If they only knew my life and how terrible it was, they would have laughed. All thought I was living a privileged life because my AD always made a spectacle out of me as if he was a decent person who cared. Yeah, my AD played the part of savior out in public, and everyone told me,

"You're so lucky." Really... they were all so phony. It was apparent that most saw through his act, but didn't care. Their concern was appearances, and they're not the one who's suffering. However, with me now aware of his actions, it was agonizing. I wanted to be normal, but didn't know how to stop him. I felt trapped and fought daily for the psychological dominance of my soul. What helped was using my bargaining power at home to trade off going to the Y, library, different gifted programs, music, voice lessons, track team practice, and meets. I did anything and everything that kept me from being at home where my AD could get me. Meanwhile, going to school 24/7 every day of the year had advantages and gave me hope of getting away from that crazy situation quicker.

Finding it comfortable hanging out with the street people in my city and not the gated bullshit suburban community where my AD lived, I tried to stay in the city with the street people. We lived in places we called Islands, which were abandon buildings. Four Islands throughout the city served as refuge and protection for anyone in need. The Islands had just about every nationality of men, women, and children. All of us were in need and orphans from the large world system for whatever reason. We lived in vacant buildings trying to survive and care for each other in a system that cared nothing about us, The Throw Aways.

The island system worked better for us. Most were runaways, but the older runaways took care of the younger runaways. All took care of the thrown away sick and elderly who were there or at home, and each Island had a King who made everything work. Everyone had a hustle or talent within the Island I belonged. I was somebody, Little Bit the Brain, and my Island was the best because we networked with other Islands in other cities. We could get anything the black market would have. That was my expertise. I made and saved money that way, plus the Island received its cut. When things became too rough at my AD's house, I ran to my island and they welcomed me there mostly, but around the city, I was just a freak. I kept my mind on getting away from that crazy situation quick and worked harder.

As I grew, the son of my AD felt, he could do everything his father was doing... and more. I never had a problem with my AD and sexual intercourse; that wasn't his thing. He liked a certain look that was young children mostly, but boys definitely. My AD had promised never to let his son have intercourse with me until we're married, so I would be a virgin for him, but almost every day I had to fight the son off me, and then those Kung Fu and kickboxing classes from the Y paid off. Most of all, I was fast at getting away since FUCK NO I wasn't going to marry his son, and making it out of this situation with my virginity had become very important to me. It was all I had to offer, and I wanted to be special in some way for the man I fall in love with since I had dreams of falling in love. With all that was going on, I wasn't sure if I ever could be normal, but I looked forward to try away from my AD's rule.

Day dreaming of how it would feel for a person to care about me; then, to love someone and they love me back was a favorite pass time, but the son always watched getting my attention with a slap and his order,

"GET BACK TO WORK." I had to wash, and iron his clothes, or clean for him in exchange for the privileged of going to my dance classes in the evening. That day when I returned, my AD grabbed me as soon as I walked in the door. The other person was one of his important friends and I smelled alcohol as they took turns performing oral sex on me. When someone tried to rip my clothes, I fought and got away. Then someone chased me through the house; then, out the house, and then back in the house until I hid in the downstairs closet.

The next morning when I heard a service person, I came out to get to school. My AD saw me, but later that day when I came home to cook and clean, he met me at the door; beat me and forced me to give him oral sex for hours in the closet where I hid. He made that my room from then on. I didn't have much, but what didn't fit in that closet, he took away. Prior to that, my AD allowed me oatmeal in the evenings, but I could no longer eat their food free. I had to pay and was hungry all the time.

When I ran to my Island, My AD would seek the police and workers from every social agency in the city on my friends. So, my friends asked me only to come if my life depended on it. I let day trips to my Island do afterward so I could eat. Then my AD left the Island alone when I stopped staying gone for days at a time.

The last reason I ran away staying gone, I was eleven. My AD brought a 3-month-old baby home, and the little boy became my total responsibility. I didn't know what to do, so I took him to my Island to get help. My AD made it so bad for the island; I had to go home with the baby. From then on, I had the responsibility of a baby 24/7 accept for when he was at the babysitters. This included me providing food and clothing him too, but a nice woman at the Island kept him during the day. I named him Richard, and he lived with me in my closet. I grew to enjoy him like my child, and I always wanted a doll, so I had a real doll baby, but let no one know that I enjoyed it for fear something would happen to Richard.

When Richard or Rich started talking, he called me Mom. It made me feel like I was someone and gave me strength.   My instructors and teachers accepted that I took care of him. He was so cute with everyone loving him; I could take him wherever I went. He learned too.

As years went on, I slowed down taking some nasty medicine I had been taking since I could remember. I had bad fevers or spells that made me pass out for hours. I wasn't sure if they resulted from my birth condition or the head injury; however, I weaned myself with smaller doses until I was strong enough to fight most the fevers. When I had a spell, people found my Island Friend Rod.

Rod was my street brother whom I met at eleven. Rod came through life fighting, so when we met he was 17 and making money as a boxer. He fought thru our Islands Production Office. Rod had it so our Island would profit from his talent. After all, the Island raised him with him braking away from being an orphan and was independent.

I must mention, Rod was 6ft 2 inches with the rugged looks of a boxer, but cute enough to be a model. He did that too and started me modeling doing catalog work when we met; then, Rod and a photographer convinced me to create a photo portfolio. Modeling was cool, and with all the positive things they said, I wanted to continue modeling elsewhere after I finish school.

Rod was the only person who knew about my secret he said I told him during one of my fevers. I couldn't remember that, but I had to go to Rod one day and tell him some of my problems at home. It was hard to hide things from him since he worried and cared about Richard and me, and I was proud of Rod. He helped at the island and didn't forget where he came from.

Older and almost in full control of my world, I notice my AD went off on long trips. He used to leave for two weeks twice a year with many weekend trips, but had more long business trips all during the year. It made life easier; however, I noticed weird happenings at my AD's house and it was still spooky there. I sensed the apparent danger for Rich and me. I made sure we're gone by 5:30AM; then, ran with Rod, took three classes, went home while everyone's gone except one daughter; cook, clean up, do whatever work while reading. Then by 2:45PM, I was on campus starting my late afternoon and evening classes. And... I stayed gone until late and I hoped all were sleep.

My schedule varied, and I napped eating when I could, with only a few friends, which were all boys who understood my situation. To them my father wouldn't allow me to have company, I could only go out if it had to do with music, dance, or education, and Richard could come. I didn't hang with girls because they turn on you over petty shit that was stupid. Most of them were jealous because of my friendship with Rod, but I had finished all my high school courses leaving their stupidity behind.

Working on first and second year college courses, I elected to go to college only so to stay on campus, but I was too young to live in the dorms. Advance Preparatory Tech allowed me to continue my enrollment there for some of my college courses and the rest I took on the college campus with people still staring or treating me like a freak. I think it was because I was so young. However, I compensated myself with my greatest love, physical activity. The freedom I felt running and the confidence that dance gave me, made me passionate at learning the art of dance, jumping higher, and running faster. So I practiced more. I was my own master and the creativity that came through my body made people respond favorably. From Hip Hop to Ballet to Ballroom dancing, I did it all so well I had the option to attend The School of Performing Arts in New York. I had my AD sign all the paperwork and sent it in.

The opportunity for my studying and training in the arts at one of the most prestigious schools in the US, Advance Preparatory Tech, was a blessing that came out of nowhere for no reason. I found out much later that my AD went to College in Berkley, California, and was in a famous band with Brian Schulman, whom he called BS, and Mr. Kapulani. BS was still playing music, touring, and had awards like two Grammys, Platinum, and Gold Albums for his contributions to jazz and pop music over the last 16 years or more.

The huge Polynesian man, Mr. Gerald Kapulani, first came to my AD's house when I was eight and started my lessons in voice, dance, and piano, but I remembered seeing him before then. Mr. Kapulani was nice and a mountain of a man. He came to see me, but not as often as his son, Adam, who came twice every month during the year since I was 8 and gave me a phone that my AD took. They always gave me money, gifts, and told me not to let my AD know, but my AD knew they gave me things and watched them intently so he could take everything. My AD hid me a few times when Adam came telling Adam I went to live with another family, but Adam and his father continued to visit looking for me finding me still there.

Adam played Pro football and his father had retired from pro football. Both were huge, handsome, and cool with me. They didn't get along with my AD, but encouraged me by making any payments for my voice, piano, and dance lessons. Adam, who played Saxophone in BS's band in his off-season, offered me a chance to go to The Beach Camp for Performing Arts. All gifted students who were prominently talented as a student in a performing art wished to go there. You had the opportunity to train and receive top pay while performing on the road with established performers. The father and Adam said they were waiting for me.

Meanwhile, I was winning so many track meets running and jumping, colleges started offering scholarships for track. They didn't know how to handle the fact I was already in college and too young to participate in their league.

Like overnight, I matured, getting tall, and had what the guy's called, the pretty hair, pretty eyes, light-skinned girl thing going on (that people loved to hate) with some speed bumps growing on my chest. I didn't weigh much, which was good in a way because I modeled with Rod a lot. Actually, it was great. That year was my first runway walk during our city's fashion week that showed a line of teenage fashion and I did other fashion shows afterward. People started requesting me. Nothing major, but it was something giving me confidence and teaching me how to handle myself as a model. I signed with Rods agent to keep my jobs and me straight.

However, time flies when you're not having fun. The son was almost 20 and wanted to claim me, which I didn't want. I had almost finished the requirements for my BA degree and according to my college ID I was 17. My AD didn't bother me so much and was planning to sign a consent form for me to marry. My period was irregular, so he took me to a doctor to regulate it telling me he wanted plenty grandkids, but he wanted Richard immediately. When my AD had an urge, I told Richard, to cry uncontrollably loud and run around like he didn't have good sense.

Our situation was terminally disgusting and running away was my solution. Since this had to be a permanent relocation, I needed to save more money. I stalled by bathing my AD having his water drawn with wine and candles helping him to relax with what he liked when he came home. Most times, he didn't know Rich wasn't there, but that kept him off Richard, and I could get him to sign anything with my special attention. My AD felt he was training me for his son. I felt like a prostitute. I had many applications signed giving me permission to stay away from home, but knew I had to leave with Rich.

One day I returned late morning to my AD's house to do my chores and thought no one was home. I let Richard go play while I worked. Soon I heard Richard cry out for me and found one daughter trying to drag him up the stairs. I don't know what she planned, but no one in that house ever had anything to do with him. She let him go to run in her room, but I caught up with her and beat her down; then, I grabbed Richard with what we could carry and we ran. I knew we had to leave that day. It was Richard's only chance for a normal life. I ran to Rod's house very upset and told Rod everything that was happening and I couldn't keep them off Richard anymore. We had to leave right away. Rod flew into a rage.

Outside the ring, Rod was a cool character, but he was getting ready to throw his life away. He said he would kill all of them. Now, I had been thinking the same thing, but this is not a Rod, Allysa, and Richard kills everyone in the house; then leave and lock the door story. We calmed down, and Rod walked us to the house to get the rest of our belongings. Richard and I had already moved the most of our stuff to Rods house a little at a time. Plus, I had saved every penny for nine years from our hustles and gifts. I took it out the security box at the bank my agent arranged for me. It totaled $7,136.60. I had $3000.05 in my bank account and $1500 in Adja Bible, so we had enough to take care of ourselves for a little while.

I figured to go home and let Rod come with me so we could get back out without a problem. This would be better than killing everyone. I told Rod my plan to get him to cool down and not throw his life away over something so stupid. Plus, it was my problem.

CHAPTER TWO

The Escape

We walked toward my AD's house getting soak in a cold January rain to find the house lit up. Usually people were stalking around in the dark waiting, but today there was a pretty SUV in the driveway with conversation and laughter coming from the house. What in the world I wondered as I stepped in to see two well dress handsome men. One said,

"Oh, there she is now." I looked a tangled up mess with my hair doing the wet curl frizz thing.

It was Adam, and he introduced his brother, Jaison, who had long curly dreads down his back. Adam had a 6 foot 7-inch frame with a linebacker built. Jaison was shorter, a slimmer built with pretty hazel eyes. I couldn't hear for looking, but I snapped out of it when I found out they were there to take me with them. By then two girls, Bubbles and BB, had gotten out the SUV, and came in behind us. They introduced themselves and said they will be working with me.

BB was outspoken and funny while Bubbles was more reserved. They fussed and joked with each other. They were beautiful and funny. I imagined if I had sisters, I would want them to be like that. I hoped they would help me with my appearance because their makeup and clothing were on point. Then I heard my AD say I was too young to go off alone, but Adam pulled out the signed application giving me permission to do just that. Plus, Adam was making the greatest argument ever. Be they lies or whatever; I figured I would jump in my closet and get the rest of my belongings, but Richard cried saying,

"Mommy don't leave me. Don't leave me alone." I looked at his toy in our room, the closet. My stomach turned. I sat there staring at the toy truck trying to keep tears from falling. A few fell.

"She can't go because she has to take care of the boy." My AD reasoned. Our guests looked at each other and me. Adam didn't know about Richard or my responsibility to him and seemed confused, but the others who came made it a point to continue getting our belongings together and packed into the SUV; determined it seemed.

Jaison and Rod realized our room was a closet in that large house. Jaison said while picking up Rich,

"We'll take the boy with us and give her a chance to get settled." Bubbles hunch BB while whispering,

"Hurry, get the rest of their stuff out of her room." Still looking at my situation BB said,

"It's a fuckin closet."

"Shut up," Bubbles whispered as she hit BB. They both left with hands and arms full. Richard and I grabbed the rest and followed.

Meanwhile, my AD's son said I was engaged to him and I couldn't go. About then Adam noticed everyone had piled up in the SUV not concerned where or how we were sitting. Jaison pulled out the drive then opened Adam's door and everyone peeped at him. Adam said bye on the run and jumped in; then, we left. I didn't look back.

With Richard calling me mommy, I knew they thought he was my child. I didn't care if it meant I was getting away with Richard. I was so embarrassed about them observing my little life I planned to run away later anyway.

Rod got out downtown. He gave me a kiss and Richard a punch.

"If anything happens to them, I will hunt you down." Rod said looking at Adam. And I thought now I get to go with them, but Adam replied,

"I feel you man. I've tried to look out for Allysa and we have our Little Bit. She's our little sister now. I promise you her life will change for the better. You know her talents. We're just going to help her," Jaison second that saying,

"Nothing will happen to her."

"I don't think you have to worry about that NOW!" BB joked with an attitude. Then, we rode for a while in silence. Richard was looking at Adam and Jaison excitedly with his big bright eyes. The cute one with the hazel eyes, Jaison, continued picking at Rich, making him laugh. That helped me feel less apprehensive. Then Adam said,

"It's the beginning of my baby brother's team's run toward March Madness." So, they were on their way to a college basketball game in which the youngest brother and cousin were playing.

My AD continued calling Adam as we traveled, so we stopped to eat in a distant town. I ordered soup and for the first time Richard and I experienced Pizza. They couldn't believe that however, we were saving money and couldn't afford it. I kept my eye on Adam. Then Adam pulled me to the side while Bubbles and BB entertained Richard.

"Ok what's the plan?" He asked. Then looking stern and suspicious Adam said, "Also, I'm not taking my eyes off you enough for you to run away. I don't want you feeling uncomfortable, but please be honest with me because we want to help you and the boy. Think of a plan."

They all had different personalities like the different flavors of ice cream. I was curious wanting to know and become friends with them. They didn't seem phony, but I was scared shitless. So, I figured it would be best if I let him help us for a while.

We finished eating, and I had them take me to a small Island in that town made up of abused women and children. They had legal livable apartments in their island, plus the elderly couple who ran it told us they could keep Richard or both of us legally after a city inspection in 2 or 3 weeks. Adam said,

"It will be just the boy." That troubled me. Richard would be by himself.

We got back on the road traveling on a wide highway. At the moment I was tired, but happy to be away from that situation. I didn't want to get sick, so I stopped stressing and enjoyed listening to all the happy chatter which proved to brighten my outlook somewhat. I nodded while riding.

"My babies are tired," BB yawned, while getting comfortable herself. "You're safe now so go to sleep." BB felt comforting like Adja, so I relaxed. I remember waking up with all of us curled up sleep like puppies. I felt... safe.

We arrived at the motel where the band was staying, and I became acquainted with the other members. I also met the baby brother's girlfriend of 3 years, Marlena, and her best friend, the brother's mother. Everyone was so close knit and just chilling, so Richard and I acknowledged everyone with a greeting, and then I sat in the corner observing. I notice Adam pacing and talking on the phone. He glanced at me several times then went into the hall to continue his conversation with Jaison following; then, their mother followed. That looked bad for Richard and me, so I made sure we had our emergency backpacks and carryall. When they returned, the two brother seem confused and sad; however, the mother went back to her little group laughing, talking, and telling my business. Adam called me over; then, quietly said,

"BS decided to use only one female dancer, Bubbles, but let's wait until my father calls back."

Some in the group made calls, and found a few gigs, but not for a teenager with a small boy. Everyone thought Richard was my son and most were nice, but the girlfriend was in a loud group with the mother making jokes about how I had to come out with my legs open to have a son that old. Then Marlena loudly asked,

"What are they gypsies... or zebras?" Their group laughed with the loudest girl saying,

"They found them in a closet. They got to crawl back in their hole," and they continued to make noise like Hyenas, however, others in the room felt embarrass and apologized.

"Don't worry," Adam clarified, "We're not sending you back to that place. Just ignore all of them including my mother. My baby brother and my cousin play on a team that will win their conference championship..."

"Yeah and get more money for me." The girlfriend, Marlena, interrupted. I thought what a gold digger. She rolled her eyes because the little brother, her boyfriend, had called to find out if I was there. That was nice, but her attitude spread through her little group like the infection they seemed to be; making me uneasy about the situation so, I planned to use the game as a distraction to leave.

I sat with Adams wife and children behind the teams' bench. They were nice. The mother and her crowd sat elsewhere. Jaison had bought Richard souvenirs, and they were eating as normal trying to force me to eat with them. Everyone said I was too thin, so Jaison wanted me to eat. I enjoyed the family atmosphere. I saw this in other families where I lived and wondered how it felt. Adam called me pointing to two men saying,

"That's my baby brother and crazy cousin with the iPod." The cousin, Delano, was the tallest person on the court and had to be trippin I thought. He's on the court with his iPod jamming while everyone else shot around.

The baby brother, Jacob, was 6ft 9inches, but handsome. Everything about him was... in balance. I found it hard keeping my attention off him. While he walked to the side and waved, I realized he was so hot, my world, as I knew it stop rotating. I could only think of him and stare. His smile was warm and inviting. He had slightly slanted light grey eyes with long hair down his back that Adam said his mother cut with a scissors all his life. My world started again on a different spin. I waved quickly and looked at my magazine, sweating. Bubbles and BB were talking to me, but he was on my mind with everything so perfect. His body was on OMG! He looked like Tarzan with a goatee.

I tried not to look at him, but he was staring at me. Before beginning the game when the coach talked to the team, I noticed Jacob looking at me moving his eyes quickly when I looked up. I couldn't help from smiling while feeling happy looking at and thinking about him. I liked that feeling too. Trying to stay focus on my plan or even look at my magazine, I could only manage thoughts of him and just turn pages when I thought it was time to do so. Then his team fell behind.

The team looked like it was uncoordinated and needed to calm down. Plus, Jacob had some problems with the ball. That wasn't good. His brothers and everyone was shouting at him and I noticed his coach telling him to settle down; then, Jacob peeped at me. Use to giving Rod signals as he boxed, when Jacob went back on the court and looked at me again, I pointed to where he was standing, and then made a shooting gesture. He started shooting from behind the arch in three-point land scoring 18 points by the half and took over the second half scoring 31 more. I almost had a heart malfunction watching him as he played. His efforts encouraged his team to play better and win the game with him getting MVP. I stayed long enough to see that, then I took Richard, our bags, and we left. Richard cried. He really liked the family atmosphere. I did too making it hard to leave. Regardless of the idiots, it hurt, but I had contacted an island in that city. I called there a few times before while acquiring items for my old island and the King was waiting a few blocks away.

It was January, cold and snowing. We met King Freddie, and he looked us over taking us. Looking at the king, he was young and sleazy looking meaning the Island was mostly teenage crazies. That's the worst. Richard and I came up with plan A, B, C, and D. I figured in the morning or sooner to move on. As soon as we arrived at the abandoned half burnt apartment building, we got D out the way when Freddie said,

"Come GIVE ME ALL YOUR SHIT." King Freddie had first dibs. After looking at our stupid mess, he said while sizing me up. "Give me the money and keep your mess." I gave him the $183.00 I had in my pockets. He grabbed me. With his captain holding me and dealing with Richard Freddie checked for more by going through my pockets; then, in my bra and underwear where he found two more $50 bills. I couldn't dwell on that. "I'll figure what to do with you two in the morning, but I got some ideas and may need you to help me keep warm." He finished saying and made a skinny joke while he continued to look at me. We had to leave.

We put our stuff together in a carryall I threw over my shoulder and snuck out with people chasing us with it becoming hide and seek, but not a game. Rich jumped on my back as I ran for our lives back toward the stadium with me hoping to see someone I knew. Everyone had left with me knowing we had to get out of sight so I quickly used a fake ID to get us a room in a rundown motel. I had money hid on Richard and found Jaison cell number on a card.

Two days later, I realized life was too rough in the street for Richard. It was snowing out and so cold that morning in our room,

31

so I called Jaison's number. The phone rang once and Jaison picked up. I asked him to meet us. I knew I could talk to him that's why I hid all my money in his SUV. Plus, I wanted Jaison to get us a warm safe place for two weeks, and a way for Rich to get to the Island with the elderly couple. I figured I would leave too, so to take care of Rich until he gets older, but the three brothers came with the cousin. Richard was so happy to see them he ran and jumped into Jaison's arms, but Adam was very upset with me. He had said he would help us the next day.

It was stupid and selfish for me to run away spoiling an important family event, and Richard was sad the whole time. I wanted to get him with decent people. He had a chance, but I wasn't use to being around decent people who cared. However, I ran feeling it was better to do things independently. With my AD calling, I felt he knew where to find us, and I was anxious. The ordeal with that guy Freddie made me realize I was alone in a large dangerous world. What I did was so stupid I couldn't look at the brothers and cousin, feeling all their eyes looking at me. I continued repeating I'm sorry, but remembered how I felt when I heard that phrase, because it made nothing better.

I felt heat go to my face. Then a tear fell while Adam led me to a back seat of the SUV. Everyone became quiet, and I sat there afraid and confused. At that point, I wanted to die. I stepped away and threw up. They said nothing else, but back at the band's motel, the girlfriend and the mother took their turn with me. The mother said little, but the girlfriend called me a stupid big-lipped nigger... Yeah she went there. I tuned out and tried to find somewhere to hide. Richard threw a bottle water at her and then Jaison took us to another room.

"Chill and don't leave," he said. Richard asked him,

"Are you leaving us by ourselves?" Jaison said,

"Yes, I'll be... " Not listening anymore, Richard wined,

"We didn't mean to make you mad," and he wanted Jaison to come back. Jaison came back and played with Richard as Bubbles and BB came in upset by the girlfriend's remark.

"Lie down, Allysa. You looked tired. We don't want you to be sick." BB told me; then, said to Jaison "The child's eyes have changed, and she looks weak. Leave it be!" Bubbles and BB made me lay down on BB's bed. Afterwards they took Rich and left.

Aware that I was going into a spell, I tried to calm down to avoid passing out. I forgot how bad the spells were and worked them that day. I came to in Adam's room in a wet wife beater and some underwear. Adam and his wife were cooling me with ice, but after resting that night sleeping on a cot in Adam and his family's room, I felt better.

The next morning, I had a talk with Adam. I told him about my medical problems and the money I left in the SUV; then said,

"Adam please get Rich and myself a place to stay until it's time for Rich to go, and I'll leave too." He responded,

"Yeah, I thought about you a lot last night and this morning. You know BS told me to send you home, but my father said to find you, keep you with us, and take care of you like a sister. I will, but you have to let me help you if you have a problem."

"Adam... I don't think I can do that. I want to. It's just...."

"Allysa, I promise to keep and protect you if you promise not to lie, play games, or run away again. My dad feels you're a special person and a talented dancer, but after last night, I wonder if you're healthy enough to handle everything. You will have to prove yourself more with BS not feeling you deserve a chance, but remember my father does. So there are battles going on concerning you. We're going on a six to eight-week tour that is also a competition against other performers. Now get some rest and let me know if you feel you can do this." He waited for a response, but

I had none.   Adam continued, "My wife disagrees, but with your talent I think this way will be best. I know you are finishing your academics for your bachelor degree, you want to go to The New York School of Performing Arts, and I'm sure you have a few ID's, but you have a legit college ID that states you're 18 and you're super smart, but I'm aware that you just had your 15th birthday. The next youngest will be twenty in two months. So grow up and stop doing foolish things. There are no kids here. We send them home."   I realized this was Rich and my chance for a better life.

CHAPTER THREE

Getting to Know You

Little by little, I became acquainted with everyone. Some were phony, some haters, and the others turned out to be family. The brothers and cousin was the band; however, there were violins, horns, and a keyboard artist I hadn't seen yet. Everyone Mr. Kapulani selected was multi-talented. The brothers and cousin Delano have been studying and playing music all their lives with Lynn and BB as backup singers for their band. Adam wanted Bubbles and I to sing with them. All were trained vocalist, thanks to Mr. Kapulani, so our harmony was on point.

Jacob came to see me after Adam's wife made me go take a nap and surprised me when he apologized for his girlfriends' remark.

"Sorry that upset you," he said, "Don't pay it any mind." I could barely look at him and it was hard speaking with him. Then he stayed too long and his girlfriend with her crew came in to collect him. The loud mouth girl, LaQuanda, whom I renamed Klondike, made a joke about chasing me back to my hole. I felt better when Jacob refused to leave and then pushed them out locking the door. He came and felt my forehead while sitting on the floor by my cot. When he touched me, I felt this... funny feeling, but eventually dosed off listening to him tell me about everyone and his father. When I woke up later, the cousin, Delano was about one inch from my face.

"I was about to steal another kiss, but I remembered you threw up," he said while still looking at me as if I was a specimen. WHAT??? I checked to make sure my clothes weren't disheveled, but realized the group took turns watching me. With all the attention, I didn't know how to react. Later, I told everyone thanks, and they looked at me as if they didn't have a clue; then, talked about going out to eat. So, with me in tow, we left for dinner.

I trailed behind under the watchful eye of Adam when everyone except me decided to eat at this expensive restaurant. I said,

"Adam I can't eat here. I don't have money for that." Adam looked at me then said,

"You are now employed. We pay for all your meals now, and you eat with us." As he talked, I looked in the window to make sure I was dress correctly and saw Jaison, Jacob, and Rich seated and eating everything. Rich who had on new clothes and a fresh hair cut literally jumped out of his seat and ran to me grabbing my hand saying,

"Mommy, look," as he showed me his outfit and new, Timberland, boots. The whole restaurant became quiet. I felt everyone was looking at me including Jaison and Jacob.

"This way madam," the Matron De said leading me to Jacob.

"There's my Barbie Doll." Jacob said as he pulled out the chair beside him to seat me. When he helped me out my coat, I think he looked me up and down then smelled the air around me as if he was getting my scent. His shy smile made me nervous while setting next to him. I had a habit of fidgeting with my clothes when nervous and I fidgeted my panties into a bunch.

"Why are you changing colors?" Jaison asked, "You're not passing out again are you?" Jacob hopped up as if I was giving birth and asked,

"Are you all right?" Then he put his arm around me for support and Oh my God. I could only imagine, but I didn't have time to answer before Rich said,

"She likes you." I wondered what my face looked like at that moment. Jaison said,

"I guess all kids embarrass Moms." I excused myself to regain my composure.

Bubbles and BB were in the bathroom waiting. BB jokingly said

"Wouldn't sit with us, huh! Got to set with the three handsome guys, so we got to talk to you in the bathroom." I managed to smile. Bubbles reassured me,

"You shouldn't pay Marlena or LaQuanda any mind. I'm Pilipino and Black, the brothers are Polynesians and White." Then BB proclaimed,

"I'm mix too... with a little of my daddy and a little of my mommy." They helped me realize how stupid it would be to pay attention to Marlena's attempt at racism. BB who was the closes in age at 19 expressed, "Marlena's a joke, but it's unusual for Jacob to pay any attention to new girls, and just about every new girl that comes in here wants to get with him or Jaison. Jacob shies away. He is quiet, but Jaison... he's just a dog like in BIG BOW WOW." I said,

"Yeah, I could see that, but they both seem nice." BB went on,

"Jacob's girlfriend just wants him for his money when he goes pro. Right now they expect him to be Number 4 or 5 in the first round of the draft this June." That surprised me, and I felt happy for him, but remarked,

"Yeah, I see that too and I haven't heard anything stupid lately. Where are they?" BB said,

"Marlena's gang travels in a pack and opted to go to an expensive Mid-Eastern restaurant... at Jacobs' expense." Bubbles remarked,

"When Marlena and mother are here, they eat at expensive restaurants every day." I realized all of them went with Jacob's mother; Marlena, LaQuanda, Rafael, Jen 6, and one called Twister. That upset me with a funny feeling I didn't understand; however, BB let me know,

"Jacob's mother and the girlfriend, Marlena, are scheming partners to do what's best for Jacob." I noticed the whole family was protective of the baby and a momma's boy came to mind, but he was too nice for Marlena. We continued our conversation, and I accidentally called LaQuanda, Klondike. I explained the spelling.

"We get it." BB said giggling.

I went back to the table with Jacob doing everything all over again, and so did I. I figured he felt sorry for my situation.

Richard was excited wanting to show me all his new gifts. I was astonished! The back of the SUV was full. He had a kid seat, books, toys, a bike, and bags and bags of new clothing. I peeped in some of the bags feeling apprehensive when I notice women clothing. There were shoes, a coat, PJ's, and some sexy underwear and nightgowns. The items I saw were very expensive. Figuring it was Jacob's girlfriends stuff, I stopped looking wondering how much they spent on Rich and became upset when I couldn't spend my money the way I needed.

Figuring Rich needed warmer clothing; I reached under the rear seat to get the money I hid. It was all there. Then, I heard a voice. No, it wasn't GOD.

"Is that yours?" Jaison asked. He looked at me suspiciously.
"Yes," I said, "And I want to pay you something for Rich's..." Jaison cut me off asking,

"Where did you get that amount of money, and what else have you put in here?"

"Nothing." I said and Jaison asked,

"Do we have something we need to discuss?"

"No!" I said, but then Jacob walked toward me. They were huge and intimidating, plus Jaison seemed mad at me. "It's my money I saved." I thought about running, but Rich was in the front seat. Feelings of being attack by my AD flashed in my mind. I covered my head as I was use to and stepped back to soften the blow a little. Jacob grabbed my arms, pulling them down and asked,

"What is wrong with you? You think we will hurt you?" The look on his face was confusing. He looked irritated and hurt, but went back to his seat. Jaison sat down in the rear with the doors open and said,

"Come here. Talk to me Little Bit, and tell me what is going on?" My head was in a tailspin. Too many questions causing stress and my head hurt so bad.

"Jaison, I need to go somewhere else." I then said to Rich, "I got to go." Rich came asking,

"Why? They like you." I couldn't even tell him.

"My heads aching Rich and I'm getting sick," was the only thing I could say. I took my medicine and laid down on the seat. Everything went from brown to black.

Waking with Rich on my mind, I felt sweaty and mumbled,

"Where's Rich," while trying to remember. I was sharing a room with BB who I understood shared rooms with no one. She came over, and plopped down on my cot, which almost took us to the floor; then, she felt my forehead,

"Good you're much cooler. Girl you about scared me to death. You were saying some wild shit over here. Sound like you got the chanting for a minute and I thought lord they done put me it here with someone crazier than I am." She said that while rocking back and forth looking crazy. She was funny cheering me up a little. "Anyway," BB continued, "Rich is hanging out with Adam and the guys put your stuff in the other room. We have a formal with promotional pictures that starts tomorrow evening. Then we pick up transport the next morning, and Little Sis, we will be on our way." I didn't have a clue. "Take a shower and get into your PJ's I'll explain later. Oh yeah, Jacob took an hour picking out a robe and some PJ's. He put them in the bathroom for you... and he was a little to concern if you would like them."

In the other room, checking for my bag with my girlie stuff and my purse I saw all the bags and boxes from the back of the SUV. Realizing Jacob bought it for Rich and me after I read the note, I had to ask,

"BB is Jacob always this nice? I mean he bought me all this... stuff."

"Girl, I don't know what you did to him. He is treating you very special... and looking at some of the stuff he got you... hmm... he is doing some fantasizing too. I think it's a little more than being nice. He wants you to go to the hospital when you get sick. I think you should too and stop worrying about shit. BB, your big sis, will take care of you. Now take a shower and leave the door cracked in case you get sick. I'll clue you about everything."

Jacob gave me this sea mist green blue set. It had a silk crop top kind of see through, a short robe that matched with short girlie boxer briefs. I imagined the different ways I could wear the outfit. I could wear the robe without the top. Then I looked at all the different cosmetics, oils and perfumes Jacob bought me. I looked at everything eager to shower and check out a few of the cosmetics. What he bought was on my wish list. I liked them... and him.

My shower took me more than an hour. BB knocked and checked on me 5 times, but I adorned myself and never wore anything that felt so good. Fantasizing myself, I wondered if Jacob would like the way I smelled and looked. Well... I didn't have to wonder. Jacob was waiting for me when I came out the bathroom. I was nervous; the material was sheer, so I went back and put on the robe. Jacob said,

"Wow, that looks so pretty on you," and he took my hands asking, "How do you feel?" Oh My God! I didn't hear a word he said. I just saw his mouth wiggle while his magnetism took over.

Jacob was truly the meaning of handsome. The way his hair hung down his back with a few curls. His slightly slanted eyes, shy smile with dimples, and a Fu Manchu with a little soul patch that made up a boyish face which signified he just turned into a man. He made me forget everything. I was so transfixed by him I didn't answer. "Are you all right?" He asked, again. His voice was deep and soothing. I felt strange, but I felt comfort too. Between him and BB, I felt much better; however, I asked,

"Jacob, are you doing all this because you feel sorry for me?"

"Well... it's not that I feel sorry for you, but I know you and the boy have been treated bad, and I want you to feel good when you're with me... um us," Jacob said blushing. I felt that weird feeling in my stomach again and Jacob rushed off. BB looked at me, and shook her head while saying,

"I see something brewing."

BB told me about everybody and everything.

"Adam's 29 and married. He's the oldest of Mr. Kapulani's sons. They have no sisters. He's been in the pros for eight years and he and his wife have three daughters, ages 2, 4, and 8. This year Adam's team wasn't in the play offs. So, he's developing the Band Camp for his father and only taking orders from Dad. He is the undisputed leader, boss, of the road band. Next, is Jaison who's

more of a drifter, lover, and dreamy. He's a model, an actor, and 24."
I said,

"He's tall for a model." BB went on,

"Well... he's a model. He used to be a wild party guy, but his friend and their baby died during childbirth. He calmed down and now he's very laid back. Then Hu who is the drummer and writes music when he's not playing pro Baseball. When he's not doing that, he's a pirate and lives on an island in the South Pacific." Laughing BB said, "What else would you do in your spare time? And last is that guy who likes Allysa, Jacob. He turned 21 this month, and he's expected to go #4, 5 or 6 in the draft in June." I asked,

"BB, what's the deal with him and Marlena?" She replied,

"Well, there's not much to it with Jacob, but it seems his mother wants him to marry Marlena. His brothers boss him around too, and Jacob can get crazy when he's fed up with something. It's just hard to figure what's bothering him because he's so quiet, but very respectful of his mother. The others have little to do with her because she so meddlesome." I said,

"Yeah, she's something else." BB said,

"I think Jacob likes you though. I have never seen him apply himself like he has with you and that's good Allysa, because his girlfriend is mean and treats him like dirt with him being so sweet to her." The thought of that pissed me off, and I realized I liked him. "Allysa, you got both of the finest guys here waiting on you, hand and foot." BB continued while I watched her fill out some paperwork. Then she said, "Now for Delano who is the character among them..."

"I think he's a pervert BB."

"Oh, you know him then." We laughed, and she went on saying, "Well at 7 ft. 2 inches he probably never had any because his shit is always on point." I asked,

"Like.... Erected?"

"Yeah," BB said, "He'll go pro next year. Now, Lynne is 23, Bubbles and Klondike 24. Lynn and Klondike have been coming here since they were 14. They're the head of all the females on the road. As you know, Klondike is Marlena's BFF best female flunky who enjoys picking at people, and she'll take any Kapulani, but at camp, you'll find her with BS in dark places doing him. That's been going on for six years. I've been at the camp longer myself for voice and violin, and I know Lynn's cool." I asked,

"What about Bubbles?" BB said,

"I like Bubbles and... I think she's cool, but she hangs out with Marlena and Klondike too much to be fully trusted."

BB and I had to see Adams' wife. After the meeting, I became BB's roomie. We both were happy. Then BB grabbed her cigarettes, the keys for Jaison's SUV and we made a midnight snack run for everyone. Afterward, we made the deliveries and returned to our room and our conversation with BB saying,

"My mother use to sing in BS's band, but she would only work for, Mr. Kapulani. My mom wants me to be a singer, but I want to be a model. I'm filling out my application for TMP now." She told me about a new TV reality show for girls who wanted to model called The Total Model Project, and then she asked, "Have you ever modeled Allysa?" I told her about all the work I did with Rod and BB said, "I got an extra copy; let's both apply." If it kept me away from my AD, I was game. The next few hours we spent talking, laughing, and hooking up our applications for TMP.

I had just gone to sleep good when Adam called at 6:30 am.

"I need to see you in an hour."

Adam was in the conference room with the group leaders. Adam announced,

"Kondyk... um I mean LaQuanda is to make sure private practice is taking place when scheduled, Bubbles is in charge of the dancers, and Lynn handles costumes and oversees all female students..." Jacob eased closer and pinched me as Adam went over rules and regulations; then, he dismissed everyone as I hit Jaison. Jaison looked at me wondering and Hu left laughing at Adam for calling the girl Klondike. Then as I tried to figure what, Adam asked me, "Do you feel comfortable with us speaking freely around Jacob?" I nodded yes and Adam got to the point asking,

"Is Richard your child? Please be honest." Trying to figure why he asked me I hesitated. I wanted to be honest, but I didn't want him to send Richard into the system of adoption. That system worked somewhere sometimes, but it didn't work for us.

"No," I answered becoming guarded. I exclaimed, "Please he can't go back there or in the system!" Standing, ready to go I said, "We'll leave. Just please...."

"Please... just don't you get upset," Adam said looking at Jacob then me. Jacob grabbed my hands, which caught my attention and then said,

"Calm down. Stop... or you will get sick. Please, we just want to help you. Adam's not sending you or Rich anywhere." Jacob moved his hands to my arms and pulled me a little closer. I felt indescribably strange, and calmed down. I couldn't help myself. When I studied Jacob's face and looked in his eyes, he looked in mine saying, "If he is your child, please, don't worry you don't have to give him away." I said,

"He feels like my child because I took care of him from an infant to 4 years old. That's why I wanted him in a decent, safe place and I can't stay with your group. I have to make sure he's safe." Adam said,

"That says a lot about you Allysa. We want to help you, Allysa, and you're a child yourself. In fact, that's why you are here. My father wants to help talented at-risk children, and we have watched your progress for years." By now, Jacob was standing there smiling as Adam walked over noticing us and I didn't hear a word Adam said. Removing my hand and backing up Jacob didn't want me to leave his touch, so he grabbed my hands again. I didn't mind, but I had to stop looking in his eyes. With me paying attention to Adam, he continued,

"We will be in a competition for positions at this year's Beach Camp. My father felt that BS was overlooking talented people, so this year my father placed together a group to represent his ideas. I understand you applied to The School of Performing Arts in New York. Well, if you make the band camp, you will become a featured dancer and your acceptance in that school is automatic. You will receive the exposure that is due you as a young and very talented artist. Your life will change for the better."

"Really?" I asked with Adam replying,

"Yes. I have watch films of you dancing. You have a very classy sex appeal that is so captivating you transform the stage with your presence. It's amazing, and with little effort, you are our best dancer. Working together, we will make sure your life changes for the best." I felt better about my situation until Adam said, "Allysa, I know you can dance, but... I will not lie to you. It will not be easy since you have many haters that go all the way to the top, and they will make things difficult. What you have to do is believe in yourself, and that my family, me, along with a few others you have met and will meet is your family now. We've waited for a while, but we will love and support you. Yeah, you're our Little Sis, and believe me when I say that. It's all good."

I was geeking about now because Jacob was still holding my hands looking at me, and what Adam said was about accomplishing my dreams. I prepared myself for this, and it was all good like he said, but then Adam captured my attention.

"However, we have some obstacles before we can get started. BS is determined not to let you try out for the camp. So my father had to agree to some conditions, but only agreed to the following:

- You must pass a physical or you are gone.
- Richard must be gone, or you are gone.
- You cannot get in any trouble where the authorities are involved, or you are gone."

The conditions upset me. I was concern about Richard, and if I could control my sickness.

"We will get you through this so don't get upset. That's what's making you have those spells or whatever," Jacob said. Then Jacob's girlfriend came in with Jaison. She demanded,

"Jacob! What are you doing holding her hands?" Jacob said,

"I'm just trying to keep her calm." I moved away from him. Jacob became upset leaving as she looked me up and down while making proclamations. She called me a street tramp. Then, Jaison called her a gold digging whore while pushing her out and closed the door on her. Adam confessed,

"Now she's the one that needs to go."

"Cool down Little Bit. Big Bros will look out for you and Rich," Jaison said as he came and put his arms around me; then he asked, "Did Adam tell you? Rich is going to live with Adam and his family... permanently. We asked Rich this morning. He said you would have to let him, so mom, are you going to let him?" I looked at Adam in disbelief, but Adam had this big broad grin on his face and I knew it was true. In shock I knew I had to say something, but I was so happy I couldn't think.

"Will he have to leave later?" I blurted out. Oh GOD, I felt so stupid. I could have asked something more intelligent. Adam chuckled,

"When he's grown and can take care of himself." I had to set down with Adam saying, "I need another man around the house and don't worry we will make it legal. We're all happy to have him." I was happy, but became alarmed.

"Adam... I don't think Rich has a birth certificate or any records."

"Don't worry about that. Adjani is on it and he's with us now to stay too regardless." I liked Adam's family and the way his wife took care of them. I fell on my knees Thanking GOD, and then kissed them both, and wished for Jacob so I could have kissed him.

It was almost 8:30AM as I waited for Jaison to take me to the doctor, but Jacob showed up in this old truck he said he used at school.

"I took care of Marlena so you don't have to worry about her," he said as he stepped out and rushed to open my door. Softly I said,

"So, you killed her?" When Jacob got in, he looked at me. I could just barely keep from laughing. Then Jacob picked to make me laugh, so I did... and it felt good.

"Look at there," Jacob said, "That's too pretty for words so I'm going to look and enjoy this for a while." Yeah, I was enjoying him too.

Jacob was getting ready to go pro, but he drove a slightly banged up truck, and his surfer boy style was old regular clothes. Yet Jacob spent his money so others would feel good about themselves and he was so down to earth, I enjoyed every minute with him, but I had to talk to him about the items he bought.

"Jacob, thank you for the items you bought us. We're enjoying them. I know you spent more, but I want to give you some money..."

"No please don't. I enjoyed getting it for you two." We were quite for a moment. Then he spoke again saying, "One day I want a beautiful person like... you and then I will marry her and have lots of children. So, I'm just practicing." I sat there quiet confused by his dialogue and felt he was directing comments at me. So I said,

"Thank you, but please stop spending money on me. It's making me feel... uncomfortable." Jacob asked,

"Okay, Allysa... so you don't want the gown I have waiting for you? Can I at lease see you in it? Do you have something to wear to the formal tonight?" Concerned I said,

"I didn't know I needed anything."

"Allysa, you have to be on point because you're new and we will be introducing you to professionals from the entertainment world scouting fresh talent." He looked at me saying, "I want you to look good... because... you are so beautiful." No one had ever told me that before, and the fact that it came from Jacob left me speechless. Then Jacob took my hand calming me and said, "Look... Allysa, take the gown and after that we'll talk. You're my Barbie Doll... yeah... and you will dress to represent." I didn't know what he meant by that, but he smiled, and made my stomach feel funny. I didn't want to assume, but he seemed to have claimed me.

At the doctors' office, I had to wear a bathing suit for measurements the nurse took. I thought of how Jacob's girlfriend was so shapely with everything bigger. I look like a pencil compared to her, and Jacob had to be there with the nurse copying all my personal information on the paper work for Adam, while looking at my emaciated body, and then the doctor finished by saying,

"We have a problem. She is severely underweight for an almost 5ft 10 inch growing female and I don't think her frame will allow her to put on 50 lbs." Then the doctor asked questions I couldn't answer. Jacob took the doctor to the side and spoke with him. I heard the doctor say,

"Was this child living on the streets? She weighs slightly under 100 lbs. and you can see her ribs. I can't say she is fit for a road trip." Jacob whispered,

"I know and we will correct that, but we need your help." The doctor looked at me for a while then told Jacob, "I will conditionally pass the young lady since I see she still has growing room. This is border line Jacob. If she picks up ten pounds in the next four weeks, she'll be okay, and she must be monitored after that to keep her healthy, but for now she must take these vitamins, follow a diet, and monitored daily." Jacob agreed then called and explained to Adam about the condition. I was fidgeting. Jacob grabbed my hands.

"Calm down we will get through this." Jacob said while looking at me smiling. "You have a nice body to be so underweight. Put on your clothes." I dressed, and when I returned, Jacob let me know, "Adam said you're in."

"I can stay?" I asked wanting to get excited. He smiled, and felt like finally... I have a chance to make my life better. The solutions to my problems overwhelmed me, and I cried.

"Oh no Allysa... don't cry." He wrapped his muscular arms around me and held me until I stopped. Oh My God. That feeling went all over me at once. I had been around guys, but none of them phased me. With Jacob, I felt so safe, so secure, and so good. I wanted to stay there in his arms, but I knew I had to make a move or I was going to be in trouble.

Jacob took me to the gown he picked for me that was breath taking. How did he know I would like it? It was perfect in every way.

"Well, do you want it?" He asked. I motioned for him to come down closer and kissed him on his cheek. Well... I caught him on the corner of his lips which he seemed to like. Then we went shopping for shoes and accessories, and Jacob said he needed to pick up some things too.

Shopping around we found all we needed, but everything he wanted me to wear was so expensive. "Allysa, it's paid for. You just need to get the right size." Yeah, he said that, but I saw him pulling money out his wallet. I gave him an arched eyebrow the first time, and he looked off in space whistling. We were enjoying a new friendship, so I ignored the money thing. Later we inventoried what we bought. I expressed,

"I've never shopped like that before. It was exciting." Jacob only smiled and took me to get something to eat. We ate and talked fashion, basketball, school, and him going pro. "Wow Jacob... now I can say I know a Pro Basketball player. I'm honored... and thank you again for everything."

"Whoa! I play college ball not pro, and the honor is mine Allysa." Jacob kissed my hand while I looked at him puzzled when he said,

"Allysa, I respect the person you are. You took care of the little boy as if he was yours. Some mothers wouldn't do that. Plus... I have other reasons," he said smoothly stopping short of explaining; then, he went on saying, "I like children and want a house full at least six. Do you like children?"

"Yes, and that's a lot of lovin. I mean with such a large family of six, but... that would be fun." I said thinking of how that could be with him. "Jacob, do you plan to get married soon after you turn pro?" He answered,

"My mother wants me to..., but I got to make sure I have the right girl. I don't want to get children involved and then have to get a divorce." Then I asked Jacob,

"How long have you and Marlena been together?" He answered,

"About 3 years. Our mothers use to be good friends, but her mother died 4 years ago, and she became best friends with my mother. She became interested in me after my freshman year when I became nationally ranked." I asked,

"Were you interested in her at the time Jacob?" He said while looking rejected,

"Well, I was eighteen and this hot twenty-two-year-old took me home with her and its' been on since, but she doesn't want to have children now and only one or two whenever. Also, I feel it's only a money and status thing for her. I don't feel comfort or trust with her." and I questioned,

"Something happen to cause that Jacob?" Jacob answered,

"Quite a few things, but she took $2300 out my travel bag when she thought I was sleep. She didn't care to leave me with a dollar while trying to convince me I lost it. Also, guys call and text her all the time and then she won't let me see her phone, but she checks mine whenever she wants. I know she doesn't appreciate what I do for her. It's like I better or else."

"Oh." I said with him looking distressed. He stopped and noticed me looking at him.

"I don't like how she treats you Allysa. She called you a zebra because you're mixed. My mother's white, but my father is a dark skinned Polynesian. So I guess I'm a zebra, and our children will be too. Maybe that's why she doesn't want to have any." We sort of laughed, but it wasn't funny and we thought for a while when Jacob asked, "Do you have a boyfriend Allysa?" I told him,

"No, my AD wouldn't allow that." I thought for a little while noticing he perked up my spirit, but his was so low. I touched his hand saying, "Jacob... I appreciate what you've done for us."

After that, everything stopped, and he was quiet for the rest of our trip. I thought I said something wrong. Jacob dropped me off at hair and makeup; then, smiled after riding back with such a serious face.

"I'll see you later," he said with me thanking him again, and he drove off into the sunset because he was certainly my hero.

People fussed over me as if I was a famous movie star. Bubbles, BB, and Lynn asked in different ways, "What took so long?" I smiled not answering with people taking my packages. Afraid it would get back to his girlfriend, and she'd give him a hard time, I started wondering when Marlena was leaving.

CHAPTER FOUR

Love Dance

Dressed and ready for the formal I looked at myself in a full view three-way mirror. The way my gown fit made me look like I had more curves and my breast had grown just enough to show cleavage. I felt a surge of self-awareness I never noticed before. Richard showed up in his tuxedo looking sharp and told me I looked pretty when he gave me a rose. This feeling was new, and I was going out to my first party without a thought of having to come home to abuse was encouraging. Most of all I was looking forward to seeing Jacob in his tuxedo with the accessories he wanted me to pick for him. I couldn't get him out of my mind, and the more I thought of how well my gown fit, I crossed his mind too.

Rich and I walked into the lobby and the doorman opened the door to the limo then told us to have a nice evening. I made a pact then within my soul I would die before I return to my AD's house or let anybody use or abuse me again. Rich was very aware he had a family and a decent home. We were geeked talking about our good fortune; then, we arrived. People screamed, while cameras flashed and when I exited the limo, I realized the carpet was red. Then I saw my name and a larger-than-life size poster of me dancing on the wall along with all the other new acts. Rich and I were astonished. Adam, Hu, and Jacob signed autographs and posed for pictures with their significant others. Hu had a movie star as his date. I forgot they're celebrities because they were... my brothers. Bodyguards protected them as they signed autographs. I wanted to ask for one myself, however as I caught up with reality, I became thrilled as fans screamed my name and waved at me.

Jacob looked hotter than I could imagine, and Marlena was hanging all over him, while posing for pictures in his arms, but the photographers snapped pictures of all of us. I was on the red carpet with movie, recording, and sports celebrities who were supporters of The Band Camp. It took a minute, but I posed with Jaison, BB, Bubbles and her boyfriend Danny who was a 6 foot 3-inch professional dancer and almost as handsome as Jacob. Finally, I felt like ENJOYING life.

When Jacob and Adam saw us, they gave us an approving smile. Richard went with Adam as Jacob came over smiling and held out his arm to escort me. I told him,

"You only have room for mom and your girlfriend... but I want to." Jacob coming to me pissed Marlena and mom off. Marlena tried to cause a scene, but I ignored her. I planned to look good for the cameras. I let them go, and Jaison came with his arm extended.

"You ready Little Bit?" I smiled and nodded yes. Jaison escorted me whispering what to do as I walked and I thought we were so smooth. Cameras flashed from every angle. We posed for Photographers. It all was so exciting, and I was smiling then.

Richard walked in ahead of us escorting Adams four-year-old daughter. They were so cute, I almost cried... So I cried.

"Now what's wrong?" Jaison asked. I could barely say,

"I'm happy." He pulled me to the side and gave me a hanky.

"Stop now, you're messing up your face. Fix yourself. Hurry!" I made believe I blew my nose and gave him back the hanky.

"I've never been to anything like this before," I said to Jaison. He gave me the hanky back handling it careful and said,

"What you saying Little Bit, you don't know how to party?" At that moment, he spun and dipped me; then, we danced. Jaison surprised me he could dance so well. DUH... he's an entertainer! We styled and profiled. I liked him too. Jacob and Jaison looked so much alike, but they act so different, almost the opposite.

Our total group was on the stage with people I hadn't met, while Klondike and her group sat with Marlena in the audience. Then introductions came one at a time. When it was my turn, the master of ceremonies, Adam said,

"This is another new addition, Miss Allysa M. Carrington, a dancer if you hadn't noticed, but let's peep at some of her sexy moves," and a film of me dancing came on a large screen. I had seen myself in a mirror, but this was different. The film surprised me. I didn't know I looked so graceful. Adam continued, "Legs for days and don't get it twisted. This is my special little sister," and he hugged me. I felt so honored and I told him.

After Adam introduced everyone, he announced the plan to revamp the Beach Camp's Program introducing our group as representation of that change in talent and guaranteed our group would win. He invited the selective audience from the media and entertainment industry to all our shows and asked them to judge the talent within our group. I thought those were some strong words, and I hoped to understand soon, but for that moment, I planned to enjoy.

Our group sat down in a special section and the party began. Jaison thought he was a lover. I told him he was just a big dog, and he howled like a wolf. Everyone enjoyed the festive mood, and then there was Jaison and his champagne. When Jaison put his glass down after taking a sip, he turned around to talk, and I finished it. Then I sat the glass back in the same spot. I turned around laughing feeling no one was paying me any mind. However, Jacob and Richard were.

"HIC." Then, Adam came and told me a reporter wanted to interview me.

The reporter was from a teen magazine and they asked questions with this bright light shining in my face.

"Did your family inspire you to work hard and achieve your goals?"

"Yes," I said without elaborating. I couldn't think of a better inspiration than abuse. Halfway through the interview the champagne kicked in, and then I bull-shitted my way through the rest of the interview. Later, I couldn't remember what magazine, much of the interview... or why they were even talking to me.

Returning to the party feeling good about everything, I noticed just about everyone's dancing. As I sat down I heard and saw Jacob trying to get Marlena to dance, but she was talking to her flunkies, and ignoring him. He asked again getting her attention this time, and she scoffed at him saying,

"Jacob, you know you're too tall and look goofy dancing making me look goofy if I dance with you. No! Now stop bothering me and go away!" She turned her back to him and continued talking while her friends snickered as he stood there and it didn't bother his mother. Jacob tried to grin it off, but that was cruel. I felt so bad for him. Jacob had consoled me so many times, and now he needed consoling. I watched as he looked down disappointed. When he looked up, our eyes met. He started toward me. I knew my action would cause a problem, but I stood up immediately and took his hands when he asked,

"Allysa, will you dance with me?" I whispered to him,

"Yes Jacob. Are you all right?"

"I am now," he said as Marlena watched the scene unfold. Then realizing her conversation wasn't that important after all she jumped up wanting to dance saying,

"Ok, ok I'll dance with you. It's a slow song so it won't be that bad, and I told you to leave that little girl alone before she screws up our money." I couldn't believe she said that, plus his mother laughed. As Jacob looked at me, he told Marlena,

"No, I've made other arrangements." I continued to gaze in his eyes, our souls met, and from then on, the feeling we shared became a dream. Yeah remember though, there are good and bad dreams; however, Jacob was a man I could only fantasize about, and I was in my fantasies' arms. I wasn't ready for that, but my body responded well.

I felt his muscular arms pulling me close, and we started dancing slow; then, he asked,

"What color are your eyes?" I gasped, but managed to say,

"Brown." Jacob said,

"No they're not. They're hazel green, like now. They're... you're so beautiful." His voice was comforting, and so sexy. After a while of us lost in each other's eyes, gently he pushed my head to his chest pulling me closer. I could hear and feel his heart beating. Then I felt his manhood poking me. He started breathing hard with him stroking my back just enough to make me wiggle... a little. I closed my eyes enjoying the moment wondering; then, imagining how I would feel with him loving and holding me throughout the night. My soul became hot, and I relaxed in his arms wanting to know. Then Jaison snapped me out my fantasy asking,

"Do you two need a room?" That brought me back from a place I shouldn't have been. He had a girlfriend. I excused myself and went to the ladies' room. Bubbles and BB followed me. Lynn was already there. BB asked,

"What's up with handsome?"

"Well we all know what's up on him," Bubbles said. "But Allysa what are you thinking? His girlfriend was right there. You're making trouble for yourself." Wondering what I said,

"I didn't do anything wrong; I only danced with him. Marlena refused; then, laughed at him and I wanted him to feel better."

"You're right, Allysa, but she'll make problems and seek her Harpies on you." Lynn commented, but BB said,

"OH NO, it's not going down like that, cause I got Ally's back. That shit was cruel. I'm glad you were there for him Allysa. Marlena wants his money and the poor guy is too nice for her. Jacob has many venues that makes wheelbarrows of money and could be enjoying life like a celebrity, but he takes his money and treats everyone. His brothers treat him like a baby, and moms trying to make a momma's boy out of him. I've known Jacob for years. During the times I've seen Marlena at camp with Jacob, she has done every vile thing a girlfriend shouldn't do to her man; and I mean everything. She even injured him." Spontaneously I asked,

"Injured him? How?" BB expressed,

"She knocked him out with a vase. I'm telling you... she needs to disappear. Nah... I'm backing my roomie. I'm glad she danced with him. They both can use some real love." Bubbles said,

"Yeah Allysa, you had me worried about my man coming here because there is one thing Marlena is right about. You're jail bait."

"How old are you?" BB asked. While looking at Bubbles I said.

"I don't like to be call names," and I continued in thought about Marlena hurting Jacob and Bubbles dumb ass comment. It became quiet with me staring at Bubbles wondering was she that insensitive or trying to be funny when BB expressed quickly,

"I didn't mean go to bed with him, but they can develop a friendship that will help them both. She loved Rich all those years cause he was a child and couldn't help himself, but no one cared she was just a child too." Shocked to see BB's tears, I tried to comfort her while she continued, "But she took care of Rich and loved him better than most mothers would have, and got him with a decent family. GOD got a hand in this. Naw, I got her back. This whole thing has been amazing." Thinking I was the only one who noticed all the astonishing things that's been happening, I hugged my friend BB, and everyone group hugged. I felt finally, I fit in with normal people, and I wanted no one to know what my AD did for all those years. I promised myself I would not let anyone abuse me in any way again with me determined my life was going to get better.

Getting back to the party, BB said something about meeting a guy from the caterers. She went one way, I another. Lynn and Bubbles went off into their own thing. I sat down chilling until Jaison came over.

"What's going on?" Curious Jaison asked as if he wanted to join us and said, "You were in there for 38 minutes. You missed all the drama that went on, and Little-Bit, did you drink up my champagne... twice?"

"No, I only hit it once, and I want some more." He looked at me shaking his head, but said,

"That's what I told Mom. You were a little tipsy."

"Why," I wondered aloud with the music thumping.

"Little-Bit, you sent them packing." Jaison said with a snicker. I noticed Jacob and most of that group had left. Then BB returned with a bottle of champagne she found for us young ladies and Jaison. It was time to party, and I hung out with BB and Jaison until morning learning how to do just that.

I tried marijuana for the first time. Some stuff Jaison said grew on his father's island. I took two hits; then, another two exploding in cough again, while passing it to BB with her doing the same, and then we giggled. Jaison finished it saying he felt it was too strong for us, but he was looking at me... and he may have been right. When I wasn't moving, I nodded out. BB and I stayed on the floor dancing with Jaison, Delano, and a Chinese guy who followed us all night speaking Chinese. He tried some too. I couldn't understand what he was saying. After a while, it didn't matter, so we danced and had fun anyway.

As the party progressed, we formed Soul Train lines; then, Lynn had us line dancing, but toward the end of the party we just cluster danced since everyone was high and didn't know what the hell we were doing. Jaison, and the Chinese guy hung out with BB and me till the wee hours of morning experiencing some of life's pleasures, a party, and new friends.

We arrived at the Hotel last at about 4:30am. Jaison was plastered and Lynn designated me as a not drunk person. Well I made sure everyone was in his or her room except Jaison, but I wasn't sober, so it took a while. Jaison fell out on our floor with his pants down. I threw a blanket on him and went to bed thinking about my dance with Jacob.

Transport was outside waiting at 9:00am, which was three custom buses, one tractor-trailer, Jacob's truck with a cover, the SUV and a few cargo vans. Adam, planned to follow Jacob and Delano to as many towns they're playing so he could go to their games and they could practice with the group. It was time to get started.

Jaison was out his clothes and asleep on the couch when I woke. I dressed; then, I had to dress Jai, and he was all right... well sort of and that was interesting, but we had to pack in a hurry to check out. I never could have imagined that I would be involved in what was happening; it was like a dream we almost over slept and missed.

Everyone except Lynn, and I had a hangover or still high. I tried to help Lynn, and it was fun, but I still felt a little loopy, so I wasn't much help. Jaison, who was walking around like a zombie acting the fool with me holding his hand, didn't help our immediate situation when he went in the compartment under the bus and laid down. After I convinced him to come out, I looked up to see BB walking around the back of the bus wearing a pair of flip flops, men's briefs and jacket holding a bra saying,

"This shit's too... something. Where are my fuckin clothes?" Oh GOD... I had to get our luggage packed in a hurry to get on the bus, and things became slightly confused. That was my bra. I packed hers... and my pants were too short. They were BB's, and I packed mine. Like I said I wasn't much help, but I got them on the right bus. Then I tried to stay out of sight. Adam was shaking his head while everybody laughed at us until Bubbles came out late shouting orders and running, but she had put on some jeans she wore before with some panty hose. She came out the door with them sliding out her pant leg swinging as she ran throwing debris with people running away. I saw a pair of happy face draws too. Danny got her.

I had no reference of a party, but THAT WAS A PARTY. The following morning was something else too. I figured if this experience continued to be like the last two days, it would fill my mind with good memories and help me stop feeling and thinking about the bad ones.

Snow and ice was on the ground and the weather took a turn for the worst. The Mother and Adams family were going home before a forecasted blizzard after only a day of traveling. We said our goodbyes. However, when the taxi came, Richard ran on the bus and jumped in my lap crying,

"Mommy, I won't see you anymore." I told Rich,

"You'll be with Adams family and I'll be with Adam. I'm not going anywhere." Desperate, Rich blurted out,

"Mommy, you're big enough now. I want Jaison to be my daddy. You like him and he likes us."

"Um... Rich, it's more... complicated than that." When Adam came to get him, he assured Rich,

"She will be at The Beach Camp with me and we hope Miss Allysa will come home to visit us." Home? Adam told me I could live with his family, but I said nothing giving Rich a kiss; then, Adam took him to the waiting taxi, and I started on my next journey.

The buses were fantastic, and I fell in love with them. There was one for meetings, practice, or just chilling. It had two, 42inch TV's, a small kitchen, and 2 bathrooms with one shower. I didn't know you could do all that to a bus, and everyone was on the meeting bus except the Captains who were Jaison, Big Al (a flunky), Klondike, and Lynn who were to give assignments and help keep order. They were on the sleepers getting them straight with supplies. The beds on one bus were longer to accommodate our tall guys, and the back of the sleeper buses had wide beds for couples. The guy's bus and the meeting bus were enclosed double-deckers, but the smaller sleeper wasn't as posh as the other two buses

We made our first stop three hours later when Adam called a meeting. The captains joined us on the meeting bus for assignments. Adam commanded,

"Let's get order," and then he said, "We will assign captains by drawing a name out the hat." Pissed that I drew first drawing Klondike's name I said nothing, but I was happy when BB drew her name too. She wasn't so happy though.

Marlena was still traveling with Jacob and she made a scene about Jacob using his money to buy things for Rich and me during the meeting. Adam quelled her ad lib by telling her to go home and get a life since most noticed Marlena was going through some insecurity issues. I agreed she needed to get a life. She wasn't a performer or anything associated with our group. Only a troublemaker with Jacob spending more time avoiding her than being with her, so why was she here? Jacob and Marlena slept on the large bed in the back of the small sleeper bus and Klondike assigned my bed next to their area.

Mr. Kapulani, considered us the elite of talent, and he invested in us. Adam issued us an iPod with the music we were responsible to learn, and a lap top computer. All in our group were extraordinary scholastically, so we were in different programs that allowed us to travel, study, and receive credit via internet correspondence. The leaders had completed their studies. I hoped to complete the credits for my Bachelor's degree in a few months, but planned to take my first summer off from school to deal with the Beach Camp and plan the rest of my life.

The New York School of Performing Arts had accepted me giving me a full scholar ship for tuition, room and board. I only needed to make money to live, so I planned to work in restaurants as a waitress and model to support myself. TMP required I give up my agent when I applied, but I planned to re-hire one afterward. Belonging to the same talent agency as Rod, I received plenty calls for print work. That's how I saved money and wished I could have kept all my money, but I had to pay my AD for the privilege of his abuse. However, I looked forward to my life and planned to model since the exciting Fashion Industry encouraged me to believe in myself. Also, the art of using your body to present clothing so people would want to purchase what you showed was a job my agent and clients felt I was just right for, so I welcomed that challenge.

Adam dismissed the meeting. Eager to finish planning, and learn about setting up my electronics, I forgot about the stupidity. All my friends had warned me that Klondike and her group had vowed to get me sent home or harass me until I run away. All because Marlena didn't like me dancing with Jacob, so when I stepped off the bus, their little gang of five knocked my computer and me to the ground, with my iPod stolen when it fell. One of Klondike's flunkies named, Twister, jumped on me taking liberties by feeling up on me until Jacob and Jaison removed him. Learning the lesson I needed to stay aware of them at all times, I figured if any of them ever crowd me like that again I planned to grab one and fuck that one up good.

"Who did this?" Jaison asked while he looked at the broken box with my damage computer inside. Klondike exclaimed,

"I'm docking her pay for that, plus if she doesn't know the music, we're sending her home. I know she's on probation." Jaison shouted,

"Yeah, and I saw you, Klondike, take her iPod. So give it back." They laughed and walked away. Very disturbed, I went to my sleeping cubicle to find that someone urinated on the mattress and smeared shit all over the ceiling and walls. Wow... that took the wind out my sails. I realized this might not be fun after all.

I told Adam what I found, and it wasn't hard to figure Klondike was responsible for the mess since she managed the area. Adam made her scrub the whole bus down and started a war between Klondike and myself I didn't want. Yep, that curbed my enthusiasm and other's too. She scrubbed that bus with Jaison watching, and we had to check in a motel. Adam had to sanitize the bus, and Klondike had to pay that bill, but we had to pay for our own rooms. Jaison felt Klondike was trying to sabotage our group by sending us over our budget or breaking up the group Mr. Kapulani had formed.

During the three-day layover, Jaison took me to get my portfolio I kept at Rod's house. BB and Jacob came with us. Marlena wanted to go, but Jaison told her,

"NO," and pulled off with her hanging on the window as she tried to kiss Jacob goodbye. BB and I tried not to laugh, but was happy she stayed with the round trip being ten hours. So, BB and I were in the backseats with Jacob riding shotgun. Then we stopped at a mall. When we returned to our trip, BB rode shotgun and Jacob sat beside me. Jacob started talking and said,

"Allysa, I don't want you to feel uncomfortable, and I remembered what you said, but I read the bio that Adams wife, Adjani, prepared about you." As I paid attention to Jacob, his magnetism took over. I noticed his face observing how his lips moved with his shy smile. Then my mind wondered to his body. What did it look like? I could tell by his arms he was muscular. Is he hairy? What did he smell like without cologne? What would it be like kissing him? I was curious. My mind wondered south on his body. I wondered if his manly package was short and fat, or skinny and long. However, if he loved me, it wouldn't matter. I looked at him dreaming like a million other girls... but he was there talking to me.

"Hello... Allysa are you listening," he asked while stroking my cheek with his finger. "Pretty eyes, did you hear me? Do you feel sick?" He took my hand; then, felt my forehead and said, "You're not hot." I thought yes I am, but in another way. Realizing I hadn't heard a word he said, I asked,

"Huh?" And smiled at him. He grinned and moved closer easing his arm around my shoulder gently pulling me closer while saying,

"To be so young you have accomplished so much. You're pretty, smart, and I know treated badly by your AD. That bothers me. If someone just treated you right, you would feel better and happy." I accepted Jacob liked me and wondered if it was as much as I liked him when he continued, "With the respect of someone, your accomplishments would be endless. My father thinks you're very special and I feel he's right." His deep sexy voice sent tingles up and down my body. Then he asked, "Allysa is Rod your boyfriend?"

"No." I replied wondering what's next when Jacob asked,

"Can we talk about that later?" I laughed and said,

"Yes, Jacob, we can... I don't have people watching me." BB turned around with Jaison's Coke Bottle glasses saying,

"I am." We laughed; then were on and off different subjects for an hour, but with Jacob wanting to have a private conversation with me continued,

"I remember what you told me about the money and I respect what you want. I know you will do well, and I want you to have a fair chance in life. You deserve it, and you need a little help. I don't want you sent home. I would have to come get you. So Allysa, please accept these items." I noticed his sincerity when he gave me a computer and iPhone.

"Oh WOW Jacob. Thank you, but I don't know how to set this up."

"Don't worry I'll help you," he promised smiling, while moving the items to the side. He smoothly slid his arm around my shoulders and played with my fingers. "I like seeing you smile. You don't do it enough, but when you do, it makes my soul smile too." Trying to figure him, I felt he was sweet talking me and I figured he was a player. He had a girlfriend... but I still liked him, so I asked,

"What does it feel like when your soul smiles?" Jacob thought for a minute and then said,

"It makes me feel like... I... I have the wrong girl." BB broke in,

"Do we need to stop and get you two a room? Like shut up!"

"Was it getting deep?" I asked.

"Da shit was deep." She said, and Jaison added,

"We still can get a room and all 4..."

"Shut up right there," I said joking, and I pulled his hair.

"And we see a little more personality. I like that." Jaison commented.

They made me feel comfortable. Without Rod and Rich, it was good to find someone else with whom I could have fun. Even though, BB and Jaison were joking, I noticed Jacob wasn't. They went on talking,

"Baby sis," BB said, "Watch yourself around Bubbles because she hangs out with Klondike's group. She seems to be cool, and I'm all for Cum by ya or whatever, but that's too close. You got to draw the line somewhere."

"Little-Bit if you have a problem, let us know. We'll look out for you because you are not coming back to this place," Jason stated as we turned off the interstate to my old hometown.

Rod had a nice house 15 miles away from my AD's house in another suburban community where he had a gym and plenty room for his son who lived with him. He was 21, and number 2 in contention for the title in his weight class. He paid for his house from prize money he won boxing. Modeling paid the bills. He ran out and greeted us. Rod had met Jaison and BB, but this time they met his little boy. Kelvin came right to me and I picked him up. We were happy to see each other, but for some reason I took Jacob's hand when I introduced him. When I realized what I had done, I tried to let go, but he grabbed my hand taking Kelvin with one arm. Rods little boy smiled at him amazed at how high he was off the ground. He played with Rod's son and then locked arms with me.

"Let me escort my Barbie doll." Jacob said in his deep sexy voice. The only thing I could do was look and blink with my heart thumping. I thought he heard it. Again, I was guilty of gazing in his grey eyes with him lost in mine. Somewhere in the eye gazing, it felt like our souls linked, mixing, intertwining, and becoming one. He made me forget everything, and the fact I didn't believe in love at first sight, relationships, or marriage, but he made me desire to only look at him and breathe. He seemed to observe and feel the same with his shy smile. BB hollered,

"Will you two cut it out; you're making my love bug horny." Jaison grabbed her saying,

"Here I am darling," and she told Jaison,

"You know what.... I'm not going to acknowledged you said anything cause... ya just don't look right." Whining, Jaison said,

"Well they made me horny too." Like BB said, Jaison was acting extra special. Rod interrupted,

"Allysa, I worried about you adjusting, but I see you have met some cool Island People." I upped the phrase ISLAND PEOPLE while Rod put his son to bed. It meant people who were trustworthy. I told them,

"Some people who live within our Island's support are not Island People. We call them INLANDERS or assholes. They take and refuse to give back. It's not a money thing. It's a matter of heart." However, the most important lesson I learned from our Island was in a system you want to work, you have to work with it to keep it giving, and keep it in balance or you will use it up. I believe when you receive you must return no matter how small. Most times, it's needed. I imagined a relationship was the same, but one person or both stop giving in the relationship and it fails usually at someone else's expense like a child.

Jaison and BB were talking about me when Rod returned. Jacob said,

"Yeah she goes off like that. Just staring into space real pretty like, but it gets eerie."

"Allysa's thinking. She does that a lot." Rod remarked after he made a Sci Fi sound; then Rod asked. "Will you be in town tomorrow? I'm going on a job tomorrow and the photographer needs three more girls. Are you girls interested? Its print work and pays well. BB said,

"He needs one now." Rod laughed and asked,

"Ally, Mr. Monique said you quit the agency. What's up with that?" BB and I told him about TMP. Meanwhile Jaison called Adam.

"Can we wrap it by 4:00pm?" Jaison asked and Rod replied,

"It starts at 7am so, we'll finish by noon."

"We'll catch up with them," Jaison said. "At the moment, they're still dealing with the bus situation. Can you drive Little-Bit?" Excited I asked,

"You'll let me drive your pretty SUV?" That took my mind off I didn't want to stay, but BB had made plans with money we hadn't received and Jaison had made arrangements. Then Rod broke my thought saying,

"I have two guest rooms with king-size beds, a cot in my gym, and a queen size pull out couch if you want to stay in this room. You guys can figure sleeping arrangements. Ally knows where everything's at."

BB sat in Jaison's lap while they entertained each other with conversation and wasn't paying us any mind, but Rod notice Jacob's attention was all on me. Rod gave me his what's up smile. I shook my head because Jacob had been sitting beside me using the time to grin and inch closer until he had me corralled in his area on the couch. His attention was hard to ignore since I felt attracted to him. He played with my fingers looking at my broken nail and whispered in my ear,

"I'll get this fixed for you." His hot breath on my neck sent a hot chill through me that provoked every muscle in my body. Then he lingered there hovering checking out my neck, ear, and hairline as if he was taking a picture in his mind when Rod broke the silence and mood saying,

"Excuse me man, but this is killing me. You're Jacob Kapulani the basketball player and one of the top draft picks; right?" Jacob face changed as he broke his attention from me. He looked at Rod with a curious frown and said with an ever so slight attitude,

"Yeah... sort of, just like you're, Lightning Rod, the boxer and number two in contention for the middleweight title." Not sure what upset him, I privately questioned,

"Jacob is it the fame that's bothering you?" He answered,

"There's plenty time for that. Right now I just want to be me setting here having a conversation with Allysa, without all that." I whispered to him,

"Jacob that is you and you are so handsome." I put my legs to the side in the chair to get him to move away a little. Then I realized, what I said and the sultry way I said it. At first, Jacob expressed shock.

"Wow, Marlena thinks I'm goofy looking," while his face changed to a bright smile. Gazing at him again and thinking about what I said, I noticed my words came out so natural. Jacob used the time pulling me to him with my knees touching his leg making us cozy again. Feelings of him ran all through me, and I could only imagine how we looked.

"She's not seeing the same man I see," I said. Rod broke up the moment again; and he knew what he was doing.

"Ally come here I want to show you something." I looked at Jacob as I left and noticed him frowning at Rod.

Rod had a new stair stepper in his large garage gym. I couldn't believe he decided to assemble it now, but I helped him because Rod had problems with instructions. When I volunteered at The Children's Learning Center, I showed Rod a routine that helped him. He had a learning disability, but functioned well. That's how we became friends, but finally he asked,

"Ally, what's the deal with Jacob?"

"I don't know. He has been acting like that since I met him." I replied and told Rod what Jacob did for Rich and me. Rod was happy, but asked,

"Has Jacob tried anything yet?"

"No," I said while I checked Rod's reaction. Jacob was coming on strong and noticed Rod making funny faces like he had to know what was going on. I didn't want to read into it too much, but became concerned how Rod was taking the attention Jacob was giving me. My thoughts made me feel off balance; however, I said while smiling,

"He's very polite. Rod, I think he's just a nice person and so handsome."

"Damn Ally, I didn't know you noticed the guys. I knew they would be after you soon when you left, but the number 5 draft pick? All right, Miss Ally. My girl has grown up, and I'm happy for you." He pinched my nose breaking my attention and concern.

I went finding sheets, blankets, and towels for our guest. I felt good, because in this little time, I felt I fit in. With them anyway, and it gave me hope. Rod looked at it as we had moved on and away from the abuse.

BB and Jaison had retired to the guest room. I found Jacob dozing on the couch. I took a shower and then woke Jacob. He was cute sleeping and smiled at me. I imagined his children would be cute and had to smile; then, he kissed me. I kissed him briefly for curiosity's sake. I never kissed anyone before and wasn't sure how, but it came so easy with him, however I said,

"Wake up, I'm not your girlfriend," but he held me there and kissed me again. "No, stop Jacob." I said a little irritated. Things were happening too fast.

"Allysa, I know who you are, and I enjoy waking up to you. Will you give me another kiss?" I felt things and him and couldn't give in to the momentum of the moment, so I cut it short and told him while walking away,

"Go to the bathroom in the other guest room and take off your clothes so they won't wrinkle." Just saying that gave me a chill. I gave him a towel and bath cloth while telling him, "You can shower too."

I tried to take my mind off his kiss as I made my bed on the couch and figured not to pull out the queen size bed. Jacob came back wearing Rods' robe I hoped he wouldn't see, but told him,

"You can sleep in the guess room Jacob," but he asked,

"Um, I don't know. Where are you going to sleep Allysa?" As I set on the sheet on the couch I said,

"Right here."

"I thought the couch was a pull out bed," he said looking confused. I didn't respond and there was silence for a few minutes while he processed the situation. Then he asked, "If I'm a good boy, would you keep me company... on the floor? I want to show you what I did on your computer while you left me." I noted his comment and joined him on the floor.

Jacob showed me how he down loaded the pictures from the formal and explained the electronics. Then he said,

"I enjoyed dancing with you Allysa."

"I did too Jacob. Why did you leave?" I asked.

"While you were in the ladies' room talking, it turned stupid, embarrassing. So, I figured it was best to take that group back to the hotel. Tell me what I missed."

We looked at the pictures talking for more than an hour and I notice the fun we were having.

Jacob didn't like Jaison giving me the marijuana. Then he was quiet, but his attention stayed on me. Finally, he said,

"Allysa, if I'm being too nosey please tell me."

"Okay." I responded wondering what when he asked,

"How you get that scar on your head? Did someone... hurt you to cause that?"

"I don't remember." I responded wondering when he saw it. "Does anyone else know?" I asked. He answered,

"Yes Allysa. All my brothers, Adjani, BB, and Devon in makeup know. I saw it the first time you fell out. Then Devon said something about it to Adam. Marijuana may cause you problems and you shouldn't get high."

"It's more than that." I said thinking of my condition at birth, but I felt they revealed something I preferred to keep to myself like they inspected me when I couldn't help myself. Feeling exposed and violated, I moved to the couch. Jacob asked,

"Did I say something wrong?" Wanting to be polite, I said,

"No, I'm sleepy." He came to the couch asking,

"Allysa, what's wrong?" I said,

"I get confused, Jacob, it's nothing." Jacob responded,

"Relax Allysa let's forget that and lay your head on my shoulder. Let's just sit awhile. I'm sorry if I did something you didn't like or want." Cautious, but I trusted him doing what he asked. Jacob continued saying, "Don't worry I won't get fresh with you. I want you to feel happy and safe. Let me hold you in my arms... please." When I relaxed a little in his arms, which felt good, he finished saying, "Yes that feels good. Rest with me for a moment... an hour... perhaps... a lifetime." Then, he kissed my forehead and tried to cuddle me. After that and the lifetime part, I sat up. I had to say something. I was feeling him, but then I wasn't, and asked,

"Jacob, tell me to mind my business, but what's the deal with you and your girlfriend?"

"Um... well um..." He stuttered, and I continued,

"Jacob, you bought me things I needed, but some were very personal items, and you have been extremely close all evening, then you kissed me. Now, you want me to relax in your arms so I'll feel happy and safe; then you want me to trust you not to get fresh, but I'm not sure if I can." He frowned and asked,

"Wait a minute, Allysa, what do you mean?" I asked,

"Can your girlfriend trust you?" I looked at him with a different gaze. He moved back to the floor and got quiet. I only needed him to back up a little and help me understand.

"I don't know what to say," was his immediate response, but then he said, "My girlfriend is more of a relationship of convenience. She's my mother's friend. At first, she looked so good it made me feel special to see everyone looking at her when she was with me. I was so tall I felt like girls were afraid to be with me. They whispered when I walked by." It was probably about how cute he was, but I asked,

"Do you feel you love her?"

"I'm use to her, Allysa, even though I don't get much attention until you come around, but it's ok. My mother wants us to get married and my father wants his first grandson." I told him,

"Well... considering all that Jacob, you shouldn't do things like kissing another girl or act like you want to comfort someone else. If I had a boyfriend, I wouldn't want him to play me like that." Jacob became weird, but said,

"I... I don't know what to say. You are the first female that..." and he shook his head. Then I said,

"Why not finish Jacob? Do you mean I'm the first one who didn't fall for your... whatever that was?" Defensively he said,

"I wasn't... Look... Allysa, just excuse me and forget about it," but I told him.

"Jacob, I appreciate the attention, your concern, and the things you bought for me, but you know Marlena's little group is giving me a hard time because of your attention toward me." That wrinkle came in his forehead. He had that wrinkle when I ran away too, and I felt bad. I didn't want to hurt his feelings. I sat in the kitchen wondering why I said all that.

I went to Rods' room and balled up behind him in his bed like normal when troubled.

"What, you don't like him?" Rod asked,

"I didn't want to be with him like that." I said as Rod rose up quick.

"Did he do something improper to you?" He defensively asked. Quickly I told Rod,

"Oh no, I think I said something that hurt his feelings. I don't know why I said all that." Rod said,

"You know he likes you, and I think you like him." I admitted,

"I do Rod, but he has a girlfriend and his attention is causing me problems." Then I told him about what happened before we left.

"Wow, Allysa, that went deep and I'm a long way from you and can't help. I don't like this. You can stay with me or we can get them straight." He said while thinking. Then I said to Rod,

"My AD will find out I'm here, and besides, I don't want to give up this opportunity because of a few idiots." Rod said,

"Allysa, I'm always here for you, but I feel you will do much better with their help too, and I don't think your AD wants to mess with those guys' father." Rod looked at me; then, said, "Most females would look at a chance for romance with Jacob Kapulani as an opportunity, but Allysa... do what's right for you." I laid there thinking deciding to go to Jacob, apologize, and try to explain to Jacob we like each other, but things were too obvious.

Waking to Rod's alarm at 5:00am, I realized I nodded after my thought only to fall asleep. Rod was up and he wondered,

"Why didn't you go back down stairs with your friend?"

"I meant to." I said feeling bad.

"Allysa, after you went to sleep I went to check on our guess and Jacob was still up wondering where you were. I told him you were in my room sleep, and that pissed him off. He laid down on the couch, but he didn't go to sleep." I said,

"Rod, if I'm friendly with him, I will have a hard time."

I felt tormented by my soul because I cared about Jacob and wanted to know him, but I was degrading myself not believing a decent person would want me. Feeling that way after Jacob made a comment about Klondike's habits, while we traveled to Rod's. He said,

"When my girlfriend leaves Klondike tries real hard to have sex with me," then, Jaison said,

"Once upon a time, she wanted to polish Jake's snake with her tongue, and when we get to camp, you'll see her hanging around BS because she polishes his worm on the regular." Then Jacob commented,

"I don't want to kiss anyone that's like that, yuck," and he shivered. So, I had a complex emotional situation. Moreover, I figured I had a little girl's crush that would go away, and so would Jacob.

We went to the photo shoot, and it took 5 hours. It wouldn't have taken so long, but people recognized Jacob. Everyone wanted to take pictures and talk to him. Jaison and Jacob were having fun with all the girls around and I was the only one Jacob didn't talk to. Jaison sensing something wrong, tried to talk with me, but I hung out with Rod like normal. When we had a break, Rod told me that Jacob said more to him about me.

"Allysa, he asked if we have or ever had a relationship. I told him no. You're a beautiful person, but not into relationships and trying to improve your life away from here. You needed some help, so I was trying to help you. I mention nothing else."

I remembered a night I had to confide in Rod. It was so bad at my AD's house with the sexual attacks I couldn't go home after my late classes. I would stay out until one in the morning and hoped everyone was sleep, but I still had to fight to keep my AD and his son from raping us. That night Richard and I came home washed, changed into our nightclothes in our closet, and went to bed. Then they attacked us. My AD wanted Richard and his son was after me. I footed my AD, and he dropped Rich then I screamed for Richard to run. Rich and my emergency meeting place was a field house in the park that wasn't close. Terrified for him to go out in the dark by himself, Rich ran, and I fought and fought, but I couldn't fight any more so I got loose leaving the house running in torn nightclothes and barefooted during winter. I found Richard in the little house so petrified he defecated on himself. We ran to Rod's house, and I told him my AD was abusing me. That's all I told him and Rod asked nothing else. I needed and found a true friend in Rod. He told me I could live there, but after a few days, my AD sent people from his agency to harass all the Islands and I knew that soon someone would tell him were to find me, so I went back. The only thing that kept them off me after that was I tutored a police officer's son for math. The day I went home, I had the father take me in his patrol car. He sensed I needed him since he said I had to tell him what was wrong. There was so much, I couldn't tell him for our own safety. I needed time, so every month until I left, the boy's father came in his police car asking about us. He knew I was fine because I saw his son every day. That action stopped everything for a while. From then on Rod kept me busy in the public eye spending more time in community work, helping children with learning problems, and modeling. I had to give my AD money when I went on modeling jobs. Sometimes I was just staying out, and Rod would give me money to give to him.

Now I worried my AD would hear I was in town and show up. Jaison stood watch by the door; however, I was happy to leave. I kissed Rod and told him,

"I'll call you later when I'm far far away." He laughed waving as we rode away.

CHAPTER FIVE

I Feel You

I wasn't looking forward to the trip back. Jacob silence let me know what I said upset him and the fact he thought I was a liar upset me. He asked Rod the same questions. That made me feel terrible, and I was so inexperienced, I let my mind work against me. There were other ways to handle my situation with Jacob, but I didn't understand my feelings enough to deal with them. I wanted to be his friend, but everything changed and he continued to ignore me to the point BB said,

"What's up with you two? Jacob you haven't said anything to Allysa all day." Jaison said,

"Jake don't tell me you showed her the snake and scared her away." OMG. Jaison made the situation worse and Jacob snarled,

"Shut up with that stupid shit." Ignoring him, I tried to look out the window, but I still thought about him and the situation. I didn't intend to upset him. He needed to understand his actions were unappealing and confusing.

As Jacob drove, I rode shotgun, Jaison slept in the third seat, and BB was cuddling her money sleep in the middle seat. About 175 miles and 3 hours later BB took over driving. Jacob went straight to the back. I stopped at the second seat. After traveling for a while and Jacob woke, I asked,

"May I speak with you Jacob?"

"I don't think we have anything left to talk about," he said, but I told him,

"Jacob, I'm sorry. I appreciate you, but you confused me. I didn't know what to think of what you were saying and doing, but I didn't want to make you angry and said too much. Please accept the money for the items because I need them." However, when I gave him the money he shoved it back at me and said,

"I don't need or want to be bothered with that or you." Then he turned away from me and looked out the window. After the shock of his words, I laid down in the seat under my blanket. What he said distressed me so much I got sick. I took my medicine and asked,

"BB, stop please, I need some ice." While I stepped out the vehicle sweating profusely, Jaison said,

"Oh man. Damn it Jacob! You didn't have to be rude to her. Why you do that?" Jacob just twisted his mouth. I walked. BB came with me asking,

"Allysa... what happened and where are you going?" I pointed toward a strip mall. I needed to get away, but BB said, "You don't feel good so get back in the truck."

"No. I need the fresh air, and this is not going to work." Jaison rolled the truck to a stop in front of us. Jacob and Jaison jumped out and asked where I was going. They seemed mad. I was about to give up a dream my soul didn't want to let go, but I said, "This is not working out. It's too stressful here around so-called normal people." Meanwhile my head was hurting so bad I pled with them, "Please just leave me alone, please..." Things turned brown.

I woke in the hospital, 10 hours later very upset. The Doctor diagnosed,

"Between the head injury and your other condition, you need to take it easy young lady. I want to see the results of the CAT scan and more of your labs. Who are the people waiting for you? Where are your parents?" I answered,

"They're part of a group of entertainers I perform with. I'm an orphan."

"Young lady, you must stop stressing." The doctor expressed. I asked,

"Doctor, please explain to the one called Jaison." The doctor did, and Jaison conference called his father and Adam. Jaison came back saying,

"Little Bit we can't stay. Can you call Rod?" I exclaimed,

"I can't go back there!" Jaison said,

"Allysa, we can't..." Pissed off I continued,

"I'm sick because Jacob wants to two-time his girlfriend, and now after he stresses me to sickness, I get sent back to my AD." The more I thought the more disgusted I became. I removed everything they had attached; then, a monitor alarm went off and a nurse came.

"What's going on here?" The nurse asked; then, made Jaison leave. She put me back in bed. I cooperated with her and when she left, so did I.

Once outside, I ran. It was dark so, I tried to keep off the road. I felt better when I ran or danced. I WAS FREE. Trying to get lost, I turned down this road, and an hour passed with me seeing one car. I was in the country. Figuring nobody was looking for me, I left my phone off feeling all I had to do was survive. I had some money and my pocketbook. My thought was if somehow I died, things would be better. I wish for it not having the nerve to end my misery.

Coming upon a dirt road, I noticed a large old farmhouse hidden by trees and I found an Island. Only my Island, so that meant I had to make sure it was safe with a fingernail clipper knife and a little flashlight. A lady should have a little of everything in her pocketbook, but I wasn't that optimistic. I was scared shitless, but in a back window, I went. When I got inside, right after I fell on my head, I checked everyplace. It was empty and a little dusty, but very nice. The full moon made the house light up. With some evergreen branches and my blanket for my bed, I made do, but knew I had to find some suitable shelter soon.

Looking around the large house, I thought about the families who may have lived there. It had a cozy warmness to it. They probably had plenty of children since there were so many bedrooms. I could feel the laughter and joy of the house. With a long picnic like table in the dining area, the house still had the essence of being full with people and love. I prayed one day I'll get married to someone who loves me and have a large family; then I thought about modeling. I imagined the family would come later.

My mind drifted to what I told Jacob. It was the right thing to say, and I figured he was a spoiled pretty boy who could get any girl he wanted, so I wondered if I hurt his feelings or his ego. Either way, I didn't want him feeling bad. I thought he was a nice person, but then I remembered how he said he didn't want to be bothered with me. My heart hurt and I cried, but I didn't get sick. I felt that with my sickness I was a problem for them.

I dozed off and slept light waking at any strange noise. It was very quiet. When I woke again, I had gone to sleep for hours. I looked out the window, and it was snowing with the ground covered. It had been snowing for a minute, glistening on the trees and so pretty. I was concerned, but I took the time to play in it, while I reminisced when I taught Richard how to throw playing "Snowman." We would build a large snowman at the bottom of a hill; then, use a large piece of cardboard, a piece of linoleum or something to slide downhill while throwing snowballs at the snowman who we imagined was our AD. I missed Richard and felt abandoned. I was.

My battery was low, so I had my phone off, but turned it back on to call Rod. Surprisingly, I had text messages from all the brothers, and an e-mail from their father, but I read BB's who accepted the fact I didn't want to be there. Saying she would get all my mail from TMP, but needed me to call so, she would know that I was safe. Then, she wanted to know where I was staying so she could get my stuff sent to me, and she would keep up with Richard, and asked me to please call. My phone rang. It was so loud I answered. I heard Jacob's voice,

"Hello, hello Allysa... don't hang up. Please say you're all right."

"Yeah, I'm good and please just leave me alone. I'm sorry I upset you I just didn't want you to be... phony, but I guess you are."

"Allysa, I'm sorry. My behavior was selfish and uncalled for, and what you said was right. I guessed the truth hurt, but I didn't mean to stress you." There was silence, and I said,

"Okay, I have to go now." He asked quickly,

"Go? Go where? Allysa, please wait. Don't go. Hear me out, please. I'm sorry for my actions and enjoy your company. I feel free and without life's burdens when we're together, but I reacted out of character from frustration because I rather get to know you than be with Marlena. I have feelings for you... but I will not act on them anymore. My advances were too strong. That was the problem. I'm sorry for acting like that. Please... excuse me Allysa. I want to know you... always." Patronizing him, I said,

"I'm cool without all that. Just do what you said, don't bother me." He exclaimed,

"Wait Allysa! I messed up! My father is disappointed and mad at me for chasing you away. I'm mad at myself. Please, can we start over again so we can help one another and be friends? I will give you your space, but I need to find you. I don't want you in the streets trying to survive. Allysa, are you by yourself?" When I didn't answer, he said. "Please, don't trust anyone, and tell me where you're at. I don't know why I treated you like that. It was wrong. My father doesn't want anything to happen to you, and he will get the police involved. He's concern, and I'm about to go crazy. Please... I have to find you; tell me where Allysa."

"I want to go about my business and I'll be fine." Then Jacob quickly said,

"Don't worry about going home Allysa. Adjani wants you to come and live with them so you will be with Richard. You are amazing, a survivor. Just please... please come back. I'll never be right again if you don't." I cried. "What's wrong Allysa?" I told him,

"I don't know where I'm at and tried to get lost, so forget it, and leave." Upset, Jacob said,

"Look, I'm not leaving you and I will look for you until I find you. Just calm down and trace back the way you went." As my teeth chattered, I reasoned I needed to get money and warmer clothes. Then I'll leave. I told Jacob,

"I ran through the woods behind the hospital parallel to the road until I came to a road; then, I turned right onto Mayberry road. I ran for two or three miles to a dirt road. I'm in this large old abandon farm house that setting back in the woods on the right side of the dirt road. My battery is low. Bye."

"Wait! We're on our way, but if you don't see us in 30 minutes, call me; Allysa, 30 minutes." I hung up feeling better that Jacob apologized, but I wasn't sure about going back to stay.

Looking through my exhale, I could see twilight. I was freezing, and it seemed warmer outside, but snow was falling blizzard like with six inches on the ground. Then, I saw a bear or something moving outside. I went back in the house, and watched for what was in the woods figuring it would try to take my shelter, but in 20 minutes, I heard a vehicle. It was Jaison's SUV turning into the yard honking. I left quickly. The snow was serious. Jaison came and grabbed me saying,

"Come on baby girl we have to out run this blizzard."

No one said anything in the SUV. I was frozen. Jaison turned up the heat, and I went to sleep under my blanket. After a while, Jacob woke me saying,

"Excuse me, Allysa, my father wants to speak with you." I thought oh no and took the phone back under the blanket with me.

"Hello," I said timidly.

"Hey Barbie Doll, is everything all right?" Mr. Kapulani happily said, but I told him,

"I want to leave, but I'm not going to my AD or Adam's house." He said,

"My sons told me what's going on, and I told them to protect and watch out for you. I'm not letting you go off by yourself. You're mature, but you're sickly and too young. There's a lot in this world you don't know about and people worse than you have encountered. I don't want you learning that the hard way. Plus, baby-girl you don't know your worth. You are a very powerful woman yet you're just a girl. I have been watching you and trying to get you from your AD for years. Finally, we have you. I knew what was going on at his house because I know him. Please, don't let him win. You have come through hell and yet you stand strong. Those people who are bothering you now are just a walk through the park to distinction. I feel your soul, my child, and I can't let you go. You will achieve your goals and do great things for people who are in need." I thought his words were powerful, yet calming. Then he went on, "Do you believe in me... sincerely?"

"Yes." I said and Mr. Kapulani continued,

"This is weird, but I feel I must tell you. What I told you, and what I will say, I have seen in dreams over a period of years. My ancestors and I are from a line of Polynesian Kings. I am the King of an Island chain. My boys are Princes. My wife and love of my life is Adam, Jaison, and Jacob's mother. Hu, is my son by my Island

Queen. Jacob just saw his 21st birthday, and he is with this woman, Marlena, my wife is trying to push on him. Young men like Jacob make judgment mistakes while they are boys, but as men, they correct those mistakes. Jacob marrying Marlena would be a terrible mistake. His mother has pushed him reluctantly to agree to be with Marlena and promise to announce their engagement after the draft. I want to tell you something Barbie, one night long ago when I was distraught because I couldn't make sure you were safe, I fell into a restful sleep and saw you and Jacob with plenty children. These dreams have reoccurred for years. Jacob has called and talked to me about his feelings concerning you. Knowing Marlena was wrong for him, Jacob wondered could someone fall in love at first sight. He just got to get his head from between his legs and make responsible decisions."

"O... kay," I said, "That is a lot... but..."

"Yes it is Allysa; however, I have never talked to Jacob about my dreams and amazed that he talked to me about you. So, please do not fight your feelings. Do not tell him anything of our conversation and stop running from your destiny. Remember this, things will get rough, and Satan will put you though a test, but good things are worth fighting, and waiting for. Tell me something with a yes or no because I don't want you to feel forced. Do you feel the way he feels for you?" I responded,

"Um... I don't know," but then Mr. Kapulani said,

"Ok, but make sure you understand your feelings; then, fight hard and I will do the same. Barbie doll believe me my thoughts are my own and not his. Now if you need anything, just ask. I know you and your life will change for the better. Now, be you and don't change a bit. You are different, special and that's my girl! Be good. Bye." I said goodbye thinking that was the weirdest conversation I had in a while, but I felt stronger about trying to make things work, and I believed in him. Therefore, I decided to go back and work with this blessing, but I wasn't interested in trying to be with Jacob. However, if this was a destiny thing, I figured he'd come to me.

Eight hours later, we caught up with the buses losing two days of practice. Our first show was in Texas in four weeks. So, we had a lot of traveling and practicing to do. Jacob kept his word staying away mostly. I paid him for the iPhone and computer arranging with Adam to pay the bill from my salary. Then, I tried to ignore Jacob totally. Even when he said something to me, I gave him my vague look, but every night for the next 3 days, I had to listen to Marlena having sex with Jacob with her making sex noise.

"AHHH shut up." Jacob said often, but most the time he flat out turned her down (yay). However, I could hear everything, and it bothered me since I still felt an attraction to Jacob, but my thoughts were to check out guys and have fun as friends. I didn't have to deal with hearing her sex noise long though, because Jacob and Delano went back to school, and it was time to get to work.

Adam wanted to have a girl group featuring Lynn, Bubbles, BB, and me making my schedule hectic. Every morning the bus stopped at the YMCA, where the group had memberships. All four of us hit the gym together for three hours. from 6:00 am to 9:00 am. We had to sing our parts while on the elliptical for 90 minutes and work out for the remaining 2 hours; then, while BB and Lynn had time afterward to do whatever; Bubbles and I had to practice dance, next practice with the band as a group, last finish schoolwork.

Every night and spare minute I used for studying, but I must take a moment to tell you about our keyboard artist with whom I practiced. He was a Chinese Exchange Student and the guy at the party that hung out with us. I loved this guy. I mean homey love. He didn't speak English, and I spoke no Chinese, but we communicated and understood each other. Instead of eating dinner, we played the piano trying new things. He played the key boards for the brothers group and I mean he could beat the dust out the keyboards. We hung out together along with the group and called him Wang.

The brothers worked hard at creating the shows to include music, music with dancing, acrobatics, musical skits, and comedic skits. It was almost like a circus, but fun with me helping and learning everything.   The brothers' theme was sexy, and The Sexetts, us. Jaison explained our job was to provide sensual persuasion for the brother's band. We made up dance routines for each song and performed our jobs well creating a following of fans after we started. They were small shows at small clubs where we picked up pocket money that helped with our traveling expenses, but Adam was preparing us for our first show.

Our group worked hard and showed no mercy at our first judged competition. The other contestants weren't ready for us since they only had bands. We had a full featured show. I was nervous before the show and then thrilled afterward. Yes, I was happy that I stayed. It wasn't easy since Klondike and her cubs continue to mess with me, but Dads words remained within. Also, to see how our show's appeal was spreading ahead of us, I became determined to succeed or die trying.

Time passed quickly as I kept busy. Adam told me Jacob's team was in the final four in the NCAA Championship. Between Jacob and Delano, they were averaging 54 points, 25 rebounds, and 15 block shots per game. Delano came and picked up the assignments. Both were big news, and it wasn't unusual to see or hear about them in the media. A feature for CBC Sports Network showed them in the locker room before a game playing their guitars. They said the music relaxed them, but Delano was usually the one interviewed. Jacob was quiet somewhat shy and interviewed alone after the games because of the upcoming draft he said he didn't want to speak on. The reporters were also asking Jacob about his impending engagement to Marlena since reporters questioned if it was his idea. Jacob told the reporters he would make a statement after the completion of the NCAA tournament, and then he stopped talking to them. Adam told the group they would be back to help us with the final judged show.

CHAPTER SIX

Is It Love

We did a show to make extra money. We didn't sing; however, we worked with the roadies and put together a light and sound show to prepare for our final judged show. Chris, Gino, and Cisco were our lead men for the lights, effects, and soundmen with their own crew of roadies. We called them The Crew and upstairs on the practice bus belonged to them. It was all electronics above and they were there working while we are down below practicing.

Adam wanted to test some new equipment, so he let Klondike and her group, earn money by themselves at a club her group booked. The club thought it meant our group until Adam clarified. Her group had talent, and Klondike had an awesome voice, but she was LOUD, uncontrollable actually overpowering everything. So they didn't have a good act. Sound fixed it the best they could, but the show was awful. The light and sound crew was successful at getting things together for our show feeling they had experienced a horrible test of fortitude. Adam never let her group be associated with our group, or his father's name. He thought about leaving them while they were performing and had us laughing.

"Why are all of them here traveling with us?" I asked Adam, and he replied.

"I don't know. It's a BS thing and I believe they're spying for him, so I'm sure they are here to make problems for us."

Even Bubbles had developed a little animosity toward me because Adam selected me to dance with her boyfriend Danny who was so cool, and could dance his ass off. He had a superman build, but he wasn't who was on my mind. I figured Adam paired me with him because I was the taller female dancer and I danced the same in heels as barefooted while keeping up with Danny since Bubbles couldn't. Danny was a professional dancer, and no joke. Bubbles thing was choreography. Danny held back when he danced with Bubbles and it was very noticeable. With me, Danny and I enjoyed the challenge we brought each other. We had fun together and evolved with our ability to dance and that's what Adam noticed. So, I knew Marlena and Klondike were telling Bubbles I was after Danny because I couldn't get Jacob. I heard all three of them talking about me several times. When that started, Bubbles stop talking to me so much. She stared giving me nasty glances constantly. BB and Lynn noticed since it became obvious when the Sexetts practice, but at shows, we were on point; so no one said anything concerning her actions. I felt the situation was a time bomb that was going to explode when least expected and figured Bubbles hung around Klondike and Marlena because she was sort of like them... stupid. Every time Danny and I were together for practice or anything, Bubbles was there. I didn't see him otherwise so I think she knew, but with them constantly bitching at her the more she acted strange.

Adam let us take the meeting bus to the beach since Jacob and Delano had joined the group during time off from school to relax before the championship game. We had Oriental, Mexican dishes with Jaison and Jacob bringing lobsters, shrimp, hotdogs, fried chicken, corn, potatoes salad, and my soup just to mention a few of our goodies. I've never been to the beach or had a picnic anywhere. Hardly sleeping all night waking to find out if it was time to go yet; BB and everyone on the bus told me to shut up and stop running around bouncing off the walls.

Finally, we arrived at the beach. After we unloaded everything, Jaison with Danny and some of The Crew started setting up the picnic and cooking area. I stayed with them to learn and help. Danny and Wang considered themselves my big brothers, so they explained everything. First, Danny in English, and then Wang mocking the always serious Danny in Chinese, while Bubbles continued giving me nasty looks. I didn't let that bother me when I danced or then since it was my first time at the beach and seeing so much water. It was scary, and the first thing for Jacob was to jump in the vast ocean and swim off. I was cool and said nothing, but Jaison told me he was a lifeguard on one of their Island's most treacherous beaches since he was 15 and trained while working as a lifeguard in Australia for the last 4 years.

The blue green color of the water was my favorite color. I tried to enjoy it all day. We played volleyball on the beach. Then I played in the surf letting the waves hit me. Next, Delano, Jaison, and Wang took turns dumping BB and me off our floats while we tried to chill bouncing around on the waves. Then, the Sexetts with Jai and Wang rode a giant Banana through the waves with other people we met. I saw that on TV and never thought I would have that opportunity, but most of all, I enjoyed building this giant sand castle with Wang. It was huge, but Jaison tripped and fell on it. Jaison was the crazy brother and kept me laughing.

When twilight came, Jaison made a bonfire with Jacob still swimming. He was staying away from Marlena, but he swam way down the beach and I couldn't see him anymore. I had made it my business to keep an eye on Jacob all day, but it was dark and I lost track of him. So I walked way down the beach were I saw him laying on a sand bar when the tide was out earlier, but the tide came in and the sand-bar was under water. There was a full moon that night and I franticly looked for his head bobbing in the rough surf as I walked pass him setting in the dunes tall grass watching me. As I walked out in the water after not seeing Jacob anywhere, I became distressed. I called for him, but he didn't answer. With my heart in my throat I ran back down the beach to get help. I passed by him crying and running; then, he came out calling me. When I saw Jacob, a relief came over me so fast I almost peed, but I jumped in his arms hugging him, and then I kissed him... hard. Shocked for the both of us, I couldn't even figure, so I said,

"I thought you drowned," while trying to control my cry. Emotions I didn't understand crowded my thoughts confusing me and I felt sick. I quickly excused myself and went to the bus, but I phoned him.

"Please, Jacob, don't get back in the water tonight."

"Okay," he said, and hung up.

A headache made me lay down with some ice; however, feeling Jacob would be safe, soon I felt better. I watched cartoons and had the bus all to myself. Then, my phone rang interrupting my popcorn moment. It was Jacob.

"What!" I asked sharply. He stuttered for a minute, but said,

"So Allysa, it's all right for you to do what you asked me not to?" Knowing what he meant, I said,

"I'm not in a relationship." Jacob continued,

"But you will mess with somebody's man?" Irritated I said,

"Jacob I wasn't trying to do anything. I thought something bad happened to you." He asked,

"So why were you looking for me?" I stressed,

"Jacob, no one else was." Then Jacob asked,

"So.... okay I see, Allysa, you're my keeper, but why the kiss?"

"I'm not going to do this," I mumbled and hung up. The next thing I knew; he was on the bus very upset.

"Why did you hang up on me?" He asked with me saying,

"I didn't want to talk about that anymore. Why are you bothering me anyway?" I went to another part of the bus, but he followed me saying,

"Now you're being rude." I said,

"Jacob you have an attitude and you're taking it out on me."

"What you expect? You keep teasing me!" He said with that curl in his brow, but I stressed to him,

"Jacob I'm not trying to tease you and I'm sorry I reacted that way, but please... leave me alone. I don't want to get sick." He stood there for a minute then said,

"I'm sorry, I don't want you to get sick. You... it's just... " He stopped and sat down. "Allysa... I want to call you, and talk sometimes... as friends, but I can't." I asked,

"Why not? We're talking now; even though, it's not friendly."

"I'm sorry Allysa, and I'm embarrassed at the way I acted toward you when we went to your friend's house. You're so different. The problem is I find you more interesting than Marlena. Just saying your name inspires me, but everyone tells me to stay away from you, and I've tried, but I care about you. I know Marlena never cared about me; however, like you said by your actions, you do. Allysa, you were upset because you thought something bad happened to me. Then you called because you were sincerely worried. No one else did any of those things, and you were so happy to see me, you kissed me. Allysa... what I saw was more than just a concern." I said nothing for the lack of what to say and sat down feeling vulnerable in some way. He came and sat beside me and lifted my face with his finger.

"Please talk to me. If I'm bothering you, I'll leave." He started getting up, but I touched his arm and said,

"No... wait." I didn't know what to say, and I was afraid of telling my feelings. Usually people use that against you, but I said, "Jacob, when I first saw you on the basketball court at the game you noticed me and I noticed you. You looked at me while you played, and while the coach gave you instructions. You struck me as being so handsome, and I noticed I felt an attraction to you then. When I told you to shoot, you trusted me shooting from behind the arch and started scoring. I felt happy like never before because you smiled and trusted me, and I was there with you having so much fun that I meant to run away earlier, but you distracted me. Never have I felt that way about anyone I met, I wanted to get to know you, but um..." I didn't know how or what else to say, but then Jacob said,

"Yeah, when I came looking for you, my angel had disappeared. I thought my mind was messing with me, and I feel the same way now. I want to talk to you... anytime. Will that be all right Ally and may I call you Ally?" I nodded yes while looking in his eyes. He kissed me. With my curiosity aroused by his kisses, I kissed him not sure how, but my kisses became a natural and easy function; then, my stomach had that funny feeling.

His kisses were smooth, not sloppy, but just a little wet with the tip of his tongue, which seemed to transfer a little part of his soul. In his arms feeling the warmth of his body made me want to stay there forever feeling his passionate comfort, but I thought about a few things. What he said concerning Klondike's habits was most prominent and I moved away.

"Did I do something wrong?" He asked. I only looked at him confused not knowing what to say or do. Then Jacob seriously said, "Allysa I need to get something understood while I'm gone, but may I call you and we continue this when I get back?"

"Jacob, I want to be friends. I'm not sure of what... this is." I wanted to kiss him again, but I wondered would that be teasing him... or something?

"Allysa I worry about you all the time. Please stay out of trouble." I asked,

"Why?" He said,

"I don't want anything to happen to you while I'm gone. Watch your back. There are people here who hate you and want to hurt you. Do not trust Bubbles. She's not a bad person and we're good friends, but she hangs with Klondike. Klondike hasn't gotten over cleaning the bus, plus they're saying things to turn Bubbles against you." I expressed,

"Yeah I know, but why people think I'm after their boyfriends?" And he said,

"Allysa, you're thin, but you have a pretty girl swagger going on. Did you know you have mood eyes? They're red gold when you're mad, gold when you're thinking; then they're hazel green when you're happy, like now, so I can tell when to stop, go or maybe. They turn pale gray when you're getting sick. The last time was before my father talked to you. You'll like him." I happily listen noticing Jacob who's not a talkative person was just talking and happy which made me smile. Then I said,

"Jacob, no one has ever given me a chance or had faith in me like your father so I love him for it and feel close to him; even though, I think he's a little peculiar, I can't disappoint him, and I don't want to disappoint you." Our eyes met, and he kissed me again. Just as I really became involved in the kiss, Wang walked in hollering,

"BITCH!" He quickly closed the bus door, but not quick enough. Jacob and I stopped kissing; then, Marlena burst in with a group of people and her mouth wide-open saying,

"I should have known the bitch was here." I asked,

"What's wrong Marlena? Don't you know where you're at any more?" Everyone laughed; then, she came charging at me. I moved away, but I balled up my fist and kept my eyes on her. She hesitated for a moment; then, threw her telephone at me, and charge while trying to punch me in my face. As I knocked away the telephone and ducked her swing, I planted a solid spin kick up side her head. She knocked Klondike down with them falling like bowling pins. I thought, oh shit. Jacob stepped in front of me; then, BB pushed past with high heel shoe in hand while I retreated behind Jacob. I wondered what BB was getting ready to do with the shoe. BB started everyone laughing except those on the floor. Marlena stumbled to her feet.

"Oh, so you're protecting her now," she scoffed at Jacob.

"I think I'm protecting you," Jacob said while snickering.

"So, it's funny now. Ok... I'll get her," Marlena shouted, "She assaulted us," and she instructed one of Klondike's bear cubs, "Call the police and go tell Adam." Adam arrived and fussed,

"You're fighting, Allysa, and I will not tolerate that."

While Adam fussed about involving the police and how BS would make me leave, Wang speaking Chinese and broken English told Adam,

"Adam shi... shi Lan. you look." Wang made Adam look at his camera and had a video of everything. Adam looked, laughed, apologized to me, and tried to stop the police. They did too, but the police came anyway. Marlena met them at the door pointing at me running her mouth.

"She's fighting us over my boyfriend and kicked me in the face knocking me and my friend down." Now the officers looked at me confused asking,

"This one?" While I could barely hold back my laughter, and it's not that I was trying to be bad. Marlena presented herself stupidly, but the police cuffed me. Marlena had a shoe print up side her head that looked like mine. Then Wang showed the video to the officers with others telling on Marlena and Klondike. Adam spoke with the officer in charge who saw the video asking him to remove the handcuffs. "We have the wrong one," the officer said; then, he cuffed Marlena. "The little girl was protecting herself from you. So you are coming with us." I told the officer,

"I just want them to leave me alone."

"Well, we will press charges on this one for you. That should help." The officer said chuckling, and Marlena went to jail. Adam and Jacob bailed her out in the morning, but Adam told her she couldn't return, and I didn't know Jacob had ended their relationship after our trip to Rod's house. Marlena didn't accept it and followed Jacob around making it seem they were together.

Everyone broke up in two separate social groups. Klondike and her cubs and then our close group with Bubbles hovering between the two, but she voiced her disapproval of the way Klondike and her cubs treated me and wanted everyone to get along. Klondike would have no part of that.

Friends were the only thing I had that was like a family, and I knew Klondike and her bear cubs told Bubbles on the regular she better watch her man since Adam had Danny and me dirty dancing. It's just a show. When all of us chilled together, seeing Danny and Bubbles together made me happy, but I became concerned for them as a couple after Bubbles attached herself to Klondike and Marlena. They're using her and wanted to keep something going to cause problems, but I was happy to see her enjoying the love of her life, Danny.

During a break one day, the Sexetts talked about how Bubbles walked around in a bliss she was so in love. Trying to imagine how it would feel I commented,

"I want to know what it feels like to be loved." Lynn said,

"We love you and enjoy you being with us. You are a hard worker and so much fun to be around. I know I respect that. We can see you been through hell and I want to be like your sister, and work with you so we can do our thing." BB said,

"Yeah me too. You're our little sis now cause we will help and advise you the best we can, and I want us to always work together." Then they hugged my head. Why my head? I hugged them, but I pinched after a while. I couldn't breathe. Not sure if I should say what was on my mind, I did and said,

"I love all of you too, but I sort of had in mind... a guy." They laughed. Bubbles only looked.

I had written poems about my feelings for years so, I was happy to work with Adam and Jaison arranging them into songs. Also, Danny and Bubbles, asked me to help them with the choreography for the shows. I stuck with Adam and Jaison and was finally alive as a teenager having fun learning with people treating me as if I was worth something and not a curiosity. That felt good.

Jacob called me every night and just hearing his voice served as an inspiration to do well, and I looked forward to seeing him again, but I wasn't ready to deal with him the way he wanted. Talking to him, I realized he was under pressure. Everything he had worked for depended on how well he performed as a basketball player. He did everything we talked about and was doing fine, but I figured everyone needs encouragement. I was surprised it came from me.

One night while I laid in my cubical thinking about Jacob, I noticed the shadow of Klondike's big ass showing through my cubical curtain. She would bust a walk by and listened when I used my phone. I had to do something about her. I thought about creating a ploy with a small cheap loud-toned keyboard I could patch my CD player through so I could play along. It was extremely loud without the headphones, so... I plugged my CD player into the keyboard without the headphones. That night I faked talking with Jacob. She did her walk by and stopped right by my cubical. I laid there and waited until she had her ear down toward my cubicle and really into her ease dropping, yep, I waited for it; then, I blasted her full volume. It literally scared the shit out of her. Well... a fart anyway that stunk so bad people abandoned the bus in a pouring rain. She needed to wash her butt. The humidity wouldn't let the smell go away and the driver told Adam her odor wouldn't allow him to concentrate. Adam just laughed and told everyone to chill on the meeting bus, but no one wanted Klondike there. It was hard not to laugh with everyone taking their turn. Then Klondike countered by complaining to BS I was talking on my phone until 4am. My conversation was my business, and that was my phone; however, BS told Adam to take my phone every day and only return it when I left base quarters; then, collect it when I returned. I was livid, but Adam calmed me down later when he gave me my phone back. Then Adam explained the way his father intended for the Beach Camp competition to work saying,

"There were 3 groups of potential students that permanent members form after scouting throughout the year for the best and worthy talent. Next, we travel and go into competitions to win the spots for our group, and gather information on what our audience wants. Our total show goes through a critique and each potential student and act will receive a critique. So opportunities for improvement will exist, but your overall average must be close to the group's overall average. If our group wins, everyone is in the camp from that group. However, sometimes we must deny a performer's acceptance for a spot at the camp even if their group wins because their talent doesn't measure up to the rest of their colleagues. If that happens, we'll give a member of a losing group with a higher critique average whose talent fits the criteria the opportunity to attend the camp. Remember this Little Bit; a score above 87.5% will get you in the camp, but I think you will have a problem even if you do well."

I realized Adam was telling me this for a reason, so I listen as he continued,

"The camp and BS is supported by the rich who enroll their children to be taught by recording stars. However, a certain portion of that enrollment fee and all the contributions made were to finance inner-city youth to attend the camp for the same privilege, but rarely does that happen. This year my brothers, my father, and Lynn brought together the talent that made up our group by following my father's original guidelines. This is our first time in a long while getting a group according to my father's vision when he created the camp.   My father's intention is to give the talented under privileged performer the support needed for success. Therefore, we have a lot to prove this trip."

Beginning to understand what's going on, I realize this guy, BS, to be an Asshole. Adam confirmed that when he continued explaining,

"The other groups must pay BS a hefty fee to compete. Then BS campaigns for money so inner city underprivileged youths can attend The Beach Camp, but that rarely happens. BS keeps the fees, contributions, grants, everything; then, gives little back by having this very visible program in a couple cities where he supplies free music lessons and old instruments. All of it donated to him. My father wants to show him up for what he is and take back control of his camp and recruit talented underprivileged at-risk youths." I asked,

"Adam what do you mean by at-risk youths."

"Allysa think about your own situation at your AD's house. You're exceptionally smart with talent to match, but you were at risk of a wasted life. There's many like you; abused by this world system of greedy, corrupt people. The children go in the street and prey on each other to fulfill their prosperity. Then they're killed, imprisoned, or just living a dead end life with the world's governments controlling and feeding off them. They never have the satisfaction of reaching their potential. My father is trying to help that special person." Thinking about what was going on, I asked,

"Adam how did BS get control of your father's camp?"

"My father had an obligation to the Island and BS took over making a large image for the camp with known talent. I know my father could have done the same or better with unknown talent and give them the boost needed to be successful which is why dad started the camp. I don't like BS and he has developed a phony operation in my father's absence including my fathers' name in his schemes and lies. Our contributors have notice, and my father promised to do something."

"Wow," I said getting pissed and a total understanding of what was going on. Adam made me feel better by saying,

"From our recruiting, we have the elite group, and you are one of us. So if you're in the group that wins, you will have learning opportunities, receive credit for the courses you take, receive exposure while touring with us, and continue receiving a high salary all summer long. Jaison and Jacob also operate a functioning production company through the camp. They book independent assignments for the camp's premiere group and work as talent agents after students leave the camp. Last year we performed televised at SUN FUN FEST in Jamaica with other notable musicians that JAJA Productions booked. So, you can get exceptional recognition."

With the last competition show approaching, our group had the highest combined percentage. My average was 98% and higher than the overall group. At each competition show, the most prominent artists strive to judge our competitions to be the first to recognize new talent. Adam also let me know that sometime things can get political. I can run into a judge that BS plants and my score can change quickly. So, I realized some Judges were still looking for exposure plus an ass to kiss. Understanding the process explained by Adam, the exposure alone in the competition was a prize.

It was time for the NCAA championship game. Jacob and Delano's team was playing. The hype was the #1 and #2 draft pick, who was Jacob, were playing on the opposite teams. The reporter said Jacob's consistent 3-point shooting made him a complete player and improved his position in the draft. Delano was receiving a great deal of notice too because the #1 draft pick was a 7 ft. 2 inch 280 lbs. center and Delano who was over 7 ft., but with a smaller frame had to keep him in check. Adam and family, Hu, Bubbles,

Danny, went to the game, and the mother and Marlena met with Klondike and her cubs there. I wanted to be there to support Jacob and Delano, but Adam told me to stop being the subject of problems. With all Marlena's group there, that was a problem, so I didn't go. I prayed, and felt very anxious as I watch the game on TV with BB, Jaison, and Wang who stayed as well.

Jacob's team fell behind by 15 points in the first 8 minutes of play. Then Jacob found his rhythm, and I coached and cheered so hard from the little towns only sports bar, the team heard me. The team caught up and tied by half time and made the game very competitive in the next half. The score was back and forth and kept us cheering. Jacob stroked the 3 and slipped in so many times to double team the center with him or Delano grabbing the rebound. I was so proud of Jacob who made it a point to cosmic dunk on their center 4 times. Thrilled as I watched his every move and he played like he said he would, a Wild man. Jacob scored 41 points, 12 rebounds, 11 assists, with 5 blocked shots and MVP. Delano blocked 12 shots in the paint with 16 rebounds and 15 points. When Jacob accepted his award and the champion ship trophy, I had an indescribable feeling of happiness, and felt extremely proud of him.

However, by time of the championship game, Jacob had slowed down calling, and apologized for kissing me. He said he felt like a pervert. I accepted his apology. Adam gave me a sex talk about causing Jacob problems. I figured he was right. I just had a little girl crush and other plans. Besides, I didn't believe in relationships. So, we agreed to stay friends. I was a little uncomfortable with a healthy 21-year-old guy talking about my body and kissing me, however, there was a side of Jacob I liked, and wished for us to be close friends.

Our final critiqued show that had Judges involved happened. Our group won with me being a part of the group and we headed for West Palm Beach and the Beach Camp. We were in Los Angeles and the trip was to take a little more than 2 weeks since we had scheduled shows in Las Vegas, a little beach show in Texas, then New Orleans, and the last show in Alabama. All generated by JAJA Production Company, which booked the gigs to represent the change on its way to the Beach Camp. The thought of touring with a band was epic. So as we headed to Las Vegas, we received new songs to study and created a different show. The meeting bus became a cramped practice area, but served its purpose.

Despite the problems that Marlena's flunkies had with me, everybody planned to hang out together during our two-day layover. Like always, we tried to figure what to do with two hot 7-foot guys tagging along so no one would notice, but knew after the championship game, it would be impossible. Everyone stopped Jacob and Delano for autographs, or pictures. Not to mention all the girls that hit on them, slipping them their numbers. For Jacob the flocks of girls became worse with the speculative story of him being out his relationship with Marlena.

Reporters and Paparazzi questioned Jacob about his personal life. Every reporter's write up concerning Jacobs' personal life, Marlena had made it her business to be involved and listed as his long time fiancé. As a couple, they did a photo shoot for a sports magazine a few months ago, and after the championship game, the magazine hit the newsstands making it seem they were still together. However, without the news of Jacob announcing their engagement, and reports of her arrest during an assault on a girl Jacob was with, Rumor Mills were churning out information concerning problems in their relationship. Therefore, he had eyes on him wherever he went with reporters trying to pry into his private life.

The first free night in Las Vegas Adam wanted to celebrate baby brother's success and us winning the Beach Camp competition.

So clubbing was on the agenda. There was an exclusive club in Las Vegas that catered to sport celebrities with a 21-year-old age requirement. Well Hu was a pro baseball player, Adam was a linebacker for a pro football team, and went to the Pro Bowl 5 times. Then there was Jacob. I only expected to see pictures, but Adam sent me to hair and makeup for an older look so I could hang out too, but Klondike got pissed saying,

"We're not going to get in because of her." She made a big announcement how she will leave me by the door. Well, we dressed, with Klondike running her mouth nonstop even while Adam spoke with the gatekeeper and security. Then we went in with Adam and Jacob. The only problem we had, security would not admit Klondike. I don't know why, but it could have been that ugly orange red lipstick she was wearing, and her Loud and obnoxious personality. Security told her to get in line. She got mad at me and told the guy,

"She's under 21 and her ID is a fake." Security didn't ID anyone in our group. Just shut up I thought; then, the gatekeeper told her,

"Yeah, she's a cutie, and you're REAL FUGLY which equals... Fucked up and UGLY. That's why you're getting in line," and that was that.

Petrified with so many celebs around me, I didn't know what to do. Some huge names in sports you saw on TV, read about in magazines, or heard the names in News reports were there. With all knowing Adam who introduced me as an entertainer/model, which made me sound interesting, I couldn't be a little girl. I tried to act like BB talking, socializing, and networking. But BB's special, so I did me. However, after Wang and Delano, danced with me, soon I had several admirers waiting for dances. That was fun, but Delano was too much of a pervert for me to slow dance like he was sweating me to do. Jacob, who was entertaining a few girls, broke his attention chasing Delano and everyone else away, but reserved all my slow dances.

"And don't come back," Jacob said as girls threw themselves at him while following him around. It was funny. However, when a slow song came on, he was there waiting and grinning. After a while I said,

"Jacob, my feet hurt." He led me to a two-person seat in the lounge. As soon as my hips hit the seat, I popped out of my shoes. Laughing, he pulled my feet in his lap and massaged them. Every female there that tried to hit on him peeped at us while Jacob gave me all his attention.

"Allysa, if your feet feel better will you dance with me one more time before we go?" I agreed, and we talked about people's outfits, which led to us talking fashion. We continued talking about fashion and basketball. Jacob massaged my feet, ankle, and then calf for a while, and then I danced with only him for the next hour or so under Adam's watchful eyes.

Arriving back at the hotel Jacob walked BB and me to our room. BB opened the door while Jacob and I said good night and the smell hit us. BB went in.

"Dammit to shit. Don't go in yet. Let some air in," BB said as she came out holding her breath. We smelled bleach when we approached the door, but didn't think it was coming out our room. Jacob went in and opened the windows. We waited a while; then found someone had bleached four blouses, three dresses, four pairs of jeans that belonged to me, and part of the room that belonged to the hotel. One dress Jacob had bought for me, but hadn't seen me wear yet. He blew up and went to the manager. Jacob came back in a half an hour bringing Adam, Klondike, and the manager. Klondike was ready to fight me claiming I blamed her for something she didn't do. Adam and the manager walked in and inspected the damage to the room and clothes. I told Adam,

"I don't know who did it."

"Klondike knows she did it." Jacob said while looking at Klondike. Then Adam told Klondike,

"You will pay for the items and damages to the room immediately. Now, admit you did it and apologize or be dismissed from this trip and fired from the camp by my father. Then make immediate payment."

"I didn't do it. They did it and she's blaming me," Klondike shouted as she pointed. The manager came out the room telling Klondike,

"Miss, you told a maid you lost your key card, and I gave you a new one." Then Adam said,

"I know who we saw go in the room with bleach showing through a plastic bag. You looked at the camera. Do you want to challenge the camera, manager, and me?" She looked at me and rolled her eyes, but Adam continued, "I will not tolerate you destroying people's property." BB said,

"Everything still has the price tag on them except the dress Jacob bought. They totaled $2,150.73." BB's math was off by about a thousand or more. Klondike paid Jacob for the dress immediately, and I had two thousand cash in my hand by 9:15 the next morning. BB and I went shopping, but Klondike with her flunkies wanted to fight me. Jaison, Jacob, Wang, Lynn, and BB stayed with me all the time, but Klondike dared me to walk around alone threatening,

"Adam can't protect you forever."

Adam moved BB and me to an area on the double decker sleeper bus before we left the hotel. Wang and Danny volunteered to change bus spaces with us and Jacob booked an extra show to help with the group's expenses, but Klondike was mad because the club requested that she not perform. So she continued to act stupid making the practice difficult with everyone feeling uncomfortable with her intentional acts. She disrupted the practice with noise and jumping threatening to attack so many times it was disturbing. I watched out for them, and kept it moving trying to ignore the situation, but before the show, I went back onto my old bus, took a razor, and sliced up her pillow.

Jacob had told us before the show we will leave immediately afterwards and while we performed, the road crew packed our belongings. Rule was to keep an overnight bag or two with necessities and a large pocketbook with you. Anyway, about 30 minutes down the highway, the bus stopped. I heard Klondike say I threatened her. Adam didn't let her on the bus saying,

"Allysa hasn't been out my sight." Klondike demanded,

"Adam, move me to your bus. I deserve to move to the nicer bus more than BB." The brother's bus was larger, much taller, and very luxurious inside, and the large area at the back meant for Adam and his family became mine. It was a large loft bed with a setting area under it and a little flat screen TV with a game console, so I was being a spoiled little sis, in my baby doll PJ's chillin hard, and looking innocent. When BB heard her name, she went to the front with me following because BB knew nothing about the pillow. Klondike saw me and tried to grab me with Adam blocking her. I pulled BB back. Then Klondike told me,

"I need to snatch your skinny white ass off the bus and take your spot." I stepped off the bus watching Klondike with BB following.

"Let this happen so we can get it over with." I pled with Adam that night as she made a big scene jumping around calling me names and swinging at me while Adam held her back. I stood there looking, waiting for her to step around Adam.

"Come on Ally," BB said, "Bull butt don't want to do anything today."

Klondike made such a big thing out of her feud with me; Adam just took her out of the show she wasn't in any way. She had no schedule appearances and no reason to be traveling with us, but she called BS lying with him threatening to send me home instead. She created the tension and problems BS planned for our group. Klondike shit rattled me... the wrong way with me wanting to put an end to her. She was sabotaging King Kapulani's program and needed to go.

The next day during a meeting, Adam addressed the disruptions Klondike was causing at practice, and during the shows. Klondike claimed,

"BS doesn't want Allysa here. She's a juvenile delinquent that's causing trouble for grown people. Send her home." Bubbles said,

Allysa did nothing but her job and then some. Her versatility has taken our shows to another level. She helps choreograph all our dance shows and the moves for the Sexetts, fill in at keyboards, perform circus acts that no one else can do, and go for what you need any time all day long. What's being asked will lose money and take away from our overall performance." Adam told everyone,

"As for her being wanted, my father recruited her." Lynn said,

"LaQuanda is going around picking fights with Ally making it uncomfortable for everyone." Adam told everyone,

"I agree, so I'm sending LaQuanda to New Orleans at her own expense. When we get there, if she wants to work with us without causing problems for anyone, we will consider it." Some thought I was too close to Jacob with one saying,

"Allysa started the problem by breaking Marlena and Jacob up." Then Adam ended that discussion saying,

"That's Jacob's business, and you need to be more professional by minding the business we're here for, the show." Adam sent Klondike packing. However, she sent word she would get more than ahead.

Jacob became a little closer. Everyone met in my area under my bed. I had pillows there for comfort. Twice Adam and Hu were there watching, but this day it was just Jacob and me. He came and laid on the floor beside me asking,

"Allysa, are you sure of your age?" I said,

"I'm not sure of anything. Why?" Jacob said,

"You act... I don't know... a little too grown. Why you cut up Klondike's pillow?" I hunched my shoulders, and he continued, "You know she will be after you." I asked,

"So what's new?" Jacob said,

"Allysa its BS's plan to send you home for any reason if you cause one more problem. Come on Little-Bit be good." I said,

"Jacob she keeps picking at me." Then he asked,

"What will you do if BS sends you home?" I told him,

"Not go." Jacob asked,

"So you'll run away like you did before? Allysa, I don't want you out there by yourself with no one who cares about you." Continuing to read, I ignored him. He looked at me bewildered, but continued, "Allysa, I need to ask you something. I need my friend Allysa's advice about a problem I have." Giving him my attention I listened. "Allysa everyone tells me what to do and expect me to do what they want. I'm going out on my own soon and still feel like a little boy, I just met this girl. I don't know her that well, but the time I've spent with her, but I've enjoyed. She makes me feel needed and she respects me as a man." Listening to him, my heart went down in flames, but he went on,

"Until meeting her I wasn't sure of myself, or how things I wanted fit in and never thought someone would want me for me, but I feel wanted and needed by her, and she makes everything come together for me. I want to know her better. Allysa, what should I do?" I didn't know what to say. Wondering... I asked,

"About what Jacob?" He said,

"Should I pursue this new girl?" I paused for a moment thinking and said,

"Jacob, do you realize you just asked me to tell you what to do? I'm confused." He looked at me and grinned, but I said, "You should pursue what makes you happy, but Jacob, let it be your own decision." He surprised me by announcing,

"Danny has planned a romantic dinner for Bubbles to give her an engagement ring. So... would you mind trying to find something to wear that's as pretty as you are and be my date?" I felt excited for Bubbles because the man of her dreams was going to make her happy, so I accepted Jacob's invitation, but soon became unenthusiastic. I realized how much of my thoughts depended on how much I liked him, and knowing he liked me too, but I felt he must like this other girl better. Trying to get pass the hurt while I showered didn't work and I had second thoughts about going.

I went to my friends in hair and make-up knowing how to make myself look older, but these guys were professionals. The person in charge, Devon, I bugged trying to get him to show me what to do and offered to pay him. Devon never took the money only asking if I was going out with the long-legged boy, Jacob. When I nodded yes, the next thing I knew I had scores of people working on my hair, nails, make-up. People in wardrobe helped me pick my outfit and showed me how to put it together.

"You're being hard on yourself honey. You have a little Miss Model thing going on," Devon said. Then he tutored me on proper etiquette. "Well, it's time to go. Devon is finish." Thanking Devon as I looked in the mirror, I wasn't looking forward to seeing Jacob's pleasure when he looked at me and I didn't want to hear about some other girl.

Jacob borrowed Jaison's SUV and shined it up. I found out from hair and makeup that Jacob arranged and paid for everything.

Jacob likes to share his good fortune. I liked that about him and needed to get what his father said out my head. I tried convincing myself to be his friend the best I could and help him find the woman a person like him deserved. However, from the time he opened the vehicle's door for me and the hour it took to get to the jazz club, I tried to think about Danny and Bubbles situation so to be upbeat, but my spirit was so low. Jacob sensed something was wrong and asked,

"Allysa, do you feel all right?"

"Yes." I replied, but I felt awful.

The Jazz Club Jacob picked, Swingers, was intriguing. We passed by two separate dance floors and bar with the music blaring finally going through some doors marked private. Jacob entered a code on a keypad. Then after walking down a long corridor, it opened into a lobby where a waiter escorted each couple to their own personal area that had a cozy atmosphere. Each couple had their own private area to enjoy the evening. Your waiter was the only person who came in your area when called. The seating were luxurious swinging love seats with pillows and throws. It was a little past romantic and after setting, I asked,

"Jacob, how did you find this place?" He said,

"Us college boys know about everything." I wondered if he planned to bring the other girl here.

I continued to try and stay focus on Danny and Bubbles situation. She was 24 in her last year at the camp as a student. She was a scholarship person the brother's father recruited. Danny at 22 completed two prestigious schools for the arts and had traveled with dance troops all over the world, but needed the exposure in the US. Jacob continued talking about Bubbles and explained,

"Bubbles' was a gifted dancer who received her break late. She's the youngest child and had to take care of her whole family by exotic dancing. My father pulled her away from that situation and she has been going to College and the camp for the last four years. She just received her BA. Danny wants to marry her and figured the time was right."

"That's amazing. I'm happy for them." I said, and then Jacob asked,

"Why don't you believe in relationships Allysa?" I told him,

"I haven't seen one that worked yet. People aren't together for love anymore and don't seem to care about the children produced." He asked,

"So why do you think people get together?" Thinking for a minute and said,

"I don't know. Everyone has a reason I guess, but it will not work unless each one work at the relationship and that's the problem. So I don't believe in them."

We looked at the menu for a while then Jacob called the waiter, but said,

"Allysa, I know you want vegetable soup, but let's try something new. Do you eat fish?" I nodded yes. He continued, "I'll order and if you don't like it, I'll eat it." While we talked this killer slow song came on. Fighting with my feelings already, I hoped Jacob wouldn't ask me to dance, but he did. I struggled with myself wanting to enjoy this loving and handsome man's company. It took me a minute to get started I felt so nervous and Jacob said,

"Allysa, I know you can dance so...,"

"Jacob... I'm just a little confused. Thinking too much I guess."

"We don't have to dance." He said quickly. I didn't want him to think I was getting sick; then, after getting in his arms, I said,

"I want to dance with you, please." Then, we started our slow dance as Jacob said,

"My father told me to stay away from you since I upset you, but I think if I approach you slowly, I can tell a little about your likes and dislikes. Is that OK?"

"Yes." I replied confused and wondered should I talk to him.

"That sounds like... but. Is there something you want to talk about, Allysa? I want you to feel comfortable and you're not. Allysa, you can talk to me about anything."

"Jacob, what about the other girl you met?" I asked serious, as he began to laugh, but he replied,

"Oh her. I tried to tell you about her earlier, but you cut me short, and made me feel stupid." Alarmed at what he said I replied,

"Jacob, I don't mean to say things to hurt you or make you feel stupid. Normally, I don't care, but... I care how you feel." He didn't say anything right away, and we danced. Then Jacob looked at me and said,

"You didn't do anything Ally; it's me. I've been saying and doing some stupid things I've never had a problem with until I met you, and... I wondered should I say something or hope this feeling would pass, but this feeling has been going on for a while... growing and I don't want this ever to pass. The girl is you. I have very strong feelings for you Allysa." I was geeking in my soul that I've been spoiling my evening. Our eyes became one gaze again with him holding me close, and I sighed in relief, while relaxing in his arms.

The waiter knocked and brought in a bottle of wine, serving it, while reminding Jacob that he carded me to be 18 and under the drinking age. We sat down and when the waiter left, we laughed, and Jacob poured me some wine.

"Drink up before the waiter comes back." He was quiet for a while; then, he said, "18, huh!"

"Yeah 18," I said.

"Seriously though," Jacob asked, "Can you and I have a 25-21-year-old conversation?"

"What does age have to do with it?" I asked with him saying,

"Allysa, you act to grown sometimes, but when you act like a teenager, you get bullied. I don't want you feeling pressured or confused." I told him,

"My confusion came from you kissing me, your girlfriend Marlena, and how to take you." He said,

"Most wouldn't care about that." I felt comfortable enough to say,

"Jacob, I don't like phony people and I wanted to like you. No one has ever kissed me before or treated me special because they liked me." He remarked,

"I find that hard to believe Allysa." Wondering I asked,

"Are you finding me hard to believe Jacob?" Jacob cautiously responded,

"No, just what you said. You're.... so appealing." Thinking and feeling more attracted to him, I went to the ladies' room needing BB in there, as my corner person to instruct and loosen me up, but it was only me. So I refreshed myself, makeup, just a little perfume, hair, took five deep breaths; then, five more while I wondered if it was the wine or the relief the girl was me, but my little girl days were over.

The waiter served our food, and we were very cozy while Jacob introduced me to different foods. Attentively, Jacob told me about the dishes. An hour later with half the wine gone, I leaned against Jacob feeding him some cake while he laid back. He asked,

"So Allysa, do you feel better after you found out you're the girl I wanted to talk to?" I ask Jacob,

"Yes, but why didn't you just tell me that?" Jacob repeated,

"I told you I've been doing things stupidly, but I saw how you felt about me so no more games, or secrets. All right?" He said grinning at me while he took me in his arms to dance which solved a problem. I wanted to be closer.

We're finally on the same page. We like each other and want to explore our feelings and I could enjoy the closeness of the embrace understanding he wants me, only me. He must have felt the same. His manhood was... poking me again. I enjoyed being close to all of him, but he was embarrassed so I excused myself and sat down. He went to the rest room coming back with his collar opened and tie loosened with that sexy little grin that made me smile. He cleared his throat taking a large gulp of wine then played with a toothpick blushing, grinning, and saying,

"Allysa you excite me. I want to get to know you better."

"Um, what do you want to know?" I asked knowing what. He smoothly answered,

"I want to take my time, and learn everything about you Allysa." We drank a little more wine. Then Jacob said, "You said no one has ever kissed you before and you had no one who liked you, and Rod wasn't your boyfriend?" I answered,

"No, Jacob, no one liked me, and no, Rod wasn't my boyfriend. He was my trustworthy friend who shared a similar background and had the same goal. Sometimes I had to run away. Rods home was the only place Rich, and I were safe. My AD didn't know where Rod lived and never found out. I only stayed overnight a few times since I knew my AD would hunt him down." The wine almost made me say more, but Jacob asked,

"Why did you have to run away?" I moved away from him putting my feet back on the floor. I felt stupid and didn't want him to question me. "Wait don't leave. Forget I asked that please." Jacob said, while setting up and placing his arm behind me, but didn't touch, "Do you want to leave?" He asked.

"No." I looked at him and said, "Really I want to forget that part of my life." I sat there feeling stupid and confused. He laid back relaxing and extended his hand for me to take with a shy smile. I trusted him with my feelings and gave him my hand. I wanted to enjoy the way he made me feel. He pulled me closer, and we were comfortable again setting quietly for a while when Jacob asked me,

"Are you cold Allysa?" I had this cleavage thing going on, and he must have seen the goose bumps because he was looking.... a lot.

"Somewhat," I said. He put the throw on my legs and put his jacket around my shoulders, but didn't block his view with me happy that I had something to look at and someone I liked looking.

"Let me warm you up a little." He said as we sat looking at each other and sharing a glass of wine. Then we talked about our friends Danny and Bubbles. I told him,

"Jacob, I feel strange Adam paired me dancing with Danny."

"Allysa, Adam did that because you're the better dancer. It's not that Bubbles is a bad dancer. You're better. Allysa you'll bust a move that look trashy when someone else does it, but your moves are so graceful you don't look slutty. You're a very appealing person and dancer. Danny and you move like one person and look good together, but I think you look better with me." Yeah, I thought that's probably how Bubbles feels about Danny too.

Jacob and I knew this was the last night before we caught up with Klondike, so we stayed out late getting in after 3:00am. Knowing I had to deal with Klondike later, I was ready to go to sleep and overpower that with thoughts of Jacob, when he showed up with his blanket and pillow. So I came down out my bed and we laid on the floor. I asked,

"What?"

"I still need you to answer a few questions." And I still wondered what, but Jacob shyly asked, "It's kind of personal. Will you be upset?" I shook my head no. "Okay... um... Allysa, are you still a virgin?" I had wondered how we would get around to the subject of sex, but didn't expect that question. Defensive I asked,

"Why do you need to know all that?" I heard him say oh no real low. "Is this the part of our date were you expect to have sex?"

"Oh, no, no.... you have things all wrong," and he laughed saying, "A pillow and blanket is not sexy. I just wanted to know if you like being with boys... or girls or if you ever been with anyone sexually." Thinking I just told him no one liked me like that, and I looked at Jacob thinking good recovery, but I wasn't sure how to answer his questions. Figuring the truth was best, so I said,

"I want to save myself for my husband. That should answer everything."

"It did." He said smiling. Then I said,

"You can stay if you like, Jacob, but I'm sleepy." I got comfortable; then, I could feel him looking at me from head to toe. He laid on top of my covers and we went to sleep.

At seven, I woke and found myself in his arms and blanket. I stayed there as he pulled me to his chest. That felt so good, but when I woke again, Jacob was on his phone talking with Adam. He seemed upset and left telling me to close my privacy curtain. I went back to sleep missing him.

Adam called waking me at 10 saying he needed to meet with Klondike and me by 11. I arrived to find Klondike already there.

"LaQuanda has agreed to get along with no animosity towards you and you will do the same; agreed?" Adam asked with an attitude. I asked Adam,

"What about the threats she made daily until a day ago?"

"I did nothing like that," she announced. "You and your friends are trying to keep something going."

"It was something you started." I said noticing her attitude hadn't changed.

"This is not a discussion Allysa." Adam said, "Now, do you mind if she stay." Sensing something wrong I told him,

"Adam you sent her away, so I'll let that be your call." She was lying, and I was sure Adam sensed this too. This bullshit was pissing me off, and I turned to leave, but Adam said,

"Allysa, you stay. I need to talk to you. LaQuanda, if you go back on your word, you will not work anymore gigs and my father will terminate you. Is this understood?" She nodded and Adam dismissed her as his phone rang. She left laughing.

Adam took a call and looked at me like he wanted to melt my head while saying,

"I will take care of it now." Then he nastily said,

"Allysa, my mother and BS has been calling me nonstop for a while. My mother said you made Jacob quit his girlfriend." I said,

"Wait a minute, that was between them." Then Adam blurted out,

"Jacob likes you and thinks you're mature enough to handle a relationship." I told him,

"Adam, we're friends. That's all." Then Adam asked,

"So why did you go out with him?" I was dumbfounded, but said,

"We hung out together. Danny and Bubbles were with us and we had dinner."

"Dinner lasted until 3:30am, and Jacob sleeping with you was part of dinner?" He said as he walked to me stopping just short of being in my face. While moving away I said,

"You're making it sound like dessert, but Jacob slept on top of the covers." Then Adam yelled,

"I'm on the same bus. I saw Jacob with you in his arms. Now, what's going on? I don't like my mother calling me upset about what Jacob's doing." That upset me and I asserted,

"Well, you need to talk to your mother about that... but I see she needs all the help she can get to make him a Mommas' Boy, so she can tell him when he eats, shit and who he loves. And really, you want your little brother with that gold digging trick? Jacob should do what he wants. I'm sure it's not your intention to control him Adam, but... I think she's controlling you too." Oh Lord, why did I say all that, and realized I was in a serious standoff with Adam about Jacob? Adam looked at me like he was going to butt stomp me, but he cooled down for a minute saying,

"You're hard headed and have a smart ass mouth. I told you to leave Jacob alone." Blamed for everything I responded negatively.

"Why? Plus, I'm not bothering him." Then Adam said,

"You know what Allysa, if this continues, you will end up back home. You are making it hard to protect you. The next trouble or problem you cause my mother my father will send you home." I doubted that, but tired of people in my business concerning Jacob I said,

"Look Adam, I just came here to learn, perform, and not be in your Momma's drama. Can you leave me out this mess to do what I came here for? I promise I won't cause any more drama by bothering Jacob." And I Audi, but pass Klondike by the door listening. However, later during a radio interview when asked about Marlena, Jacob officially announced,

"I'm no longer seeing Marlena and plan not to make that mistake again." However, I understand she and mother dear went to his graduation.

Big sis BB, received her BBA with a specialty in commerce, and I received my BA BS in economics and finance, as we made our way to the beach camp. We had four pocket money shows left to perform. I pretty much stayed to myself talking to Adam only while we worked, and I did everything he asked of me. Jacob stayed away mostly.

BB and I received mail from TMP requesting us to make a video of ourselves. Wang and the crew made us some professional looking videos.   Then Adam and Jaison took us to the mall to turn them in, and TMP asked us to stay along with about thirty other girls to interview with a man who took plain pictures of us and reviewed our videos. Then I had to wait for another man who requested information from my agent which was encouraging.

After the situation with Adam, I felt strange when I was with our group. So I stayed in my area because when everyone went out, Jacob wanted to be close to me and I wanted to be close to him, but I didn't want problems or get sent home. The situation confused and depressed me.   My buds, BB, Jaison, and Wang always came to keep me company.   Jacob would come to my area with them sometimes when the group hung out to play cards or video games. Then, I would climb up to my loft bed and chill by myself.

For the longest time I thought Jaison and BB had something going on, since they slept together now and then, but their thing was blunting and boozing, (I figured that's what BB stood for). Anyway, she had a boyfriend at home, and Jaison had girlfriends all over, but she agreed with me chilling for a while and make it to the camp. So I did... for a while.

CHAPTER SEVEN

Erotica

Arriving in New Orleans, Jaison handled everything and called a special meeting giving us a schedule. We would be there for 3 days and perform two shows. However, this was a JAJA Productions thing where Jaison made a deal with the owners of the clubs for a percentage of the door and drink proceeds if our show brought in a certain amount of people. Jaison and Jacob planned two street shows hoping to bring in more people. The third day we were to spend the day at a plantation turned into a water theme park with a horde of people that benefited from a JAJA production charity event, and other tuition students from the Beach Camp. I had never been to an Amusement Park before so I was looking forward to that, but Jaison asked me for a favor.

"Little Bit I'm going to need a dancer to do a dance with a pole as your prop tomorrow." I said,

"I never performed a pole dance before," but Jaison said quickly,

"Wait Little Bit, it's a dance with the pole as your prop. Get that straight now. You will show very little skin only your face and maybe arms. You're my baby sis."

"I'll do it for you Jaison. I'm on the thin side though. Bubbles body is more... mature."

"But Allysa, I want you to perform because you're more creative, athletic, and classier than Bubbles. You have a sexy elegance about you and I want you to use those factors and bring it tomorrow. I saw you showing Bubbles moves on the pole she never got. Then you plucked her nerve playing on the pole and looking sexier doing it than when Bubbles was serious. I believe you'll bring in more people than the club will hold, and I know I will have problems with Adam and Jacob when they find out the plan, so don't give me a hard time about the way you look. You're a honey, now go... practice."

Our first street show took place at an area called Park Place. It's an area near the club where we were to perform. It was a parklike setting that had a large crowd formed already watching a group entertain. We rolled in and stole that crowd; then, had a nice crowd at the club for a Thursday night making more money from JAJA Production's negotiations. The next morning, we had our meeting, and it was my turn to dance. Jaison was in charge, and he didn't change his mind.

I liked working with Jaison, because we had fun with his very vivacious shows, but the club where we were to perform was just a block away from the red-light district, which explained the dance with the pole. Jaison had told Adam I would be the feature for our preview and he moved the time for the dance closer to show time. When Adam called to meet with me, Jaison and Jacob were there. I knew Jai (Jaison's nickname) had told Adam about the dance with the pole as my prop. Adam didn't buy into it and Jacob felt no one would take me seriously saying I was too young and skinny in so many ways it hurt. Jaison talked up for me smiling like a pimp saying,

"She will pack the house." It went back and forth for a while with Jaison winning out. With all said, I couldn't let Jaison down.

My friends at hair and makeup called me to come hours earlier than I thought necessary. Devon saw me coming and I could hear him.

"Oh my, here she comes. Look at the pretty little girl. Let's help her out," he finished while sizing me up. Devon who was from New Orleans had his friends waiting. I had my routine together, but they showed me how to walk, vogue and stop pose and helped me worked that into my routine so that most my dancing was off the pole. All performed their jobs keeping me up beat and didn't fail me.

Devon dressed me in a one-piece black skin-tight hot pants leotard with a skinny sparkle belt. My leotard came to a turtleneck with the shoulders and arms out. I had on gloves that went a little pass my elbows with part of the fingers cut out. My High-heeled boots went about 6 inches pass my knees and stopped mid-thigh with black stocking showing between the top of my boots and the bottom of my hot pants. The boots had thin sparkle rope chains about four inched from the top to make them gather with a sparkle bracelet around the ankle of one boot. Except for the boots, my outfit was seamless; like in skintight. BB and Lynn came to explain things and keep me company.

"How do I look?" I asked. They looked me over and fixed a few things. Lynn said,

"Yes this is cool." BB said with her thumbs up,

"Yeah baby sis, you're gonna brake their hearts. You go out there and just do what you normally do." Then Devon gave me a beautiful robe to wear and all his friends came with us on the bus. All the laughing and Joking calmed my nerves. BB and her blunt help too.

We drove up into a parking lot packed with people. Jacob went to the local radio station after our meeting and did an impromptu interview and the DJ announced the dance and show. I thought if I only could dance not lewd, but enticing enough to bring people inside the club, that'll be what Jaison wanted and the group needed for this to be a success.

Under Jaison and Cisco's direction, the roadies set up the pole, stage, and effects, which extended off the bus. Jaison and BB planned it so I would step off the bus to the music with security all around. I almost lost my nerve waiting, but kept it cool. I stopped thinking about Jacob not having confidence in me, and his young and skinny comments that hurt when my brother Jaison came and helped me out of my robe. He asked,

"Little-Bit, you ready?" When I thought about how Adam and Jacob said no one would take me seriously, my confidence came back and I said,

"Yeah... let's do this."

Stepping out the door to the music as planned, I heard a woman laughing loud. I figured it was Klondike and ignored it since I planned to make this my moment, and people told her to shut up anyway. Adam, Jacob, and Wang were running security with others on hand if there was a problem. I made my entrance and by time I touched the pole I had everyone's attention including securities and stretched using the pole doing walkovers. Just when their attention peaked, I did a walk over springing up onto the pole catching myself with my thighs only. While there, I gripped the pole with my hands and did a vertical split aligned with the pole; then, I swirled around fluidly like a snake. After that, I slowly pulled myself up the pole with erotic hesitations keeping my toes pointed, and elongating my neck letting my head and hair fall back like Devon said. It was like playing on a jungle gym at a park playground and I enjoyed myself. When I was near the top of the pole, I flipped into an upside-down Russian and did a quick whirly bird down the pole to a walkover, and then it was on. Dancing without the pole I had and kept every one's attention doing what Devon showed me. I heard BB say,

"You got them baby sis." Enough said, and at the end of the song, I danced back to the bus with people hollering for more. Jaison came out announcing,

"Miss Erotica, will be singing and dancing at GINOS in an hour... without the pole. You need to get your tickets now because we expect a capacity crowd tonight." Jaison was right the place

GINOS had people waiting to get in with the large size club getting packed.

I thanked all my friends in hair and makeup, and Devon's group from New Orleans for helping the little girl that came to them. Devon said while hugging me,

"Girl you represented, and that's all we wanted."

All my friends were acting stupid doing a show and tell about what I did, how I did it, and asking for my autograph. I felt ecstatic thinking before I was so afraid I would let people down. Then Jaison came saying,

"My girl, my girl," while he hugged me up off the floor, "I knew if anyone could do it, my little sis Erotica would." Everyone applauded and wondered where, when, and why Jaison came up with that name. Jai answered, "I thought of it while I watched her dance. That was a nice pole as a prop dance, and the traditional pole dance will never entertain me again." Then he kissed me on my forehead while he slipped me a letter Jacob sent. I slipped the letter back thinking I didn't need or want to know what he had to say and said to Jaison,

"Tell him it's ok." Feeling myself in one way, but sad Jacob didn't believe in me. I told our group, "It wasn't only me that made this successful. The only thing I did was dance, which was a small part. Jaison and BB planned the idea together, Devon you and your group created my look, and my routine from a vision in your mind, the stagehands positioned the stage together making sure it didn't rock, Jacob went to the radio station, and that's just mentioning a small amount. It was all your support. That's what I saw, realized, and understood from this overwhelming success, and I hope we continue to work together and support each other always." Everyone made a toast to that.

"Ditto for life." Jaison said clapping his hands, "Now let's get it on." Then we partied while we performed. Without Klondike's influence, some of Klondike's followers worked well with everyone with no animosity, so everyone worked together, and all had fun. Klondike, and a few of her faithful ones were in the audience setting with Adam who was only making a guest appearance.

We chilled on the meeting bus with the party following us as we rode to our motel. Adam who rode in front along with Klondike seemed disturbed. They were talking more than ever, and glanced at us continuously, but everyone else enjoyed the party atmosphere and ended up either blunting, drinking or both during the hour and a half ride. All talked in one group with every one into each other's business. Then someone asked who people thought was still a virgin. At first, everyone said Delano, but all agreed on three people, him, A Korean Gayageum player with thick glasses, and me. My name was almost first. Then the conversation moved to the guys talking about what they liked about each female in the group. Hu had joined us after his team lost their game in Atlanta said,

"I like setting in back watching the Sexetts bodies move." Jaison stated,

"Man you're watching their butts moving this way and that." Hu snickered with this little shit-eating grin on his face saying,

"There's a lot of bouncing going on too. I love it." BB said,

"We have our share of sexy manly parts to look at too you know." Jaison announced,

"Okay, this question is for the ladies. What part of a man's body you think is the sexiest?" Then he covered my ears. With a tied vote of butt and the way men are hung after it went around to all the females except me, everyone looked at me saying I had to break the tie. I thought for a moment.

"Honestly," I said, "His arms." People said Aw come on in different ways. Then Jaison said,

"Wait, hold on... Why the arms Little-Bit?"

"Well, if a guy holds you right, it will make you feel like exploring other things with him." There was silence for a while; then, while going cross eyed BB said,

"OH WOW, that's DEEP." She's so special I hunched her while Jacob shyly peeped at me. I could tell he wanted to talk, but I kept my distance.

Bubbles announced this would be my first time at an amusement park. Everyone told me what to ride and not to ride. I figured I would wait and see. The gang said they would look out for me. Oh boy. So the next morning we got up at 7am and traveled for two hours to an old plantation turned into a water theme park. I kept bugging Jai,

"Are we there yet?"

Once there, we met other Beach Camp student groups. Some of BS's rich tuition with their families, about 1,000 children and their families who won various contest dealing with the arts, plus the two schools JAJA helped. King Kapulani reserved the park and part of the prize was going to the water park to meet The Brothers. I found out then Jacob has been a singing heartthrob since he was 12 and wondered how I missed that. His mother shopped his talent at eight and he became part of a children's show at nine. So, he was very busy with his brothers talking, signing autographs, and peeping at me.

Next, Adam spoke. With everyone tired and nodding, we wanted to get on the rides to wake up. Plus, it was hot, muggy, and something else. I was sweating just sitting there looking, and it felt like we were all going to be little and big grease spots if Adam didn't rush. After that, for the next three hours the gang introduced me to different crazy rides. A few I didn't go on, but we did the socializing thing with the other groups which was cool, and one thing everyone agreed on, it was too hot and humid for us not to be in the water.

Changing into our bathing suits, we went to the water park that was open to the Beach Camp groups only. We went to a section called The Hatfields vs. The McCoys and had a battle that turned out being the girls against the boys. There were stationary water cannons that had enough force to knock off your clothes. We had all different shapes and size water blasters and let me not forget my favorite, the water balloons. We fought our battle on a slip and slide with a small stream of water that covered the whole area. I had crazy fun that went on all afternoon and became so serious we had to sign up for leave. We fought getting wet; then, put on our shortest cut-off jeans, and went on the fastest rides. With the other groups there and the prizewinners, there were long lines, so we had to wait. BB and I had so much fun at the water fight we forgot about our hair. Everyone did, so we had the soft curl going on. Hu said,

"You girls look exotic."

So I lied. It disappointed me that Jacob didn't believe I could be alluring, which pissed me off. But with all the fun BB and I had flirting with the other guys in line and Jacob peeping at me, I laughed it off. After a while, Jacob cut the line and pushed people out his way until he was next to me. He placed a flower in my hair and asked to take a picture with me. I agreed, so Jacob asked Hu who was right there in our face to take a picture of us in front of this beautiful plant. Pulling me close he wrapped his arms around me; then asked,

"Am I doing this right?" I smiled because it was too right. After the picture, Jacob didn't move that far away. "Are you having fun?" He asked next and I smiled and nodded yeah to both questions. "I will remember the water bomb you busted upside my head because until now, Allysa, it's the only attention you've given me." As I giggled, Jacob wondered, "Why are you avoiding me, and are you going to talk to me?" When I looked up, Hu was closer and looking down our throats. It was like Adam told Hu to watch us. While looking at Hu I said,

"I'm sure Adam and... your momma... don't want us together."

"That's silly," Jacob responded, "We're all here just having fun with friends Allysa. Come on... ride with me, and then let's get in the water it's hot." Jacob took me by my hand and by now, we were looking at each other with him playing with my hands. However, I asked him,

"You sure you want to be seen with me? I'm still skinny and young you know." By time we were next to ride, Jacob had apologized profusely, and I got over my attitude. Well... sort of.

We socialized as a group, but Jacob's body language let everyone know we were together. We did the ride. It was scary, but I had Jacob; then, we strolled to the water park section sharing a cotton candy and pictures with a photographer. Klondike's slight attitude arrived with Jacob's attention towards me, and my interest became Jacob regardless of who Adam and his momma wanted to control. So we rode the lazy river inner tube together. The course went around the water park with us drifting. I took a nap while people snapped pictures of us. I had become a project of Hair and Makeup, so they made sure I looked exceptional everywhere I went. Devon taught me the proper etiquette of being a lady, and that day he dressed me in this sexy two-piece James Bond 1960's era swimsuit.

Drifting took almost an hour because Jacob stopped us. When I woke, he was just looking at me and trying to cover his chubby. That made me smile, but at the end of the ride, Hu was there trying to get his fuss on wondering what took us so long. So I went with BB, Bubbles, and Lynn on a water slide ride. If it hadn't been for that situation with Hu, I know I wouldn't have gone on that ride and waited. We walked up so many flights and slid down hill forever. When we finally slid out the bottom of the tube, the attendant had to quickly duck out the way with BB launching out the float head-first, like a torpedo diving from a ship with Lynn and me flying out attacking by air. Poor Bubbles just laid on the bottom of the float with it spinning. By time we could get off the ride, the guys were laughing most on their knees saying we were screaming in harmony all the way down with me screaming lead. After everyone in sight laughed, we pulled ourselves together and signed autographs as a group, The Sexetts.

Next, we walked a distance to the swimming hole, which was part of a large lake that had large boulders all around by the edge were you could enjoy the sun. Most the boulders were around a wall of stone that sprung up at least 20 feet or more also situated by the lake's shore. I could see the water was clear by the edges, but murky and dark in the deep areas, and there were many murky areas. A huge tree that had grown by the water's edge alongside the large stone formation had thick, knotted ropes tied and hanging from the branches for people to swing on out to one of those deep areas and let go. It looked like dangerous fun, but knowing all the wild life like snapping turtles, snakes, Alligators, and a large fish with the same name that lived in Louisiana, I planned not to get in the water anyway. Jacob swung out on the rope three times, which bothered me and I held my breath until his head popped up from that murky hue. He noticed and stopped. Jacob started watching how people hit the water, but he was watching me lying on the rocks below with another group of girls trying to get a tan.

Danny and Bubbles kept asking me to come up since our group was hanging out on top of the rock formation we called The Wall. After about an hour, I did. It was fun watching people jump off, but scary climbing up. It was so high I struggled from fear and didn't know what was going on up there or how to get down. I went up there because Danny and Bubbles helped me and to be closer to Jacob.

A photographer Jacob's agent sent over to do a free-lance article for a sports magazine was working with him to get pictures, so he asked Jacob to get a few girls with nice bodies to take some pictures. When we finished the climb, Bubbles said as she smiled,

"Ok Jacob, all the Sexetts are up here so we'll take a picture with you as a group; then, you can take your pictures with Allysa." The photographer had asked Klondike to join us, however, Jacob told the photographer,

"No this will be me and my backup singers as soon as that beauty there comes over. They are the Sexetts and get the spelling right." Jacob and the photographer motioned for me to come while all of them corrected the photographer's spelling. I headed straight to Jacob because I needed him. I was petrified being up that high wanting to crawl, but what happened made Klondike mad, and I notice she started asking her friends something. They were shaking their heads no while moving away except for Twista. He told Klondike,

"Yeah, let's do it." Twista who was over six feet and 300lbs and Klondike, who was almost as large, moved towards me fast. He snatched at my top while grabbing me off the ground. I only had time to grab Twista's skin before Klondike punched me while snatching off my top. Then both pushed and threw me off the rocks while she told the photographer,

"Take a picture of that."

It all happened in an intentional instant with no one close enough to help. I fell almost 30 feet and hit the water face and chest first. I didn't swing out and jump like designed. Thank GOD, they threw me hard enough to clear the rocks, but the water stunned me. Jacob came out of nowhere grabbing me under water and brought me up. I leaned against him for a few minutes to get myself together, but anger and the terror of falling was all I could feel. I always had bad dreams about falling forever. Now every time I closed my eyes I experienced the sensation of falling into a black hole. Klondike and her group knew from us going on different high rides that day I suffer from acrophobia.

Jacob helped me to the shore while Jaison covered me with a blanket and scooped me up. Delano acquired a park golf cart. They took me to my area on their bus. I was so mad and embarrassed I couldn't talk.

"Allysa do you feel sick?" Jacob asked. When I didn't say anything, he told Jaison to stay with me. Jacob found me some ice, and then left to see what Adam did because he saw everything, but never checked on my condition, but Hu came on the bus asking me,

"Jacob touch you?" When I ignored him he asked, "Did Jacob get fresh with you?" That wasn't even the issue. I moved away. His stupid ass asked that dumb shit, and I had just fell 33 fuckin feet! Then I heard Jacob and Adam auguring.

"You saw what happened and Klondike is responsible for starting shit by trying to kill her. This shit is escalating Adam," Jacob said and Adam responded,

"This is not about Klondike, but it's about you staying away from that girl." Jacob replied,

"That girl Adam? Her name is Allysa... remember her? Allysa? I only wanted to take one picture with the Sexetts and then a picture with Allysa. There was nothing wrong with that, but there is something terribly wrong with LaQuanda and Twista's actions and your fucked up attitude. You need to mind your business and do something with Klondike and Twista." Then Twista came walking up to the buses with his little group around him talking loud, but not saying anything. When Jacob jumped, all Twista's friends ran away. Danny, Hu, Adam, and Jaison were trying to hold Jacob when crazy ass Delano walked up unconcern, but grabbed Twista and made him twist and shout. Delano kicked his ass all beside the bus with Jaison helping until Twista got away. Then Delano told Adam,

"I want you to get in my face with some shit. What they did could have injured or killed her." Adam walked off with Jaison following him. Bubbles, who was fighting tears of anger apologized saying,

"I didn't know. Please believe we didn't know."

Jacob came back on the bus concerned and wanted me to go to the hospital. I refused by moving away to a corner to feel secure. I had a terrible headache and held my head to keep it from exploding. It wasn't a normal headache. It was like the ones I experienced when I was small after a severe beating by my AD. I laid back closing my eyes and stopped paying attention. BB said,

"Oh no! Allysa..." She put the ice on my head and kept calling my name. "Allysa you must go to the hospital." When I didn't respond, Jacob moved BB and pulled me in his arms getting my attention.

"Allysa, what day is it?" Jacob asked, and then it was quiet with everyone looking at me. I couldn't remember right away, but tried to play it off saying slowly,

"Leave me alone. I'm all right." with Jacob saying,

"Okay, you said something now tell me the day."

"Saturday," I said feeling like I had to throw up. Wang came in angry slinging Chinese; then said to Jacob,

"You come you help brother."

There wasn't anything done concerning the matter. Adam had this smirk on his face with an, I told you so, attitude. I thanked my friends for being good friends, but I needed to be by myself for a while. I believed Bubbles didn't know, but really, I wasn't sure whom I could trust anymore and didn't want to be disappointed. BB told everyone to get out, but didn't leave making me talk every five minutes. After a few hours, my headache slowed down and Adam called me later saying,

"If you retaliate I'll take you home." He raised his voice as if he was my father and wasn't concern about how I felt or if I was hurt. That made me cry, but I told him,

"Adam, you went back on you word and I no longer trust you. I believed you, but the punk ass way you handled this will make my life miserable. You're not doing anything because you think she'll stop Jacob and my friendship, but that will backfire."

Yeah, and I had decided I would not suppress my feelings for Jacob. They were there and very strong; just barely controllable, and I wanted to be with him and experience this... feeling; however, I felt like I was going into the unknown and afraid. I knew I had to keep control and not let my feelings control me, but they were getting stronger. I wanted to keep myself for the man who loved and respected me, but how can you tell who really loves you. The feelings we had if it was love... I wanted Jacob to show me how love feels.

CHAPTER EIGHT

Charisma = Change

We started for the camp early that morning with one last pocket money show scheduled in Alabama. Before starting, Adam called a meeting and said some shit; then, dismissed everyone except for Klondike, three of her faithful flunkies, and me; then he reminded me,

"Remember what I said Allysa."

"Your personal word has no meaning anymore," I said trying to leave, but Adam who was standing in my way told the driver to pull off with me and Klondike and her flunkies on the meeting bus. I turned on the TV. Adam turned it off, so I sat there and looked out the window ignoring him while he told me things he thought I needed to do. Klondike was there and heard everything. Adam looked at her, but sat down shook his head and laughed as if it all was their plan. He didn't say a word to Klondike, but his laugh signaled her to pick calling me names, making offensive comments about my race, the way I looked, and then Klondike said she planned to teach me respect for my superiors. I thought she didn't know what any of those words meant. However, I took out my earrings, tied up my hair, and put my cap back on while she ran her mouth joking about what I was doing, and then boasted about what she planned to do to me.

I was terrified, but my mind wondered to Rich being with Adams family and I became concerned, so I called to make sure he was all right. Before he left, I told him to take a taxi to the bus station and call me if things didn't work out. I hid get away money in his wallet and told him not to let anyone know. So I called Richard and talked for a little while. Then I asked Rich,

"Are you being treated OK?" He said,

"Yes mommy, I can eat and my mom love me like you."

"That's great Rich." Then he excitedly said,

"I'm having fun. We have a big park with a playground, horses, and a tree house. I help my family, and I'm on the honor roll again with my sisters. Mommy I can ride a horse." He was excited, happy, and I wished I could enjoy his joy. Then he asked, "Are you having fun mommy?" I hesitated not knowing what to say. Rich whined, "Mommy, Mommy where are you?" And then he cried. I tried to calm him, but Adams wife took his phone and asked,

"Who is this?" I answered,

"Allysa," and I hung up, but Adam's wife called him to find out what was going on. He told her something. Meanwhile Klondike threw shit at me and hit me in the head with something hard. It hurt so bad I move to the front wanting to get off the bus pleading with the driver to stop. Adam pulled me back, and blocked my way, again, while telling the driver to continue driving and hollered,

"Why are you disturbing my family?" And he took my phone with me saying,

"You don't have any right to take that. I want Richard, and I'm leaving. You won your competition and now you're not treating me right. Adam you're just a liar." Klondike was all in our conversation saying,

"Adam's going to take both of you home to your father so he can kick your asses, fuck you, and make you eat shit." Then she laughed and Adam accepted what she said while snickering. The driver trying to help told Adam,

"Man, get out her way! Miss I can't stop here because it is not safe. I will stop at the next rest area in a few miles. I don't know what is wrong with your boss, but he's not doing right. Set up here with me." I stepped pass Adam and sat on the steps watching and waiting.

Klondike and her flunkies threw so much shit at me the driver was having a hard time driving. He asked Adam to stop them, but Adam didn't try to get control of the situation in the ten minutes it took to stop. The driver pulled into the rest area and went to bus parking in the back. He pushed me off in front of him, got his stuff, and exited telling Adam he quit, while I continued quickly walking away, but I didn't run as the driver wanted. That would give that gang all the reason needed to chase me, but if they did, I knew the one I wanted.

The other buses stopped at the food area dispatching the group before the drivers brought their bus to the bus parking area. Meanwhile, still upset because I called Rich, this huge man, Adam, caught up with me and grabbed me fussing in my face while Klondike was loud talking what she would do when Adam finished. Terrified, I couldn't think any more and was past scared fighting madness as tears ran from my eyes and nose. I couldn't remember ever feeling so desperate it drove me to the point of craziness. Adam held me until all four of Klondike and her gang surrounded me; then, he let me go. Realizing all Adams deliberate actions, I tried to walk away, while Klondike pushed me, and her flunkies hit and kicked me. I looked at Adam and he did nothing to stop them as he watched. Then everything started happening in slow motion. I saw Wang and Bubbles get off one of the other buses when it came to park; then, Twista shouted,

"YEAH, I'M GOING TO FIND OUT IF YOU'RE REALLY A VIRGIN!" Then he tried to grab me. I lost it all at once giving him a groin kick, and then I grabbed Klondike's hair with both hands. Using her big ass as a counter weight I spin kicked this other guy in his Adam's apple and he went down. I still had Klondike's hair while spinning, keeping her off balance; then, I kicked the shit out of her. Adam tried to grab me but Wang flipped him to the ground and started Kung Fu-ing everything that moved. Cisco, a crew guy and boxer, helped him, with Bubbles running off a while ago. I continued kicking Klondike, losing part of my grip on her because I pulled out part of her weave, but she ran under the bus in a compartment. On my way in, I picked up a broken 40oz beer bottle, while never letting go the other hand full of still attached hair, and I fucked her up any way I could. After a while when I saw all the blood getting on me, I let her go and she ran from under the bus trying to stop bleeding, with me kicking her in the ass all the way. While I grabbed her again, her best female flunky tried to help. So I kicked and cut her too. I knew no one expected all that, but I've been in training all my life dealing with people like them.

When I next noticed my area of kick ass, there were so many people standing or moving around, I couldn't figure who was who. Then I saw a guy in coveralls looking at me with a fire hose when I bumped into Adam and he grabbed me. I had almost gotten free when Twista kicked me in my back knocking me free from Adam, but bouncing my ass off the bus too. Turning when I bounced to get Twista with my piece of glass, I got hit full force in my chest and stomach with high-pressure water that slammed me back against the bus. It felt like a wall of water pressing on me... forever. I couldn't breathe and prayed to die. Just then, a shadow came grabbed me and shielded me from the water. I thought it was GOD. I remember using my last strength to look up to see Jacob's face straining to take care of us.

Awaking fighting, I realized I was in the damn hospital. Lynn was there, and she held me down saying,

"Allysa, Allysa calm down. Everything is under control just calm down." Realizing who it was, I did. She asked,

"Allysa, can you remember what happened?" I took a while, but I nodded yeah. She calmed me and herself while she sat down, then Lynn asked,

"Did Adam laugh at you or help?" I didn't want to think about that so I said nothing. I only cried. Adam lied just like my AD.

Jaison came in the room with the police and a doctor who said,

"You have a mild concussion and a bad bruise on your lower back that will hurt. I'm more concerned with your head injury and prior head trauma. What happen that cause the operation?" I said,

"It happened when I was young and I can't remember what." Then a police officer wanted to know how everything started and I told them what I could remember. The officer said,

"That matches the statement the driver gave." Another officer that came in said,

"The driver was so upset with your group leader, this Adam fellow, for not protecting you and getting control, he quit. We will question this Adam now to find out why he didn't, but you... don't leave the hospital. I understand you were protecting yourself, but five people are in the hospital and two girls had to undergo operations for their wounds. One had life-threatening wounds, and you sustained serious injuries too. This mess needs straightening out. We need to find who the blame is for all this." When they left, I said,

"I want to leave and get Richard," but then, I asked Jaison, "Where is Jacob?"

"Richard is outside waiting to see you. Adam lives about 80 miles away and Adjani came while you were out of it and she is keeping it straight, so just calm down. I think she took his pissy," Jaison said laughing. After a while Jaison had us laughing telling us how she tore Adam a new asshole for how he acted plus what he did and didn't do. Jai continued, "She's still on him about the way he and others treated you. I don't know who called and told her what happened." BB pulled out her phone nodding her head.

Adjani came in bringing Richard to check on me getting mad all over again. She gave me my phone that Adam took; then, without a word left quickly in a vortex as we silently watched her leave. Jai said,

"Boy oh boy, is she pissed. I have never seen her like this, but I know she keeps Adam's big ass in line and has a non-tolerance for foolishness." Yes, she emanated the seriousness of her concern for Adam's foolishness that caused this situation, and she had a bad temper. I was happy Adam had to deal with that.

I talked to Richard. He was happy at home, but upset about finding me in a hospital. To make him feel better I told Rich,

"I'm fine now that you came and brought your Mom. She will take care of me too." Then I asked Jaison, "Take me to Jacob now please."

"Jacob is not hurt." He said, "And I'm not sure if you can leave Miss Carrington." Getting upset I whimpered,

"I don't care I want to see him." BB said,

"They told her not to leave, and she's not leaving. She's going to visit her friend in the same place." Shit, don't leave? What a joke. Jacob was the reason I stayed. I had a new commitment. Getting to know Jacob, but at that moment, my ass hurt and I was dizzy.

BB and Jaison stole me a wheelchair; then, took me to Jacob who was in an emergency cubicle waiting to check out. Jacob hugged me and said,

"I'm fine Allysa. You're supposed to be in bed resting." While Jacob spoke, I opened his shirt and looked at his back checking for injuries while he watched me amazed. I didn't think. I just did it and Jacob didn't mind, so I asked,

"Are you hurt anywhere Jacob?" Then I thought of how he was hurt because of me. What if he couldn't play basketball and I ruined his life? All my thoughts rushed me at once. Jacob sat me in his lap after he sat in the wheelchair. I held him with my face buried in his chest and cried as Jaison pushed us around taking us on a tour of the hospital.

"What happened," Jacob asked? When I told some of the story, it was so upsetting I didn't finish. Then Jacob got mad as he said, "Bubbles told me how Adam laughed as Klondike hit and kicked you," but Jaison told Jacob,

"Man, calm down. She done kicked and cut everybody that was responsible except bro and Adjani took care of that, so there's no one to get." They thought that was funny, but Jacob didn't. Neither did I. Things were uncertain for me now, but I told him I was fine and buried my head in his chest. Jacob held me until it was time for him to leave.

I read a letter Adam's wife wrote while Jaison registered me in a private room, and Jacob checked out. It stated,

"Adam was serious and determined to help you and Richard. He had to talk me into it. I knew there were missing records and didn't want to lose him with the courts. However, I took things in hand, and hope you don't mind he's Richard Ulysses Kapulani now and enrolled in private school with my girls. The school was happy to accept the tuition and birth certificate from me, so stop worrying. He's our son now and we'll love and take care of him like our girls. Also, after getting to know Richard, I know you. I only hope to do as well raising him with my girls as you in his five years. He's a loving child who's willing to help, but just mischievous enough to be a little boy and we have grown to love him in this short while. You can pick him up at any time, but my girls and I have claimed him, and we will miss him when he's gone. I don't know why Adam acted the way he did, but I will get to the bottom of it and hope that the problem can be resolved without disturbing the children, and that includes you. You'll hear from me soon." I asked no questions as tears rolled I felt so relieved Rich was legit and in school on his way to life.

Richard was with Jacob when all of us met back at my room. We enjoyed talking for hours with Richard. He told me about all the fun he was having being a little boy in a house with decent people who adored him. I felt so happy hearing and feeling his joy. After a while, Adam and Adjani came in with Adjani asking,

"Can Rich come with me?" Of course I said yes, and Richard was happy. Adam couldn't or wouldn't look at me. I noticed he had a lump on his forehead. I wondered who put it there and hoped I did.

Jacob and Adam had to give a statement to the police. Jaison and Delano went to keep the peace. Everybody left except for BB. She waited a while then she said,

"I couldn't believe Bubbles when she told us you were fighting Klondike and her gang, and Adam wasn't doing anything to help you. Bubbles said Wang and Cisco were the only ones..." I cut BB off and asked,

"Where are they?" She said,

"They're outside on the bus or in the waiting room." I asked BB to get them and when they came in, they both broke into a kung Fu pose. I had to laugh. It hurt.

"Thank you," I said hugging and kissing them when they came. Both sat down, and BB finished her story saying,

"When Bubbles told everyone what was going on, we started running to you. The guys were in the lead and I couldn't believe I was keeping up. Then I notice Bubbles took a left turn running hard. When I looked in front of me, Jacob was airborne, and the next thing I knew me and a couple other people got stuck in a mud hole called a creek. Jaison just made it across. Jacob, Delano, and Danny were the only ones who made it in a jump. Then after the fight, the police arrested Danny for knocking out the worker who used the hose on you. That's why you haven't seen him. Bubbles and Lynn got him out and press charges against the worker on your behalf. As it worked out the police dropped charges against Danny, but the police told Danny to stay away from the situation." Cisco said while shaking his head,

"Jacob went straight to protect you, but he caught Twista on the way in and slammed him against the bus then Delano beat him down, again. Jaison cut the water hose about the same time Danny knocked out the worker who held it on you. And Adam didn't do shit." Cisco continued shaking his head saying, "This mess not right." I just cried. Cisco, who was extremely upset with Adam, started walking and mumbling. Wang got up in the bed and hugged me saying,

"Shh Shh, Li Siz. Cisco crazy. Me... no today." BB said,

"He's mad Wang like all of us... you crazy all the time." Cisco went on,

"But, when Jacob asked Adam what his stupid ass was doing, they started fighting when Adam pushed him. I don't know why they're not in jail. Adam, Jaison, Delano, Jacob, and Danny were fighting. When Jaison broke Adam and Jacob up, Jaison punched Adam." BB said,

"Damn... I'm happy Hu left last night or it would be a mess now." Lynn came in the room telling us,

"The police let Danny go because the worker used deadly force against you, Ally, but I have to go and keep an eye on things. Something else is going on. Adam's on the phone and he wouldn't talk around anyone. Adam shouldn't have let it gone as far as he did. Allysa, I think they thought they would beat you up, and that would be it, but you cut and messed them up bad. They're looking for a scapegoat now, and I'm sure they're trying to blame you. So I will leave and find out what's going on." Lynn left and we continued to talk for a while; then, the phone rang scaring us.

"Wei." Wang answered; then, he talked shit in Chinese. Afterwards he gave BB the phone. With BB making a face she asked me,

"Do you want to speak with BS?" I shook my head no, and then BB sounding very automated said "Sorry she's medicated right now. Please call back. Goodbye."

We talked about that idiot, BS, for a while then Cisco left. He wanted to quit. We convinced him to stay with our group because we needed him. Cisco and his crew stayed, and he went back to the bus, but BB and Wang stayed in my room telling Adam before, they will catch up with the group and bring me. So, we went to sleep, and around two hours later Jacob called me saying,

"I want to make sure you're not by yourself. Lynn and I are running things because Adam and Jaison are still out. Something is going on." I woke BB and Wang while Jacob said, "Allysa I know you're hurt, but I want you to get out of there and come to me. Never mind. I'm coming to you." I told BB and Wang,

"Jacob said something's up." Scared I got up to get dress. I felt dizzy and the pain throbbed. So I sat back down, but the next thing we knew, bright lights came on, and two officers came in the room with the doctor, Adam and Jaison. BS called the police after calling my room. An Officer stated,

"Miss Carrington, you are free to go because you have no record. However, because you are a minor and the severity of the action, you must be release to Brian Schulman who has custody of you, and he wants you transported to the camp immediately or we will classify you as a runaway. Then, we will take you to jail until he picks you up."

BS arrived at the camp from a tour the day before and gave permission for only Adam to transport me. I wondered what the police meant by the minor and custody part, but getting my ID I pleaded,

"I'm 18 and don't want to go." Then the doctor said,

"You can go," as he gave me some papers.

"Get dressed, now!" Adam said and snatched my I.D. BB helped me while complaining and fussing at Adam. I couldn't think my head hurt so bad and my balance was off. I had to take breaks sitting and not dressing at all.

"Where is Jacob?" Wang asked in good English, but Adam ignored him. Wang left the room using his cell phone since the police insisted that he leave.

"Can we wait for Jacob?" I asked. One officer found a wheelchair and brought it saying,

"Get in the chair!" Adam placed me in the chair and pushed. As we moved, the doctor explained,

"One medication is for pain and be careful not to take more than one every six hours because it will affect your breathing. I'm giving you four pills now. Get the prescription filled for the rest tomorrow. Be sure to be careful with this one. The other medication is for your head. You must take this until completely gone." Then Adam pushed me away from my friends, the doctor, and the hospital, but we ran into Wang who came back with Cisco. Wang pushed Adam saying,

"No, no! You wait!" Jaison had to break up a standoff that begun with the police detaining Wang, BB, and Cisco, but Jaison had to run to keep up with Adam because in a minute it seemed, we were in a taxi with me very concerned. I didn't know what happen to my friends and didn't know my fate.

Adam continued to act strange and slipped Jaison at the airport by somehow getting him detained. Then Adam took me half dressed in PJ bottoms and bedroom slippers on the jet. I was in so much pain I threw up and couldn't think straight. I needed to rest, but Adam decided to talk.

"Allysa, I tried to help you, but you made me sorry I did. Then you tried to turn my family against me including my father." I told Adam,

"Adam you're a liar and didn't do your job. You placed your father's whole program in jeopardy and your choice not to do your job cause all the injuries. You deliberately set me up to cause all this and everything is your fault, and where did they take BB, Wang, and Cisco?" Adam told me,

"Well, you're going home now. With the police involvement in this last incident BS has gotten in touch with your AD and he'll be there to pick you up tomorrow." Upset and confuse now, I watch that amazing dream that came true for Rich and I fade into a lie anyway. I asked Adam,

"Are you going to continue taking care of Richard?" I waited a while, but he said nothing. "Please don't throw him away Adam. He just began to feel human. He realizes that now. Richard is just starting life and young and has nothing to do with my actions." I pled with him, "No one has hurt him yet. Please give him a chance to be a decent person. My AD will make him disappear like the others. Then no one will know where he's at. I know I'm messed up and can't do this anymore."

My head and back hurt so bad I went to the bathroom half-crazy from pain and full of despair. I couldn't figure what to do because I didn't know what I did wrong. I prayed for Richard placing my trust in Adjani as I took those pills the doctor warned me about and returned to my seat with my knotted stomach churning. Then in a few minutes, I threw up. I sat there afraid as I looked out at the darkness eventually seeing the light of dawn as I felt my breathing slow down. Adam, who looked at me strangely, became alarmed when I slurred. "Sorry... I'm... messed up."

I woke up with stuff stuck in my mouth and down my throat. The room seemed dark, but I could see Jaison. He had his head on the bed. I couldn't move or see straight so I went back to sleep. The next time I woke, Jaison was still there. His clothes were different and I managed to pull his hair. He jumped up asking,

"Allysa, what happened? What did Adam say to you? Little-Bit what did you do, Allysa, what did you do?" I remembered what I did. Tears rolled uncontrollably and there were tubes everywhere. I motion for him to take the tube out of my throat.

Jaison notified the doctor I was awake and having difficulty breathing because of the tube in my throat. They took a while, but I received something to relax me. When I woke again, the tubes were gone. I asked Jai in a whisper,

"Where are Jacob, BB, Wang, and Cisco?"

"They're all right and at the camp calling me about you Allysa." The doctor came in and read my chart; then said,

"A Psychologist has to see you because you tried to kill yourself." Jaison disagreed saying,

"No she just made a mistake with her medication." The doctor shaking his head responded,

"No. She had too much in her system for that."

The next day, men in white suits escorted me to the Psychologist. He went through this long speech about how everything I said to him was private and he continued,

"I have looked at your history whereas I see you are travelling with an entertainment group. You are a very smart and talented person with everything going for you so, I need to know why you want to harm yourself?" I had no choice, so I told him,

"Some of the people I travel with continuously bully me. These people tried to harm me. When I protected myself from their abuse, the blame fell on me for everything that our group leader who was right there did nothing to prevent. That's my situation, however, my real problem is my adoptive father abused me since I was six and made me do shit that wasn't right. Then he threatened me constantly saying I could disappear with no one to care or wonder what happened to me because I was a throw away. I survived all that abuse and escaped disappearing, but every time these people pick at me, certain program leaders, threaten me with removal and placement back in that situation. So I did it because I didn't want to go back there, and I will die before I do." The Psychologist said,

"I see. Miss Carrington, I know this bullying went on for a while, however, you must manage to control your anger and your death wish." I told the Psychologist,

"I reacted from fear because they were assaulting me. The bullying was before and I did my part ignoring it, but no one stopped it, so the bullying escalated to violence. They will leave me alone one way or the other, but if I'm left alone, I'm trying real hard to fit in and think I was doing fine."

"Yes, that's what I heard. I understand you are part of a youth program that requires traveling with a group of performers. Are all of them bullying you?"

"No, only a few. Most the others are trusted friends who have protected me from them. The group leader separated me from my group of friends isolating me with these bullies and he wouldn't stop their verbal insults that soon turned into them hitting and kicking me. One said he was going to rape me; then, he tried to. I don't hate them, but I will kill every single one of them to protect myself. So I took care of it. I don't want to be around this uncontrolled and unnecessary foolishness."

"Do you want to be a performer Miss Carrington?"

"I want to model, dance, while studying more; then, later work in finances." The Psychologist smiled and said,

"I see you have a plan, and you need to be looking forward to your new life. The problem, Miss Carrington, is obvious and easily solved. You see, unfortunately losers, disguised as decent people, hate others who have more going for themselves because of hard work and the person is a quite one minding their own business. They want to distract you from your plans. I feel that's what's going on here." He wrote feverously for a while; then said, "I want you to talk to a social worker." I met with the social worker back at my room. The next day the psychologist came in smiling then asked,

"Miss Carrington, do you trust the young man, Jaison, who's been waiting daily for you? He swears out he's your big brother, and he let me know I was right in my diagnoses." Surprised Jaison waited, I felt better and told the psychologist,

"Yes, he loves me like that, and I trust him." The psychologist said,

"I'm letting Jaison take responsibility of you. He meets all my requirements." He called Jaison in the room and talk to him in front of me saying, "The only problems I see are the people trying to hurt her and send her home. Jaison, do you plan on sending her back to her adoptive father or let people injure her?" Jaison said,

"No, never. I will take care of Allysa and straighten this matter out. She will go to my father's camp without these problems. She's my responsibility now and I guarantee this mess will stop."

"Yes you must stop these people you said you're aware of from bothering her because this would be in her best interest, and from what I read theirs too. If you send her back to her adoptive father, we will have to take her in protective custody, and that will not help her. I listened to her, and she does not belong here. I believe she will be a frontrunner for many people and big brother, you must help her." The psychologist made clear to Jaison, but I looked at them concerned. I didn't want to go in the system. Jaison adamantly assured the psychologist he would protect me with his life. The psychologist looked at Jaison for a moment, and after that, I had concerns about them keeping both of us, but the psychologist dismissed Jaison, and continued talking to me.

"I spoke with the social worker you talked with yesterday. She gave me some insight and forms you must fill out before you leave. This paperwork will emancipate you from your adoptive father." I looked at him concerned about dealing with the courts, and the psychologist explained, "Don't worry you have numerous factors going for you. That man is not your natural parent. You have finished college, employed with housing, a well-paying job and they will have my report. Your accomplishments are impressive for your age and the judge will approve. I will be present to make sure of it on your behalf. Jaison will give you your medication, and when you finish the forms, I will release you in the gentleman's care. Allysa, you just keep on working hard and thriving. Grow and achieve before you deal with serious endeavors of the heart. Don't let anyone stop you and you must remember, YOU CONTROL YOURSELF. Now you, Miss Allysa M. Carrington, control yourself and do what is good. I will hear about you again and remember you have the choice if it will be in jail, a mental hospital or through the worldwide media showing others the way."

The psychologist spoke with Jaison while I filled out the forms, and then Jaison checked me out the hospital with the psychologist words echoing in my thoughts. Afterward, Jai took me to get something to eat; however, I wasn't hungry for wondering what will happen. I was very confuse feeling alone and abandon and wanted to leave, but Jaison was there asking,

"Why do you look so stressed Allysa? The doctor gave me orders to get you in to see a therapist weekly, but you need someone now. I waited for you, Little-Bit, will you talk with me?" I felt total trust in Jaison. He didn't leave me, so I nodded yes. "Why you do that?" He asked with his voice breaking. "I love you. You're my little sister. I would kill anyone I see doing harm to you, if you leave me a piece, but you're hurting yourself baby girl. What would we do if this had happened? What about Richard and how could we tell him? BB would have blown up, and Wang would have all of Asia after us. I don't think Jacob could or would go on. I know he's in love with you. His timing is off, but I know he's... we're the best thing for you. Everyone loves you. People are asking me about you including some who didn't like you because they hung with Klondike, but they wanted to apologize and stop acting stupid I hope. I'm afraid to call and tell people you're with me because I don't know whom to trust. Adam thinks you ran away and I'm trying to find you, so everyone thinks you're gone." With him perplexed and stressed now, I was sure he understood without me saying a word.

With the thought on my mind to run away, Jaison called his father. I wasn't aware of Jaison's relationship with his father, but Jaison had to make amends. They talked for a while with Jaison telling his father,

"I can't trust Adam to look out for her Dad. The doctor made her my responsibility now, and I need your help... please." His father asked to speak with me.

"Why you want to die?" The father asked. Through my tears, I told him,

"That's what I'll do before I go back to that life with my AD. Adam lied and Richard is with him."

"Richard is there to stay and taken care of fine. I'm finding it hard to imagine how things got like this. Adam is like my right hand. He said he didn't send the girl to the camp because everyone would be there in one day and you made things hard for him and yourself by being hardheaded."

"Daddy, Jacob is my friend, and he wanted to take a picture with me. It's not right for only us to stop interacting with each other. We're not doing anything wrong, and Adam keeps coercing us like a Bully; then, people BS planted to cause confusion followed his lead, and that's why this situation exist. Adam deliberately isolated me with people he knew wanted to hurt me, and then he let them.

Adam only needed to do the job you told him to perform, but he purposely didn't. So I don't trust him anymore." I cried. Dad said,

"I can see Adam made wrong decisions because he said you challenged him in every way, and he lost control. I don't know what to tell you about Adam, but what in the world did you do to my son Jaison? That boy never cared about anything, but women, roaming, and surfing. But now he has taken on a responsibility and begging for help for his little sister. That is interesting." He said with enthusiasm. "I'm coming for the Introduction Show. Are you going to be there Allysa and still work with us?" Exhausted, I couldn't think and everything ran wildly through my mind, but most prominent was how I felt about Jacob and I said,

"Yes."

Dad gave Jaison instructions to take me to the dance school to stay. Then Dad said,

"I'm going to make a few calls. Wait until I call back." Jaison sat there while I leaned on his back with my arms around him until his father called. While I lingered on his back, I felt comfortable enough to stay since Dad or King Kapulani would be there and I know I stayed for Jacob, which was a curiosity at the time, but Jai, Wang, Danny, BB, and Lynn became my real sisters and brothers in my mind. Soon Dad had arranged everything, and the King always felt like a father to me, but at that point, he became my father. I felt his protection and love so I called him Dad too.

Jaison only told my brothers and sisters he had me and wanted no one else to know. They really thought I had run away. My family fixed up my room at the dance school since I hadn't quite healed from my injuries. Then, Jaison drove to camp and snuck me in that night. He explained that Lynn would have men working during the day in the Dance school's large kitchen so stay out of sight of that which wasn't hard. Then Jaison said,

"I need to go and be seen now, but Little Bit, you need to stay inside out of sight. Wang and BB, you have to leave and not come back because we have to play it like she's still lost. No one can suspect she's here. Danny, you and Bubbles have to watch out for her, and get her in dancing shape. The doctor said her head should be fine tomorrow. We only have a week before the opening and we must keep my father's plan alive." I was like his father now. Who is this man?   I watched Jaison feeling so proud of my big brother who I knew cared about his father's program and me.

"You will have a pain in your ass for the rest of your life." I said smiling at him when we were by ourselves. Then Jai commented,

"Well, I plan to live a long time so you're not going to do that again right?"

"Yeah... right." I said hesitantly.

"Now Little Bit you're getting too little. You need to eat and get your strength back."

Jaison recorded the practices I missed with the group, and Bubbles brought them to me. I went over the material at night taking a snap shot in my mind. Then Jaison stopped by with some things for me to study and paperwork I needed for camp. All the new members had to submit them. Jaison explained the paperwork then said,

"I'll sneak these in the night before. I have to bring you to practice in three days so you can practice with the group at dress rehearsal. There is always dress rehearsal the day before so BS can add or remove acts. I'm concerned because my father won't get to the camp until 1pm the day of the show, and six hours before the red carpet walk, but we're going to do this. Oh yeah, I had to tell Adjani and talk to her. Before she left you after the fight, the three of us talked about your safety. She told Adam to stay with the show and I would bring you to their house when you left the first hospital. Adjani planned for you to stay with her to be safe. Then Dad was to fly to Adams and she would bring you, the children, and Dad in time for dress rehearsal. However, after missing calls from Adjani Adam called her from Miami and told her they were delayed because of your sickness. Adam stalled her for a day, but had to admit he didn't do as she asked and was taking you to the Beach Camp when you took pills. Adjani looked for you, and then in a couple of days Adjani came at me with Adams balls in one hand looking for you. I had to explain Adam didn't say shit to me and changed his mind at the last minute taking you on a different flight, but I made that flight with you and Adam. While we landed, Adam notified the flight attendant of your condition. After we landed, I took over telling Adam, I was holding him responsible, but fuck off. Then I went with you and rescue, leaving Adam at the airport. Adjani kicked Adam out the house threatening a separation because Adam continued involving himself doing unnecessary shit to you. The entire situation upset Adjani and the children so much, Adjani told Adam he needed to take his shit, stay away at Camp, and think about his daughters. She was extremely upset with Adam for driving you to feel that way and took it personal. So I had to help her not go ballistic." I thought wow, but then Jaison said, "Plus, that crazy boy, Jacob, has been giving me a hard time." That caught my attention. Jaison continued saying, "Allysa, Jacob packed his bags to leave and find you. I don't know what to do about him, and I'm tired of that horny boy crying on my shoulder at night all night asking, 'Where is she? I got to find her.' Jacob paces the floor all night and is driving every one crazy keeping suspicion up. So, I brought him with me. He was on his way to the airport anyway." I looked around for him when I heard Jacob talking to Danny as he walked in the door. Surprised, but in pain and tired from practice I only sat there looking. I had to cut back on my medicine since I didn't have many and no way to get more, but Jacob quickly came asking,

"What happened to you? Can you walk?" I had made Jai promised not to tell Jacob the details of what happened, but he only told Adjani. I didn't believe that and felt strange only smiling. He hugged and kissed me. Jaison told him what we planned. "Hey man, everyone thinks you took me to the airport so I'm staying here with Allysa." Jacob said, while looking at me smiling. Jaison talked to Jacob while he fixed us something to eat; then, big brother left after eating.

I worked out with Danny for another two hours, and Jacob was shocked, but happy to see me dancing. Danny and Bubbles left us to ourselves after practice peeping at us and smiling as they left. We went to my room upstairs. I took my medicine and laid across the bed hurting. Jacob laid beside me,

"Are you all right?" He asked.

"I hurt a little so I'm letting my medicine take effect; then, I'm going to shower and go to bed." I said; then Jacob asked,

"Where are you hurting?"

"All over," I responded very happy to have him with me. He laughed and said,

"I planned to massage the spot, but I don't think you'll let me give you a full body massage," Looking at this handsome man lying beside me talking about a full body massage made feelings emerge that surprised me, but the only thing I did was look in his grey eyes. I sat there mesmerized, but he made his move. (Kiss), (lip lick), (kiss), mmm, (body caress), (gentle lip suck); then, he finished (long kiss). He kissed me before, but never as seductively. Then Jacob jumped up saying, "I'm going to take my shower now," and rushed off to the bathroom... without me. I didn't know what to think wondering if the kissing was a prelude to his shower announcement? Then he stayed in there for about an hour. I sat on the bed with my nightclothes and my girlie stuff waiting when he came out with his street clothes half on, and he was still wet. I asked,

"Jacob... are you finished?" He responded,

"Yeah, but wait until I come back." He ran away, but came right back with his gym travel bag he brought and said, "I'll get Bubbles to help you bathe, and get you to bed."

"No, I'm all right, but... are you okay Jacob? You're acting a little... weird, but I'm enjoying that you're here." He said,

"I'll be here, Allysa, if you need me." Looking at him saying I need you... it didn't come out, so I took my shower and went to bed.

Jacob had changed into some Capri like PJ bottoms and a tee shirt by time I finished.

"Allysa..." I answered,

"What Jacob?"

"Um... Can I spend the night with you?" He asked nervously. I wondered where he thought he would go... but I thought Jacob was so sweet.

"Yes you can Jacob." I said with him asking,

"Can I look at your back were Twista kicked you?"

"Okay." I said as I climbed onto my queen size bed with a different feeling than our night at Rod's.

"Why did he kick you like that? This bruise is terrible." Jacob mumbled as he walked around talking to himself; then, he didn't say anything for a while and left. He returned with some ice and said with an attitude, "Here, place this on your back." He laid on top of the covers and looked upset. It seemed something was wrong. I asked,

"Jacob, are you upset with me?" When he said nothing, I asked, "Did I do something wrong?"

"... No..." he said slowly. After a while, he said sounding very disturbed, "Adam told me what happen. He said you took pills and tried to kill yourself. Did you?" I didn't know what to say or do and didn't want him to know.

"Jacob, I'm sleepy," I said and turned away when he grabbed my shoulder. I couldn't look at him or talk to him, but he pled,

"Allysa, I don't want you stressing so please tell me what's bothering you. Please, Allysa... I like you a lot." Then he let out a huge sigh saying, "Really... I've fallen in love with you. I've never felt this way before and know we're young, but I want to be here for you now so we can be together later. Could you want that too?" When I didn't react or look at him, he nudged my head so I was looking him in his eyes again as he moved closer getting under the covers with me he said, "You are so beautiful Allysa, but do you feel for me?" Almost feeling paralyzed I told him softly,

"Yes, I believe we feel the same way, but... I'm so young and stupid I don't know what to do with myself. I'm so scared of going home... or not having anywhere to go." He asked,

"Is that why you wanted to kill yourself?"

"Can we stop talking about that?" I asked as I looked away.

"Yes we can, but no, no Allysa... you can't do that." Jacob held me tighter and asked, "Do you still want to die Allysa?" Then I said,

"I'm tired and want to go to sleep." He looked at me puzzled, but cut off the light. I turned away. He laid there a minute and soon gave me more attention.

"Please don't, Allysa, I need you." Jacob whispered while pulling me to him wrapping his blanket and long legs around me. I drifted off to sleep in his arms thinking about what he said and how good it felt wanting to live for Jacob.

Pain woke me around 2 am. I was alone. I looked around and found Jacob down stairs exercising. Setting on the old fashion broad wooden stairwell, I watched him work up a sweat for a while wondering if all of his body was as ripped as the parts I could see. When he noticed me setting on the steps, he said,

"I had to burn off some energy," I told him,

"Come back to bed, please. I miss you." He said something about staying there. Wondering if I drooled on him while asleep or what, I asked, "What's wrong?"

"Nothing," he said, "I will stay down here." Shyly I said,

"Jaison said something..." I stopped and could only smile. By now, he wanted to know more, and I wished I hadn't said anything, but I continued, "Are you horny, Jacob?" I said trying to joke. "Is that the problem?" I was hurting so bad I couldn't even get into the moment and I called Danny for some medicine. Danny came in and looking at Jacob strangely saying,

"We only have three Ally. Try to hang on." OMG, I hurt so bad I just hung my head. Jacob picked me up and carried me back to bed.

"Let me shower a minute and I'll stay with you Allysa." He took an hour. I waited for him to answer me saying,

"You never answered me Jacob." He only stood there. "Jacob, we need to talk about this, yes?" He sat on the floor in front of me and said,

"Allysa, I respect your wishes to be right for your husband." However, I told him,

"I know what I said. I've thought about that almost every day since getting to know you Jacob. Now I don't think I'm going to make it because..."

"Because what Allysa? Please tell me." Jacob asked concerned as he moved to the bed beside me. I told him,

"I don't want to give my virginity to a jerk, and I realize a person like Twista will take it. So, I feel as long as the person is special, and I feel you are, they understand what's going on, and I feel you do, I believe I'll be happy with that and enjoy myself too.

That's the way I feel about you being horny Jacob." I guess the way I said that was odd, but he understood me. Then Jacob said,

"My feelings are more than just having sex with you, Allysa; I want to love you, take care of your every need, and just be around you like now talking, and finding out more about you. I like your room, but I don't envision loving you here with you hurting and please understand I want to be with you... so bad, but not now." He looked at me. "Um...I got to go!" He ran away and dressed saying, "I have to leave." Danny caught up with him and asked,

"Jacob. Man where are you going? You can't go back to the house and you can't leave like this. We have to be careful man it's 3am. People are snooping and it's not safe for Allysa." Jacob came back inside with Danny and they talked. Meanwhile, Bubbles came upstairs and asked,

"Ally, what did you do?" I said,

"I don't know what happened." Bubbles asked,

"What were you talking about?" I told her,

"Sex... and now, I'm confused, my ass hurt, and I'm horny." Bubbles laughed telling me,

"You got to work that out yourself." Just then, Jacob peeped up the stairs, apologized, and then asked to come up. Bubbles looked at us and continued to laugh as she left.

Noticing the way he walked, stood, and grinned, I wanted him to hold me in his arms again and we go to sleep. I figured yes that would do, so I smiled at him and gestured for him to come to me. When Jacob came close, I hugged him and asked,

"Will you just hold me tonight?" He stood there looking bewildered saying,

"Allysa I get... excited by you and it's very hard to be close." I told him,

"Jacob, I felt you excited before, and I don't mind because it's you." But then he said,

"And... it's just; I have this picture in my head of you without your top." Not knowing what to say I asked something stupid.

"Did you see both of them?" DUH. What was I thinking? They come in pairs. He noticed and laughed at me while he pulled me in his arms.

"Yeah, I did. They are beautiful, and I touched one by accident. You're so soft and I know sweet. I don't want to over step myself and scare you away... and I don't want you to feel pressured... (Awkward dead air time)... If I accidentally touch you while sleep will you be upset?" WOW! He was tripping. As I wondered where, I laughed and said,

"No." I watched him take off his clothes down to his Haynes longs and got in bed. I thought, oh yes, while I found a comfortable spot. He looked at my back first then seemed to have an accident. I turned and caressed his arms, shoulders, and chest. His muscles fascinated me. After me doing that a little while, and him kissing me on my lips, I looked at him needing to study his eyes. I felt closer than just holding and kissed him wanting to check out his body, but Jacob said,

"Wait Allysa... we better stop. I don't want to do things this way." I requested,

"Just please hold me, Jacob, I enjoy that." He kissed me on my forehead and said,

"You're so tempting, but I'm going to try to sleep. Good night." He held me the rest of the morning and woke me with some tea and medicine. I was stiff and in so much pain, I couldn't hardly move. After I took a hot shower, Jacob massaged my back with some pain cream. His gentle care made me feel like a new person. Then Jacob asked me,

"We have one day before stupidity catch up with us. What do you want to do?" We decided to help Danny and Bubbles get the school ready.

Jacob and Bubbles picked up supplies while Danny and I practiced. When they came back, Jacob had acquired four more pills that would take me through the show. I thanked him properly; then, we got the school straight. Danny and Jacob made repairs, and Bubbles and I organized the paperwork and lesson plans. Then I fix all of us a romantic dinner in Lynn's new kitchen that was too large and well stocked with equipment to be just a kitchen for the dance school. So I used different utensils cooking new recipes I found on the internet. My cuisine was perfect and ready around 7pm.

The men cleaned up, and we ate by candlelight on floor pillows. Well, I was in Jacob's lap feeding him. I enjoyed that. After we cleaned up, we watched some DVDs about people taking a bus trip with a monster stalking them. I enjoyed both wrapped up in Jacobs arms scared to death. He paid more attention to me than the movies.

When Jacob's happy, he smiled all the time and hummed while he worked. I wished for things to stay that way. He grinned blushing with me realizing his smile and grin represented two different emotions. I wanted to understand him more, but I knew when I saw one or the other he's happy and I liked his face better happy, but noticed Jacob was very emotional, and realized he's troubled most the time.

Danny and Bubbles lost track of the second movie while they fooled around. So they went to bed. Jacob and I agreed to turn off the movie and talk. As we laid on the pillows Jacob told me what he wanted to accomplish, and about his family's kingdom of a chain of Islands. So far, Jacob had been almost a perfect gentleman, but his ideas and thoughts aroused me. I sat there mesmerized by the total Jacob, mental and physical, and wished I could help him somehow with his dreams. I wondered what was Marlena thinking? Then I thought why was I thinking of her?

"Allysa are you okay?" Jacob asked while feeling my forehead. "Your eyes are a little different, grayish. I think I need to get you to bed. Tomorrow is the big day." When I stood up, I felt a little sick.

We were like an old couple going to bed. Jacob exercised while I read. Then took his hour-long shower, came to bed kissed and caressed my breast saying,

"Just doing a feel test checking to see if they are still soft. I can't imagine them being any other way." Now, me knowing what an erection was, I noticed a while back Jacob seemed to stay like that. BB informed me of her new equation during the trip to Band Camp, Allysa + Jacob = Erection^2. So, I asked while giggling,

"Well um, is the General still... exercising?" Defensive he asked,

"What? Why are you calling my joint the general?" Then said, "He doesn't rule me." I quickly said,

"Oh wait. I'm sorry I wasn't implying that. I tried to say he's always at attention sometimes saluting." He laughed and said,

"I think I saw a bead of sweat, but I didn't think you noticed Allysa." I replied,

"All Marlena and Klondike talked about was how they loved Jacob's... manhood. Personally, I like the whole package. Not just one part, but... Um... Jacob have you and Klondike... ever, like maybe..." Again defensive he said,

"Hell no. Number one, she's not my type. Plus, she sucks BS's worm. I don't want anything like that." I ran to the bathroom and threw up. Jacob was right behind me. I felt a little dizzy, and he started asking questions like, "Do you hurt, was the throw up a dark color, what the doctor say, did they check you for internal injuries... why did you start fighting like that by yourself anyway?" And Jacob kept going on and on asking more questions.

"Jacob, slow down," I said washing my mouth out and gasping for air, "Give me a minute." I wrapped up in a towel and stepped in the shower as I told Jacob, "Leave me alone. I'm okay." He exited the bathroom while I cooled off in some cool water. After that and throwing up again, I felt better. Wrapped in a towel, I stepped into my room to a pacing Jacob. "Jacob, the doctor said the medicine may upset my stomach." I said while slipping on a tee and undies without revealing much: then asked, "Where you get the pills?" He explained,

"I took the bottle to the pharmacy. They call the doctor, and he gave permission for more." Next, Jacob asked THE QUESTION,

"Are you pregnant?"

"Didn't I tell you I'm a virgin? Jacob, you think I lied? I hate liars." He apologized saying,

"I'm sorry, I shouldn't have asked that."

"Yeah... you think?" I said feeling he considered me a liar. I couldn't get myself to say anything to him and he said nothing, so I went to sleep, but not in his arms like I wanted to.

CHAPTER NINE

Making the Cut

When morning came, Jacob had left, and I was so not looking forward to that day, but I prepared myself since it was dress rehearsal for the show and BS was going to be there. I arrived at 12pm and called BB. Rehearsal was at 3 pm so I drifted to hair and makeup after BB told me where to go. BB was there in a crowd and everyone greeted me asking what happen. Bubbles and BB looked at me; however, I didn't answer telling them,

"This will probably be the last day I'm here. Is Klondike here?" BB said,

"She dragged her ass in from the hospital yesterday, and won't be performing for a while. Girl you fucked her up. What did you use on her to cause those wide gashes? She had to get over 150 stitches in her neck, stomach, butt, back, thighs, and leg. You almost gutted her friend. She went home, and no one has seen the other guy. Everyone said he had a broken jaw. Child, you fucked them up good... but the way she messed with you and the others laughing and saying inciting shit to egg her on, they deserved every bit and more. Twista went home after he checked out of the hospital."

"What happened to him?" I asked and BB continued,

"Jaison and Delano almost beat him to death, and it didn't help that Jacob clothes lined him on his way to you. Twista looked truly twisted in an upper body cast and will not work here anymore. The King himself terminated him, but you know BS had to keep the worm polisher." BB went on and on with everyone there laughing so hard they had to make her shut up so they could do their jobs.

As the Sexetts walked in together making our entrance on the stage, Lynn said,

"There's strength in numbers," with someone, announcing,

"Owe yeah baby... they're here! And looking so, so sexy." Then Hu smiled and shouted, "And they're all in the house." There were so many people happy to see me I received an acknowledgment. I guess all thought BS had gotten rid of me, but when Adam saw me, he motioned for me to come to him. He told me I wouldn't be singing with the group today, but just dancing for now. I figured that to be the beginning of my end.

BS started reviewing the acts. The harmony was off with Adam trying to make adjustments, but everyone noticed a voice missing, and the Sexetts didn't cover it up. BS notice too, but didn't care. Later, it was time for my performance. Jacob was to sing, and Danny and I dance. When we walked out, that's when BS let loose with,

"What the hell are you doing here, you Beige bitch? Didn't I tell you I didn't want you here?" BS shocked everyone with what he said. Ready for opposition, but not ready for what he said next. "I don't want that Crack Head or should I say cracked in the head on my stage. She's a stupid pain in the ass. Get her out of here!" His words hurt, but seemed to have meaning I couldn't figure. Everything upset me. I looked at Adam puzzled feeling hurt hoping he would say something, but Adam didn't, so I left. Jaison caught up with me back stage and said,

"Come on Little-Bit, it's time to stand strong, we're going to do this." He took my hand as I heard Adam's baritone voice proclaim,

"We want her. She's a good performer doing everything you ask, concerning performing, and shouldn't be blamed for the stupidity of others... including myself."

"Yeah, but I have the last say. Keep her messed up ass off my stage." BS stubbornly said. People booed BS, and that was encouraging, so... I took a cleansing breath, looked at Jaison, and remembered what Dad said. I figured it was time to continue my walk in the park or every hater would gain the momentum to disrespect me. Plus, it was my time to shine and not his.

I walked back out to the middle of the stage with a little diva's attitude. Checking my nails; then, looking at BS impassively, I asked him,

"So, who are you and why are you here?" BS looked at me surprised, but I didn't wait for an answer saying, "It's obvious you don't know me or my name. I'm Miss Allysa M. Carrington a musician, vocalist, and dancer. King Kapulani scouted my talent, and I went through hell to get here. I've earned my spot, and I'm going to do what I came here for and the Kings voice is all I will listen too." While I stared him down, people clapped and said yeah, we got your back, and tell him little sis. Almost all encouraged me, so I stood beside Danny to perform, and BS fired back,

"Well that's out then. Bitch, get off my stage." Ok, so he took the act out, but I went to set in my spot next to BB, Bubbles, and Lynn, and looked for someone else to leave asking,

"When's his momma going to leave, so we can get on with the show?" There was a roar of laughter. BS jumped up. So did Jacob, Jaison, and Hu. They walked next to Adam. Then Hu told BS,

"Look man, you don't want to cause any problems... My father said she's in, so... she is in, the acts in, and she's gonna sing too." Then, he lit up a huge blunt with BB hollering,

"Now that's gangster. Give me some." Everything was quiet for a minute after the laughter stopped. BS calmed his nerve, but continued with his agenda. So BS said trying not to look at me,

"Okay, the acts in. Jacob you sing and Danny dance solo or you can dance with Anita." Confused wondering why he didn't say Bubbles and she was too; however, BS continued, "This year we will showcase Danny with Anita as the premier student dancer." Danny went off.

"What! Wait a minute, King Kapulani requested me to come help him with his Dance program, and promised to showcase my talent with an upcoming talent and a true primo student dancer, Allysa. I have seen Anita dance. I don't consider her a student that fit this school's criteria in any way. She's a poor dancer and wouldn't be able to perform the routine with me if she could learn it in one day." BS told Danny,

"Well, dance by yourself then."

"I will not perform!" Danny fired back and then had an Artist Fit walking over to Bubbles. Next, Jacob shook his head saying,

"I quit!"

"We're not performing." Jaison and Hu said and walked over with Jacob and stood by Danny. Then to my surprise, almost BS's whole band left and Wang said something in Chinese taking his group, but they all came and formed a crowd behind and around The Sexetts. Lynn said,

"We will sit here for now but we're not performing without Allysa." Hair and Makeup, Wardrobe, sound and lighting, roadies all came and joined the group. Almost everyone refused to support BS's show. Crazy ass Delano made a sign, WE WANT ALLYSA M. CARRINGTON TO SING AND DANCE (THEN TAKE HER CLOTHES OFF). He stuck it between his Bass guitar strings and walked around carrying it like a picket sign to add to the confusion.

An older trumpet player, Mr. Browning, who played in the Band since Dad was in college and stayed at the school as a music teacher and performer, called for order. He didn't know me at all, but everyone hushed and listened to him say,

"I listened to the story these children came back with. Now I've heard and seen both sides. I just now saw the young lady for the first time, and wondered how she could cause such a problem, but then I listen to you, BS, call her derogatory names, and then mess up the show by removing or interfering with the talent that people want to see and hear. Only because you, BS, don't want to give the child a chance who earned a score of 98% to help her group win the limited spots in this program. This scouting competition is for worthy new talent and she achieved 98%. That's something no one has ever achieved... especially with the mundane talent you've been pushing. I'm getting the whole picture now and I'm sure she's not the problem at all. I've known these boys from birth and all of them have walked out on you, and I'm gone with them." BS had only 8 people left who were stage worker's or support, but all the real acts supported King Kapulani's program and me. Lynn said,

"Well I guess we'll leave now. Have a nice day," and we left the stage and went outside with the group following.

All gathered on the huge steps outside the building with me asking everyone to go back. Crying and upset I said,

"I don't want all of you to lose your jobs and can't be responsible for that." Then I threw up again. I felt sicker and sat down on the steps. An older lady pushed her way through introducing herself and her husband, the older guy who spoke.

"Hi Allysa, I'm Camilla Browning and this is Brown, my husband. Are you all right?" She asked.

"I think my medicine is upsetting my stomach." I said while looking at the pretty brown skinned older lady. She took my hand telling me,

"This stress is not helping. You're coming with us. We have a spare room for my niece when she comes, and you will rest well there." Then, BS came out shouting,

"This little crack whore will make all of you lose your jobs." Lynn said to BS,

"If you slur this child's name again, you will be in court proving it." BS growled,

"Tomorrow her father will come and pick her up. Do you know how many people I've turned down that will be here by tomorrow?" BB said,

"Why rush? They don't know the material and the show won't go on tomorrow or the next day or week." The whole time this situation went on Jacob said nothing to me. He didn't even come anywhere near me. I figured that was fun while it lasted.

The nice older couple, the Brownings, insisted I stay with them for the night so they could get to know me. Jaison and Brown seem to be real tight and Hu came too, but I was apprehensive. We left Adam battling with BS and I didn't know the Brownings, so I wasn't sure of anything, but I went with them. The Brownings were nice and already knew about me thanks to King Kapulani, but I needed to lie down.

My rough night continued into the morning. It was too much knowing that so many people were going to lose their jobs because of me. The pressure of everything happening made me sicker with me pacing needing to get out this cage when the situation got the best of me and I said to Jaison and Delano,

"I need to go. This is too much to take. Don't worry, but please take me to the dance school to get my clothes." When we walked out the door, Adam, Hu and Brown drove up. Adam said,

"Allysa, come on BS wants to see you." Jaison asked

"Do you feel sick or pressured?"

"Yes. I don't want to go and I don't want to be here if that's what you mean." I said very alarmed with good reason because Adam grabbed me and forced me into the truck.

"Stop!" I said and asked Adam, "What is wrong with you? Is my AD there?" I asked Adam, and he answered,

"I don't know and we will not let anyone take you or do anything bad to you. We want you to stay and continue to learn. You have started something that's good for my father's program and the only way we're going to continue is to stand our ground." Hu had to leave, but Jaison and Brown who followed were going with me. Then Jaison added,

"Come on Miss Allysa M. Carrington, lets finish this." I wanted to see Jacob so bad, and I didn't know why, but I felt the need.

It was 11:30AM, and we were in BS's outer office. I started sweating. I took my medication just in case. Brown, who was a no bullshit type of guy, sat in the office with me. So while Adam found some ice for me, Brown showed me a little gun in his pocket and while patting his pocket he said,

"Don't worry baby girl you are not going anywhere you don't want to." Jaison received a phone call and went off with the truck. Feeling very nervous, I didn't know how Adam would react and felt it was good I had the older guy with the gun.

BS called Adam and myself into his office and started by throwing pictures at us. They were the pictures of the injuries Klondike and her friends sustained. I looked them over feeling proud that they received a worthwhile ass kicking. Next came the broken equipment and hospital bills, plus an arrest report for Marlena and Klondike. The police arrested Klondike for inciting a riot and charges of assault with BS having to spend money to keep her out of jail by paying for her lawyer. Plus, she still had to go back to court. I felt good about that too. They had no business being there to cause trouble. Then BS complained,

"These two decent girls have to go to court now to defend themselves against lies this trouble maker told to get here. I told you she was trouble, and how many times did she run away? She's a delinquent and a pain in the ass who should not be here." I kept quiet looking for my AD to show up at any moment. I thought of how far I could get if I ran. Not far, and couldn't figure out why I felt so bad. I had saved my last pill for the show, but it didn't look like there was going to be a show.

BS dialed the phone trying to reach my AD hanging up after a few minutes of ringing. I felt better hoping my AD went on one of his disappearing episodes. Then BS announced,

"If I don't get John, you're going in the system... you have got to leave here. Your ass never should have been here anyway. Now I have problems with the show. I told you Adam, get Anita." Adam seemed to wake up with that statement and said,

"We never would have won with your rich student and I'm tired of hearing your little brave noise like you run things. I have tried to represent my father's interest, which is inner city, and at risk talented youth who lack a break. Basically because, they have to deal with self-serving shits like you, so you can play politics for your own gain. I've stood by for years and watch you use all their money on yourself so you can continue to be a big shot among the rich. You're spending donations meant for her and children like her." BS interjected,

"I run things in your father's absence, and he's always gone, so I run things. And I told you to get Anita. I know you just found this run away delinquent, and now she has caused problems for my program." A vein popped up in Adam's neck during the moment of silence I thought it would take for Adam to snatch him, but Adam got in BS's face and said,

"This is not your program. Anita's here only because of you. Allysa has more talent in her than Anita will ever encompass, and yeah, she ran a couple of times, however, after watching her trying to make adjustments to trust us, I know abuse when I see it. She's a child who has suffered a severe lack of compassion, love, the decency that's due a human being, and only GOD knows what else. HE has taken an account of all the things purposely done to her and by whom. And you know what's going on Brian." Adam appeared very serious and what Adam said had a confused meaning. Then Adam continued, "I see what type of person Allysa is with her showing compassion and caring for a little boy she raised from an infant to four years. You will do nothing to her. The Kapulani have her now and she's not going in any system or going back to that hell hole." While he talked, Adam got up and stood in front of me like whatever would have to go through him. He was huge with huge muscles to match and terrifying, but his demeanor change to an attitude of a determination he never displayed before. I wanted to peep around him and say, Yeah! Now Adam was acting like the oldest brother who was serious when he told you to do something with you knowing he will keep order by kicking butt. I felt better. Then Dad came in with Jaison and said,

"Now that's my boy." Jumping up I hugged Dad.

I had seen Dad before and hoped he was my father and could see all his sons in him. It looked like each one took a piece and built from that. Adam had Dad's seriousness, Hu had his Gangster, Jaison's was the Lover boy, and I knew that gentle, sweet side with a grin and slanted eyes I recognized to be like Jacob's. However, Jacob looked more like Mom than the others. It made him pretty. However, Dad was here in BS's face saying,

"When I started this camp about 23, 24 years ago, Brian, we were younger and full of ideals and ideas. We traveled as a band all over the US, and part of the world. We saw poverty, people in despair with no hope or a way out, and we saw talented young people who could improve themselves, but couldn't get a break. I worked hard to start this camp for people in that situation. I created a system of contributions and the rich enrolling their children to finance the less fortunate; however, when my attention left, you took over, and then something went terribly wrong. It became all rich with very few poor. You enrolled just enough of the underprivileged to make them your slaves working in the cafeteria you turned into a restaurant and all your other businesses so you can profit from them." BS remarked,

"Gerald, that's all bullshit," and Dad said,

"Sure Brian. That's why we call you BS. However, three years ago, Adam oversaw a plan to re-indoctrinate the original program. My boys created a production company so students could earn the money they should have been getting for working and performing. Brian you have tried to make that and my intentions non-affective, but my program will start again the right way with this young lady, and you know she deserves it. While searching for her... you remember when I searched Brian, don't you?" BS didn't answer, but looked like a weasel ready to jump on all fours and run off, but Dad continued by saying, "Yeah I'm sure you remember. I was here searching for talent when I found this young lady at 5 years old. She had stopped talking, but she could play the piano that she taught herself from listening to Mozart, Chopin, and then, every jazz pianist the director of the house gave her. You remember her; don't you Brian? We talked about her all the time, and we knew both her parents were dead. Talented children in this type of situation, is why I created the camp. I tried to get her then, but the only thing that happened for her was to end up with John. You should be ashamed of yourself Brian. Something went wrong with that situation and this. When my attention left, things got way off track. Now it is like my son Adam said, she's not going back to that hellhole, and stop threatening her with it. This is my camp, and I plan to help her and others like her, but she is someone special to me. I didn't think the small fragile five-year-old child would survive. BS you knew I had personal problems at the time and couldn't help her, but the camp was functioning, so you should have. Brian, you discuss me, and then you say she shouldn't be here, but you can justify Anita's enrollment... free of charge? Anita's 26 this year and has been coming for five years with two being free of charge since she's gotten worse. She doesn't have the talent to learn at this level. She wasn't even scouted by any of the losing groups."

"I told your boys to get her," BS said and Mr. Kapulani responded,

"My boy's picked the most deserving girl that fit the criteria this camp invests in. What will happen is she dances and attend this camp or my boys and I will pull our endorsements and demand an account of all financial records for the last 7 years. In addition, I want Anita's tuition in full from your father's friend, by time I leave tomorrow. It looks like you're not going to have a show anyway." Jaison popped in to say,

"Yup. Last time I checked you have 10 people. You'll have 11 when you hire the translator because none speak English." Then he grinned and popped back out. I ignored him trying not to laugh. However, the conversation they were having piqued my interest.

It seemed my AD John, BS, and Dad knew each other and I wondered if they knew me. I wanted to know, but why wouldn't someone tell me and why all the secrets? I didn't know my parents were dead and had hopes of finding them... to know them, but they're dead. My situation and thoughts concerning all my colleagues who worked so hard to win this competition almost consumed me. I threw up, and BS wasn't giving up. BS told me to get the hell out his office, but continued talking with Dad. Probably because a little throw up went on the floor... and the rest on his desk.

When the performers and support crews found out we were there battling with BS, most came to the office and camped on the steps of the huge building. With the red carpet walk scheduled to start at 7pm and the show at 9pm, I told Adam, Jaison, and Mr. Browning while they waited with me in the outer office,

"Talk to everyone and tell them to get ready so things can go on. They worked so hard to get the exposure the camp and the show would give them." The three talked a little while. Then Jaison went to the group and read a letter I wrote thanking them for supporting King Kapulani's real program and me; however, I let them know if we didn't show our new and returning acts as King Kapulani planned, BS would be successful. So I asked them to at least do the red carpet walk and introduce all the new and returning acts. The weight of taking away the performers' opportunity was hard to deal with. So when the performers and all of support agreed to what I asked, I felt better. However, all agreed they would not perform unless I danced. Dad solved that, but my illness became a concern for me. Brown who called Dad, Kap said,

"Kap is here, baby girl, and you are fine now." I thanked Brown and asked him to go get ready.

While I sat in the outer office by myself, Adam came back alone and sat. We sat there silent at first. Then Adam asked,

"Did you try to kill yourself because of the way I acted?" I thought for a while, and knew he had a direct input into my decision, but I said,

"Adam, I didn't want to be a problem, and I'm confused about a person I grew to love who became my only hope. My AD said no one cared about me, but I felt you did, and you came every month looking for me. I looked forward to seeing you, my hero, coming to take me away like you promised and you kept your promise, so I trusted you in place of your father... but... all your intentional actions with Klondike and Twista... destroyed my perception of you and confused me." I sat there remembering how I felt and told Adam, "Don't ever lie and abandon your children. It will change their love for you." Sadden and disappointed that he treated me that way I moved away with tears falling. It felt like someone died. I wasn't aware that I had accumulated so much love and respect for Adam that was living within. Then Adam hugged me which scared me.

"There is not a thing wrong with you, Allysa." He said with his voice breaking; then, Adam apologized for his actions and said,

"Allysa I felt that in my soul. I thought my father would kill me. I caused the problem and now I have a problem with my wife. Adjani put me out because she said my attitude caused your actions. She wants me to bring you home, and we take care of you. My whole family is upset with me, and I want you to believe I want you to come and live with us like my daughter. My wife says Rich and my girls cry for you worrying, thinking people are hurting you and I'm not helping. Allysa, I'll get you in the NYC School of performing Arts. That's where you want to go right?" Adam wasn't the cuddly type so I realize his words to be somewhat genuine, but I felt he had incentive so I said,

"Adam, you will win your wife and family back, or not, with your own merits, but not with me." Wondering how I could ever put faith in him again; then, I thought about Adam coming and calling me at my AD's when there was no one. He gave me so much hope, and even though he changed my feelings for him, I still loved him, but it was hard to love without respect. My respect and his family's he had to earn again. I told Adam,

"I think the best thing will be to conquer this system that BS established and Dad's trying to get straight. It seems like we're central players in something that will be good. Yeah?" Adam nodded.

After Dad came, I felt more confident, and I felt sure I would dance. I wanted to stay with dad and fight because it wasn't just about me. It's about people like me getting the intended and needed help. I was sure I wanted to be a part of that. What I wasn't sure of was... me. I asked,

"Adam, do you know who I am?"

"No," he said quickly. I didn't believe him and this sickness wasn't helping things with me beginning to see little spots floating around and I was feeling light headed with hot flashes and throwing up. Feeling I was going to pass out, I kept eating ice to keep cool.

Almost 6pm Dad and BS were still going at it. I was hurting so bad I took my last pill telling Adam,

"Get dress and do what you believe is right." Adam left, and I sat there by myself thinking; then, wondering where Jacob was when Dad came out BS's office and said,

"Allysa, step in and sit down." He looked like Jacob when upset. I looked at him wondering if I did something wrong. I wasn't that sure anymore. The pictures were back out and BS had shown them to Dad and lied no doubt. Dad said,

"The fighting and cutting of the girls bother me Allysa. This is very serious. There is no room for that behavior." I pushed the pictures to the side. Yeah, I really messed them up and began to regret I had to do that; then, BS laughed, and that pissed me off placing things in the proper perspective. I asked,

"Well is there room for the behavior where my property is intentionally and continuously destroyed, people constantly ridiculing calling me racial names like zebra, big lipped white girl not to include the names that... man called me; then, throwing things at me, stalking, bullying me, hitting and kicking me when they feel like it. Also, having your clothes ripped off while being threaten with rape? All the way to the Beach Camp, I had to endure that behavior from Klondike, Marlena, BS, and their little group. If what they're doing is behavior you allow, Mr. Kapulani I don't want to be here or around people like that anymore."

"Did you know all this was going on Brian?" Dad asked BS and he said no, but I know Adam and Jaison called Canada to tell him. I told Dad,

"I don't want to be here because this situation is not safe for me, but I can't go back to my AD."

"That's not an issue," he said, and asked, "Who threaten to rape you?"

"We got rid of him." BS said while brushing his suit like it all meant nothing to him. Dad stood up swelling on the way, while he said,

"Brian... I thought you didn't know, and that was the guy I fired because you didn't get rid of him the first time he sexually attacked her, and that's the same group that cause all these bills for equipment damages. This has put so much stress on her, I know it made her sick!" Dad was tall like Jacob, larger than Adam, very fit, and angry. I jumped out the way when he grabbed BS by his throat lifting his hoofs off the floor. "What's his name?" Dad asked again with BS spitting out quickly,

"Victor Bueno. Twister is his stage name." Dad threw his ass back in his chair banging them both against the wall. Now that was gangster, and I'm sure I laughed, but the way BS looked at me when his butt hit the chair, I knew BS wasn't finished. Dad said,

"Brian, you know Allysa's right when she made you part of that group. You mixed your people in with my boys group to cause trouble, but amiss your drama she's here, and it's time to leave her alone. You haven't learned yet that she is special." Dad gently grabbed my face with his hand and made me look up. "This is what's going to happen, I will escort Barbie here tonight, and she's dancing. After that, she's part of my boy's group and will sing back up, dance, and work at the dance school." Then Dad was finish, and we were out leaving hours after he walked in the office with Jaison.

My four friends in hair and makeup waited for me. Devon said,

"Honey, we're going to do something simple and quick." In 30 minutes Mrs. Browning was helping me get dressed. By 7:25 pm, I was ready with Devon and Mrs. Brownings help. Then Dad arrived to pick me up in a limo with a few photographers following. We took pictures, and then we moved quickly into the limo. His dark skin, mix gray hair, and hazel eyes, handsomely suited his black tuxedo with a silver vest and cranberry accessories. I felt bad, but seeing him made me think of Jacob. I smiled, but I felt so bad, and Dad noticed.

"You feel all right?" He asked.

"Yes." I told him. He went on,

"Jacob said you're mad at him." I didn't feel like talking about that, so I looked out the window. Dad continued by saying, "Jacob has to mature. His mother tried to baby him and he needs to get away from her." I change the subject, and I hugged and thanked Dad for all he was doing for me. With my head on Mr. Kapulani's shoulder I felt the genuine comfort of a father, but I was hurting so bad, I got confused feeling sicker and wanted to tell him so bad I cried a little. OMG. "Stop the car!" Dad commanded and then he asked, "What is wrong Barbie? Tell me." I wanted this moment to ask him if he knew my parents, which was the thought at the time... and stop calling me Barbie, but I figured he had done so much for me, there had to be a reason why he hadn't told me, if he knew. I told Dad,

"Things are confusing me, but I want to dance now." He asked,

"Are you sure you're all right?" I nodded yes, and he told the driver to continue. Still feeling sick, those energy spots floated around vividly.

All the new acts had walked the red carpet and were introduced. Unbelievably, everyone was outside awaiting our arrival. The show was ready to be or not to be. I finally saw Jacob and with that, my system perked up with expectations of being around him. Jacob rushed opening the door with his father stepping out grinning amiss flashing cameras.

"Is Allysa dancing?" Jacob asked; then, Dad stepped aside as Jacob peeped in the car. When he saw me, our eyes met, and we lost ourselves in a gaze for only the moment he took to help me out the car. After taking my hand he asked,

"Are you feeling better?" His eyes said more and almost made me forget how bad I felt. "Are you dancing?"

"Yes." I replied managing to smile. Jaison as well as others who heard cheered and passed the word.

"She's dancing so let's get started. Quick take your places. Hurry." Jaison said as he hunched Jacob. Then the four of his sons encompassed me quickly and with Dad, we took pictures. Next, Jacob looked me up and down and smiled.

"I feel like I'm dreaming," he said, "But we have to get ready." Jacob ushered me to my dressing room in silence and opened the door looking around the room checking; then said, "You'll be fine here. The Wardrobe people will be in to get you ready, and then Danny will come and get you." After he left, I threw up again. Something was terribly wrong. I felt so bad I couldn't enjoy having my own dressing room.

BS had all reference of me removed from the theatre with only my action picture remaining. Danny and I were to have one poster size action shot and one portrait along with our names on the marquee under the headliners with me receiving second billing to Danny. BS replaced my portrait photo with Anita's and place her name on my poster sized action shot, and marquee like she was the one performing in the photo and that night. She wasn't dancing at all and hiding backstage. I found out later that I didn't see Jacob, Danny or Wang because they spent time, looking for my photo and poster. When they found that BS destroyed them and ordered my name removed, Jacob made a poster and displayed it in the lobby with my name and picture as the featured dancer. I was the only one that didn't get an introduction as part of the group that won the highly publicized Band Camp talent contest, and BS made the best of it.

Mrs. Browning and her crew came helping me into my costume making sure all was right for me to dance. Then the Make Up/Wardrobe crew went elsewhere and everything was very different from the first red carpet affair. After sat there for 1 hour not seeing anyone and not sure what was going on I figured it was all a lie and threw up again and was recovering when Danny came in saying,

"Let's go. Jacob is in place and the band is ready for us."

"What? I... I need a few minutes to stretch." I told him feeling really off. Those little spots that floated freely were connecting.

"What? Allysa! Do something quick," Danny said, "Everyone's been looking for you. Why didn't you come out to the back stage area?" He asked while I took one bend and knew this would not be good. I prayed and wasn't sure how until I remembered the prayers in the Bible Adja use to leave open. I repeated them in my head.

On stage, we performed a modern ballet that Danny, Bubbles, and I choreographed. Jacob sang a ballad about a heartbroken man who was feeling blue, but he found a beautiful blue creature, me, who touches his heart and let him know that he's never too blue to love again. We practiced this to a CD of Jacob singing, however, to see and hear him perform live was very different. I didn't notice the pain or time so much as I noticed his body, his expressions, and listened to him sing. Sexy was the word, and it seemed he was singing to me, so that inspired my movements to be sensual. They were supposed to be, but I had two lifts near the end of the song I was dreading. They were close together and the last one I had to help lift myself over Danny's head. His hand supported me in the small of my back so I could snake down his arm and body, slowly and smoothly until the end of the song. The pain must have shown in my face. Jacob kept watching me. I completed my lifts, and snake as planned, but I think the stagehands noticed my pain on that last lift, so the curtain fell quick at the end of the song, and so did I. Danny helped me up. I felt lightheaded and couldn't stand without holding on. My back was beyond hurting. I made it to a garbage can and threw up. That was so violent. I think I saw some of my organs go past in that purge. On my knees, trying to get myself together when I looked up, I saw Jacob with his slightly bowed legs coming down the hall from the stage area. I figured he would start with the pregnant thing again, so I moved quick and made it to my dressing room, laid down, and passed out.

CHAPTER TEN

When I Open My Eyes

Waking with a tube up my nose, IV, monitors, and something stuck up my twat, I was very uncomfortable in ICU at the hospital near the camp. I didn't know what to think, but saw a nurse and tried to set up, but I couldn't. My head was spinning. I felt if I could stand up, somehow I wouldn't die. So, I tried when Jacob came quickly and said,

"Wait, slow down." He was still in his suit. I tried to talk but nothing was working. I thought I was dying, and tears rolled. Jacob grabbed and held me. "Calm down," Jacob said; then explained, "The place on your back Twista kicked wasn't healing." I took refuge in Jacob's arms. While the nurse injected something in my IV Jacob continued, "It caused some problems and your kidney is infected." I started feeling sleepy, but could hear the nurse telling Jacob,

"She will relax now and sleep," and I closed my eyes going to sleep in his arms... like I wanted.

Waking again later, Jacob was setting by my bed changing the TV's channels. He had changed his clothes, and I think ate my food. He looked at me, smiled; then, kissed my cheek.

"Are you feeling better?" He asked.

"A little." I whispered while looking at everything attached to me. I pointed to a bag. "Where is that blood coming from?"

"The doctor said your menstrual cycle started." Managing to be a little offended, I mumbled,

"I guess now you can believe I'm not pregnant." Respectfully he said,

"Miss Allysa, I see you didn't lose your attitude, and I was out of line. Please excuse me for asking you that." I only looked at him, but said,

"I want to take a shower," and he told me,

"Oh, I gave you a bath while you were asleep." I didn't know what to think, but wished I was awake for that. Then he said, "Oh yeah, another thing, I told the hospital I'm your husband because they wouldn't look at you right away and you needed to be looked at… right away. That place looked worst with you feeling hot. Plus, it was over your kidney. A man went out walking about on my father's Island and fell hitting his back. He didn't see a doctor and died suddenly in 5 days. He had damaged his kidneys like you and I didn't know how long you were out. It was good our performance was last." Not believing all the attention from Jacob I could only listen. "Allysa, after I asked you about being pregnant and pissed you off, I laid there. You were asleep, but your back was very warm. You were doing too much, and when you used your medication the wrong way… it didn't work correctly." I turned away with a frown feeling embarrassed that I wasn't successful at killing myself, and then I had to hear and talk about it. Dying would have been easier. Even though, I wanted to know Jacob better, when he talked about that, I felt stupid. "Ally, Allysa, ok I'm sorry. I know you don't like to think of that situation, but please understand I'm more than concerned about you. Please, talk to someone or me about your problems. I don't think I can continue without you being around me, somewhere within reach and not upset with me. Hey, come on Ally… Allysa… look at me." I did, and he smiled asking, "Promise?" I nodded ok, and he said, "Now, we got to get you feeling better, and I was just joking when I said I washed you. Adjani and a nurse took care of that. I only brushed your hair and stole a kiss. The doctor said you can have juice and soup tonight, and then he will reassess the situation in the morning if you keep that down. BB went to get something to eat, and she wants to come in and gossip, but Dad wants to see you. So I'll be in the waiting room and send him back."

"Please... please don't leave Jacob. I just got here." I pleaded, but Jacob told me,

"Only one person can visit you at a time, and I been here the whole while. I wanted to make sure you were all right."

"Thank you Jacob." I said wanting to say more.

"You're welcome Allysa. I'm sending Dad in now." He kissed me on my forehead; then, he went out the door smiling.

By time Dad came in, I had talked myself into believing he would see another bill and think I was only a pain in the butt. He came in and sat down. Whispering I said,

"Dad, I know I'm a pain in the butt and I'm sorry for getting sick and passing out," and Dad asked me,

"How long were you feeling ill?" Thinking about Jacob I said,

"I felt bad for a while. The doctor said the pills might upset my stomach, so I thought it was that. Jacob thought I was pregnant. That's why I was mad with him." Dad said,

"Really? I mean... have you..." then, he blushed a little.

"No." I responded quickly, "I'm not ready to get pregnant. I want to model and need my body for that. In maybe 7 to 8 years or maybe when I'm 24 or 25 years old, and I'm not sure if we'll get together. We're both young and going to meet other people. Right now I'm trying to get through this situation and that's too far ahead." Then Dad let me know the way he felt about the whole thing when he said,

"There are girls on my island that's married at 14, 15 years old." Responding quicker I said,

"I don't live on your island. Dad please, don't think that I'm unappreciative, or being disrespectful. I have to make a life for myself before I marry and lose myself again. Plus, married people don't stay together and it's hard on the children. Are you and your wife together?" Dad said,

"Yes... no, wait a minute! Allysa that's personal." I said,

"I guest this is personal too." Surprised he said,

"Well... okay Barbie." I had to ask,

"Dad, why do you and Jacob call me Barbie?"

"I call you that because you're a Barbie doll... perfect." He explained; then, he kissed me on my forehead and said, "Got to go, but I'll be back. The Brownings want to see you," and then he left. Dad and his sons were so much alike, but he was huge and enough to keep them in line.

The Brownings came in and made sure I was better. Brown left to talk with Dad. I could tell things were still amiss. Adjani came in with the doctor and discussed my condition making sure I understood. Mrs. Browning combed my hair and Adjani helped me wash off again. Then they tucked me in as Brown came back. I asked,

"What's going on? I know BS is in an up roar and he's blaming me... right?" Adjani said,

"Stop worrying Allysa. You need to get well and if BS get pass the brothers, he has to come through all of us." Brown said,

"Yeah, no Joke," as he patted his pocket making me laugh. Adjani left, but the Brownings stayed and talked for a minute. Brown had me laughing about how guest talked to BS concerning the confusion. I like them, but listening to Brown I realized the industry was only tolerating BS, and how important it was to get rid of this

Brian Schulman with his program. The Brownings left, and BB came in with crumbs around her mouth. She said,

"Hi crazy butt. You hungry yet? I just got finish eating a Philly Cheese Steak Sub with soup. It was good." I told her,

"You're not finish yet," and passed her some tissues. She wiped her mouth; and started talking.

"After the show finished, Jacob asked if anyone saw you since you went in the dressing room.   No one had, so we went to your room and found you, unconscious. Jaison thought it was your sickness, but Jacob pulled up your little dress on your costume and found the injury swollen and dark blue. At first we thought he had lost his mind, but when we saw the spot, everyone knew you were bad off." I overstressed,

"And Jacob took me to the hospital…. again."

BB was turning into my best friend and it really felt like she was my big sister. She was easy to trust, because she was so for real, but sometimes I had to say BB, shut up. She told me the same often, but now she was concerned for me.

"Klondike vows to get ahead not even. So, we're going to watch her." My big sis said as she took off her shoes getting on the bed and laid with her head at the foot. She had a stack of magazines. We talked fashion, designers, and gossiped all while looking at the magazines and playing with our phones. That's what we did when together and schemed.

"When you think we'll hear from TMP?" I asked wondering if BS would mess with my mail.

"If you make it to the 40 finalist, they will cast at the end of August or early September. So, I figure sometime in June." I thought that's next… EURK…. (Eric not Ralph). The tube down my nose was pumping my stomach and some green stuff passed through it. BB made a face and the sign of the cross saying,

"That's nasty." Recovering I mumbled,

"Well, that's why I'm sick." After that BB asked,

"Allysa, you know, I wanted to ask you why in the world did your little skinny ass start fighting all those people plus that big ass girl without us there?"

"I had some help, and it wasn't like I could pick a time or place. I would have loved to have waited for you to be there BB."

"Yeah, but how you cut her like that?" She asked laughing. "You got her in the butt, neck, and everywhere else."

"I don't know. Her butt was the easiest though because it was like right there, and then I thought I just cut this girl on the butt with a broken bottle. Then... I sort of lost it after that and tried to keep it moving so no one would grab me. Plus, I studied Kung Fu and Capoeira for years at the YMCA first, and then at Rod's friend's Dojo. I was his best student and won over 25 trophies. So, I used moves from both and some that I made up for the occasion. My teacher would be proud of me."

"You're sick in the head kid." BB said giggling, but I thought and told her,

"During a spin kick pass I saw Wang and Cisco. They kept the people off my back."

"Yeah, everyone who doesn't speak English saw the fight and they're just talking about it," BB said sarcastically. "Shit... I spent the whole damn time in the mud, and I know someone saw me drop." I asked,

"BB! How you get out?"

"Finally, I dragged my own ass out." She said and then told what happened to her that day. "Mud covered me up to my neck with some in my hair, but I came up on the hill runnin hard. I had to check on you, you crazy butt hole. And as bad as I wanted to hang a fingernail in one of them I get stuck in some f—king mud hole. But anyway, when I got there the ambulances with you and everyone in it had just left. I mean I missed every damned thing... but the police. They were still there. I ran by one, 'Whoa,' the police guy said. Then he asked me, 'Were you involved in this?' I told him my friend was in a fight and I wanted to check on her. I knew I looked a hot mess and I mean that literally. It was 105 degrees, humid, something had stung me on my ass, and the shit was itching like crazy. Then the policeman ran up on me and said, 'You were fighting!' I wondered how the hell he got that an asked him. So he got disturbed and called his partner telling him I was in the fight. His partner came, and then he's looking at me like he wasn't sure what happened. So I took them to that damn mud hole and showed them, there, I fell in there. That mud hole tried to suck me under. I lost both my shoes. I was barefooted, and they laughed, I mean roared. They said, 'She fell in the creek,' all country and shit. Creek? Girl there was a little 3-inch wide stream with maybe ½-inch deep water running. THAT WAS A 25-FOOT-WIDE MUD HOLE! And you could see where I jumped straight into the middle with some force to go down in it like that. I don't know what I was thinking following them long leg boys cause Bubbles took the bridge. They just left me there. I almost died." BB had me pissing in my bag, but I felt better, and by 9:30pm I was hungry.

BB talked herself out and went to sleep at the foot of my bed while I dozed. The nurse brought Jaison in the room.

"How you feel Little Bit?" He asked pulling my cheeks. I replied,

"Hungry! And what's wrong with you? Leave the face alone."

"I would kiss you, but I'm afraid you'll spill on me," He said laughing. I stuck my tongue out at him. He kissed my forehead, and then said,

"I see you're feeling better," as he tried to set on the bed, but sat on BB. She made some noise and kicked him. He looked at BB and said,

"There's people waiting to see you and she's in here sleep?"

"Who?" I questioned and Jai said,

"BB." I asked,

"What? No crazy. Who else is waiting to see me?" Jaison said

"My Dad for one. You were out of it when he came earlier and stayed for 2 hours before Jacob chased him out." I said,

"I saw Dad."

"Every one that counts were here after the show. So many important people saw you dance and wanted to meet you because of the confusion BS created when he advertised Anita as the feature dancer. Plus, Allysa, you didn't do the acknowledgment bow with Danny and Jacob at the end, and then you were in costume and made up as a blue fairy with little fluttering wings and all. I thought that was so cute." He said that while smiling and looking off into space... but Jai continued, "Anita's talking to everyone taking the credit meant for you. Some came and others called because I don't think they completely believed she danced, but you were so sick they couldn't see you. Since there is so much confusion with people requesting to meet you, Lynn's trying to keep it from getting twisted by letting the people know your name and making a list for you of concerned people. When you get out, give them a thank you call and you'll have an instant contact. We're going to keep this straight." I asked,

"Where's Jacob?" Jaison said,

"He went to get you something to eat. Hey Little-Bit, when Jacob came out earlier after staying with you all night, he told everyone you were awake and talking with an attitude. Everyone applauded and cheered." Wondering I had to ask,

"Jaison, why are they treating me so... respectfully?" He replied,

"Baby girl, you have won them over. You are the little angel that stood against that demon, BS, and you have started a movement against him. They love and respect you for that brave action. Many knew of BS's mess, and wanted to move on, but knew Dad planned to revamp the program, so they stuck around to see. It was like something to talk about with others in the business. We boys wanted to kill BS and use his body for shark chum around the island, and I still think that's the best idea. Make him disappear." Jaison gave me a local newspaper article concerning the show's success and my name was in the article. "Ok Little-Bit, I said my piece. I'm going to leave so Dad can come in to talk with you before he leaves and go back home to the island." Jai kissed me on my forehead with a wink and hit BB; then, he left.

So many people had shown such genuine concern, it made me feel euphoric. However, when I thought of Jacob vigilance concerning me, my passion deepened for him, and even though I didn't quite understand it, I wanted to be around to take care of Jacob. Feeling anxious I wanted to see him. I just had to figure something to say... that was nice instead of just staring. But what?

Dad came in looking so tired, I felt bad he went through all of this mess because of me, and I wondered why, but I opened my arms in a gestured for him to hug me please. He did, and I hugged him saying,

"Please forgive me for causing you such a problem. I see the stress in your face and I don't like you being so tired and looking that way." Really, I felt pissed, but his hug was so strengthening just like his words.

"Had to take care of my Barbie Doll." He said while smiling. "But I have to leave in 6 hours and don't like it. I wish I could stay so I could oversee this situation, because I don't like Brian's attitude toward you, and that's causing me a great deal of concern making me second-guess bringing you here. I've talked to Adam, and he's dead set against you being or staying at the camp."

"Why?" I asked. He was slow to answer, but said,

"... Well, Adam's #1 concern is the conflicts you're having. He thinks you're too young to be with this group. He wants you to live with his family and grow up without this foolishness. Adjani thinks that would be best too. Then... #2 He's worried about this thing between you and Jacob. My wife has forced Adam to be on Jacob watch when she's not around, and you know that crazy boy said you're his wife so they would look at you right away. Allysa, tell me truthfully what's going on with you and Jacob?" I didn't know what to say, so I told him,

"We're friends, and I have feelings for him... because he has turned out to be everything to me. I'm sure he just wants to protect me, but that's all it is. Adam has made too big of a thing out of it. I know Klondike and her gang doesn't like the attention I receive from Jacob, but I have my sisters, BB and Lynn, plus my big brothers Jaison, Danny, and Wang that I respect because they keep me focus. The Brownings I'm falling in love with too, but I hate BS. But please, please, pretty please, don't make me leave." I pled as I started rethinking everything I had done and thought about what happened between Jacob and me at the dance school. That seemed personal, so I didn't say anything about it, but I figured Dad had given up on me. Then he made my day by saying,

"The big plus for you Miss Barbie is I'll have a riot if you left now, and entertainment wise, your dancing, choreography with and without Danny has put us over the top. Adam said your stage presence has given the show the versatility of youth and you have attracted many supporters from the show biz world who's requesting information on you. This was something I knew would happen because I trained you and you put in the dedication. You, BB, Wang, Lynn, and then some are part of my plan that's been in the making for years, but you are special to me. It would be wrong to remove you, so get that out of your mind, and get well. We need you and want you. You're not a problem. I arranged for the school's insurance to pay for the hospital bill, and the doctor said you would be fine and dancing in about 2 weeks. As soon as you can keep food down the doctors will remove the tubes. It's a good thing you were throwing up since that expelled most the poison that escaped in your system, but Allysa... why did you dance with such an injury?" Firmly I said,

"Because everyone supported me to dance, so there wasn't an option." Now Dad said sternly,

"I understand, but don't do that again Barbie. Now I have to meet with BS to make sure he has the plan. Allysa, I will be watching this situation. So, PLEASE be good."

"Given the situation, Dad, I'll try, but why they pick at me like that?"

"Sometimes when certain people see you have a natural talent, and other things going for you, they get angry." Just then, BB woke up talking.

"Yeah, that's why they call them haters." She got up and went into the bathroom. In about 5 minutes while Dad and I were saying goodbye, she came back out in what she called her PJ's. She took a pillow, one of my blankets, tied her hair up, and then laid back in her spot while poking her butt out getting comfortable. "Bye Dad. Can you turn off the light when you leave?" She said and went back to sleep. I laughed while Dad shook his head saying,

"Lynn, BB, and one more you'll meet are the only girls to be trusted. Trust the Brownings, but I think you noticed by now Bubbles can be strange. Keep this in mind about her, she was an older you four years ago, but never will be as good, and she's aware of that fact." I asked,

"Daddy, why does BS have custody of me and not you?"

"The manager of the camp must have custody of the minor orphans for insurance purposes and the manager must be present. I don't live in the US."   After saying that he kissed my forehead and left cutting off the light laughing as he went out the door. I loved Dad and knew I would miss him; however, I felt stronger ready to fight with him, but the whole time Dad's kissing my forehead, my mind was on Jacob and I really needed to see him.

Thinking about Jacob and the way he made me feel from the first time I saw him, I kept asking myself what was going on. This guy touch my brand new boobies which I knew was an accident, but I didn't mind him touching me... anywhere, and I felt like stuffing BB in the closet so I could get him in my room. Then I thought we both had a moment, and I needed to slow down my feelings, but I wanted to see him before I went to sleep. I reasoned... you don't know what may happen, so I put my leg over BB trying to look like one person with this big round foot and I called the nurse. When she came, I asked,

"Is there a guy named Jacob..." She asked,

"You mean the cute taller one that stayed with you all night?" I smiled saying,

"Yeah, that one." Smiling she said,

"He went to get you and the other girl something to eat." Darn, she looked right at BB, but she let Jacob come back anyway. He kissed my cheek and gave me my soup and crackers.

"What's wrong with BB? Dad said something about her taking her clothes off." Jacob asked looking confused. I pointed to her sleep at the foot of the bed. While laughing he asked,

"Do you feel like eating some vegetable soup?" I thought it was interesting how I never told him I didn't eat meat, but it was as if he already knew. Shrimp and other expensive seafood I love, but had never tasted before knowing Jacob, but he figured what I would like. I didn't know men paid attention to women like that, and don't think I said anything just smiling, but Jacob said,

"Since BB is here I'm going to straighten up my room. It's messy." I came out my stupor and thanked him and we said good night. I really had to figure something to say.

Four days later, I was out of the hospital. It was almost May and the weather in Florida was beautiful. Dad had me moved to one of his beachfront mansions with Lynn and BB as my roomies. Our dorm was an eight bedroom and bathroom mansion that was two years old. We had a large kitchen that opened to a large deck with a gazebo and then the beach. We also had a formal dining area and two living areas a formal setting area, library, and game room. The smaller area we used for practice, which was setup like a studio and included everything we needed like a Baby Grand piano, a complete sound system, with a 48-inch television. A 60-inch flat screen TV with large pillows and lounge chairs all over furnished the large area connected to the game room. Our house had a sunken living room like the newer Mansion about 100 feet away with whom we shared a huge deck. Jaison, Jacob, Delano, and Wang stayed there.

The beach camp, located at the southwest tip of Florida right where the Gulf and Caribbean Sea fused. So the color of the water was breath taking. There were windows, plants, pillows, and sun everywhere. It felt good and made it easy to recuperate. The houses sat by different types of palm trees with all type of native flora around with the beach a few hundred feet from our backdoor. It was a culture shock for me.

My first day out of the hospital, Jacob came and asked me out. He fixed a dinner with a blanket on the beach in a beautiful romantic setting. We sat and ate in silence most the time, while I noticed a slight, but constant breeze refreshing us as we watched the surf, and then the sunset with its orange gold color that highlighted everything. It seemed like GOD was sprinkling gold dust all over the beach signaling the close of a precious day. Then the sun seemed to melt away into the ocean.

At dusk, the palm trees gently swayed in rhythm with the breeze that carried along the faint cry of crickets and the song of the night bird.   It felt like a tropical paradise and was very romantic except for these little... well large Beetle Bugs that lived in the palms. Now and then, you would see them scurry out stop and look, and when you move, they scurried away. They moved fast and Jacob kept them away from me, but I had to keep watch. I told Jacob,

"This feels like paradise."

"There are places on my fathers' island prettier than this and don't have these bugs." Jacob remarked while shooing one away. Then he told me about a special place on his father's island.   "Each summer since my twelfth birthday I spend time there, but it's not easy to get to... my grandfather showed me the place."

"Prettier?" I questioned. Jacob said,

"So much so, I use to dream about how I would bring my wife there to live. I never could get any of the girls to follow me there, so it became my bachelor's paradise." I smiled thinking I would go with him.... for a while. He smiled and asked, "Are you still upset with me?" By now with me caught up in Jacob's smile and imagining him in the Jungle with a little lion cloth on when I noticed, he was saying, "Earth to Ally," the second time. I asked him,

"What?" Jacob gently kissed me, and then he wrapped a blanket around us and held me. It was dark and a little chilly, but I felt secure in his arms. I would want him to hold me under any circumstance.

We sat for hours watching the surf and sky with Jacob telling me about his dreams and things he wanted to do on his father's island. We enjoyed each other's company with me still not saying much, but I listen intently to everything Jacob had to say. His thoughts were interesting, very organized, and planned too well to be just dreams. Jacob and his plans were fascinating. Then, Lynn and BB came to collect me, but asked what he was doing and didn't give him a chance to explain anything. They were just messing, wanting me to rest and get better.

Before practice, Jaison and Mr. Browning picked me up in our golf cart and took me on tour of the campus. I was off for the next two weeks, but planned to go to practice so I could keep up. I was part of the brothers' group as a backup singer so I didn't want to fall behind. The tour orientated everything for me. About ½ mile from the mansions down the beach toward the Camp's southern end, was the dance school with a little corner store, and flea market. Also, a little way further was a little tourist motel, a tour boat, and fishing charter that Dad owned and operated. In the other direction up the beach about a mile or so past the mansions, were the boardwalk, the police station, City Hall, and hospital with every type of store within walking distance toward the down town area. Past the police station were the fishing jetties and the point. That was deep water and an active seaport.

The camp was about six blocks deep on a little isthmus in an exclusive small town with mansions and luxurious hotels. On the other side of the camp behind the hospital were the camp's offices and a neighborhood where the Brownings, Adam, BS and most of the older band members lived, which was a funky cool Artisan community in the downtown area. Within the Beach Camp, there were two older dorms located behind a small park that had an outside theater where we practiced and gave shows for guest. All was in the center of the Beach Camp campus along with the outdoor pool, a full inside gym with a basketball court. Also, there was an outdoor basketball court with bleachers, a track leading into the city's park. Then the tennis courts, which connected to a country club and golf course that continued toward the Downtown area.

The Band Camp cafeteria which was by the offices. The cafeteria was also an exclusive restaurant catering to the rich year round that BS operated. Slick BS talked King Kapulani into starting a culinary program at the Camp; then, BS claimed to hire some excellent chefs to train students in the culinary arts. However, the Chefs hired prepared exclusive dishes for diners at the restaurant and the students learned from working long hours without pay. Meanwhile, BS received the proceeds from the restaurant and a paid private chef at home who followed him around on tour to prepare his meals. Students like me were to benefit from the restaurants proceeds and contributions received by the school, but we end up working without pay for the privilege of being here.

My work schedule was 5 days a week for 3 hours daily as one of the restaurant's waitress and I made my own hours at the flea market to collect rent and keep the books. I reported to Lynn and Jaison, so things worked out fine since I excused myself from working for BS. I didn't mind working. It was what BS had done that bothered me.

However, this year Dad implemented Lynn as manager of the cafeteria to protect the student's interest. After BS started the culinary classes and remodeled the cafeteria into an upscale restaurant, Dad's scholarship students ate in the hectic kitchen area or outside. BS made them eat uneaten food from patron's plates like they were eating from garbage cans. Meanwhile, Brian's rich enrollees ate from a beautiful buffet prepared fresh daily for the restaurant with them dining inside and they paid BS a living large tuition for it all. That situation was an uphill battle with BS until this year. This year as soon as Lynn arrived at camp, she quietly took charge to make things better for Dad's students and BS didn't challenge Lynn. She was quiet and never tried to cause a problem, but she did what she wanted, which in this case was fire BS's chefs, take over the fresh food ordering from BS, ordered all new equipment from BS's restaurant's income meant for the school, and started the school's catering company with Dad's blessings; then, Lynn took all BS's customers. So, all six of the scholarship students from the culinary school quit and worked for the school's catering company managed by Lynn and Bubbles out of the dance school's new large kitchen area, which gave those students a chance to make money from their efforts. JAJA hired three chefs that year, and the large dance school building housed the new Culinary School classes and offered a program for a Culinary Arts degree. Dad's students prepared what they wanted to eat and had a nice air-conditioned Dining area.

Lynn offered exclusive dishes with full service delivery orders with waiters to serve and cleanup for large parties or just dinner. Also, Lynn and Bubbles added a luncheon buffet and had a partially enclosed large garden patio built onto the dance school for the student dining, but allowed a small amount of customers to dine there as well. Soon the rich and businesses ordered from Lynn's and Bubble's catering where the students prepared Breakfast, lunch, and dinner menus daily. So BS's restaurant business declined immediately, and it became very fashionable to have lunch at or catered by, LYNNS.

Jacob came taking me for a walk around the track to get my strength back. Then he became involved in a pickup game in the gym with some other team that challenged our team, but they didn't want to play for money. Any team could play, but with our team being Delano, Jacob, Jaison, Danny, and Wang, no one ever wanted to play for money. It became a social thing with two first-round draft picks playing. I stayed for a while watching, but I went to my room and rested.

BB was at the Bookstore working until 5 pm. and woke me when she came to cook certain dishes at Jaison's request. Our group who lived in the mansions or Beach-side always ate at home and we always had guest. When supplies were low, someone or all of us went out and gig to build the supply kitty pass full so we could restock. We had all we needed keeping food, snacks, wine, beer, liquor in supply, and marijuana, but JAJA had a serious policy concerning drugs. They didn't allow other drugs and dismissed any users of hard drugs.

Almost everyone hung out at our house except BS students, and all from Klondike's group. Klondike continued her foolishness and called on the house phone making threats to all of us. They targeted BB and Lynn with threats feeling the Brothers were treating them special because they were my friends. I think the fight was over where we lived. Dad built the larger mansion over the last few years for his sons, certain guest, and extended family when they stayed. BS told Klondike that he had control of the mansions, and promised to move her and her crew into the one we girls occupied, but it didn't work out that way.

Jaison, Jacob, Delano, and Wang hung out and slept at our house most the time so, BB and I convinced them to let us used their house for charity events and to rent out for private parties that Lynn and Bubbles could cater and generate money for Dad's school. Jaison and Jacobs' production company, JAJA Productions, produced the parties, which served as a way to meet and socialize with professionals and contributors that JAJA Productions worked with to promote their father's interest. It was a very effective tool with everyone in our group contributing, which kept us in the local newspaper's social page and Entertainment Magazines. Also, our group had developed a following of fans on every level from our cross-country track to The Band Camp and those parties kept that momentum going. With entertainment magazines covering many of the parties, the professional arts and entertainment who's who expected invitations to JAJA's events. During the events, portfolios, film, and information were available on our group. Anyone could ask the brothers for help.

Inez, a woman who worked in the laundry asked Jaison for that help launching a line of her families' clothing in the US that her family had manufactured in Brazil for over 50 years. Lynn researched the company to make sure of their business standing whereas their reputation was stellar, and then Jaison arranged the Fashion show and party. Lynn, BB, and I modeled with some of the company's models. It was so cool and educational to be part of that total presentation. Inez family's company received orders that night and that started her supplying stores in the US. Plus, her company received other manufacturing jobs. The deal Jacob made was for JAJA to receive a percent of the annual business signed in the US paid quarterly. There were many deals similar to that, and I was happy seeing Dad receiving the solid financial support due through JAJA Production.

A week went by and I was feeling almost like new. Mrs. Browning fed me daily with milk and cookies at night. I gained 3 lbs. and the gang threw a party. Then that Sunday after practice, I went to see the Flea Market. Jacob helped the janitor there and said there was a little area next to the office he cleaned up for me suggesting I could find something to sell. Jacob was concerned that I would have enough money save when I left the camp. Wang and I went to look. I knew a few people from my old island's resource, but Wang told me he had little cousins who had merchandise in New York. I could get authentic seconds in brand name handbags, shoes, and clothing at crazy prices. That was new, and I wanted to check it out and NYC. The deal was to get the merchandise, open the store, and Wang had two friends in his group that needed money, so we made a schedule for work. The only thing left was to get the merchandise. I didn't want to COD it because I wanted to go to New York to pick it myself and I had the money, but I wasn't sure how to arrange my trip.

Telling Adam I had to go to Rod to get information for TMP, I had Rod to call and cover for me, but he couldn't go with me since he was in training for an upcoming fight. I should have asked Rod to get me a room, but I figured to get Jacob to do it when I told him about my trip.

Jacob came that evening for us to exercise. He seemed upset as he knocked quickly on the doorframe above my head, asking quicker,

"You ready?" With Jacob not greeting me sweetly as normal, I Ignored him figuring someone pissed him off, and he'll be all right soon. Then I'll talk to him, but it didn't happen that way. I wondered if I did something wrong, so I asked and he shook his head no. We exercised in silence. On the way back to the house, Jacob started talking and said,

"So, you're going to visit Rod." I didn't answer because I tried to talk to him and he nixed me all through our practice and seemed upset making me very uncomfortable. Then he asked, "Are you going by yourself?" Realizing that Jacob thought I wanted to see Rod and that upset him, I figured it was time to say something.

"Jacob I wanted you to get me a room in New York and let you know what I'm doing." He stopped walking and asked,

"Are you meeting Rod there?" I said,

"No Jacob. I wouldn't need you to get me a room." I had to smile at him and he grinned at me. Then Jacob shyly asked,

"May I escort you there?" Looking at him and thinking in a trance... I said,

"Yes"

CHAPTER ELEVEN

I Will, I Do

J acob booked a room immediately and left that night very uneasy. Before he left, he asked again and again for me to promise I wasn't tricking him. He even called after checking in at the Hotel. I tried to ensure him I wouldn't do that to him. He made me laugh and feel special, but I wished he believed me. Maybe all the running away made him distrustful of me, so I tolerated it, plus I liked him.

I left early the next morning taking an earlier flight to Newark Airport, and then, the train and a taxi to the room to meet him in New York before 9am instead of 1:30pm as expected. Jacob opened the door quickly. I surprised him, and he kissed me so sweetly my heart felt like it skipped a beat. After the kiss I said,

"Hi." I needed to figure more to say, but his kiss said enough. He stopped to bring my suitcase in the room. I looked around not expecting the beauty of it. The room was full of fresh flowers and done in all white. The bed looked like if you laid on it, you would just float away, but something else I noticed about the bed, there was only one very large bed.

I had second thoughts about being intimate with Jacob since he never said anything about that again. However, I thought about what he said that night about wanting us to be in a nicer place with me feeling better. Well, this was a much nicer place... and I felt better, but things felt awkward. I placed my clothes in the closet and smiled at him again. It seemed like he was waiting for my approval, but I continued to smile as he gave me a little nervous smiled back. Then Jacob walked to me grabbing my waist with that grin he has when he's satisfied.

"I hope you don't mind me sharing your shopping trip Allysa, but my agent said I needed to spiff-up my wardrobe, so I need to shop and figured you know fashion... Will you help me?" Then he pulled out a wad of money that fell in banded bundles on the bed.

"Oh my God!" I said. "Yes Jacob, but put that away. It probably will be stupid to offer you money for the room or even give you half." He said,

"No don't worry about that or anything." We kissed with me thinking we have two days together. After that, I fell on the bed. Jacob laid down beside me while pushing the money out our way confessing,

"I didn't get much sleep." I asked,

"What's wrong?" He mumbled,

"I don't know... its stupid Allysa..." I asked again,

"Jacob... what is it?" He answered,

"I worried about you not coming, and then you getting with Rod instead." I felt a little strange so I let him know,

"Rod was a story for Adam so I could leave and not worry him." I felt I had to confront him wondering, "Jacob, why don't you trust me?"

"Allysa I know your treatment was bad and you have a hard time trusting. Well, I just finished dealing with a treacherous female. I'm sorry Barbie; I need to get use to you." Laying there happy and looking at Jacob not minding at all he called me Barbie I told him,

"Yes, I have a hard time trusting too; however, since I want to trust you, it becomes easy." I tied his money into a bundle with my scarf and gave it to him. I was sure he received my message.

Placing the money in his bag, he showed me a gift-wrapped box.

"I want you to open this later, but since this is a special occasion may I buy you more things like some dresses and shoes to match, handbags, and some other outfits. I window shopped last night, and I saw so many things I would like to see on you." Looking in his eyes appreciating he had been thinking about me, so I said to Jacob,

"Okay, but remember? We're supposed to be shopping for you." He looked at me and I said, "Jacob just let things happen... naturally." He kissed me. This went on for 5 minutes or more. Then he jumped up saying,

"Let's get started. Allysa, I made a dinner reservation in SoHo for this evening and I want to watch a game on TV tonight. Are those plans okay? Do you want to rest now?"

"Yes that's fine and just give me time to shower and freshen up; then, as long as I'm with you I'll be fine."

Before we left, Jacob peeled off some of his money for his wallet and gave me the rest to hold in my pocketbook, whereas I placed most in the hotels safe, but I guessed he's beginning to trust me.

I called Wang's cousins, and procured everything I needed for my store, and finished by 2pm. Buying Lids, shoes, belts, jewelry, and handbags. Wang's cousins took us to another world inside two buildings. Benny and Herman were crazy like Wang and fun to be around. When we picked the merchandise we packed, and I paid; then, Wang's cousins helped us ship the $6,000 worth of excellent quality merchandise to the camp. I spent my money. Jacob tried to tip the cousins, but they would not accept asking for a chance to go to the camp and talked with Jacob for a while; then Jacob and I returned to the hotel room, which seemed more like a spacious one-bedroom apartment with a beautiful view of Manhattan.

As I sat on the couch plotting our next move, Jacob poured us some juice and then came setting beside me.

"Um… do you mind us sleeping in the same bed, Allysa? I really want to show you how I feel and didn't know how to ask before now."

"Like I said Jacob, as long as I'm with you, I'm fine, and I wouldn't want it any other way." After that conversation, the awkwardness disappeared.

We walked around New York absorbed in each other with people noticing Jacob, pointing, or doing double takes, but not approaching us. There were people taking pictures though. I was sure some Paparazzi would be around, so I had readied myself for prying camera lens by changing my look topping it off with a Fedora and huge shades. I felt comfortable, and we had fun hanging out together. Jacob held me one-way or another the whole time with me catching him lovingly staring at me as we strolled and shopped for each other.

This was quite different from our first shopping trip. I realized Jacob had established what he wanted as a basketball player and was stepping into his star potential with endorsements offerings from the sports and music world. He bought me everything he scouted the day before; dresses, jeans, shorts, some smoking high heels I saw in a magazine, and bathing suits along with accessories for both of us; then Jacob had all packages sent to our hotel room except for the Jewelry. I kept that in my pocketbook. Everyone who waited on us was very courteous as we shopped all the way downtown and I realized Jacob would be a special fit because he was so tall. Therefore, I had a little planning to do.

Late evening, we had Italian dinner in little Italy. Then talking, laughing, we enjoyed being together while strolling after dinner. With us attracting more attention Jacob seemed to have something on his mind while he shyly looked at me he said,

"Allysa, you must be tired. Let's get in," he said while stopping a taxi.

By 10pm he had taken his shower and was lounging around in a robe watching his game while I collected cosmetic's I planned to use. Then, Jacob showed me the gift box again from that morning saying,

"I bought these for you last week wanting to see you in them, but I didn't know if I should ask." I questioned,

"Why." He said while hunching he shoulders,

"Allysa... you're a hard person to figure and I wasn't sure if you wanted to be with me."

"Do you still feel that way Jacob?" I asked, and he said,

"No, you came to me. Will you wear one these for me, please?" I smiled taking his gift with me to take my shower and see what he wanted me to wear. They were some sexy Baby-dolls from Veronica Secret. Each one was a see through flyaway top with bikini undies and various other items, like a sexy garter and bra set with stockings he said he wanted me to wear the next day.

While Jacob watched the game, I took my shower and did my girlie thing. Then adorning myself with what Jacob wanted, I topped it off with a beautiful short Kimono, and then I balled up on the couch beside him napping after making sure everything was draping just right so my every breath was inviting. Before the game was over, I felt Jacob fumbling at my Kimono, untying my top, and spreading it open. He waited a while, looking I guess, until I moved a little after he disturbed me. The TV clicked off. Then I felt his muscular arms raising me out my kimono like the act was nothing with him taking me to the bedroom. Laying me across his lap, he kissed me. As I watched him feeling his every move, I thought, well... this is it, but I became confused and started fidgeting with my top.

"Are you nervous Allysa?" Jacob asked with me saying,

"I don't know what to do, Jacob, and you may not... like me sexually."

"Allysa, I'm past that and I like you all right." He said as he looked at me in the nightie, "Yes this looks better on you." I thought about him trying it on and giggled. "What's so funny?"

"Did you try it on?" I asked. He said,

"No, a girl modeled it for me. Now you're a funny lady, huh?" Then I thought about the top being see through and wondered if I could model outfits when people could see my naked body, but then I remembered... he liked it better on me. That fact gave me confidence as he played peek-a-boo with my breast. While rubbing my stomach with his huge hand Jacob said, "Wow you have some serious stomach muscles here."

With him saying things and touching me, he had me mesmerized. The fact I was there with him, and he wanted to make love to me was unbelievable. While we gazed at each other, he said,

"I love the way you look at me, Allysa, and you're always looking at me that way, but now I can kiss you, and love you" ... and then it started as Jacob laid me on the bed and started kissing me. Starting with my lips, he used his tongue sliding down to my thighs; then, he kissed my stomach, my neck, my breast, and my everything. Not in any predictable order. He had me excited from the suspense of where his lips were going to kiss next when he slid his tongue up to my navel and then to my nipple. Jacob was charming me like a snake and had me wiggling from anticipation. He slipped me out my top while his huge, but not so clumsy hands probed my body. While gently stroking my hair and kissing, he sat me on the edge of the bed as he kneeled on the floor between my legs. He kissed my naval while his slanted eyes looked elsewhere as he spread my legs. Breathing heavy, Jacob managed to ask in a whisper,

"What's that?" I answered,

"My naval piercing." He whispered,

"Take it out." I did, then I touched the inside of his thigh with him saying, "NO... not right now. Just let me love you and get things under control." He laid me back on the bed as he gently pulled and then pushed my underwear down until he removed them. Looking he toyed with the General and then fumbled while he removed his briefs. Realizing he was nervous, I relaxed. Slowly he climbed on the bed beside me while looking down at my body with me looking at his. Then Jacob sighed, "You're so beautiful." His body was so on point too. Sexy would describe it better; HOWEVER, this was my first time seeing ALL of his body as he revealed the General at full salute. OH MY GOODNESS! Wait a minute, I thought as I wondered where was all that supposed to go. The General was long, but chubby which made it almost look normal; however, it was huge, and I had no idea. So I moved to the other side of the bed while covering up with a sheet. I was a little self-conscious about my skinny body he thought was so beautiful. Then Jacob asked, "Allysa, is there something wrong?" Timidly I said,

"Well... um... I didn't know you were... that large." We had never explored each other's body beyond feeling while dancing or somehow being close. It didn't feel that big, but I wasn't thinking about his body parts, so I told him, "Jacob, my thoughts were to be with you in every way, but this is my first time, and I didn't know what to expect. This is kind of a shock." I was still looking and trying to figure out how to deal with doing something I had never done before. Confused by the situation that surprised me, I continued in thought while covering up like a little girl.

"Allysa are you afraid of me now? I wouldn't hurt you." Upset with myself feeling I let Jacob down, I didn't answer, but I wasn't giving up. I just tried to figure things out thinking well... he's certainly not a pencil dick.

Jacob looked disappointed and said, "It's ok. Get under the covers Allysa. I won't touch you." As he put his underwear on, I grabbed his arm saying,

"No, wait don't leave. Jacob, I'm not afraid of you. It's just...I didn't figure you were so large. That wasn't my primary thought. My thoughts were to be with you, and I want to in every sense, but I should have explored your body Jacob. Your clothes hid a lot of the General and it's just... I'm not sure if I can satisfy you... sexually."

"You're right I rushed things, and I'm sorry. I'm so eager to be with you, but let's slow things down and take our time to take care of everything. Is that okay?" He questioned.

"Okay." I replied trying to relax. Smiling again, Jacob found some smooth jazz on the rooms little Bose box while saying,

"All I want is for you to want me and not be afraid."

"Jacob I do. I have all these feelings for you, but I don't know how to tell you or express them. I feel comfortable with you. It's just... this is my first time. I want this to be right for you Jacob and be what you expect."

"Okay, okay sweetheart calm down. Trust me... this is already right for me," and he kissed me; then said, "Go ahead... please touch me." So I touched him starting with his muscular arms, his shoulders, and chest. I stroked his muscles while kissing him and he laid back relaxing. I stroked and kissed all the way to his six-pack as I ignored the sheet that had been covering me. Moving the sheet out my way I played with his navel. He became excited right away as the General popped out the top of his briefs to greet me. So I touched it and started my inspection. I was dumbfounded that I was touching Jacob Kapulani like that, but managed to get myself together removing his briefs while looking. The problems I thought I would have because of my AD's abuse, never crossed my mind. Being there with Jacob occupied me totally as he propped up on his elbows to see what was going on.

Dealing with the AD and his son, I couldn't even imagine the General being so large, hard, and desirable. That's what shocked me and for the first time looking at the total Jacob with his sexy body that was so appealing, I couldn't talk and could barely catch my breath. I continued massaging Bing and Bong trying to excite him more. I wasn't sure if what I was doing was normal, but the General continued to transform, confirming Jacob's enjoyment. Then he rose quickly saying,

"Stop!" It was as if his heart was in my hands. I did this so many times before with my AD, and never experience that. My AD had a deformed piece of meat and I could barely keep from throwing up. It was ugly and sometimes I did, but this time I experienced very different feelings like I wanted to do more, but I quickly removed my hands thinking maybe I did something wrong. Jacob read my face and said,

"Wow," with an exhale, "Allysa hold on... for just a minute."

Jacob played with my hands for a while saying,

"Your hands are so soft and warm," then he placed my hand on the General and the throbbing had slowed. I started massaging again, but he grabbed my thigh pulling me toward his body and then Jacob touched me for the first time fingering around looking. I was so excited, I figured he found what he was looking for. Then I felt my body do things I couldn't stop. My nipples were so hard and erect I thought they would blast off and injure him. As I laid there breathing hard, Jacob asked,

"Are you ok?" I nodded yes; then, he continued fingering around looking as my body continued to accommodate him. OMG I laid back from the ecstasy of his fingers with his lips now feverously kissing my breast and loving my nipples. He lost control, but he was still flawless. Yes, the General was still saluting me, but with Jacob touching and stroking me everywhere, I was about to go crazy with this weird energy that had taken over. Then Jacob got to his knees and spreading my legs he lifted me onto his body asking for a lap dance. Never having done that before, I moved to his lap and for the first time I found my favorite position, face to face, with my arms around his neck, my leg straddled and lock behind him moving with the rhythm of the music.

The friction of our bodies together started me kissing stroking and massaging his muscular chest, shoulders, and arms kissing them, loving him. Jacob sat back admiring me being aroused by him; then he grabbed the General and started stirring him around like he was mixing something until it boiled; then, he pulled me closer. The way his arms held me, and with my body feeling him, I wanted more. The next thing I knew he was inside me inching the General into new unexplored territory in a galaxy that use to be far... far... away, but the launch's success was touch and go for a few seconds. It hurt, but as I relaxed, I felt escalation. Plus, to see Jacob being so drop dead handsome enjoying himself, made me perform; then, something happened, and I wondered WHAT WAS THAT? I could no longer control my muscles or feelings. They were performing on their own, but finally, I heard Jacob say,

"Allysa, slow down your hearts racing," and so was his as Jacob embraced my body, laying me on the bed with his body following mine. He cuddled me while gently stroking my breast. "Are you all right?" He asked, and I nodded yes wanting to lay there and enjoy the moment, but he questioned me, "Allysa, are you taking birth control? We didn't use a condom."

Jacob and I had talked about disease, and we made sure we were free of that, but birth control never came up. I knew I had been taking birth control to regulate my period, but he didn't know that and never asked, and I wondered how... WE... didn't wear a condom, but I said nothing. I figured he was just eager for sex with a virgin, but my feelings for him became amplified. HOWEVER, that didn't bother me as much as the blood on the sheets, and I was still bleeding. I ran to the bathroom, and he followed me. Just another thing I didn't expect.

Freaking out, I started crying. I knew it wasn't time for my period. Jacob trying to calm me said,

"Please Allysa don't get upset. Do you feel sick or hurt... there?" Realizing what was going on, I calmed down, and I shook my head no. Then Jacob said, "Sweetheart, most all virgins bleed, and that's all it is, but I want you to remember I have what you saved for your husband, and I will cherish it and love you, Allysa, for the rest of my life," and Jacob kissed me. I stopped crying thinking about what he said. While he turned on the shower, he told me, "Come on Allysa, shower and I'll rub some lotion on you. You'll feel better soon." He held and kissed me while I sat on the toilet. That really wasn't romantic, but Jacob made me feel human and loved.

While I showered, Jacob changed the sheets. Then he came in the bathroom smiling and humming which gave me a feeling I wished to keep for the rest of my life. He asked,

"Are you sore or hurt? And Allysa, please say something."

"No." I said. That little word earned me love this time and not a slap. Then he asked,

"May I shower with you, Allysa, and will you wash my back for me?" I answered,

"Yes Jacob," and he stepped in kissing me. After the kiss, my mind drifted to him as I washed him. His back and butt was so muscular and cute. His legs were like thick tree roots, very muscular. When he turned around, the General wasn't so big.

"The General's cute that way," I teased while noting every inch of him.

"No one ever called the General cute, but he's resting right now. I think he heard you and now he's blushing cause the General likes you." That made me smile. He did that a lot; then, Jacob washed me all over noting every inch. I enjoyed that and hoped I made him feel the same way. We dried each other off moving to the bed and rubbed lotion on each other. He started on my back; then turned me over, and after he finished the front side, he made love to me again, and I bled again. Then we showered and went to sleep naked in each other's arms.

Awakening to a new day in the dawn of me, I felt a confidence I didn't have before. Jacob was up and looking at the fashion magazines for men, I purchased. He came and gave me a kiss, and another, and then another. Even though I had nothing to compare this feeling to, I knew it was something special, and Jacob became special to me. I loved the way he made me feel. I enjoyed waking up to Jacob and looking forward to spending the day with him or thinking about him and wondered why Marlena had taken him for granted or how could she not love him. Then, I wondered if he was taking advantage of me? Well, I wanted him to take full advantage.

"Good morning my love; are you feeling all right and ready to go shopping?" Jacob asked as he peeled the covers back so he could hold me closer. He started kissing me again. Seriously, I felt like I wanted to spend the day locked in the room with just him, but I wanted to have time and the resources to pay special attention to every detail for Jacob, so I said,

"Yes," and reminded him of what we had to do, because he was about to sidetracked both of us with his kisses. So, I retrieved my small notebook from the night sand telling him,

"I made a list of specialty designer shops for big and tall guys, like you." While I smacked his hand, Jacob said,

"Allysa, I am enjoying you too much." He really didn't know. I thought traveling and being part of a group of paid performers was too much to imagine; however, knowing Jacob surpassed any fantasy my imagination could ever put forth, and we started kissing with me stopping him again.

"We need to get ready." I said smiling and feeling better than any day I ever felt in my life. Feeling satisfied, I showered and wore a dress Jacob purchased and couldn't wait to see me in along with his requested present. Then we went for breakfast.

The paparazzi surprised us when we exited, and someone from the hotel must have told them, since they were waiting outside. Also, there were reporters from entertainment and sports magazines shouting stupid questions. Happy I wore super large shades, and satisfied at being with Jacob, I ignored the people and cameras... for a while anyway. We ate breakfast and then left the restaurant quickly catching a taxi.

Determined to get Jacob looking GQ, I figured that wouldn't be hard after I found where to shop for him. The problem was all day long I had to share him. It seemed everyone wanted an autograph and take pictures with most not taking, no for an answer. Paparazzi and a few reporters kept up with us, but one in particular with his cameraman followed us around all day filming or snapping pictures. Other people stopped or stared because of them. I tried to stay away from Jacob and shop while that one reporter or other people occupied him, but Jacob kept up with me shielding me from all when they moved in too close and moving us on when they asked me questions. I kept him from losing his temper twice, and he kept me from popping someone, anyone because there were so many people and girls trying to hit on him, while we tried to shop. It all bothered me. I wanted to give Jacob, just him, all my attention since he had given so much of his to me making me feel special. Even with the other bodilisious girls there wanting his attention, he ignored them. I felt claimed, and didn't mind him claiming me, but the people were too much. Still, we bought so much, most stores closed for crowd control, and then we shopped in peace. We tried to shop in those stores, but I didn't limit what I wanted for him.

Marlena's announcements and now absence caused all the attention from the press and people, since that was the topic. The situation wore me out. Jacob noticed taking me back to the hotel. It was after 5:30pm and shopping took longer with the interference.

I didn't even want to go back out for dinner. Jacob only left to pick up ordered seafood from a nearby restaurant after I went to sleep almost immediately.

I woke in three hours to the food and some roses. Jacob apologized for the days' confusion. I loved him for a minute before I ate dinner wrapped up in his arms while we watched the large flat screen TV. Around 10 pm, he received a call from some friends who wanted him to come out. He told them next time. While he talked with them, I organized our things for the trip home, and then I showered. After a while, I heard Jacob in the bathroom. WOW, he peed for 5 minutes... with echo, but soon he joined me in the shower saying,

"Aah... here's my Barbie Doll," while he put his arms around my waist and pulled me close. We made love in the shower this time with him taking his time engaging in foreplay. We continued loving each other after lotioning.

While I laid in Jacobs arms, BB called me talking a mile a minute.

"Allysa, where are you? Have you seen the thing on Entertainment Watch TV about Jacob?" Before I could answer, she asked more questions. Then BB told me, "Girl..., he's all on EW TV with a new girlfriend, and CBC Sports Network is playing other interviews of him with Marlena, but now, they're reporting he was seen going in a hotel late evening with a new girl and wasn't seen again until morning catching a taxi with her. Is he still talking to you?" I proclaimed,

"BB we're just friends." I felt hesitant not wanting to tell her more and confused why she didn't recognize me, so I asked BB,

"What did the lady look like?" BB said

"She's pretty with dark hair, a little taller than you with more curves. EW TV showed a picture of her modeling and said she's from

Argentina." Confused, I was happy the camera added the weight and someone supplied a picture, but I was with him all day and I didn't see her. I knew it was me, but BB, nor anyone knew who I was or didn't care and that was a good thing. When I hung up, I told Jacob what was going on. We figured it would take the attention off me, so we enjoyed ourselves the rest of the night and arrived back at camp from different directions on different days, and no one knew any different, but it was very hard to hide how our relationship had grown. We agreed to keep busy and away from each other. Figuring to have appeased our curiosity, I didn't expect things to go any further after the trip. Wanting to keep it real, I wouldn't mind doing that with Jacob repeatedly, but something else was going on with Jacob, and I wasn't sure what.

CHAPTER TWELVE

Time 4 Living

My week started at the Flea Market or Bazaar as the rich referenced it that was located down the beach from our house. That whole south west area of the Band camp which included the Dance School, motel, marina, Corner store, Bazaar, and our houses Jaison, Jacob, the JAJA boys, managed. BS never came near there and Adam came only on invitation. The only time we, Beach Side, interacted with the other dorms were only on invitation or not at all. The Asian House, Wang's dorm, came and went at will, but certain people from the Latin house in the crew with our Sound and Lights people were spies for BS. So everyone else had to have clearance. Not my rule, but I liked it.

Wang and his girlfriend, Shuti, helped me get the shop together. Shuti worked there and handled scheduling and just about everything concerning Dad's interest. She wasn't in school or camp. We snuck her in and everywhere because she didn't have a green card just a student travel visa, but spoke English, Spanish, Japanese and Chinese, fluidly and was very intelligent, a true problem solver. She's our personal secretary and takes care of things when we're gone and lives and works out of our fourth bedroom. Shuti was a shadow person like Wang's cousins and ran an import export company over the internet. She works our jobs for us too when we needed time off or she would schedule who's available. Shuti took care of JAJA's business also; helped with Lynn's catering and received a salary for everything. Dad knew about her and approved telling us to keep her in our house since BS checks the Asian house. So, I gave the other venders their new contracts, explained the new policies, and introduced Shuti to them. She's the fifth Sexett and cool with us.

My day started at 5:00 am with exercise, a ten-mile run and sprint. I loved running barefoot in the sand. This was the one thing I tried to do every day rain or shine, but not storms. Somehow, I wanted to run and jump in the Olympics. I always ran and trained by jumping fences from side to side and started running at the age of seven., and I ran around a track next to my AD's house every day to stay out the house and because I felt angry. The track belonged to a small university. The women track team coach saw me and felt I was a talented runner so he asked my AD's permission to train me. They started me competing as an amateur and trained me until I left. It was my first glimmer of hope so I wanted to keep up my training.

I never ran by myself though. Adam, Jacob, Delano, Wang, Danny, with Tony and my friend Cisco both boxers, met daily to run. It was challenging keeping up with those long leg boys, but I did. Jaison would run a few miles, chill and catch us on the way back. BB exercised with me a few times, but she was a bad habit waiting to happen. When it came time to run, she would run... the few feet back to the house.

Mandatory gym was next. We had to work out, sing our backups while on elliptical machines, and could not sound winded. We would lose our spot with the SEXETTS. That was our official name that everyone felt suited us. Then, band for 4 hours and then hours of dancing. Also, I spent time studying, helping Lynn with the catering business, performing at shows with the band, and dancing with Danny at different venues. Finally, I was free, alive and a teenager full of hopeful dreams.

Jacob and I kept very busy. Jacob would call and we talked every night and spend time with me when he could. We were together at the market some days, but tried to keep on the down low because it seemed everything was quiet. That worked until I had to ask Adam to come help me with a vendor problem at the Flea

Market. After we resolved the problem, the vendors talked to Adam about how Jacob was all grown up with a promising future as a Pro basketball player, and a new girlfriend... me. After that Adam and Jacob worked together daily with Adam keeping him busy recording and hired trainers to prep him for professional ball. I rarely saw him to talk, and I missed him. It wasn't a sexual thing since I could spend nights with him. He never asked. When we were together, it was in a group or for walks with us just talking.

I used the time studying sex education. I didn't think I satisfied Jacob. People thought I was hitting my homework hard. This sex thing didn't come that easy. Bubbles was the only one I could talk to, but didn't. I never told BB about us and don't know why. Growing to value her friendship or the sisterhood we had developed, and thinking I wasn't doing things the right way, I didn't want her to be upset with me. Plus, this thing with Jacob had just started which I figured could end at any time when he decided to check out one of the women that called him regularly or one of those who had been slipping him their number. Don't get me wrong there were times during walks on the beach when kisses, his hands, and my thoughts tried to get the better of me, but I wasn't ready for love on the beach with the sand stuck up your ass thing. Maybe when you got into it, it was cool, but I figured to pass on that and keep my feelings and expectations of him controlled.

Our group always had mail call before practice, and I never received mail so when Adam called my name, BB and I knew we received our mail from TMP. Everyone anticipated that mail. I mean the whole band and support crews knew we applied since Adam and Jaison were so adamant about us going to the interviews they took us to meet with TMP both times. Adam went with us as if he was our daddy, asking questions and everything. BB and I were amazed, and then Adam fussed and fussed until I sent in some information that TMP requested.

BB opened her letter up and started celebrating. There was so much excitement for BB. Now I knew things rarely went that well for me, but I was happy she made the cut and cheered for her. When Jacob and Jaison asked me didn't I apply, I hunched my shoulders and said nothing, so they didn't press the issue. During a break, I could see that Adam was on his way to talk and probably to me, and I said,

"Oh shit... and here comes Adam." Then BB asked,

"Allysa, didn't you send back the information TMP requested?" I answered,

"Yeah, but I don't think they want me." Then BB asked,

"Didn't you get a letter from them today?" I nodded yeah, and she said, "Allysa... the guy told us we would receive a letter by July if we're pick. Open your letter sis. We're on our way." By now, everybody was looking at me. Reluctantly I opened it feeling it would be bad news, and I will be embarrassed plus disappointed.

"OH WOW!" I was geeked. They wanted me. Jaison picked me up and flung me around while almost everyone cheered. When Jaison put me down, Jacob grabbed me and gave me a very intense hug. I didn't move away, so he kissed me and Jacob said,

"See, everything worked out," and he kissed me again. I had to look at him after that one, and we became caught up in each other's eyes. When that happened, everyone disappeared, and we forgot ourselves for a moment. Everyone knew Jacob, and I liked each other and just smiled at us, but not Klondike and her cubs. They noticed it and Klondike loudly told her bear cubs',

"Jacob got these young girls all over. Marlena needs to get her pedophile boyfriend under control." Then this guy named Ricardo said,

"Shit... Jacob like them young honey's, and he's going to get that one over there too. She's easy." Then Adam broke up their little chat when he announced we had the rest of the day off to celebrate. I knew Adam heard what they said, but everyone also knew Ricardo wanted to talk to me and was envious that it's not him. Adam was happy and excited for us. That was weird, but we found out his wife was a model until she married him. Afterward she designed formal wear and worked from home as a personal stylist for the rich dressing them for everything from polo matches and formal affairs to clubbing. Adam told us,

"Her work keeps her on her toes and this is great. Adjani always wanted to start Acting and Modeling classes at the camp. Is it all right for me to tell her?" We didn't care. We were excited about TMP or The Total Model Project accepting us as part of the 40 finalist. BB said,

"We might not get on the show, and if we do, we may not win the prize, but we will be on TV, and I'm going to make the best of it because that's what I want to do."

BB had modeled as a toddler until her starting school, and then some when she started band camp. Finish with school for now she wanted to concentrate on building a career modeling. My interested in modeling was as way to take care of myself while in school, but enjoyed the artistry of changing your look, selling a product with that look while using your body to do it. However, I had to find out more about modeling and wasn't sure if I wanted modeling as a career. I thought about that see through outfit still wondering if I could model that type of clothing or if I could take care of myself by modeling. The TMP experience I hoped would help me.

Having no place, I could call home to live was stressing me. I knew Adam invited me to say with his family, but that's Richard's chance, and I didn't want to spoil it for him. Plus, after the comment's that Klondike's cubs made, Adam still felt I was going to get Jacob in trouble by acting too grown, so I received lectures daily concerning Jacob, and Modeling. Adam wanted me to stay at his house, and let Adjani manage me. I liked Adjani and the children, but I didn't want to live under Adam's roof. He tried to push me around and I didn't tolerate that, so it wouldn't be good for his children.

I was curious about Jacob and myself. It was personal and something we shared. I knew I wasn't starting too early to model, but it was too early for a relationship I knew would be sexual. However, the way Jacob made me feel was special. It was weird since guys weren't on my mind at my AD's house. The situation at home stopped that, but I had plans of working on having boyfriends when I left. So having Jacob Kapulani helping me was a dream. However, I couldn't figure why I felt like I did toward Jacob, or explain my developing dependency for the way he made me feel. I found him fun to be with and talk to, but I told him I thought it was too risky to continue to be that close. Our time together made us closer, more familiar with each other and I was sure people noticed it was more than being just friendly. I realized how my feelings for him had grown and needed to keep them in check, but that was getting difficult.

There were weekly basketball games that became a fashionable social event since the basketball worlds most talked about pro prospects, Jacob and Delano, were playing. We used the social media to advertise the games and created a tournament of sorts. This attracted other college players and pro players who watched with some forming teams to participate. The games attracted a crowd from the sports world, occupants of the city, and tourist, but we didn't worry about selling tickets. The games sold out quick, which Shuti booked on the internet. This was just another plan from the drawing board of Jai, BB, and me who everyone calls Triple Team Blunt Force because of our constant money-making schemes... and probably other reasons too.

Lynn and Bubbles sat up concession stands for refreshments, but had a huge tent on the lawn in place for a dining area. The seating was exclusively for dining on different culinary cuisines that the areas rich paid $$$$$ to enjoy and the evening on the lawn watching the event. Adam had a few off-duty police run security and hired referees for the games. Shuti organized the event with entertainment which amazed me to see it all come together with all proceeds going to The Band Camp after expenses. Of course, we took bets secretly, and that was our gang's money.

During one of the week's game one player accidentally scratched Jacob on his back. I was minding my business setting there in a trance because Jacob was on the skins team, and that's what I was looking at... skin... so hard that when he walked straight to me and asked me to check his back it surprised me. I took a few seconds to respond, but when I did, I saw there was a small deep scratch. When I touched his back and that mischievous grin took over his face, I realized then that was all he wanted. Just my touch and he did this in front of everyone. I finished taking care of the scratch by kissing it, and he kissed my hand. OMG. He's so sexy. Caught up in his eyes only for a moment because the guys were whistling for the game to proceed and the females... they were just looking. I was past geeked. We hadn't spent time together for about two weeks and that was a movie together with the gang. So, he had been watching me from a distance all day making sure I knew he wanted to see me.

After the game, Jacob walked me back to the house telling me he liked my outfit. I attired myself in a mini skirt with a halter-top made from a beautiful floral silk scarf. Jacob asked,

"Allysa, you mind coming to my room to put a band aid on the scratch."

"Okay," I said oblivious to Jacob's thoughts. I should have been suspicious when he asked me to come to his room. Jacob showered first, so I sat down and read a magazine while I waited.

When he came out, Jacob just had a towel on that the General was trying to take off. Then he asked me to rub lotion on his back. I did so trying to stay cool, but I guess it was the view and my mind that started my blood boiling. I continued to rub lotion and peeping with the back rub becoming more sensuous as I exhaled. Then Jacob let go of the towel and turned to me. With all his body exposed he pulled me to him which got us on his huge bed making love... and that's where Jaison and Delano found us. In the ecstasy of sexual pleasure, I had laid back with my eyes closed and didn't notice them until Jacob stopped to cover me. I wondered where they came from and how long they were there, but I didn't know how to take the way Jaison looked at me. Very much unlike Delano who seemed to have been getting off. Jaison had a disappointed expression at first, but Jacob became upset with the fact they were there, and told them,

"Man... get the hell out of here and why didn't you knock before coming in my room? I respect you," but Delano said,

"Hey bro we did, but we heard all this... noise." Jaison hadn't said anything yet and looked very serious. I tried not to look at Jai while Jacob retrieved his shorts. Jaison gathered my clothes and threw them on the bed.

"Get dressed," he told me finally saying something. Then Jai pushed Jacob and told him, "Bro you know why we came in, man, you left with Allysa. You have these other women and you're playing her... it's not right." Jaison shook his head telling Delano to leave since he sat down as if he was going to watch. Jaison made them both leave the room with him.

I threw my clothes on fast and thought about going out the window, but we were on the second floor. Then I tried to run out the house fast too with Jaison almost dislocating my shoulder when he grabbed my arm saying,

"We need to talk."

Jaison took me into the library and lectured me forever it seemed, but he became silent abruptly while staring at me like I was a specimen. While staring at the floor, I fidgeted with my hair and clothes as he continued, "Jacob likes you a lot, but..." Jaison stopped again looking at me harder, and then said, "Allysa you're the girl from the magazines who was with Jacob in New York... aren't you?" Reluctant to say anything, I didn't. I peeped up at him. "Allysa... I know you care about him, but your timing's off and Allysa you need to concentrate on other things concerning your well-being. It would be best for you two to at least wait and mature more. Jacob's established. You're not Allysa." He thought for a minute and said, "I don't know what to say." Then he sighed and walked off, but what Jaison said about waiting made sense so, I tried to avoid being alone with Jacob. Then I avoided him. Jacob stayed away, but seemed hurt and we had to talk about us.

"We need each other," Jacob said with me telling him,

"Jacob, what do you need me for, and where do you plan for this to go now?" He didn't respond. I continued, "We both have things to do and I think it will be best if we wait awhile, and just be friends for now." Jacob didn't want that saying,

"Girls on my fathers' island are married at 14, or 15." I thought, WOW, I heard that before, but he upset me. I told Jacob rather sharply,

"I don't live on your father's island. Can't you see I live in this stupid place and I'm an orphan, so I have to take care of myself and I want to be a model not barefoot, and pregnant. I need my body and don't plan to have children until I'm 27 or 30, and we need to be realistic." Jacob seemed disappointed, but said,

"Allysa I understand you want to model and I'm 21. I'm not interested in having children now, but I want you, and it will be hard waiting for you because I need and want you now."

Jacob's comment made me realize how difficult it would be for me to give him up. I realized Jacob occupied my mind totally.

Everything I ran past Jacob in my mind to make sure I felt he would approve. Knowing him inspired me to do and try different things, but what he said bothered me because I didn't think I had anything to offer him but my body. Plus, I didn't want to get involved deeper in what I felt was a summer infatuation for him and make it harder for myself.

Jacob was growing on me, affecting my thoughts, and I loved the way he made me feel, but I needed to stop my thoughts of him and my dependency for his love. So I isolated myself from him and figured that would give Jacob time to realize. After a while, Jacob approached me and said,

"I miss you Ally and promise to be just a friend and won't push a relationship." I accepted that because I felt a need to be his friend.

CHAPTER THIRTEEN

Stupid Is As Stupid Does

The Beach Camp, was in a little town established by the Spanish in the 17th century as a rich deep-water seaport. The area has always catered to the rich and famous with Opera houses, Theaters, and boasts to have more Art Galleries than the entire south. When The Beach Camp came to town, The Annual Show, the Band Camp presented every summer rejuvenated the area with the fame of the Kapulani's, BS, and others that were camp alumni along with the modern flavor of future stars. Tickets sold out months in advance. Professionals knew that fact and pre ordered.

The Annual show the camp presented was a competition to recognize being the best talent that year produced at the Beach Camp and went on for three days with different events. Trophies and a plaque with your name would go on Trophy Lane and displayed forever. That was an honor. Then you became an up and coming talent that the industries' professionals strived to work with. That year there was a great interest in the dance competition and the camp, with many influential people's interest focused on the event.

The Beach Camp Annual Show started, and I was more than ready. BS caused confusion when he gave Anita the credit for my performance in the Introduction Show. Many interested professionals from the entertainment industry felt the performance was exceptional and wanted to know the artist who truly performed. Anita continued to accept credit for my performance, and who danced in The Introduction Show depended on with whom you spoke. BS told interested professionals it was Anita, but Adam gave them my name. Some called the Dance school, and Bubbles told the truth. One interested person, Randall, was very serious about finding out.

Randall was a big name in productions, choreography, dancing, videos you name it. When he started he was an at risk teenager involved in gangs and the thug life; however, he loved to dance. Someone started a program at his local Boy's club where they invited dance groups to dance out their differences. Randall started there street dancing over 20 years ago. He danced his way to the top and stayed there with his award winning productions. He's not dancing anymore, but he choreographs many productions that are ballets, modern jazz, etc. You name it in dance his name was all over it; also, he worked with Dad and the brothers to help at-risk children and knew the family very well.

After Randall saw my performance in The Introduction Show, he hunted me down to the hospital because of the confusion, and was very interested in Danny, Bubbles and me. He spoke with Adam about me because he wanted to know what was going on. So, Adam told him everything about first finding me living in a closet with Richard, and my sickness. Randall came to the hospital, but I was out of it, and he had to leave before we could meet; however, Randall called until he spoke with me the third day and continued to call me every week to talk keeping me grounded. He told Adam he wanted to be one of the judges for the dance students this time along with five others who called. All wanted to see both of us perform and find out who really danced in The Introduction Show.

Jacob had his last competition at the camp for 5 & 6 string bass guitar. BB had voice, Bubbles had choreography, and I had dance.   Bubbles worried about competing against me in the choreography category making our relationship strained. Yeah, and BB knew I had a big mouth and the King with Adam made sure I could sing with voice lessons, but I didn't bother her. We're not bitchy, so we planned not to rain on one another's parade by competing against each other. The three of us talked about it and wanted to make it a win, win, win situation. However, I had to tell Bubbles again I wouldn't be competing in that category, since she didn't understand.

Piano was first for me and you know I came in second to Wang. Both of us knew it, but he asked me to compete since I made him play better. We had fun, and then we found BB who was geeked because she won the voice competition edging out a BS planted professional from Australia. Bubbles won the choreography contest just barely edging out someone Danny said he worked under in Boston who fulfilled BS's criteria, which was payment of a tuition fee and an under the table contribution as a gift. All for BS's pockets then BS allowed those entertainers already established in the business to use the recognition of the show to perk up their careers by taking our spots at The Band Camp. The show was monumental in the entertainment world.

All knew King Kapulani was making a bid to take back control of his program that BS made into a mockery among fellow serious artist, and talent agencies looking for true new talent. Our group wanted to sweep the competition to help in BS's controlling demise, which had gone well so far. All the students King Kapulani selected for our group won in their category. Professionals who came to see checked the judging results of each show and noticed. My competition, dance, was last, and we knew BS would try every trick in his bag for Anita.

BB found Wang and me; then, we peeped in on Jacob and he was doing fine. I had to smile when I saw him. He was so awesome at everything he does; then, to watch him and Jaison on stage together was a sight anyway because they're so ridiculously handsome, and the hall was packed. Yep! That was our JAJA boys.

I couldn't stay until they finished, since it was my turn and I left going to dance, which was the last competition.

The dance competition was the climax of The Annual Show and Art Extravaganza Month for the City. The Band Camp displayed an all-day showcase of talent that took place in the large building that housed the school's administrative offices, practice rooms, 4 stage areas, and Trophy lane, which was a large hall that housed all the previous winners' trophies and awards.

In the dressing rooms backstage at the dance competition, Mrs. Browning and Devon dressed and styled me for the first phase of Danny and my presentation. Devon placed my robe on and I checked to see whom the judges were, and saw all the people who contacted me after The Intro Show were present. Anita was talking to some of them and I notice she had invited two backstage, so when I walked pass, I said,

"Hello." Anita said snobbishly,

"Oh yeah... hi!" Then she walked away and immediately continued her conversation with her guest pulling them away as if she wanted them to ignore me. I wondered what the hell. Then I noticed Bubbles and Danny standing in a corner looking weird. So, I walked over while asking,

"What's up?"

"That bitch is trying to take my position after we got everything in order," Bubbles said.

"Who?" I asked and Bubbles said,

"Anita, with BS's help. You know how Adam and I notified all participating dance couples they were to perform two predestinated styles with the couple dancing as a pair. Next, each would dance separately to guest choreography; then last, would be a selection choreographed and danced by the student dance couple.

At the end of the show, all the couples would perform a production together choreographed by the school's students that we've worked on since being at the camp this year. Mr. Kapulani wanted the performance by each couple to produce a brilliant show of talent and worthy climax of the camp's total show and Art Extravaganza month. But now, at the last minute, BS changed everything to no one will know the music, each couple will dance free style at the same time, and he's just notifying the contestants." I knew that would be utter chaos of BS's designed to make everyone look bad, since he couldn't make Anita look good. We were expecting BS and Anita to do something to cover up their lie. Bubbles said, "Allysa, we know hands down you and Danny are the best dancers." While we talked, Randall came to us and introduced himself. He said,

"I know you're Danny." Then he asked Bubbles, "Didn't I speak to you over the phone?"

"Yes you did." She replied, and Randall asked Bubbles,

"What's going on? Why has things change, and why is Anita telling us about it? She is a student, right? I mean I saw her dancing at the Intro show and she is a fantastic dancer, but why is she taking over?" Pointing at me Bubbles said,

"You saw her, Allysa, dancing. That wasn't Anita." Randall turned to me and while he looked me up and down, he said,

"I wanted to speak to you in person that night. When I arrived today, BS told me Anita was the one dancing at the Intro show."

"No it was me," I said. While he looked at me, Randall said,

"You have a different physique than Anita and a pre ordered tan, but it was hard to tell who was dancing because the person was in costume and blue. Plus, the dancer looked shorter." I smiled at him with Danny laughing. Then Danny said,

"Real youths mature and Allysa has gotten taller." Then Randall asked,

"Well then, what happened to you after the show young lady?" Danny answered again,

"She had a prior injury that she aggravated by dancing that night and Allysa stayed in the hospital 4 days." I think Danny upset Randall because He was answering for me, but Randell let Danny know,

"Yeah, I went to the hospital that night, but didn't see anyone. Mr. Kapulani gave me her digits and I've been talking to her, which sounds like you, Allysa, but I told you I would find the underlying cause of this and I'm not joking. I am!" Randall turned and watched me warming up for a while. Then he said, "I've been told some bad things about you by BS, and I don't care to repeat everything, but just for my records do you mind if I ask you a few things, because I'm confused, but curious. It seems like something else is going on here, and somebody is lying." I nodded OK and walked to him as Randall started his questioning.

"How old are you?"

"That's personal." Bubbles said, which curled his edges a little and he directly questioned me.

"Do you run away a lot?" I answered,

"Yes, when I'm not treated right." Then he asked,

"Do you have a sickness that's drug related?" I looked at Randall in disbelief he talked about my personal business in front of everyone. That somehow seemed unprofessional, so I ignored him walked away and started stretching.

"We need to get ready," Danny said, and walked away with Bubbles and stretched too. Randall seemed upset, confused, and definitely suspicious, but he said,

"Danny, I want to talk to you and the girl who danced the introduction show after you dance because I'm not sure which girl is that person. That girl was smaller. I will be judging and I will keep it real. If you are halfway, Allysa, I'm going to tell you."

"That's what you're supposed to do," I fired back staring down at him. He was shorter than I expected. Danny said while laughing,

"We'll be looking forward to seeing you."

It was time to take the stage for our performance. As he anticipated our competition Danny said,

"Ally, we will own the stage by not holding anything back. You and I know who you are. Let's have some fun and blow them off the stage."

"Ok," I acknowledge with a smile. Danny said,

"Yeah... that's what I want to see; that smile Ally, now let's do this."

Danny and I were modest dancers in class not showing off, but we planned to show off that night. There were three couples dancing. Five couples applied, but two dropped out at the last moment after they heard about BS's rule change. They were serious competitors, but they dropped out because of the foolishness BS had going on. Even though they were BS's students, I saw the importance for King Kapulani to make this stand and change things or BS would destroy this program. No one would take the talent produced by The Band Camp seriously, so Danny and I planned not to let that happen, and dance our ass off.

First, the introductions, next, BS, who was also judging along with Randall, Mrs. Bieul from American Ballet and two others gave us the instructions.

THE THROW AWAY Book One

"This will be free style and you are to start with the music. During your performance, any hesitation or missed step will disqualify you, and you will have to move off the stage. Only the couples completing this task will be judge for the available trophies. You'll be dancing to Supreme Love by David Wells," and I thought to what and who? As the audience murmured questions of confusion, I realized BS's plans design was to trip Danny and me up with one mistake to try to make Anita look good. She probably had been practicing to the song all week since she didn't show for any dance classes; however, Danny and I were determined.

Dancing freestyle was to our advantage. So we planned what to do by whispering to each other. He didn't say we couldn't. If we didn't know the technical terms or what they meant, we wouldn't be successful. If the music was fast, we planned to Coupé jeté en tournant in opposite directions around the perimeter of the stage, catch the music, and when we cross make plans for when we cross again. Next, go around the second time then start. If moderate to slow, we planned to lyrical dance until we catch the music. Once we're dancing together, we planned to play off each other.

Danny and I had dedicated long hours daily dancing together for months in prep for this show. It was also ironic the song BS chose was a strange named song that neither Danny nor I recognized by title, but we recognized the music. It had a fast tempo and a weird beat. So it was difficult getting into the song's rhythm, but Bubbles made it our warm up song and we danced to it every evening. Danny and I achieved our perfection warming up with that song during our daily extra practice in the evenings. Anita wasn't around since the practice wasn't mandatory. See GOD doesn't like ugly souls like BS and Anita.

Our competition was the last judged, and by now, the whole gang was there and watching. We all knew he would try something. So, everyone wanted to see what, but I figured to have fun, so I wasn't nervous, and we rocked it hard. After we started, it was obvious the other couples were in the way. Our first pass was so powerful we took their hearts and saw the first couple dropped out almost immediately. Anita and her partner Ricardo were dancing a little and hesitating a lot. I notice Randall saying something to BS. They both looked pissed.

Danny and I took over the dance starting with barely known Latin steps. Then we took our time modifying them. Halfway through the performance, we performed the moves that made Randall famous. Even though I wasn't dress for that, I made it look good. Of course we did our power jumps and lifts. We could hear and see the gang waving scarves, handkerchiefs, paper, tee-shirts (Delano took his off for the occasion), and whatever they could get above their heads to the beat of the music cheering us. When the song ended, Anita and her partner were watching us too.

Mrs. Bieul came straight to the stage when we finished and talked to us. She wanted us to join her dance company. We weren't interested in that or a contract at the moment, and there was so much excitement going on it was hard to concentrate, but just then, Jacob walked up to the stage all cool like and motioned for me to come there. I did, and he kissed me on my cheek; then gave me the most impressive bouquet of white roses. Each one had a little blemish of red in the middle. I looked at them and kissed him on the cheek, but the more I looked at the roses the more I thought about the night Jacob... well took my virginity for safekeeping. When I looked at him with an arch eyebrow, he grinned.

At that point, BS tried to get order, but no one paid him any mind because everyone knew he was a liar and found out via Bubbles how BS tried to set us up. Plus, what he was doing to her. However, when Randall spoke, everyone gave him their attention.

"Danny and Allysa, I promised both of you I would keep it real, and realistically the two of you are the most fantastic dancers I've ever seen. Your power is enormous." Then Randall addressed the audience stating, "I've never seen such a formal talent expressed this powerful at such a young age. Easily, they won since they were the only dance couple who followed the rules set forth. The other two couples shouldn't have been on the same stage Brian. Danny and Miss Allysa were too knowledgeable, too powerful, and just too perfect. Allysa gave Danny instructions, but never did she lead during the performance. This is the couple I saw dance at the Introduction show." Mrs. Bueil said,

"I agree with Randall. Danny hit all the steps with an accent, but all his moves were masculine, and Randall was right when he said Allysa told him what to do, but she never led. All her moves hip hop to ballet, everything was the true essence of femininity. They are fantastic." Then, she looked at BS shaking her head saying, "Daniel, you are a fantastic dancer and you know that, but until now, few people knew of you. That will change overnight and I hope we can work together, but I must say this Brian, as a professional your actions were deliberate and prejudicial. The originality and execution of Allysa's work that night was just like this performance and merited a great deal of fuss and attention for the discovery of a fresh new talent, and you lied giving the credit to Anita who doesn't have a portion of her talent. Brian, the situation you created at The Band Camp almost turned me off from this resource for fresh new talent, but I knew of Mr. Kapulani's project and had faith in his intentions." All other judges said ditto. Mrs. Bueil who was one of the most respectable voices in dance continued by saying, "I know why everyone calls you BS. You tried to Bull Shit the dance world out of a stunning new talent, which seems to be your legacy... BS. I must inform my constituents of a fresh new talent and this... error, which is you Brian Schulman. Miss Allysa M. Carrington, all in the professional dance world on this planet will know of your deserving talent." Everyone applauded her statement accept for BS. He hadn't said anything. He was turning red and looking stupid because Randall was cussing BS for what he did. After Mrs. Bueil made her statement, she left in a whirlwind taking her entourage of about 25 with her. After that, Randall pretty much ignored BS like everyone else because all knew BS was a liar and recognized him as the scourge that was afflicting The Band Camp.

The two other Judges that Anita was talking to before we danced were looking and pointing at her, whispering to others with all laughing, and shaking their heads. Everyone watched as she disappeared from embarrassment. She didn't have to flee like that, but she made her only scene. Then Randall came on the stage getting everyone's attention announcing,

"I agree with Mrs. Bueil. Brian you are the scourge afflicting this camp and the intended program. It's just like how you afflicted this dance competition, which has always been a 2 hours or more show of spectacular entertainment, but you degraded it for Anita's benefit to be a one-dance show, and not even 10 minutes of entertainment. So, to our audience my apology for the lack of a show, but this is the end of the dance competition. Now we have two trophies to award." Everyone booed BS calling him names and said get rid of him. It took a while, but Randall calmed things down again and continued, "The first trophy is for the winning couple of the dance competition, and that goes to Mr. Daniel Meyers and Miss Allysa M. Carrington." I didn't think there would be a trophy issued and still felt cheated since we didn't get a chance to exhibit our true talent; however, Danny and I would be in the trophy case and on the wall of fame with some fantastic people. The gang and audience stood clapping calling our names. The honor for me was immense. All the students that were the best of the best and made it at his or her art were on the plaques there. Dad, Adam, Jaison and Jacob to name a few and now our group who traveled together to win our spots at The Band Camp will continue together on trophy lane and the wall of fame. Randall called for order; then said,

"Everyone settle down. Next, we have a trophy for the best overall dancer. When I say overall, I mean for their overall knowledge and ability. Their engraved name will go on a plaque and will be on the wall to fame plus this huge trophy will belong to them... and this young lady has paid more than her dues for this trophy and plaque." Randall called my name. I received a standing ovation, but before Randall presented me with the trophy and plaque, BS raced on the stage and acted ugly declaring,

"This is my school, and I will say who will receive..." The applause stopped with everyone surprised by BS's outburst, but Randall cut him off,

"Number one, this is not your school which you have tried to ruin and if you say Anita, your credibility will be totally gone." BS was fuming mad and came on the stage, and he looked at me like he could kill me, but I was happy his dishonesty became apparent. BS was so red and swollen from anger I thought his head would pop open. Well, I was hoping anyway, but his mouth popped open instead with him saying,

"I'm giving everything to Danny because this girl's nothing but a crack head whore, a tramp who is worthless just like her skanky ass mother." Then, he snatched the plaque from me as he pushed me in my chest hard. I stumbled backward with Danny holding me so I wouldn't fall. No one expected that; including me. The brothers and some others tried to get on the stage; however, understanding the inevitable, to keep order Adam ran at heavy security for the Mayor who was present along with every influential person in town as well as the dance world, and they witnessed everything.

Astonished by everything BS said, I tried to absorb some of it, but heard too much. I felt embarrassed for myself and bewildered concerning King Kapulani's program. I tried to move away from BS, but he followed. Randall had to push BS off me since he stood in my face with his alcohol laced bad breath hollering and spitting on me to say,

"This little tramp bitch shouldn't be around respectable people. She's been trying to get in the #2 draft picks pockets by spreading her legs to break up him and his fiancé and she caused this." Randall told him to shut up, but BS just kept spewing. Adam, Delano, and Jaison were holding Jacob. BB who stood in front of Jacob said,

241

"Jacob... stop. All he wants is for you to hit him. Then BS will be the real bitch that's in your pockets." After Jacob looked at her crazy, he understood and calmed down. It took a while. Adam told Jacob to find and comfort me after I calmly retreated and hid in the curtains. Upset, embarrassed, but confused by what BS said and did. So many people saw and heard BS, but I couldn't figure what was going on to make BS say all that. Plus, I lost my flowers. I just cried.

Jacob found me and Randall gradually approached us asking,

"Oh man... Jacob what is going on? Why did BS do and say all that?" Jacob who was trying to comfort me answered,

"He lied about Anita dancing at the Introduction Show and Allysa just showed him up. Plus, BS hates her anyway. He didn't want her here because of her talent and prove what an unknown can do if given a chance. BS wanted us to carry Anita with our group so he could continue to have his control in everything my father does. My father recruited Allysa and had to make a special trip from the island to keep her at the camp so we would have the premier group we formed, but BS has been dragging Allysa through shit trying to chase her away." I buried my head in Jacob's chest as he held me and then he kissed the top of my head while whispering,

"Allysa, everything will be all right, so hush, and stop crying. Don't let him make you sick. Everything will be all right."

"Man, is anything BS saying true?" Randall asked while looking at us curiously. Jacob gave Randall a nasty glance and snapped at him,

"It didn't fuckin happen like that!" There was a little while that Randall let Jacob calm down. "Come to the party later man and I'll tell you what's going on if she wishes." Jacob told Randall then mumbled, "She needs to be left alone." Randall who looked at Jacob guardedly said,

"I would like to talk to your father about this first and then hear Allysa's side. Take care of her, and I'll see you in ½ hour because I don't feel it's safe for her here and this is crazy. What the Hell."

We had an after party going on at the larger Mansion like usual, but I didn't feel like socializing. I wanted to be alone with Jacob, but Jacob wanted to go to the party. I thought about the large audience that paid $150 per ticket for the dance competition. It was a critique, but has always been a yearly production that all wanted to see, and we had planned to give the audience an excellent show. Realistically, all they saw was a stupid freestyle 5-minute dance with BS calling me names plus talking about my mother like a dog; then, he told everyone I was a crack addict, but I was a baby, born addicted. I didn't know my mother, but felt it must be true and now I had to deal with people who probably knew her with me wanting to know the truth, but not this way. I said quickly,

"Jacob, I don't want to go," but he expressed,

"I don't like the accusations BS made concerning you, Allysa, and I want to talk with Randall."   So, after I changed to a party dress, I went with Jacob and the gang.

We found out that Mr. and Mrs. Browning quit along with some of the older band members. Jaison and Randall planned to line them up with jobs. The band members made it clear they couldn't stand to see BS treat Bubbles and I like that, but we realized BS was still breaking up Dad's camp. Jaison was still speaking with the ones who quit, but he also had to deal with complaints from City Hall and people who wanted a refund. Jaison directed the complaints to BS since all present heard him announce the change in the competition.

Randall had spoken with King Kapulani when he showed at the party, and the three of us retreated to Jacob's room. I remember setting there thinking that somehow my family was involved with this school. I knew that BS and Dad, knew who I was. However, with what BS said and the way he treated me, I didn't want him saying anything else, but I wondered why Dad wouldn't tell me. Confused I didn't want to hear more lies. My head ached, and I was too upset to talk. I figured I needed to slow my roll, or I was going to fall out so I took my medicine when Jacob asked,

"Ally, are you all right? Your eyes look weak." Randall said,

"Let's take a moment to slow down. Just breathe, Allysa, don't think. Jacob, get her something cold to drink please. With plenty ice." Jacob looked at me to see if that was what I wanted. I nodded yes. "Take your time because I have a few things to ask the lady in private." Randall told him. Jacob looked at me for approval again, and I nodded yes again. Randall looked back and forth at us while he smiled. Shaking his head Randall assured Jacob, "I'll take good care of her man."

There was silence for a while with Randall looking at me. Then, Randall told me some funny experiences he went through while traveling. It helped a little, but then he said,

"Allysa, the King told me you were born addicted and didn't mess with drugs and I'm sorry this has happened to you. I feel BS slandered you and I think the King needs to do something, but do you have any real relatives you know?" I shook my head no feeling despondent.

Randall waited a while then asked,

"Were the people you lived with abusing you?" My reaction I guess answered the question. My defenses were down and things were chaotic in my mind. All I could feel was my vulnerability with my AD and how BS would take revenge. I told Randall,

"That's why I ran away so much... and I can't go back there. I will die first, but now I'm afraid BS will try and send me home." I couldn't help from crying. Everything seemed so hopeless and I wanted my chance to live. Randall took my hand saying,

"Hush calm down now. I've been concerned for you ever since you went in the hospital. Mr. Kapulani gave me a little history about you prior to the Intro show and asked me to come and check you out. What I saw thrilled me, but I became concerned when I didn't get a chance to meet you in person and wondered what was going on. When BS said it was Anita, I didn't half way believe it. She didn't walk like a person who could dance with that power or look athletic enough to make the jumps you made. Then I watched you walk on the stage and you walked with a confidence. Plus, your legs are the same long shapely legs I saw at the Intro Show. They were just a little longer, and you had a robe on. So I couldn't tell when I first saw you tonight, but when you walked on the stage, I realize then you danced that show before this performance. Plus, you're nothing but one muscle and you have matured. I'm sorry for not believing you," I nodded in acknowledgement; then, he continued," However, when I spoke just now with King Kapulani, he told me all about finding you in an orphanage; then trying to keep up with you. Allysa, I know how it is when life's so hard that you're never a child, plus how easy it would be for you to disappear without someone who cares that have your back. That's why I called you, and every time I called you, I called Mr. Kapulani and BS to let them know I was keeping both eyes on you because someone's lying. I didn't know what was going on, but something was and I didn't want to lose you after you survived that hell. However, I see BS is the problem here. I know he made a damn fool out of himself and lost a lot of credibility among his peers. Why did he do all that?" I hunched my shoulders and shook my head because I didn't know BS's problem, but told Randall,

"He's always like that with me. He's angry with me all the time and I'm doing what I suppose to. I'm being good like you told me Mr. Randall, but nothing works. It's like he knows something I don't. I don't want to run, but he acted so irrational because everyone knows he's a liar. I know he will get my AD involve just to punish me." As I stood up panicking, Randall grabbed my arms and said,

"Slow down. Take it easy. Calm down, Allysa. I know I'm not going to let that happen, and I hear you have most the people here in your corner. So just breathe, relax, and please don't get sick. Jacob will kill me." Randall tried to calm me for about 5 minutes; then he said, "I need to ask you a question that may be none of my business, Allysa... but I have to ask. If you don't want to talk about it, just let me know, please. Allysa, I'm concern about you. I want a business relationship with you and want you to feel the benefits of your ability... Also... as beautiful and mature as you are, I know you're fifteen, young lady." I looked at him wondering the question and he asked, "So, what's the deal with you and Jacob? He's going Pro, right?"

"Yes." I said and Randall continued,

"I can see Jacob's really concerned about you. He's outside the door pacing now. Girl, you must have put something on him. Yeah, I know about dancers, but I've heard BS's take on it and Jacob's view. I would like you to tell me. Are you two intimate?" I wondered for a minute; should I be answering this? I trusted him saying,

"Jacob's my friend, my comfort, and my lover... at times; however, I don't know where we can go with our friendship at this time, but I know by what he does he has feelings for me and I feel the same for him. I'm not familiar with two people being together, but I don't know what I would do without him."

"Allysa, I'm glad you said that. So you don't think he's taking advantage of you?" Randall asked and I explained my view by saying,

"No, I feel Jacob is a very caring person who's going through pressures too, so we comfort each other, and we enjoy being together. We don't sleep together that much, but I feel safe when I'm with him." Randall smiled and seemed satisfied.

"Well, all right young lady I believe you, and I will keep our conversation private like always. Happy I finally met you. You are mature for your years. I'm going out here, and jump in the middle of Brian's mess and run some interference for you because I understand what Brian is trying to do, and I will send Jacob in... And Allysa, I know you're not sure where your friendship with Jacob will go, but stop worrying, and stay with Jacob. I will feel better about your safety. This is crazy, and I'm concern." We exchanged information again with Randall saying, "I'll keep in touch, but call me when you feel like talking to someone out of the loop, and don't walk around by yourself." Thanking and hugging him, I felt Randall was genuine and understood.

Upset at what happened and furious since Brian or BS talked about my mother. I don't mean like in your mother jokes, but like he knew her. It was confusing, and I needed to know why he treated me so bad. I couldn't figure to know what to do and had reduced myself to tears. Jacob walked in sat next to me whispering,

"I have you now Allysa." He situated his arms around me and then stroked my hair. "Come my little princess, I want to take your mind off BS and how foolish he made himself look." I continued to cry and told him,

"I don't feel like partying Jacob." Jacob said,

"What are you so upset about? You showed BS up!" I questioned,

"Are you joking? Jacob BS talked about my mother so bad. It seemed... like he knew her. I want to know what happened to us, and why he talked about her like that. And he treats me the same way. I need to know and I believe your father know what's going on too." By now, I was troubled since I felt people associated with this camp knew my mother, but angry because BS was nothing but a sneaky liar and he was saying derogatory things concerning my mother. No one defended her. Jacob held me saying,

"Whoa Allysa, calm down! This is too much on you. Please, just stop thinking about it. I don't want you to get sick." All his touching and kissing could only calm me a little, but he didn't understand my feelings about my family. He had his all around. I wanted to know about mine, but I understood that Jacob cared about me getting sick. My heart felt a little better since Jacob was with me, and I planned to stay with him like Randall said.

We join our friends at the party with me still not feeling it. Everyone there looked at me like... I don't know what. Jacob had left to speak with Adam when BB came and grabbed my arm asking,

"Sister, are you all right?"

"No." I said, "I think people know who I am, but won't tell me."

"Yeah, that dumb fuck did say something about your mother, but you know what? There's this incredibly handsome guy with you. Give him some attention Sis. He's so concerned about you and that's more than a brotherly love I see. He has girls all over the place, but he's crazy about you, and you never know. Later on... ya never know."

Jacob came back with Adam and I went to Jacob apologizing for being a killjoy, even though, I knew I had the right. Jacob asked me to dance. When he put his arms around me, my whole thought process changed to him and us. This was what I needed and didn't know, but really... it was what I didn't need and did know. It wasn't so much dancing to the slow song as it was being with Jacob in his arms, knowing he feels for me, and how I felt about him gave me comfort. It didn't seem like a summer thing for him.

With my mind racing on thoughts of Jacob I almost forgot what happened, but I started wondering what was happening. Figuring, if this ends after summer, we would move on in the fall. I knew I would never forget him, but if it's more, like BB implied, I would never know if I was too afraid to explore my feelings and thoughts with Jacob. Yeah, that was nifty reasoning with me realizing I had fallen for this man. His arms made me want to become a part of him so I could feel his love all the time. So I buried my head in his chest after I sniffed and caught his scent. I could feel and hear his heart beating as I slid my hands down his back, around his waist and up his chest slowly feeling every loving manly inch. Kissing his chest through his clothes; they were in the way, and I didn't care who saw me. Jacob held me tighter breaking the silence by asking,

"Will you do me a favor?"

"What," I wondered, and he said,

"I would like a sexy picture or two of you in a night gown. I want to put them in my space when I go to the Pros and look at you before and after the game. They'll excite me, and I will play like a Wild Man. I've looked at pictures of you before all my games since knowing you. They... you inspired me. You gave me comfort when I was troubled, courage when I needed it and I wish for more. And I better have stroked that 3 pointer like you told me." Surprised by his comment and wondering how I did all that, I said,

"I don't want to take nude pictures." Knowing the comment didn't fit the moment of inspiration, I didn't want him to get things twisted, but he replied,

"Oh no, I don't want nude pictures for other people to see my ladies naked body." He said while gently rubbing my back. "I want to show off what makes me feel complete. Remember the job you did with Rod. You had on this sexy short nightgown with a long opened robe. The picture and you were so beautiful and I sat there with the attention of everyone except you. It pissed me off more that you wanted nothing to do with me and I wanted that picture and you so bad you can't imagine." Remembering the moment, I said,

"Jacob, you confused me. Plus, you ignored me very well." Jacob said,

"No, I wasn't ignoring you Allysa, and I'm sorry I treated you that way," and he kissed me.

While Jacob and I danced, I noticed some iffy people at the party looking at us and whispering. Jacob noticed me looking. So when the song ended, he looked at me and as our eyes met, I felt a definite need to be alone with him. I guess he felt the same, and he said,

"Allysa get some things together. We're going to get away for two maybe three days. I want to have some alone time with just you and me. Is that all right?"

"Yes," I said and quickly went back to my room to pack running into BB who was sneaking off to be with a friend from New York. She asked me to come and hang out. I lied telling her,

"I'm going to visit Rod and take care of his son while he trains." BB commented,

"Allysa, I don't know. You've been hangin out with Rod a lot... I think you may be taking care of Rod." We laughed, but if she only knew, and I don't know why I didn't tell her.

Jacob borrowed Jaison's SUV and came by to pick me up at the dance school. He helped me in, took my bags, and put them in the back. When he got in, things felt like a dream, but I told Jacob,

"I think Ricardo followed me and he's been spying on us." Jacob looked and saw him in the mirror, but nixed it. I knew Ricardo liked me, but didn't know he wasn't part of Klondike's cubs. With his strange attitude, Ricardo following me or watching Jacob and me, made it seemed like he was spying. Jacob had noticed, and they talked. I figured it was a man thing. Anyway, I was geeking in my soul to be with Jacob and he wanted me, so I tried to accept that I made him feel good. It became easier to talk with him.

"I plan to drive 100 miles down the coast to this little quiet village and I want to spend 3 days and 2 nights at a beach cottage I rented. Are you up for it?" He asked. I fastened my seat belt and smiled at him.

CHAPTER FOURTEEN

Deeper

It was quiet as Jacob drove with us glancing at each other smiling. Jacob was a quiet person, and so was I, but I wanted to talk to him. I knew he was interested in me, so I felt I could get him to talk and picked something simple, I thought.

"Jacob what do you want to accomplish in the next 5 years."

"Allysa, do you want to hear everything?" I nodded yeah. "It may take a while." He responded, and I said,

"Ok, I have more than a while for you." He looked at me and started smiling and talking.

"First, I want to establish my importance and feel confident I have a future with the team that I go to because I don't want to move around from team to team. I want to buy a house where I call home and raise my family." Wondering I asked him,

"Do you have any children?"

"No. I'm going to have them with my wife," he replied knowingly. Then he continued, "After I'm establish, I plan to help Adam and Hu improve the conditions on the Island."

"Tell me about that Jacob. Are you really a prince? I mean do you live in a palace on your fathers Island?" He replied,

"Yes, I am a prince, and no I don't live in the Palace, but I stay there sometimes." I told him,

"I've been around Princes before at my school. They were decadent with people waiting on them and kissing their butts. Your father never acted like that. You and your brothers don't act that way either. It's hard to believe your family is royalty." I said; then he told me,

"Sweetheart, that's because the governments and most of the rich people who make up the world worship money and promote that behavior. We got our asses kicked if we acted like that. My fathers' ancestry dates back to what history calls the first Polynesian Kings who sailed to a large chain of islands many thousands of years ago. Our Klan vowed to be servants of The People on our island. Our government and its people are different. I talked to our village historian to trace where we came from. The historian talked about a world and lands I didn't understand, so he told our history before the move to a large chain of Islands in the Pacific.

"We were sea explores who originated around and settle for a while on the Malay island chain. Our tribe historian said we sailed to North and South America many times for trade. Our clan was tall, big, and considered giants to the native people on the other islands; however, our people grew mighty among themselves, and were not getting along so we split into four Kingdoms.

"Our, The Kapulani Kingdom, were representatives of The People we governed and were peaceful people on our part of the island, but attacked often by the other larger Kingdoms trying to kill our men and take our women and children for slaves because we were the smallest kingdom. So a fighting system developed that became our spirit and way of life. Our people became such fierce warriors, the other kingdoms, hired us to protect them and we became rich from our exploits. However, some centuries later my ancestors noticed our island was part of an active underwater volcano. The Kapulani led 40 families who had one tribal elder for each family, from the island knowing where to go. The other Kings joined with the Kapulani and The People; then, sailed to a large chain of islands in the Pacific. The Kapulani with 26 remaining families settled on a smaller island in that chain and continued our way of life." I said,

"It sounds like all the Kings had planned to move anyway, but how did 14 whole families die?" Jacob continued his story saying,

"Our Historian said they had plan to move, but it was a long and dangerous journey. Each family had their own boat they lived on as we sailed and the sea took many families during storms and other hazards. The boats were small compared to the ocean. However, over time all the kingdoms grew into a mighty nation that inhabited the whole island chain with a King on each island. Then the Europeans' came and stole our land in the 1700's. Spears were no match for treachery, cannons, and guns. We lost many warriors men, women, and children in that battle, but with the help of the European religious people we moved the remaining woman with most of their children and a hand full of wounded men to an Island in the South Pacific that was not much." I asked,

"How many times did you move to get where you are now?" Jacob said,

"Three times and somehow, the Royal family survived through a strong Princess who left their island pregnant with a son who grew to over 7 feet called the Warrior King. He took us to the Island we govern now. My father was the first from our island to get into the pros in the US. He played football for 12 years and married mom whose father owned some of our original land on that Island chain the Europeans stole. My mother wanted me to marry Marlena because she inherited the other part of our land this year when she turned 25. That's how my mother wanted us to get some of the land back in the Kapulani family where it belonged." My mouth was wide open in shock to hear his people's struggles and realized Jacob's mother had placed her personal struggle on Jacob. He had to be struggling within from his own history. That was so deep, I wondered if it was true, but said,

"Wow Jacob, that's deep. I knew your father to be a King, but I had no idea... Were you going to marry Marlena?"

"At a point in time the arrangement satisfied me, but just maybe later. I like to think you can grow to love a person?" I looked at him and said,

"It sounds like there is a, but, in there somewhere." He lovingly said,

"But... I bumped into you." We looked at each other, and I knew what I heard, but I wondered what he meant.

Jacob stopped to get gas. Thinking of him, I watched him move. Jacob was so sexy and different when we were alone. Not quiet or shy, but very sure of himself, what he wanted and how he planned to get things done, but I noticed that we stopped in a bad neighborhood. There were people hanging around the front of the store and one guy looked intoxicated. Some drug activity was going on while Jacob was in the store. I became alarmed for him. He was so tall and nice looking, he was noticeable, and dressed in evening wear driving an Escalade. I thought of how I would feel without Jacob. When he came out the store, one guy asked him something, and then, he came and opened my door. I wondered why and he said,

"Allysa, stop looking so worried and lock the doors when I leave."

"But..." I said wanting him to get in before the doors locked. Jacob pumped the gas and posed with the guys at the store so they could take a selfie and then that was that. Unlocking the doors so he could get in quickly, I began to understand just how important Jacob had become to me. I couldn't imagine my life without him. This was very different from the close feelings I had for Rod. When we were back on the road, I asked,

"Jacob, what did you mean by that but?" He glanced at me saying,

"When I heard about you, and saw your picture, I felt like I had to get to know you. I found out what was going on in your life, and... I didn't feel sorry for you, but I felt you deserved a better chance in life; then I miss-understood what Miss Carrington liked. I took for granted that every woman liked men to give them expensive things and lots of it, but I realized that overcrowded you."

"Jacob, I took what you wanted me to have for your pleasure and the other items to keep me in your father's program." Jacob said,

"The point is I notice you're happiest just being with me. We had fun shopping in New York, and we made love all night. The next day you didn't even look at anything for yourself. You happily picked out items for me that was my taste too. You keep up with me, looking out for me, and you worry about me. The same as I do for you. Allysa you are the strangest fem I ever met." I didn't know how to take that, and asked,

"What do you mean by that?" Jacob quickly responded,

"I didn't mean that in a negative way. You think differently than all the other females I've known, and you're so mature it's hard to believe you're so young, but you give me so much comfort, I feel the strength of it. Being with you, inspires me, giving me confidence elevating my life." I was stunned we felt the same way... and he noticed. Then he said, "That's why I want to establish a relationship with you, Allysa, and hopefully... in some manner be around you for the rest of my time."

We sat quietly for the rest of the trip. I thought about what he said and couldn't imagine him thinking of me that way. He even understood me, which made me feel better, but for the moment, Jacob's thoughts were overwhelming. My soul needed to be with Jacob and I didn't want to think of anything other than how he made me feel. However, his comment started me wondering how deep were the feelings we shared when I noticed Jacob fighting sleep, so I drove the last 20 miles.

Jacob was exhausted, so I deposited him and our belongings inside the cottage that had a floor plan for lovers and started the water running in the huge tub. As Jacob laid on his back across the bed dosing, his body enticed me bulging here and there. Excited I figured to practice some of my sexual studies to awaken him and the General. So in front of him, I undressed down to my lace garter belt, panties, and stockings wondering if I was getting his attention. Then I slipped into a long kimono leaving it open with Jacob peeping. As the tub and his pants filled, I turned off the water. I walked to him and he stood up and rushed trying to jump out his clothes, but I stopped him shaking my head no while placing my finger over his lips. I slowly removed his shirt and undershirt first, to get to his muscular chest and arms stroking them while he watched everything... quietly. I opened his belt unzipping his slacks to give the General more room and pulled his slacks down; then underwear and sat him back on the bed. As he sat manly with his legs open, I kneeled removing his shoes, socks, slacks, and underwear. Moving away intentionally, I replenish the tub with hot water by letting the water run slow. Jacob raised to his elbows as I hung up his suit. He watched as I removed my garter, panties, and then stockings. I walked back to him letting my kimono slip away. I kneeled between his legs spreading them wider; then, I teased him with just my hot breath to find most of his trigger points for arousal. That was educationally necessary. Then I crawled up between his legs and slid on top of the General, while bending down to kiss his lips and whispered,

"Lay back and close your eyes." I felt the General throbbing, so I stopped. When things slowed, I slid back and forth. After a while, Jacob looked at me noticing my arousal, and he grabbed my hips moving me to his delight. Soon Jacob closed his eyes and moaned. Then the General shot off his gun and it was time for our bath.

I washed and loved him playing submarine until a torpedo almost got me. Then we relaxed in the tub for a while. Realizing my sex education, I continued enjoying my time with Jacob. When he stirred, I asked him,

"Do you want to take your pictures tonight?" He grabbed me saying,

"No, I'm enjoying this too much." He held me wondering, "Are you feeling better?"

"Yes Jacob. I love being alone with you." We kissed, and I let him rest more while I continued to entice him, by licking his nipples, kissing his lips, neck, shoulders, chest, and stroking the General until Jacob's excitement got the best of him and he took over... sexing me wearing the general out. We moved from the tub to the bed, and I continued to entice him as we rubbed each other with lotion. With Jacob dosing off, I continued to explore, but playing with his hair and looking at the way it framed his facial features. I could still see the baby in his cute boyish face with such a muscular body. His everything was perfect.

Thinking of life before, I never thought I could have an intimate relationship with anyone after my AD's abuse. I've always had problems knowing what to say or do around guys and never desired to explore a guy's body before. Rod and I slept in the same bed sometimes, which felt good, but it wasn't sexual, and liking girls wasn't the issue or confusion. Until meeting Jacob, I thought sex was a bad thing that people did to other people when they wanted to punish or control them. I didn't know sex was a pleasure enjoyed when you're with that special person and you share a desire to be closer. It's also mental and not all physical. I wondered why I never felt this way before and I really liked Rod, but I never thought about exploring his body and probably would have freaked if Rod approached me in a sexual way. Then I wondered why I was so totally attracted to Jacob and not Jaison. It was interesting that I love Jai with all my heart, but I felt so different about them. I wanted Jacob to touch me and feel his body next to mine all the time.

Thinking about everything; my feelings for Jacob, what Jacob said and figured I had to slow this roll. Our feelings were getting deeper and I couldn't be in love. Then pregnancy crossed my mind. I couldn't do what I had to do with a baby and figured Jacob would probably leave the child and me alone because we both were young and needed to mature.

Suddenly, I thought about the responsibility hidden in the pleasure of screwing, having sex, or making love, etc. With the many names for the act, I didn't believe men worried about the responsibility because the pregnancy would affect the woman's body and bend it out of shape and he wouldn't have to carry another human in him for 9 months. It would be in me, and then… it would have to come out. On that thought, I went and sat on the couch in the other room. I wanted to leave thinking I shouldn't have come with him. It was 5:45am almost light, so I stopped my panicking and went for a run. I had some thinking to do.

I ran on the beach for miles and felt trapped by my own feelings that led to my desires. The running helped me to feel free when thoughts crowded me, but before I noticed, it was almost 8:00am. I felt a little better figuring we needed to talk. However, when I arrived back after 9:00, Jacob was standing in front of the cottage upset.

"Why you leave like that?" He asked with his voice elevated. He frightened me because he was angry.

"I… I just went out to exercise Jacob." He hollered,

"For three hours? I've been looking for you since 6 o'clock. You could have left me a note if you didn't want to wake me, and why didn't you take your phone?" While I stood there in shock, he threw up his hands saying, "I can't deal with this. I don't know if I did something, and you ran away or you got sick and fell out somewhere. You're about 103lbs soak and wet. Someone could have hurt you and I can't get the police involved." His actions scared me and I moved away from him, but Jacob grabbed me, and asked, "Why did you leave and do that? You don't exercise by yourself or go away alone in a strange place for 3 hours. What is wrong with you?" He continued to holler while I pulled away from him almost in tears with my heart in my throat.

"I'm sorry," I managed to say while going inside and nervously packed. "Please take me back to the camp." Jacob frightened me so bad; then, ignored my request. He changed to his swimsuit and said,

"Allysa, I told my brothers I wouldn't let anything happen to you. That's why they let you come with me, but you... I don't know what to think about you," and he waved his hands at me and walked off! Terrified and upset, I told him,

"I'm going back to the camp if I can find a way."

I was so upset I couldn't think straight. Then he left me, and I sat there not knowing how to feel after finding out the only bus traveling up the coast left at 7am. After a while, I showered and dressed crying all day jumping at every noise. At 3:00pm I went looking for him. I was so worried and scared I started getting sick. I tried to rent a water thing, but I didn't know how to operate it. When I told the attendant my concern, the man closed his shop and went out to look for Jacob. The man came back and pointed to Jacob letting me know he was fine. I thanked and paid him for his time, and then went back to the cottage took off my bathing suit, changed into my dress, and waited on the porch. In about an hour Jacob came and went into the cottage without saying a word. I felt sick, so I balled up on the couch while he showered and dressed.

"You want to come and get something to eat?" He asked coolly, but by now so much emotional junk was flowing through my head, I felt sick so I shook my head no, and then asked softly,

"Please take me back to the camp."

"When I get back," he said and left. Meanwhile I cried because I was unsure about how he really felt about me, and I didn't want to be alone. I had more than developed feelings for him and it hurt.

Receiving one call from BB, and two from Jaison, I didn't answer BB, and I wished I could talk to her. BB always straightens me out without trying or sometimes not knowing what's wrong. She's an honest person and knew Jacob, and I liked each other, but I hadn't told her about us because I wasn't sure if I was correct in my endeavor with him since I realized Jacob doesn't trust me or believed what I say. I didn't know why, but I knew trust is very much a part of love and he trusted me like he did with Marlena. He left me alone all day not wanting to be around me. I cried and cried.

The first time Jaison called, I answered.

"How are you feeling?" He asked.

"OK" I said, and we hung up. Jaison called back 10 minutes later. I didn't answer, but I thought I should have. Jacob left me in this strange place alone, and I knew Jacob was mad with me. I figured he's probably enjoying himself with someone else. An hour later, I called Jaison.

"What's going on with you two?" He asked like a big brother. "Jacob called me earlier wanting me to check on you. He didn't think you would answer his call. Are you all right?"

"No," I told him crying. "Jaison, I'm afraid, alone, and I want to come back to the camp." Jaison told me,

"Calm down Allysa." Then asked, "What's the problem?" I told him,

"Jacob frightened me and then he left me alone."

"Ally, you left without telling him." Jaison said.

"I didn't know I had to check in and out with him Jaison, and why do I?" I asked getting angry.

"This man worries about you. He wants to take care of you, and be with you every minute," and then he asked, "Why are you afraid?"

"He's angry with me. I don't know what I did wrong, and he raised his voice at me all because I went out to run? That's something I do every day. He so big and I know he has a bad temper, but what gives him the right to holler or touch me negatively?" With alarm in his voice Jai asked,

"What did he do to you Allysa?" I answered,

"Grabbed and shook me like he was out his mind. I got away, but... I'm not playing that anymore." Jai said,

"You're right Ally; that's not right. So... do you still want to come back?"

"Yes." I whimpered with him saying,

"You two should learn to talk over your problems and Jacob has calmed down, but he wasn't mad at you just... overly concerned; plus, he has my vehicle, you know. He wants to bring you back to the camp like you asked, so is it all right to send him to you? I mean... Allysa, don't hurt my little brother. People make mistakes. I'm sending him to you now, okay?"

"He rented the place so why ask me." I told him and hung up. Really, Jacob hurt my feelings more than he angered me and I couldn't believe Jaison thought I would hurt Jacob... like I could, but in about 5 minutes, Jacob showed up. He said hi, and I nodded back keeping my distance.

"Did you eat?" He asked. Nodding no I apologized for upsetting him.

"Jacob, I'm not use to people being that concerned about me, and I didn't think." I said and was afraid to say what was on my mind.

"Come and set by me Allysa." Jacob asked. I didn't move and just looked. I wasn't sure what to do. When he came to me, I stood up and moved away. "Allysa are you afraid of me now?" I said,

"I want to go back to the camp. You left me alone like you did Marlena that day on the beach. I don't feel you want to be with me, and I don't want to be here... with you."

"Ally please forgive me," he pled, "I didn't mean to frighten you or make you feel bad. I left because I... I became too overbearing and didn't know how to correct it." He went and started packing up his stuff. Jacob had his belongings everywhere like he planned to stay, therefore I said,

"Jacob you rented the cottage and I don't want to disturb you, I'll catch the bus in the morning and stay in here tonight... please. I'll get out your way soon and you can enjoy your time... with someone else." He looked at me then sat with his head in his hands. "I'm setting on the porch." I hollered to him, and I sat there thinking about what happened.

After about a half hour, I heard this bumping. I moved around trying to figure what it was when I realized it was Jacob knocking.

"Come in... out." I said as I stood keeping some distance and the pole between us with an escape route behind.

"May I speak with you, Allysa?"

"We're talking." I answered feeling leery.

"It's 10pm now and I know you haven't eaten, and I know something upset you this morning before you left." He walked out to the truck while I stood and watched from the corner of the porch. As he walked, I looked at how huge and intimidating he looked. This guy looks like a much taller Tarzan, and when he's upset, he walks around like a manly animal on the prowl with his handsome face still handsome, but looking like an angry Genghis Khan. However, he wasn't like that now. He had a very distressed look on his boyish face, but also a look of hope, which made me want to hope with him, and now his walk, was his normal sexy saunter that made me feel like going to him.

Jacob opened the passenger door and retrieved a bouquet of blue roses. They were so pretty and a little wilted as if he rode around with them a while. I rushed to him, took the roses, and went in the house to get them in some water. He came in and stood by the door saying,

"I'm sorry. I didn't mean to frighten or confuse you Allysa, but I'm not going to sleep in the bed or stay in the cottage without you feeling comfortable. There's no one else I want to enjoy my time with except you. I wanted to take you away from the problems at the camp, but now you rather be there then stay with me. So, I'll take you back now and I'm sorry for getting so upset this morning." I turned and looked at him and shyly said,

"Jacob, people that usually holler and scream at me, hit me, beat me... or hurt me in some way." Moving a little closer Jacob said,

"I would never hurt you like those people have Allysa, and I talked to Adam all week because... I wanted to spend some time with you. Adam needed to understand what I feel for you and my intentions. I don't want to sneak around to see and be with you, but he's acting like he's your Daddy, so I talked to him and our big brother. When you took those pills, we became concerned. Adam and Adjani want you to leave the beach camp. They feel given the situation with BS and those other people, they want you to finish growing up at their house. I think you could because with so many people seeing you, people in dance want you to work with them now. You came out of nowhere like a storm and blew them down with the surprise of this new unknown talent. So, you're known and with Randall working with us who's crazy about your talent, that's all you need."

"I want to help Dad's Program get rid of BS and the mess he's doing with the school. People see what he's doing now with Dad's talent sweeping the competition. No, I'm staying!" I said sternly. Then Jacob quickly said,

"Look, Adam let me take you and suggested I should talk to you about going to live at his house with Rich, but forget about that. I don't want you to leave because I feel you will do just what you said. I agreed to talk to you about it so we could get away, and I picked this place since this town is a small retirement community. There are no paparazzi or people asking for autographs. They look at me as some tall handsome dude." I sort of smile at his humor. He came closer. "I only want to be with you Allysa. I can't eat knowing you don't feel right, and I should have talked to you calm and not worry or leave you in this strange place by yourself. Please forgive me. I was upset with myself for failing you last night and not giving you the attention you expected. If I had, this wouldn't have happened." Thoughts were cluttering my mind all at once too. However, I said,

"What are you talking about?" He replied,

"You tried to love me and I was so tired and couldn't give you the attention you wanted." I said,

"That's not what upset me." Jacob asked,

"Can we finish talking about this over dinner?" I nodded yes. He warmed up the food he had in a large bag so I prepared the table. "Allysa, do you feel a little better about staying here with me?"

"Maybe." I said while looking at him knowing I needed to say more, but I wasn't sure what. I figured it was best to be honest. "Jacob, I understand why you were upset, but you were a little too adamant to be upset with me. I don't want you upset at all; however, you don't have the right to touch me negatively, holler at me or dictate what I do, and I will tell you where I'm going if I feel like it. No one will ever control me again. You need to understand that I control myself, Jacob, and you don't know what a person will do from fear. Never do that again." It was his turn to stare, but Jacob said,

"Yes, Miss Carrington; however, I'm serious about you feeling and being safe." I told him,

"Yeah, so am I."

While he ate, I just drank some tea watching him and thought about how protective he was with me in New York. Really, he was like that everywhere we went. I also noticed that even though he stays busy while we're at camp I see him watching me. He positions himself at certain places he knows I'll be at or walking by, and I see him, but just then, I thought of Adam's reaction to the BS situation. I questioned,

"Jacob, did Adam ever tell you it was all right for me to come with you?" He answered,

"No, not when I asked, but after BS upset you so much he told me to take you away from The camp for the two or three days. I had to go through a lecture about being careful with you, and the first thing that happens... you run away."

"I did not run away or I would be gone now," I said very pissed, but he told me,

"Okay... okay, calm down, Allysa. Everyone cares about you so much, and we just don't know what to do because people have treated you bad for no reason. Yeah, I heard BS, and he made a comment about your mother I plan to talk with my father about. Allysa, I don't want to upset you again, but I believe something else is going on too. So much is happening, and it's hard to understand why. I'm concern for you Ally and I need to keep up with you 24/7." He slowly walked to me. Thinking of what Jacob just said reminded me of what Randall told me to do and why. I didn't move, and he timidly took me by my hand and led me to the couch. "Please relax with me like before, Allysa. I'll never raise my voice at you again," and he hugged me, holding me while stroking my hair whispering, "I'm so sorry. Relax now, please. I love you, Allysa. Please trust me again." I kissed him. I thought what am I doing? That was so impulsive. "Is that a yes?" I smiled at him and said,

"Really Jacob, I don't know what that was."

Like always, Jacob took my mind off all my problems, thoughts, stupid things that shouldn't be anyway. We had sat in silence when I said,

"Thank you for the roses Jacob. They're so beautiful. I never saw blue roses before." Excitedly he sat up and said,

"Allysa there is a beautiful garden with all types of flowers and plants, and they take you on air boats to see Alligators. I want to take you there tomorrow." While he talked and talked, he was so excited telling me about what he wanted to show me, and what he wanted us to do together. Really, I still planned to catch the bus in the morning. However, I tried to reason we both were wrong, and we were finding out more about each other. I felt compelled to try and understand Jacob.

Dinner was over and while Jacob and I moved around finishing our clean up, I noticed he left his stuff all around like pieces fall off as he comes in from where ever. So, I made him pick up his pieces, everywhere. Then I asked,

"Jacob, do you still want me to take the pictures?"

"Yes, if you don't mind me having them," he answered, and I said,

"I'm happy and honored that I inspire you. Yes, I'll take them as long as they're not nude," but Jacob said,

"I want to set and talk for a while, Allysa, if you don't mind." He came out the bedroom gathered me and sat us on the couch and continued, "I'm sorry for being so tired last night, but I loved the way you took care of me.   Yeah... I enjoyed that, but did you enjoy yourself Allysa?"

"Yes. Very much so," I said. Then Jacob asked,

"So why did you stop and go set on the couch?" I didn't know how to tell him, but said,

"It was nothing... just thinking."

"I have to ask, Allysa, do you still want to go back?" I shook my head and said,

"No... I don't want to..." He said,

"It sounds like a, but, is in there somewhere. Feel free to tell me what's on your mind."

"I'll see how I feel in the morning, and if I leave, I'll catch the bus since you could have done that when I asked, or talked to me rationally, but you left me alone in a strange place. I'm not fuckin Marlena," I said getting upset again. Walking away I said, "You need more time to learn to respect me. Look, I'm not going to make you, but let's get these pictures out the way if you want them because I promised you that, and don't post them on the internet." I took the box and tried to sneak a peek at what he wanted me to model, but he took the box as if he didn't want me to take the pictures.

"Allysa, I respect you." Then, he came while looking at me saying, "No, I won't do that these are for me only. Please honor me, Allysa, by taking them. They're only for me." He said that while moving closer enclosing me in his arms with his hot breath stopping just short of meeting mine; then, he presented the box again. I took it and slowly rushed into the bathroom anxious to examine the outfits.

I showered and dressed in the first outfit while noticing he also gave me a naval ring with a thin but heavy gold waist chain. The sexy outfits showed just enough to leave the rest for... I guess your imagination, but I felt so uncomfortable around him again. I was nervous and started fidgeting. While I worried Jacob came kissed me and grabbed my hands, saying,

"You look just like I want you to... sexy." Well... that helped.

Each time I changed my outfit I change my hairstyle and makeup to create different looks. Jacob liked that saying, "That's another reason I love you because you amaze me how you look beautifully different each time I see you. Sometimes I am waiting to catch a glimpse of you, and then I see this hot female walking my way. Wondering who it is because I never saw her before, I feel I must meet her; then, she walks directly to me smiling and I find out it's you." He started kissing me and I had to remind him about the pictures, so we took the pictures and I hit poses to the music until I changed into the last outfit. I had to say,

"Jacob, this outfit is too revealing. I don't want to take pictures in this one." He responded saying,

"This is only for me... now. Please, come out." Leery, I peeped out saying,

"Please don't take any pictures." He promised, so I came out peeping with my robe on; the cameras were gone. Soft jazz played with lit aroma candles and Jacob in bed waiting. With his hand reaching for me Jacob asked,

"Are you too upset to sleep with me, Allysa?" I wanted to run and jump in his arms, but with him leaving me alone, the pregnancy issue came to mind, so slowly I walked to the bed and sat on the edge saying,

"I do have some concerns about what we're doing." He sat up and moved toward me enclosing me in a little valley with him as my rap around mountain range.

"What are your concerns Allysa?" I felt the vibration of him speaking in his deep sexy voice, and with the heat of his breath on the side of my face and neck, I could barely tell him,

"I'm trying to make adjustments to you being in my life. You are important to me, but Jacob I know what we're doing has some liabilities that can become a responsibility you can just leave... like you did me today." He surprised me by saying,

"Yeah, I want to announce and be with you now, but people place such a stigma on stupid shit that's none of their business. Reporters and People are calling me a cradle robber because I gave up a mature female. So I feel strange most times and I'm trying to deal with that." I was shock and said,

"I don't understand... what you mean?"

"The reporters say you are a 16-year-old model from Argentina."

"Jacob, stop worrying about that since I'm not that person or a child. I'm a young lady, and I want to mature mentally, spiritually... sexually with you. I wanted my first love making experience to be with you since I believe you're here for that purpose."

"Really, and what purpose is that?" He asked, and I said,

"To help me understand love Jacob; I feel like I want to be with you romantically always, but I want to continue to be your friend even if the romance is not there. I realized today how quick things could go crazy because of misunderstandings, and the absence of respect. So we must be careful to understand the other's feelings and take care of them. And... I believe I love you too, but we're so young. We must do this the right way so not to destroy this special... situation we have growing." He reached out for me and I noticed he was grinning and naked while he pulled me to him and held me saying,

"There is something very different about this... affair we're having Ally. I don't want to call it a relationship, but I experienced nothing like this before. I mean the way we share our feelings. The only thing I could share... no that's not right, I shared nothing with those other girls. After sexing them once, I felt nothing. I just gave those girls gifts and money because I thought life was that way. It felt like the sex was just a service by them so they could continue getting. That's all they wanted and bragging rights, but you, little Miss I'm not a child, demands more. You need and want me more. You want just me and not for sex and definitely not for money like the other girls. I can look at or talk to you, and get a greater thrill than I ever had with them, because you only want me to love you, and I love that fact about you Allysa." He looked at me while pulling me closer, whispering, "Yes, there's something special about this... and you." He kissed me, and then he took his big hand and palmed my butt. "I have you now and I'm not going to let you go," he said jokingly, but then seriously he continued, "No, I don't want to control you. I just want you to love me... and I feel your expressions of love... just like you feel me." Then he peeled me out my nightie kissing in places and in a way, he never kissed me before. And Oh... My... Goodness.

After he cut the craving, we talked about things. Thoughts of him were still flowing through me while we laid there admiring each other's body, and then I asked him,

"Jacob, why did you think I would run away from you?" He answered,

"I didn't, I was just trying to figure what happen. You went off in thought. Then you woke me going to the couch upset. I dosed off and when I looked for you again, I couldn't find you." He looked at me strange then asked, "What's wrong Allysa? What were you thinking about?" I said while moving away,

"Jacob I know what you said about finding it hard to trust because of Marlena; however, even though you say I'm not like those other girls, you don't trust me, plus I'm wondering what happens... if I get pregnant? Would you leave me alone... in a strange situation and act as you did earlier today?" Jacob froze in thought and I continued, "Jacob, if you couldn't deal with the fact I freely came here with you and didn't run away, I doubt if you would give me consideration dealing with a pregnancy, you didn't want." He moved closer touching me saying with a funny expression,

"I don't want to ask, but... do we have that problem?"

"No, I'm not," I said; "However, there's a liability behind having sex. I take birth control, but you never put anything on, and like you said it would be a problem." Jacob explained,

"Allysa I love going bare back with you. Feeling your love is important and I would love having a child with you, but not now. If it happens though... I would love and take care of both of you." He put his arms around me and continue, "I only want to be with you and wish Marlena's mess wasn't confusing things. I would announce our engagement." He was quiet for a while; then he said, "A baby? I like that. Maybe in five years let's have a baby," he said proudly as he pulled me close kissing my neck. Noticing he seemed to be happy with the thought. That felt good, but it didn't solve my doubt or the problem and I said,

"Wait, let's stay focus in the now time zone."

"I am," he said, and we started loving again, but I gave Jacob a rubber to wear that he snatched off while he made love. He finally went to sleep around 3:30 while I thought about the baby coming out part.

We both exercised that morning and managed to keep an eye on each other, but showered separately to save time. I found it easier not to undress or dress in front of him too. We lose track of time, but we managed to stay on schedule with Jacob's plan of going to the Alligator farm and gardens, but I was so tired and napped when I could. I didn't want to miss any of my adventure with him, plus the plants and flowers were breath taking.

Surprised to see Jacob writing the names of the flowers and plants we both liked, he also took plenty pictures of me with them, and we shared the same likes and dislikes that even reached into plant life.

After the gardens, we went out looking for Alligators on an Air Boat. The boat was hyper, but a little too close to the water for me, because we found a few. Then we watched some fool wrestle one. That was funny. The poor little Alligator almost won.

We left the cottage going to the beach and stopped to eat; then, walked around checking out things with no one staring or stopping us. Jacob held my hand or me, stopping to apologize. Then he asked,

"Allysa do you believe that I'm sorry?" I hunched my shoulders and said,

"... Yeah Jacob, it's okay." Jacob stopped walking kissing me intimately apologizing again for the previous day. Then he said,

"Allysa I want you to believe me, but you don't." I told him, "I want to, but what you did hurt, and we had a setback. Time and situations will allow me to believe again or not... and I appreciate you apologizing, but I don't want a man that have to say I'm sorry all the time either."

I wanted to try a margarita, so we shared a super-sized one while walking on the beach. It was hot and muggy, and Jacob took his shirt off he was wearing with his cargo shorts. Sometimes Jacob didn't wear under clothes. So he was showing enough skin to let all know that only the General and his cute butt was holding his shorts up and had every female we passed enjoying his body and swagger including me. I noticed his tribal tattoos and asked,

"Do your tattoos have a tribal meaning?"

"The one on my neck means I'm of Royal blood and the one on my shoulder and upper arm is my warrior's tattoo that will grow with my accomplishments," he explained. Then after walking around a bit with that strong margarita, Jacob talked me into getting a little tattoo. I decided to placed it on my upper right butt cheek. Jacob directed the guy by drawing the tattoo first which impressed the tattoo artist. Then the guy transferred it to me under Jacob's observant eye, however, Jacob, didn't like the way the man was touching my butt, and told him a few times. I kissed Jacob to calm him, so Jacob asked this lady tattoo artist to tattoo me. Jacob really shouldn't drink. He was acting up and told me,

"This will help you with modeling. If anyone can see this tattoo, you have gone too far. Put some damn clothes on." Anyway, it wasn't like I had my bare butt in someone's face. She tattooed it on my upper right butt cheek, so I only had to pull the top of my skirt down. Jacob asked for his artwork back and paid her. Then she let Jacob know,

"By the way, I'm gay!" I didn't know if that should have been funny, but the look on Jacob's face made me laugh.

Personally, I didn't want the tattoo in a place that looked like I was demonstrating my freedom. If I got a tattoo, I wanted it to have a meaning, but I didn't know how tattoos on models worked. So, the fact that I would almost have to be naked in order for someone to see it was good. Looking at it in the mirror, I thought the small tribal circle was a strange tattoo to have. I had thoughts about it, but didn't say anything since I had a freehand drawing by Jacob Kapulani tattooed on my body.

Planning to stop at this club before we went back to the cottage, my butt was sore, but I figured I could shake it. So, we strolled there. While walking we figured to spend another day and party tonight at this club that was so crowded, the entire county's young adult population had to be partying there. They knew who

Jacob was, but they were more interested in parting and having fun with us. That's just what we did and had an enjoyable time. The management never checked our ID's, so we drank just a little more. We walked back to our cottage at 2:00am feeling satisfied.

At the cottage, Jacob took a shower while I gathered my stuff together and went to sleep. Jacob was much louder than usual and needed a nap, but he turned over reminding me to take care of my tattoo. I showered and went to bed to find Jacob asleep. I woke him, and he wrapped his arms around me holding me all night.

We planned just to relax on the beach our last day and started moving around 10:00am. Then, showered together for a while, ate, and fooled around some more, and then went out to the beach and waited for Jacob's friend who he has known since he was 13 and traveling with AAU Basketball. They kept up with each other throughout college and now both were awaiting the draft. I think there was a mix up and he brought a girl for Jacob. They saw Jacob and me intimately romping in the surf with no doubt we were together, but she stepped to him and tried anyway. Jacob said I gave her a mean girl stare, but I didn't have to do much. Jacob did it all making me feel so special since he had a part of his body on me at all times, but I became apprehensive since we not only had an extra girl, but the paparazzi found us too and they got a lot of intimate pictures. I thought that scenario was strange since Jacob and I been there for two days without them.

Jacob's friend had a camera too and wanted to take pictures it seemed like all day. I posed for a few pictures with Jacob and a few without at his friend's persistence. The friend wanted to take off my sunglasses. I became suspicious as soon as he showed with all his extra guess, so I didn't let him or answer any of his questions truthfully. I just played off whom he thought I was, but stop taking pictures when he touched my Tom Fords. He almost lost his hand, but feeling very leery about the total situation, I retreated to my floppy hat along with my sunglasses, and chilled under a beach umbrella. I read while Jacob did some swimming, and I continued to hide me all day, being very anti-social or sleep. It was crazy, but as long as Jacob didn't mind it, I was fine.

Around 5:30pm, we decided to say goodbye and leave. The extra girl tried to slip Jacob her number. I mean I saw her and everything and she didn't hide it, but what do you do? If your man doesn't stand up for you, I guess... you have no business being with him.

"Didn't you see I am with someone... and I'm satisfied?" Jacob said like a gentleman, but sharp enough for me to hear. "I didn't ask you for that." Jacob threw the number away. "That's disrespectful," he muttered while turning, kicking sand on her. Then, he came over and helped me gather all our stuff. After all that, I didn't know what to say, but he gave me a kiss and we went back to the cottage with Jacob carrying everything. "I'm sorry for what happen," he said, and I kissed him. Then I said,

"Thank you for standing up for me Jacob." I think he thought I was mad at the number thing. I wasn't, anyway not at her stupidity, but it seemed the paparazzi came with his friends and I couldn't enjoy Jacob like I wanted, which bothered me.

Jacob and I planned to arrive at the camp early when everyone was sleep. So, I made Jacob lay down for a nap before we started on our trip since he did a lot of swimming. He took a shower and while I lotion and loved him a little I told him,

"Thank you for bringing me here Jacob and spending the time with me. It was... interesting." I kissed him again. "I feel refreshed. Now take a nap and I'll wake you when it's time to go." While he napped, I made us something to eat for the road to keep him awake. I enjoyed taking care of Jacob. He loved that attention, but he didn't want it from mommy any more. I figured it's a man thing.

I woke Jacob a little early so I could get my attention. So we kissed goodbye before we left the cottage. That took a while. On the trip back, I let Jacob know,

"I'm concerned about the Paparazzi. I think your friend brought them and tried to spy for them."

"What's bothering you sweetheart?" He asked, and I said,

"We took all those pictures, and why did he want those pictures of me? I'm surprised you let him take them."

"He's cool, but he can be wild," Jacob said. "He thinks you're that model from Argentina and kept asking who you were."

"Exactly, why did he need to know all that? He asked me all these questions and to pose this way and that way. Then he would look over his shoulder to see if the Paparazzi were getting their pictures too. He tried to take off my sunglasses, and that's when I stopped. It was obvious," I told Jacob all the questions his friend asked and all the lies I told. Then Jacob frowned saying,

"Hmm, he was kind of over inquisitive about your name and what work you done as a model." I laughed and said,

"He probably didn't believe I was a model." Jacob exclaimed,

"Allysa, you look like a model and he believed it.   I'm sure you will be successful as a model and dancer. Plus, you're going to school for other things, but I've been taking and looking at your pictures a lot the last three days, Allysa, and you have what it takes. You're young and need to work on your confidence, and I would like JAJA, to look out for you after TMP." Jacob made me feel better about continuing my plans to support myself modeling while finishing my education, but I said,

"Jacob, I'm concerned about your friend's intentions."

"Don't worry about it sweetheart," but I did as we rode in silence for some ways.

Reflecting on the time we spent together even through our rough times I became more familiar with Jacob, which seemed to increase my feelings and care for him. Smiling and thinking about Jacob he looked at me saying,

"Allysa I'm happy you stayed, thank you. I really enjoyed the time we spent together and I love the way you take care of me. You're a very compassionate person." He had a smile on his face the rest of the way back and hummed a new song he was working on most the way. We cruised into the camp early with everyone asleep.

CHAPTER FIFTEEN

Secret Lover

We reported for practice at noon which started with an announcement that JAJA Productions booked a weeklong working cruise to Aruba via the Western Caribbean. We'll take a short jet hop to Miami Friday morning and board the cruise ship by 5pm when we're scheduled to meet for practice. Next stop, Cancun Mexico, the Cayman Island, and then Jamaica to the last stop Aruba. We're to perform for the daylong outdoor jazz concert for the beginning of carnival. We're the house band and would be on stage from 3pm to 5pm, and then 9pm with various artist, and then our show until the end. All the brothers could sing including the idiot Delano. He's like the fifth brother and they had an album out that featured each one with their own songs, plus a few with them as a band. The album released last year was making its' way up the charts.

This was a RB jazz fusion show. The schedule stated that Danny and I will dance for the main show at night, once together that evening, and the three of us in a group during the day with carnival. So, Adam told the dance crew, Danny, Bubbles, and I were to depart the boat on Friday, meet up with a dance troupe in Aruba at 8am, work out with the dance crew, and fitted for costumes; then, Band practice from 3:00 to 5:30pm that evening and curfew at 12 midnight. The next morning the dancers would dance in the carnival parade while the band members rode the floats; then, the show Saturday afternoon.

It was all Jaison's doing. He ran up on the opportunity for the paying concert while getting jobs for the people who quit after BS messed up the show. To arrange transportation Jaison called one of his father's Island residents that Dad mentored whom was now the Captain of The Elite II, which was a new cruise ship that sailed the Western Caribbean on the Royal Cruise Line for Passage. The Captain booked our small group as entertainment so to offset the cost, and so all could make some money and enjoy. It was a favor for Dad and needed to keep momentum going for our group and Dad's program. Plus, our group had a following which booked more passengers for the cruise.

Jacob and I were looking forward to more together time on this cruise and the days in Aruba. Also, my store in the flea market netted almost $16,000 in three weeks. Shuti and I hustled on the internet, purse parties, in the square selling to tourist, and once word got out, people came from everywhere. After I paid my help, and took out money to restock, I had almost $10,000.00 to bank. I had no rent because my store was the office.

It was noticeable that I grew gaining 8 lbs. and was clearly taller than BB and Shuti now. All my designer jeans were high waters. That hurt, but Mrs. Browning who was a fantastic seamstress or tailor, and supervised wardrobe until she quit, tailored me three miniskirts, and three hemmed Shorty Shorts. The rest Mrs. Browning made into cut-off shorts. I felt better after we recycled them. So, I had to shop for some more jeans, and the cruise.

I gave Adam some extra money for Rich and the girls because Adams' family was coming too. He looked at me strange wondering why and I hunched my shoulders, and smiled, walking away. Some of my pay I had going to an account to help take care of Rich, but felt he and the girls needed to shop and have spending money. I know they didn't, but it was a habit, and couldn't leave out Adams girls. Since my problems, Niecie calls me with all of the children talking to me, and I call them. They felt like my little sisters and I love them too. I always sent them something through Adam.

Toward the end of the week Lynn, Bubbles, BB, Shuti and I collaborated to get supplies for the trip. We were happy because

THE THROW AWAY Book One

Shuti was going too, so we talked about the trip and all agreed the only downside... someone requested Klondike's act. She will be there with three from her group. We tried to figure who would request such a thing. My hoped was for none of those idiots to be there since Jacob and my affair had gotten hot. We didn't want to sneak around on the trip, and I planned to let BB know before we left. She's been sweating me about where have I been disappearing to. Telling her Rod's was okay, but I disappeared when Jacob does. With Adam knowing we were together I figured BB knew too, but I knew I had to say something soon.

Since this last trip, with Adam, Jaison, and Delano being aware of us, I was with Jacob every night before the trip at his request. Some evenings I stayed leaving early in the morning as soon as everyone settled down around 4am and go back to my room, or other days leave when everyone's sleep spending the rest of the early morning with him; leaving just before day break on our run. Jaison said he could tell our relationship had grown by our body language. I wondered what he meant by that, but the trip we took made me want and need Jacob daily. There wasn't so much sex going on. We just wanted to be close to each other. I didn't want to get closer, but we did.

On the day before travel, I fixed breakfast at their house after we ran. Jaison picked that time to talk to us saying,

"Seeing you two together anyone can tell you're more than friends, so with Klondike being there you guys need to stay away from each other until you're alone. They're snooping because the day Delano and I came in on you two with all that moaning and groaning, oow oow aah aah," Quickly I said,

"Shut up. I get it."

"Okay," Jaison said while laughing. "But I chased Ricardo from behind our house listening to you two and he may have told

Klondike. She's mad at you Allysa, and it could be bad for you and Jacob if they figure out you're the Argentine model." Delano said,

"Man, just wait until you get your contract it's only one month." Then Delano being an asshole blurted out, "Then you'll have more ass than you can handle." Well, after that statement, I left.

I felt terrible since my feelings had grown for Jacob, but that snapped me back to the reality that our affair couldn't go anywhere now and only cause trouble I'll be blamed for; then, feel the hurt when Jacob moves on to another. So I started wondering why do it, and I didn't give a shit about Klondike's miss directed anger, but really, I didn't think she knew because she had been quiet since Jacob and I went to New York. I figured the whole horde didn't know who was with Jacob. He called me later and apologized for what his cousin said.

"You know he's right." I said; then asked, "Why are we doing this?" Jacob answered,

"I'm acting on my feelings. Allysa, you said, 'I love you too.', and that's what I feel coming from you. Plus, you said, too, so you know how I feel." I opened my mouth, but he continued, "You make me feel needed and in control of my life. As I said, Allysa, you inspire me. My life falls into place with you and gives me the confidence and drive to do what I have to."

"Yeah Jacob, I'm feeling like I never felt before too, but it's getting like a drug. Being a couple is becoming a habit that's not helping either one of us now. We talked about this Jacob. We both have things to do when we leave here, and I want to be your friend to keep in touch with you, but..." he interrupted me saying,

"So, Allysa, you're going to break my heart like that, and I get let's be friends over the phone?" Jacob made me feel bad, but it was 12 noon the last day before travel, we didn't have practice, and BB and I had some serious shopping to do. So I said,

"Think about it, Jacob, and I'll get together with you around 7 or 8 this evening."

While we shopped, everyone ran their mouths about what we were going to do on the cruise. BB announced,

"My boyfriend, Fernando, booked a suit for us using an upgrade coupon. I know Jacob booked a suit that overlooks the sea." BB was really running her mouth excited about the cruise. My feelings and thoughts concerning Jacob phased me out until she went on about how the brother's mother, Marlena, two uncles on his mother's side, the Dad's younger brother their spouses and all their children would be there. It was a fuckin family reunion, and I knew Jacob had reserved a suite for us, but didn't he know his family was coming? And BB continued running her mouth saying, "I think Jacob's bringing the girl from New York or the new one so the magazine says, but I think it's the same girl, The Argentine model. I bet if the model chick is there, Marlena's going to go after her since she knows he's sleeping with her." The whole time BB's talking, she's looking at me watching my reaction. I didn't give her one, but listening to BB made me realize how the camp was looking at the Jacob situation and certainly explained why Klondike hadn't been picking. It's like the attention is off me because it's on me. It was crazy. "HELLO ALLY, ARE YOU LISTENING?" BB said very loud. I nodded saying,

"Yeah."

"Where's Rod training anyway?" She asked,

"About 150 miles from his house," and that was all I said. She looked at me curiously; then asked, "And where are the Flat Irons?" I remembered leaving them in Jacob's bathroom.

"They're at the brother's house. I'll get them later."

BB and I went on a shop till you drop mission with her meddling and teasing me about disappearing. We get along so well, it's easy for us to ignore each other at any given time, but continue talking about something else with the previous lost forever... sometimes.   Plus, BB didn't persist for answers about questions like where do I disappear and go? Why can't she go? What do I think about Jacob? What do I think of Jacob and his new girlfriend? etc. etc. There were too many Jacob questions, so I cut myself off to them and secretly ran as usual. I don't know why, but I wasn't ready to talk to her about it. I think it's because I didn't know how or what to tell her.

At 8:15pm, we had packed everything except for the flat irons. I wondered why I hadn't heard from Jacob when I thought; I had been with BB for more than 8 hours and hadn't said shit about Jacob and I being a couple. It's probably because she was running her mouth the whole damn time; however, after her questions, I think she knows, and it's a matter of us talking, but now I must talk with Jacob first. He finally called at 8:30 and asked me to come to his room breaking up BB talking about Fernando. I hadn't met Fernando, but hoped his heart didn't break easily. BB was not a monogamous person, but I announced,

"BB, the brothers are home and I'm going to get the flat irons."

Jaison and Delano was there like always when I went to Jacob's room, but this time both of them were quiet and stared at me strangely as I walked by. When I walked into the room, I notice the look on Jacob's face.

"What's wrong?" I asked and Jacob said,

"My family's trying to interfere in my life. I booked a room for the two of us. Now I find out my mother, Marlena, and 15 other family members most from my mother's side will be there."

"Oh. I mean besides that!" I didn't know what else to say, but Jacob went on telling me,

"Look, I know we have to slow down because the intimacy started way too soon for us and the relationship... we are not having, but the needs we have made our affair happen." I wondered what he felt my needs were; however, I knew the pressures of the draft, playing pro ball, and playing to the potential of the world's opinions was bothering him. Plus, having someone needing and believing in him, as a man was why he said he needed and wanted me. All he really wanted to do was play music, work with his brother Jaison, become an architect, and establish himself. Then get married and start having his babies when he's 25 or 26 years old. I know I didn't want the glamour of a pro player's career, but my feelings for him had enslaved me. I believed I gave him the confidence he needed to do well, but he was such a natural at it. Jacob said he loved playing basketball, but he didn't like all the attention and politics that came with the game. That took the fun out of playing, so he wanted to quit, but somehow, I believed Jacob playing pro ball had a further significance.

Jacob broke the silence with,

"My mother wants me to marry Marlena, and I knew Marlena was only interested in me because of the money and lifestyle that pro basketball would give her. I knew she was taking advantage of me, but I figured to marry her to get our land. If she started loving me in a few years, I would get the land and stay with her. If she continued to be herself, I would stay in the pros for a few years then quit pro ball and I'm sure she would leave, but I'll have claim to our land and she'll be gone. However, I knew I wouldn't be happy with a leech. I have a dream to build." I told him,

"No, that wouldn't be the right way." I was leery to tell Jacob what I really thought of his mother for asking her child to do that. Then Jacob said,

"Allysa, all I wanted was an honest woman who's not phony that I could love who would love and inspire me, and I knew I had very slim chances at finding that type of woman becoming a pro basketball player. I about gave up. Then we met at Adams concerning gathering our group. I didn't know the history, but knew dad was having a hard time getting one girl who was so important to him. I had heard this and that about you for years, but then was the first time Dad showed me your picture. It excited me, lifting my spirits, so I stole it; then, before my next game I studied your picture with nothing on my mind wondering, who is this Allysa who made me feel inspired? I felt so at ease playing while thinking about you just wanting to see your picture again. That urged me to ask my father more about the girl in the picture, and he told me about your situation, which alarmed me greatly. We had to get you away from that, and I was afraid something would happen before Adam could get you. I worried the 3 weeks, but was happy when Jaison called saying you were in the back seat nodding. Then we met, and my feelings for you, inspired my life. That's when I decided to go pro because it would be a way to help you right away if you needed it. When I got to know you, I realized you were a smart, honest, unselfish, down-to-earth person who is so beautiful in so many ways, but getting prettier every day. You act more mature than any female I've met. Allysa I know you're the woman I want, and that's why our affair is so important. I want to find out more about us, and let you know what you mean to me, but I feel constantly pressured." With everything Jacob said, I had so many questions, but told him,

"Jacob, I don't mean to pressure you." Jacob replied,

"It's not you pressuring me Allysa. My family is doing it trying to control my life, and I just want to be with you because you're my drug of choice." OMG. I thought of how Jacob who was quiet and shy was spilling his guts on the regular about his feelings and seriously telling me how important I was to him. I knew I wouldn't have gotten this far without him, but I know most of my problems stem from the roots of our feelings for each other and then they grew.

Keeping his seriousness in mind, I thought about the different stages of life we were in as far as love goes. I was just finding out about guys and he was trying to find the woman he wants in his life to start his family. My problem was I didn't know that much about sex, love, or myself and how it all would come together for me; I had questions. Would my feelings continue to be this strong for him, would it grow or what? It felt like I would want and need Jacob forever. I believed my feelings would continue to grow since they had, but was this what I planned, needed, or wanted? I knew I wanted him... but I knew I didn't need everything that was happening. The sincerity of his love and intent certainly weren't in my plans, but Jacob was so correct and I didn't want to lead him on or tease him since I still didn't believe in relationships. It seemed like another tool people used to control your feelings. So I said,

"Jacob, I want to be with you, but right now is not a good time for us. People are intentionally making our experience miserable. They want us to be unhappy together, and we have to slow this down to a stop." Both of us became silent for a while. Feeling I needed to say more about the situation, I said, "If we place time, like wait until I get a little older, distance, we're away from here, and space, let me find out about myself in this equation, I think things will work out favorably." He was quiet for a little while and looked so bleak, but then almost murmuring he said,

"We need each other, but I understand Allysa." Jacob sat quiet for a while, and then he asked decisively, "I want to spend tonight with you, one night on the cruise, and if possible, one night in Aruba. Then I promise after this trip I will back off the intimacy part of our affair... but I can't just be friends with you Allysa. You are special to me and... um I want a better life for both of us... together." He made me feel strange. I didn't agree or disagree. We sat in his room thinking at first, but after a while, we started talking about different things, laughing and joking forgetting about our problems. While thinking about Jacob and enjoying his company, I chose to go along with his immediate plans.

Feeling comfortable and happy to spend time with him, I kissed him and decided to shower in his bathroom, and that's when things heated up. I missed being with him for eight hours and felt happy I was the Argentine model. So we showered washing and loving each other for the next hour or so. While we were busy, someone knocked on the door. So when we finished, Jacob slipped on some sweats and peeped out. He said he saw no one and we continued on the bed rubbing lotion, kissing and massaging each other. Jacob put on some music and asked me to give him a lap dance. It turned into a little more. I couldn't understand how or why I would lose all my inhibition, all my thoughts except for Jacob when with him, and I wasn't sure if that's the way it should be. What's my point??? Exactly! I didn't know what I was doing and that's why I hadn't told BB.

We laid down in each other's arms to rest. Jacob kissed me on my forehead and we dozed. Since the incident when he thought I ran away, he keeps me in his arms all night long. Kissing me each time he wakes to change position. When I wiggle out to go to the bathroom, he grabs and holds me until I tell him I'm coming right back. Thinking, while I dozed in his arms, I felt how hard it would be to give him up. Feeling the dread of that, I felt the need to get closer so to enjoy all of him. I turned and kissed him while he dosed. He stirred grabbing my butt pulling me even closer so I could feel all his body with The General and his long fingers resting between my legs. Then someone came in the room and went in the bathroom, but turned and left quickly. As I went back to sleep, I heard BB's voice asking Delano,

"Why the hell you send me in Jacob's room when you knew he's in there with his woman?" Then, I heard Jaison and Delano laugh. I covered us up and figured as I dozed off back to sleep I would tell her about Jacob next time we talked. Sometime later, someone closed the door and woke us. Jacob went to the bathroom. When he came back, he pulled me back close to him and kissed me. As we laid under the covers, he cuddled and kissed me. I loved that.

"Are you cold?" he whispered while touching me. I nodded yes, and he said, "Let me warm you up a bit." Then he started loving me in a way that would make any woman lose her mind from pleasure. Next, it was my turn and Jacob pulled back the covers with me first exciting Jacob with a massage. Afterwards, I climbed on top with the General ready and waiting and got into my rhythm that soon became our rhythm; then, someone grabbed me from behind and pulled me away. I couldn't figure what the hell was going on because the only thing Jacob did was blushed and covered up. My climax became a climnull. Then I heard BB's voice.

"Girl put some damn clothes on! Do you know what you're doing and what's going on?" I thought, no. She scared the shit out me. Where did she come from? I wondered as I fumbled around trying to gather my clothes to no avail. They were all over the place and in the bathroom. I sat back on the bed upset with the interruption and shared Jacob's sheet. BB saw our problem shook her head and left. I jumped up getting dressed while pissed and very finished with people walking in on us, so I asked Jacob who just laid there looking at me,

"Is the door lock working?" Jacob said,

"No, I got to fix the knob." I thought I really didn't need to know after the fact. I dressed wondering what to say since BB was still fussing at Delano and sounded like she was ready to fight him. I know I kept hearing BB say 'Give me the fuckin computer;' then, we heard shit falling over. We peeped and then rushed to get downstairs. Mr. and Mrs. Browning came after Jaison called them since it looked like spunky BB went to Delano's ass to get the computer. Poor Jaison was standing in between them with the computer looking a little tattered, but Delano looked like he had been in a fight with a razor. Jaison was still telling them to stop and shut-up. It was 2:30 in the morning. Lynn and Shuti stood by the outside door peeping and wondering what the hell was going on because they could hear them fussing next door, and I wondered too. BB fixed her hair noticing me and said,

"Girl... do you know what's going on? They got cameras in the room and have a video of you two fucking." Jaison intervening said,

"BB, you keep saying they. I had nothing to do with this and Jacob was with me all day. Stop saying that." BB called me,

"Allysa!" I thought oh shit. "You're acting way too grown. Do you know what's going on in Jacob's life with all these girls he's been within the last month? Do you know what you're doing?" She fussed and fussed. I was getting a headache and becoming very confused and didn't know what to do or how to feel threatening to spas out. I started fidgeting and crying feeling my modeling career was over before it got started, and I have naked pictures out all over the internet while wondering if Jacob knew. However, Jaison had the computer and was looking at it hard saying,

"I knew nothing about this... hmm." Brown snatched the computer and closed it; then, Brown and Jaison took Jacob in the library. Jacob felt upset and bewildered that his cousin would do that to him. Brown and Jai worried about him going off, but he seemed to feel like me.

Mrs. Browning took me back to my room and told me to stay there when she went to get the computer after Brown called. Meanwhile, BB and Lynn just looked at me shaking their heads while lecturing me about my actions and asked me all these questions at once. When did you start? Is he taking advantage of you? Do you want to be with him? Are you taking birth control? Why didn't he have on a condom? I was so embarrassed and upset I just looked down and said nothing. I didn't believe Jacob knew about it because

Jacob was with Adam and Jaison all day until he called me. No doubt the stunt hurt me, but Jacob looked like he was too. Shuti said,

"Ally, Don't worry Wang has removed the hard drive and can tell if he uploaded it to the internet." I cried thinking people were watching my naked butt in Bang-kok Thailand and I wondered what to do now. Shuti, Lynn, and BB tried to comfort me, and backed off with the questions. Lynn said,

"Look Allysa... I figured you and Jacob had been together. When you and Jacob are together with us, your body language shows you and Jacob are intimate with each other, but that was your business until you wanted to include us. My only concern is people taking advantage of you the way Delano did."

We went downstairs when Jacob came in with Mrs. Browning and Wang. Delano's computer was in about 6 pieces. Each of them gave me a piece or two of the computer. Jacob wanted to speak privately with me, but Mrs. Browning wouldn't have it telling Jacob,

"Son... it's best for you to say what's going on now and right here." Embarrassed, Jacob whispered,

"Allysa I'm sorry. Delano did this on his own, and he filmed us while we were together tonight."

"Meaning?" I privately queried. Still whispering, Jacob told me,

"The only thing he did was watch because the last time he logged on the internet was yesterday." However, Wang said extremely loud,

"No internet. We fix for Hot Mama." BB who had been just looking at me lately with her mouth closed finally opened it after Mrs. Browning fussed her out about her temper and fighting. She said,

"I didn't lose my temper. You see what happen was when I came in, Jaison and Delano was working on some music and I came over to find your butt and the flat irons," and she punched me hard on my thigh as she continued saying, "When I asked them about you, Allysa, and the flat irons, Delano said 'They're in Jacob's bathroom.' I heard him, but didn't hear him. So I went in the room since the door was cracked, but I knocked first. I heard the shower going, so I left. When I came out, Jaison, and I smoked a blunt and talked. Delano had the screen half way down on his computer, but he would come over take a few hits; then, go back over to the table looking at the computer... nervously. Jaison and I noticed he was acting funny, but so what's new? We are talking about Delano. Meanwhile, it seemed he was trying to watch something on the screen, but he wouldn't completely open it up. I kept watching him. I asked what you looking at; then, he told me to get the flat irons and get the hell out. So after the blunt, I thought maybe Jacob wasn't there and maybe I didn't hear the shower, and I went back in his room and that's when I walked in on you two balled up together naked sleeping.   I would have never guessed you were with him or Jacob was in his room with someone. I don't know why Jaison didn't tell me, and that ass hole Delano was still looking at his computer when I asked why he sent me in the room. He laughed, and I ignored the idiot. About 20 minutes later, we were halfway discussing the music Jaison was working on, but during that process, Delano got mad at me because I was trying to see what fascinated him, and he was sweating. Jaison looked at him and asked Delano why he was sweating like that. Then Jai told me he's probably looking at some porno and asked Delano to let him see. Delano got upset because we walked towards him to see and he tried to go upstairs with the computer. That's when I got a glimpse at what he was looking at and recognized you, Miss Allysa Melody Carrington. I told Jaison and went and got you." Next, BB confronted Jacob telling him, "Jacob, even if you didn't have anything to do with the filming, what the hell are you thinking fucking Allysa and what are you thinking with? We're supposed to be taking care of her. You didn't even have a condom on. Jacob you got all those other girls and you're taking advantage of her. You could give her a disease and mess her up for life. This is Allysa... Allysa, you asshole." Mrs. Browning grabbed BB while telling Jacob,

"I'm disappointed in you and know your father will be too." Jacob put his head down peeping at me as he left. Then, after BB told everyone about Jacob and my sexual endeavors that night, Lynn and BB started the lecturing and questioning again. I couldn't help thinking I should have told BB and Lynn and was impressed Bubbles kept my secret since she knew. And then BB started.

"Ally, do you know what you're doing?" BB asked me again. I shook my head a little agitated, so I moved to the library. Lynn told BB to calm down. There was a little while of silence. Then Lynn, BB, Shuti, with Mrs. Browning came to me and Lynn said while BB continued to look at me curiously,

"You know he's in an older crowd and very sexually active, and sometimes when young men get in the pros, it goes to their heads, and they start taking advantage of women they know." But BB said,

"Ally, you do know Jacob is all over the news and in Gossip magazines with different women. He was in New York with a girl and I just picked up a magazine with pictures of another girl last weekend. She's supposed to be 16 and you're 15. Why is he doing that?" I know BB had to know I was finished with all this lecturing and questioning about my business and talking about Jacob. Both subjects pissed me off. So I surprised everyone by first giving them a nasty look, and then I went to my room slamming the door. After a while, Mrs. Browning knocked. She apologized, but explained her concerns in a short sex talk. Then said,

"I know this is private between you and Jacob, but I think you should talk to Lynn, BB, and Shuti. They consider themselves your big sisters and I know they're seriously concerned for you. Talk to them Allysa. You know by now you're safe with them."

"Yes, I know, but they need to stop." Mrs. Browning said,

"Allysa, talk to them. They think Jacob is involved with other girls, and I'm sure you can straighten things out for them." I didn't know what to think of Mrs. Browning, but she knew.

Walking downstairs with Mrs. Browning we found BB still standing there with the magazine talking with Lynn and Shuti. I asked her,

"What the girl look like BB?"

"I don't know... and you asked me that before." Looking at me strange, BB continued, "I think they're the same girl, and we need to look," so we did.

The cover headline stated Jacob Kapulani seen in Florida with the Seductive Goddess from Argentina. When BB came to the page of the article, she looked at it then jumped up with a smile saying,

"Oh Yeah. I thought so. That's you Allysa. You're the sexy girl in New York too!"

"Yeah," I said, while I looked at all the pictures of us in the magazine. All were the pictures Jacob, and I posed for that his friend took. Plus, some the paparazzi took of us playing in the surf and intimately kissing while laying on our blanket.

"Read the article." I said; then, I told them all the bullshit I said to Jacob's friend and the girls with him. It was all in the article, and I clued them in, "When I'm not with either of you, I'm with Jacob. I'm surprised one of you didn't figure it out." BB said,

"I just asked you today, Allysa, because you and Jacob usually disappear at the same time. That's what everyone at Beach Side noticed, however, you do throw people off the way you leave and come back at the different times." Mrs. Browning spoke with a very concerned look on her face.

"Allysa, I want to mind my business, but... look I know you care about Jacob, and know you have respect for King Kapulani. We have BS were the king needs him, but if it's found out who the mystery girl is, BS, with the mother and Marlena, and whoever BS can get to help keep his mess going, will make it terrible for all of us." Lynn said,

"BS already figured something and tried to tell everyone the night of the competition." Remembering that night, and BS's comments about my mother, the embarrassment of that night occupied me totally and I failed to consider what he said about Jacob and me, but I wondered why was everything so quiet and why hadn't BS used the information. So contritely, I said,

"Yes, I know it would be bad with those stupid, meddlesome people involving themselves. That's why I told no one... but I have feelings for Jacob. I was curious at first, but this... affair has grown and we tried to keep on the down low. Even still, it's our business but everyone is in our business like Delano tonight, Jacob's friend who took all those pictures, and he had to tell the magazine what we said. I can't explain it, but... our feelings I can't ignore. Somehow, I believe I'm important to him and it feels right that we're together, but I have to speak to him about BS and this article."

Jacob came and looked at the article with BB and me, but it upset him the way his friend sold him out and Delano hurt him. I felt bad for Jacob and comforted him while he told us,

"Allysa, Delano apologized for his actions, but really apologized for being jealous. He said he wasn't going to put it on the internet. This was something we guys just do to each other, but that's not true either. We never done anything like that, but he realized he hurt two special people to him and the gang. Now he feels sick and not the way he thought, so he's sorry he did it. I hope he learned a lesson." I said,

"The freak's sorry he got caught." Then BB said,

"Jacob, look I understand, and I want you two to be happy. I knew you two liked each other and... this is cool... BUT BS knows and said something the night of the show. I know you have a nice room, and you planned to be together, but you don't know who your friends are, and too much shits happening. You need to be careful."

TO BE CONTINUED IN

THE THROW AWAY, Book Two

www.ingramcontent.com/pod-product-compliance
Lightning Source LLC
Chambersburg PA
CBHW071300170626
46809CB00001B/292